LANDBRINGER

KAREN LUCIA

- 1 -

PART 1:

HARD HANDS AND TARRY LUNGS

1:

It wasn't time yet. That I was sure of. But as the airship drew closer, I started to wonder. Was this it? Was this the one? No other ships were supposed to pass this way at this hour. Air traffic control had been strict about maintaining their gaps at the underpass of the Grand Cross Bridge ever since the Great Collision. Fifteen hundred lives had gone out like sparks when the gas bags holding them up had ruptured. The friction of two ships passing too close igniting fabric, wood, and bodies all in one fell swoop. No. Air traffic control would not allow another ship this way this hour. They couldn't handle the bad press. Not now. This had to be it. Or was it?

I palmed the talker hanging at my waist. The magical contraption would bring my voice to the ringleader. I could ask. But I knew just as well that we were supposed to leave the talker clear. Leave it quiet. The ringleader would be getting into place now. As would the others. Breaking the silence could compromise them and this was too big a heist to compromise. No. I let the talker hang back at my hip. This had to be it.

I checked my rope as I clung to the shadows of the bridge. I was all too aware that if the knots securing it to the girders were to slip, I would very likely plunge thousands of feet to my grisly death. Thousands of terrifying feet with nothing but air on all sides as I descended the distance between our slice of land where it floated and the blanket of clouds shrouding the entirety of the planet below.

First the mists would be cool as I entered the upper alts of the cloudline—or so the scientists claimed—then they would turn corrosive the closer my body plummeted to the planet's surface. No. I didn't want that to be my end. I checked the knots again then looked out of my gloomy hiding place at the approaching airship.

I pulled my goggles tight over my eyes and my bandana close over my nose and mouth. Tucked up into the struts as I was, I was somewhat sheltered from the raging winds I would have to traverse to hit the airship's bulge. This wasn't my first rodeo. The descent could be treacherous. I knew that others, less experienced than myself, would make the mistake I had of youthful cockiness: disregarding the advice of experience and diving through the divide at the airship with their faces bare to the wind and the occasional wafts of planetary fumes that reached these climes. Those fumes rarely melted the insides of those who braved them, but they had a terrible noxious quality that would put even the tarriest-lunged vagabond into a stupor and send them plummeting to the planet's surface. They were likely so out of sorts by the vapors that they couldn't even perceive their imminent demise. I liked to tell myself that, at least. If I had to go from a dive gone wrong, I wouldn't want to be aware of the long seconds of falling. No, sir. But I had no plans for meeting my end for another few years.

I looked to my left and right. There would be others making the dive. I would know pretty quickly if this was the wrong airship, but by then I would be caught in the winds and fully committed. No. There wasn't much I could do if this was the wrong one. It really was just like one of these gas bags to be early the one day I needed it to be on time.

I let the rope slide between the sturdy leather of my gloves. Gloves thick enough to protect my hands from the burn of the rope, but supple enough to give me the dexterity I had no doubt I would need in a moment's time. It didn't really matter how hard your hands were at the end of the day if you got unlucky with the winds.

I said a quick prayer to Devton, the God of the Deviants and Vagabonds. Not a very nice prayer, but a quick one. If any of the gods were going to favor this dive, I was sure it had to be him. Maybe I shouldn't have bothered. Maybe I was just drawing undue attention onto my little venture. I couldn't be certain what the right answer was. I had never met any of the gods.

The airship lumbered closer. The beast was a massive swell of faded red fabrics all sewn tight and pulled taut by their lighter-than-air contents. As it passed below, even from my height, I could see the many patches, the discoloring of fabric where it had been exposed to fumes a little more corrosive than usual, the streaks of water damage from storms weathered and the constant damp of life above our hellion of a planet. The sight never inspired my confidence in the airships, but the rich and powerful swore by the things.

I gripped my rope. I wore it fastened to my waist, but loosely so. I couldn't have a tight knot on an overly secured rope be the thing that caused me to miss my landing. I needed to be able to be free of the rope, and if that meant falling to the winds, that meant falling to the winds.

Death was better than being caught hanging helpless from your own safety line when the Enforcers came around. Death was better than capture. That's what I had always been told by the older vagabonds growing up. Death over capture. Too often though, that mantra had been their swan song. Now that I was among the ranks of the older members of the gang, I wondered how right the vagabonds who had come before me had been. Still, it was tradition, and the mantra of the vagabonds left my lips.

I jumped. The rope slid between my fingers and in the moments before the full force of the gale hit me, I saw others start their descent. If I was wrong, so were they.

The winds caught me, whipping me like a ragdoll on a line. And really that's what I was, wasn't I? A tiny doll fighting the forces of nature, clinging to a rope. Years of dives, of braving the gale, had given me the label of one of the Hard Hands of our little troop, but everybody knew even Hard Hands fell.

The rope continued to slide between my gloves, warm and burning, but not my flesh, at least. I had control still as I was lashed and tossed forward and back and side to side with the ebb and thrust of the gusts. The winds howled and hissed and snapped, but I still thought I heard a scream in the distance. Maybe one of the other vagabonds. Had they fallen? It was hard to know one scream from the next as the dive itself could be enough to bring a jumper to the edge of terror. I had screamed my first time. Oh, how I had screamed. But I had made it, somehow, teetering on the edge of fear-induced unconsciousness. This time, though, I gritted my teeth and plummeted; the rope only slightly arresting my fall, its lead only just keeping me over my target.

The airship loomed closer. I could see the surface. Some of the other vagabonds had dropped too fast, scrabbling for purchase on a slope of fabric that would give them little or none. I saw one small figure hit the fabrics and slide away into the mists. Had they lost consciousness? Fumes or fear? I held my breath, though the buffeting winds were enough to stop the breath in the chest anyway. The small body was gone from sight now. Had they been one of the younger ones? Maybe a first jump? Death was better than capture. Still, I felt the pang of the loss. One more to the winds.

My hands gripped and released, controlled—if it could be called that—in my descent. I was whipped violently, then the torrent tearing at my body abated slightly as I plummeted into the slipstream of the airship. Above me the rope still fought the winds, tossing me here and there as I undid the loose knot securing me to the bridge above. It tossed and jarred and lashed and I released it, falling the last several feet to the fabric of the gas bag.

Even calmed slightly, the winds were still violent and could tear a vagabond off the surface of the ship in seconds if they weren't careful. I rolled, a gust pushing me along as I clawed at the mottled, greying fabric under me. Condensation, or maybe wetness from the storm the ship had battled to arrive here, had soaked the fabric, laying thick swaths of water on top of the grease that coated the balloon's exterior, another layer of protection against the elements.

I fumbled and flipped. I was going to fall. Even the hardest hands and the tarriest-lunged vagabonds fell sometimes. And that was it for them. Only the abyss awaited them below. I was skidding on my back, staring up at the underside of the Grand Cross Bridge and the hard stone of the landmass of Vale. The fear started to build as I found no purchase, as the winds grabbed at my clothes, tight as they were for this very reason, and worked to force me from the airship.

With a flick of my wrist and a twist that brought me belly down, a set of talons whipped forward from where they nestled against my upper arm and slammed hard into the fabric of the balloon, punching into the ripstop and bringing my fall to a jarring halt. My arm protested as the metal hooks of the talons dug in; the sudden stop risked dislodging my shoulder and breaking my bones. But my arm held. A thin whisper of gas escaped its containment where my talons pressed in, but the airships were not so fragile that a small hole would sink them. Still, we tried not to use our talons unless a fall was imminent. The ringleader had no interest in a successful heist being ruined by the landing party popping too many holes in the balloon to keep the ship aloft.

I took a few steadying breaths, still feeling the deadly winds pulling at my back, then pressed close to the fabric and started my crawl. With another flick of my wrist, the metal talons that had lanced forward to save me snapped back, their tangs resting neatly on both sides of my forearm, the savage teeth now harmlessly tucked away.

I crawled, knowing my objective. Knowing how to get access to the passenger compartment on the behemoth of a ship. I hoped not too many of my fellow jumpers had fallen. There was a scent in the gale that had me swooning, and I knew that this heist was going pear-shaped right quick and in a hurry.

A moment of clarity had me draw back my arm and slam it down, the talons flashing in front of me as they bit into the fabric once again. My body was limp, my mind reeling from the planetary fumes. Oh, others would have had the wherewithal to sink their talons in too, but I knew in the back of my hazy mind that many wouldn't have been so lucky. My body thumped and flapped against the side of the gas bag, all rigidity gone from me, only the talons holding me up from certain death.

The sounds of shouting roused me from my stupor. My talker was firing off curses and threats. The ringleader's call to action. He knew his landing party had been taken out by the fumes and was whipping everybody back to their senses with a string of profanities so vile I would never allow myself to repeat them. Still, the cajoling worked, and I pulled myself back together. My brain still swam in its soupy haze, but I was able to crawl the rest of the way to the access. I wasn't the only vagabond to make it. A small boy with a faraway look stared at the port with a stone-faced girl beside him. Another handful of kids and teenagers made their way to where we were poised for the breach. I looked at the two oldest vagabonds who had made it. Our ages were similar, but they had survived this life three months longer than me. Age was a jumper's seniority. The two oldest nodded to the rest of the group, the howling winds making any attempts at talking useless, and we threw open the hatch.

It was quiet inside. Dark and quiet. Everybody turned down

their raging talkers and the oldest, a woman twenty years and one month old, hefted hers to her mouth to calm the riled ringleader. It couldn't be relief I heard in the man's brusque response. Beater was not a man to show anything other than absolute brutishness. No, it couldn't have been relief.

Still, we had made the drop. Some of us, at least. We were in place. The ringleader was in place. Our talkers hummed as, around the ship, other teams of vagabonds confirmed they were ready. Then we moved.

We were like a swarm of locusts hitting the passenger carriage. Pistols went off all around, batons were brandished, and we surged on. We had numbers—though fewer than expected after the fume waft—and an underlying desperation that had always fueled our success in the past.

The power flickered and the lights went out. We continued on in the chaos as passengers shouted and screamed. I knew that only the lights were out, not the steering controls. Nothing that would risk us sinking down into the mists below. Eda would be with Beater, and I was certain that with that woman at the helm, hitting the cloudline wasn't a risk.

In the darkness we managed to get our foothold. To drive the fear-filled masses to the floors. We grew up in the dark where these poor sods had likely never left the yellow glow of their electricity.

We corralled the fretting passengers in the corridors, droves of street kids wielding fearsome bludgeons. Some of my fellows were more than willing to work a little frustration out with thumps and thwaps of their billy clubs against the upstanding citizens of the Society.

I caught one of the clubs as it was about to fall with a little too much gusto and shook my head silently at the boy wielding the weapon. Bumps and thumps to keep the passengers in line as we pilfered their belongings was one thing, but an ill-fated fall of a baton could spell disaster. The well-to-do could forgive a small bruise, hold it up at their parties and proclaim themselves heroes for surviving such a savage attack. A broken bone, scar, or worse would only bring raids and retaliation. The younger members of the gangs would learn that eventually, I was certain. A few of the youngers watched me pass, their shouting and cajoling pausing only slightly with their regard for my age.

My time and options within the gang were dwindling. It was

time to get mine and start looking to the future. I needed to find some piece worth enough for me to make my way. In the dark it was a hard git, but metals tended to have value, and rings were often fitted with their share of jewels. I quickly stripped a man's hand of his bands and stowed the load away into the small pack on my back. I found a pocket watch in his vest which he fought to keep, but when I leveled my billy club at him, he quickly yielded the bounty. A watch could help me escape Vale; all it did for him was tell time and raise his esteem among his friends.

I moved on.

I was still a little out of sorts from my brush with death on the exterior of the airship and couldn't quite comprehend the clear white glow of magic tearing through the corridor. When understanding struck, I threw myself to the floor, grabbing the girl who had been patting an older man down and pulling her to the floor with me.

The whiteness passed, immobilizing pain taking any who it struck. In front and behind, passengers and vagabonds alike collapsed in sobbing masses. In the wake of their magic, casters filled the corridor ahead. I had always thought the Aberrants looked ridiculous in their sweeping navy robes and high collars, but now, they looked like death.

I grabbed my talker, any hesitation at using the contraption gone. "Abbies!" I shouted the warning, hauling the girl back down before another immobilizing wave of magic passed overhead. I lost my talker in the bound for the girl, but I could hear it behind me echoing my warning in the various voices of the boarding leads. The shouts. The fear. The sudden turn of the tide. This airship would be our demise. The trap had been set and we dove right in.

I grabbed the girl, she grabbed a boy, and we hauled those of the vagabonds who could still move from the corridor, narrowly evading the blasts of tormenting magic. The Aberrants and their magic were an endgame, and we knew it. Whoever Beater had pissed off had high connections and our ringleader was bringing the rest of his gang down with him.

"We have to get off the ship," I said, trying to believe that would even be possible with Aberrants aboard. If the Society had committed their precious few Aberrants to this trap, it would only be a wrong turn and a matter of time before I was being hauled away, paralyzed in pain. Still, I couldn't resign myself to that fate.

With enough of us, maybe we could overwhelm them. But maybe then their magics would turn from the savage to the lethal. Already they had shown their willingness to harm civilians if it meant getting their hands on us. It was only a small step.

An image flashed in my head as the youngers followed me, whimpering through the darkened corridors. A girl, her mangled body and tortured face left where only the street kids roamed. A testament to the Aberrants' darker magic. A warning for the gang that had owned the child. Those of us who were old enough had all seen her. Every street kid over the age of fifteen had seen her. We had made a point of looking. It had been due her. She had been one of ours, no matter the gang. The bloodied froth of saliva trickling from her mouth lodged in my mind. It would have been better to have given in to the fumes and fall.

I shook my head and continued moving.

Twenty and one month came across us, leading a group of her own. We had been in Beater's gang together for years, yet her name always seemed to slip from my mind. Maybe I had inhaled too many fumes in all my dives. She grabbed my arm, her fingers too tight with fear as she tried to sound strong. She was half a year my elder, if even that, and the only reason she still held a place in the gang was that she agreed to share a bed with the ringleader when the desire so struck him. Still, she was my elder, and that meant she now took charge of my small posse.

"Come on. We are mounting a push." The heavy lilt of her Dorado accent quavered slightly, but she managed to stiffen her spine. "We can clear by force. I need everybody." She shoved me forward and, I couldn't help but notice, in front of her.

"Where's the ringleader?" I asked quietly, letting her use me as a shield as she drove her mass of vagabonds ahead of her. I didn't care about Beater, but Eda would be with him.

"I don't know," the woman's voice cracked a little. "Dead for all I fucking know. I need to get off this damn ship. Get me off this ship." Her hand clenched, fingers tangling in the fabric at the small of my back. Her death grip wouldn't let her human shield stray too far as she shouted orders at the vagabonds.

Batons were raised and more than a few talons flashed as vagabonds prepared for battle.

I knew the only reason Twenty was holding me toward the back of the group was because I was the tallest shield she could find.

"What's our altitude?" I asked.

"What?" Twenty asked sharply, confusion in her wandering eyes as she drove the vagabonds forward into attack.

"Our alt. There's nothing but acid clouds below us if Beater didn't get us in line for escape."

"I don't know." Her panic was breaking through. "I don't fucking know. We need the control room then. There's no way that bastard held it against Abbies. Go, all of you! Fucking go!" she ordered the vagabonds crowding the halls.

There was a reluctant surge, then a synchronized charge of children and teens.

Enforcers and vagabonds came together in a clash of pistols, batons, talons, boots, and fists. With their compatriots so entwined in the struggle, the Aberrants must have been ordered to keep their wide-sweeping magics to a minimum. Still, I saw the flash of drawn symbols and flare of savage magic in the clash ahead of me.

I knew without a doubt that there was death on all sides now as Twenty continued to cower behind me, only appearing to fire the infrequent shot from her pilfered revolver.

The press of the corridor was too tight. The chaos too widespread. The baton swinging on my hip went forgotten. There was no chance for me to grab it in the crush. Children screamed and fell. The larger bodies of Enforcers succumbed time and again to the beating masses of vagabonds. The desperate body of vagabonds fighting with the knowledge that if they did not die in this struggle, they would face the torture of the Abbies.

Another flash and the line of vagabonds in front of me collapsed in gasping and bloody sobs.

Twenty's ragged breath caught behind me as she watched the scene and finally realized the rules of the battle had shifted. The Aberrants weren't looking to immobilize us, to capture us, to take us in for punishment and torture.

Her hand leaving my jumpsuit, Twenty ran back the way we had come, a throng of retreating vagabonds all flowing away on my right and left in frightened shrieks. Another wave of death hit and I felt it in my core like the suffocating choke of a pillar of fumes. My dance with the gasses outside must have kept me slow-witted because instead of turning with the rest, I stood a moment too long as I watched an Aberrant face me in full, his pointer and middle fingers poised together as if bound, dragging down, arching, curving, climbing. The glyph the man cut into the air etched in my mind, the intent behind his swift motions clear.

Frozen, the symbol carved in the air firmed in my mind then slipped away as the man thrust his fingers forward in release. The savage attack of magic seemed to leech the energy from me as death swept toward me. Then the Aberrant's chest exploded and he collapsed. His magic had backfired.

The shock of the realization stilled his companions but melted the ice on my limbs, finally freeing me to run as the others had. I grabbed the arm of a boy who was staring at the bodies of his friends as I passed. I couldn't do anything for the other children who remained trapped by their shock or their injuries. All I could do was drag the boy after me as we fled.

"I … I … I …" the boy was saying. He was in shock. He was a liability with his babbling. It would be better for me to leave him behind, but my hand stayed firm in his.

In a moment of calm, I pulled the boy to a stop and crouched in front of him. His clothes were tattered and bloodstained from the mass of cuts caused by some Aberrant curse. I cupped his face in my hands. He was cold with shock. "You need to be quiet, alright? You need to stay close to me. Can you do that?" He was nobody I had known well. Just one of the youngers in a gang where youngers tended to be short lived. I struggled on his name. "Marco. Can you do that?" I repeated, his name having roused him just enough to hear me.

Dully, the boy met my eyes and nodded. Once again, I took his hand and led him along. Whichever way Twenty and the others had gone, I didn't know, but maybe it was best to be away from the mass.

One wrong turn, though. I had known it would only be a matter of time. I made the one wrong turn in my haste to find some hidey-hole to stow myself and the boy away.

A line of Enforcers stood guard over a corridor filled with panicking passengers. When I rounded the corner, they pounced with batons swinging and fists flying. I shoved the boy away from me at the first realization that I would die here, beaten to death by a gang of Enforcers with the screams of the airship passengers to mark my passage.

I hit the carpeted floors of the corridor hard. There were no Aberrants among the Enforcers, or, if there were, they were enjoying the thrill of the blood sport. I didn't know what was worse: to die by their magic or under crushing blows. I searched for any sign of help among the crowd. A women's empty eyes were all that met mine. She offered no help and no solace. I curled in on myself. I saw the boot come up and wrapped my arms around my head. It wasn't protection enough, though, because with the crash of the boot, I lost consciousness.

2:

When I woke up, it felt like a cold piece of beef was slapped over my swollen right eye. I could taste blood from my cracked lip and my bit tongue. I felt a beaten mess. I *was* a beaten mess.

The cabin was dark, but not dark enough that I couldn't see. The white clouds outside the small porthole cast a hazy light into the cabin. A young woman sat beside me, dabbing away the blood that streaked my face. She saw me looking up at her in the gloom and smiled.

"Look who's back in the land of the living." She had the accent of one of the rich, proper young things that frequented these airships. My head throbbed. "My name is Katarina Norwood." She looked at me expectantly.

The only response I gave her was a panicked grasping at whatever was laying on my face, covering my swollen eye. My hand came away with what was indeed a slab of beef. I looked horrified at the hunk of meat and the utter wastefulness of simply laying it on my eye. This wasn't my first black eye and it wouldn't be my last. Unless it would. I swallowed as a sudden wave of dread swelled. Had I been captured? I must have been. Katarina prattled on as though she couldn't see my sudden wariness.

"My mama always said that a good slice of prime steak was the best medicine for a black eye," she said wistfully, staring off into space. I didn't know what occasion this woman would have for remedying black eyes, but I took her word for it. She looked at me again. "Katarina Norwood," she repeated, as though she hadn't already introduced herself.

"You should stay away from that dirty thing. You don't know what diseases it has."

I jumped, realizing another woman was in the compartment with us. I knew without a doubt that the woman was talking about me. She scowled at me over the brim of the tawdry noir novella she had been reading. There was no denying the two women were sisters from the similarity in their appearances. The two looked the same in every way, except instead of Katarina's expectant smile was a mirthless sneer. "I don't know why you insisted on dragging that heap of filth into our room."

"Now, you just keep your own matters to yourself, dear old Deara," Katarina said with a hint of malice sneaking into her rosy little voice. Her sister huffed and turned back to her reading. Katarina looked down at me again, still holding the slab of beef dumbly in my hand.

Where in the abyss was I? I hadn't been captured. This didn't feel like capture, at least. If this was an Enforcer trick, I couldn't understand its purpose. My eyes darted around the space. Definitely a passenger cabin, though kept unreasonably dark. Deara must have really been straining her eyes to read with only the porthole as a source of light. My eyes returned to Katarina. She watched me: patient, but expectant. That patience was slipping, though.

"Sade," I blurted. The full smile returned to Katarina's face, but still the expectant look remained. "Just ... just Sade."

"Sade," Deara snorted. "What sort of name is Sade?"

"Hush," Katarina chided her sister. "You are not exactly one to talk, *Deara*." She looked at me. "Now, Sade. I pulled you out of the hallway not too long ago. Don't worry, nobody saw me do it."

"Why?"

"Because I can't stand the idea of throwing promising youths out the side of an airship while it's over the abyss."

My breath caught and Deara snickered. "More room on the streets for the rest of us, I say."

"Well, thankfully, nobody asked you," Katarina shot, still smiling down at me. Her voice softened again. "I might recommend you find your way into one of my dresses and out of those ... things," she said, picking at my ruined, rain-dampened, oil-slicked jumpsuit.

"She's only going to ruin your dress," Deara pointed out. "It won't take the Enforcers two seconds to realize she's a gutter rat playing dress-up."

"Well," Katarina said, appraising me now. "She may have a

point there." A terse little pout pinched her lips. "In that case, I'm going to need you to fit into this footlocker. Be quick about it."

I looked at the box she had indicated: the metal casing and rearing elks on the seal, but mostly the lock on its outside. I could get into small spaces. I had for years. Still, the idea of folding myself up to squeeze into a chest barely larger than a small dog's kennel that latched from the outside in a room of strangers had me hesitating.

"Death over capture," I said weakly, my voice only a whisper as I decided.

"Death over capture," Katarina said in an appreciative hum. "Well, now, as darling as that little slogan is, it's not very practical, is it?"

"You're going to get us in trouble with this little stunt," Deara said, bored.

In trouble? My life was on the line and this woman was worrying about getting a slap on the hand.

"Death over capture," Katarina said again and shook her head. "Honorable as that sounds, I am certain there are better uses for you than death. Now, the Enforcers are coming around making certain none of you rascals were missed in their first sweep of the ship. If you are not in that box, I'll be forced to tell them you came in here trying to hide, all the while threatening this poor young virtuous maiden with your big scary claws," she said with a dainty swoon and a wink at my talons. I was starting to get the feeling this woman was not the delicate flower she presented herself as being. "I assure you, you and your friends were doomed before you landed. The Enforcers were expecting you. And here you arrived. You look like you've been around a while. Like you might withstand some torture. You've got a sweet young face under all that balloon grease, anyway. They won't just throw you overboard like they will your softer-souled kin. No. They will make *full* use of you before throwing you to the abyss. So. Are you going to get into that box and trust me? Or are you going to turn yourself over to the Enforcers and their pet Aberrants?"

I swallowed and, with a glance between both of the women, I moved toward the box. Katarina pasted a self-satisfied smirk on her painted lips. I stepped in, tucking and curling and wincing as bones and bruises protested. All the while, Katarina stood over me and Deara sat reading in the corner. I was starting to feel I had made a deal with some malicious demon of the winds.

Still, the sound of hard-soled boots thumping down the halls of the airship and men shouting orders drawing near had me curling up tight. Katarina cast me one more smile before closing the box over my head. I heard the latch click and knew I was locked in. If she meant to turn me over, I had packaged myself up nicely to be thrown overboard without so much as a last look at the light.

My ribs hurt. My back hurt. My legs hurt. Hunched up in the cedar-lined chest as I was, I could feel the rumble of the great propellers forcing the terrible gas bag forward and the staccato *tap tap tap* of boots marching the halls. I fought to keep my breathing even. When the knock came, I stilled, my breath holding while I waited for the betrayal.

It must have been Katarina who answered. I couldn't imagine Deara lowering herself to speaking with the Enforcer standing at their door.

"Madam." The man's burly voice was muffled. His accent told me he was from Junction, though not the rich part, as the hint of Dorado creeping at the edge of his voice suggested. "Excuse us. We have to search your quarters. Make certain there are no vagabonds holding you hostage in here." His gruff tone almost verged on flirtatious mirth.

"Oh, certainly. Be my guest. Though I imagine I would have noticed if anybody had come into my room unannounced," Katarina said, returning with a playful tone of her own. "I haven't left all day. And with all that dreadful commotion in the corridors …" I could hear the sound of an officer tearing through the room. No doubt the Aberrants were too busy with their torturous interrogations to use their magic on such a menial task as searching the ship.

I broke into a cold sweat. I could see my own end coming in the mists below. I had come into this with all the confidence of a vagabond who had survived nineteen hard years, three gangs, eight ringleaders, and fifty-seven dives. I had been more nervous going into fist fights than I had this job. With nearly the whole gang at my side I hadn't seen the risk in it. The likelihood of failure. We had descended into a trap. The Enforcers had known, or at least suspected we were coming. Maybe they had even been tipped off. And now I was hiding in a dark little box just waiting for one of the brutes to look inside and find me. The footfalls drew closer.

"By the way, do you know how long until the power will be back on? It really is dreadfully dusky in here, don't you think?"

"I'm sorry, madam. I do not know, but I do know the engineers are working on it now. The little cretins that boarded cut the cables and started pillaging the copper before we were able to reach them." Even with the muffle of the box, I could tell the man was putting on his best facade for the young women in the cabin. They were cute enough to warrant such treatment, I supposed. Even if they weren't, their money surely was.

The boots drew nearer. Katarina gasped a small gasp. "My, my, Sir. You can't mean to inspect a lady's petticoats!" She was righteous indignation flaring with embarrassment.

"We must search everywhere."

"I assure you, no little rapscallion snuck past me and climbed into my drawers. I feel faint at the very thought of you and your men digging around in my underthings." And indeed, she did sound ready to swoon.

"If you have not left your room all day, I suppose I don't see the necessity in it. Corporal."

The boots started shuffling away again.

"We will hold off making port until morning. Need to make sure the ship is clear of the little demons before we dock," the sergeant said.

"I feel so comforted knowing your men are being so very thorough."

"Have a good evening, madam."

The door closed and for a long moment Katarina didn't move. I waited, knowing she was listening for the Enforcers to make their way further down the hall. My legs protested and my beaten muscles cramped worse and worse. I had endured pain through my youth; I could endure this a little longer. Still, I caught myself swimming in anticipation at the sound of Katarina's dainty steps drawing near.

For a while there was nothing, then finally the latch was undone, and the lid of the footlocker was lifted away. I struggled to unfurl.

"Why, you look like you have seen a ghost." The woman laughed, but I didn't understand the joke and only stared. Katarina glanced over at Deara, still reading her book as though a troop of Enforcers hadn't just barged into their cabin, then looked back at me with a pout. "I am starting to think you don't entirely trust me.

Did you think I would just throw you to the Enforcers after all that hard work dragging you in here and getting you all stuffed up in that box?"

"Why did you do those things?" I asked, finally finding a semblance of my voice.

Katarina glanced at Deara again with a small smile. "We are returning home, you see, and, well, it's a little embarrassing but, hmm, I was supposed to bring a guest. Now, I will admit that you are not exactly suitable, but we will make do. We've been away so long already," she said exhaustedly. "In all my months of searching I didn't happen to find anybody fitting and then there you were, laid out and unconscious right in front of my door like an offering from the gods and I thought to myself, 'what the deep and dark, let's see if the girl's got the Moxie.'"

I was uneasy. A cold shiver wriggled down my spine. Deara looked up from her book.

"Offering?" I said in a thin voice, suddenly very aware of just how strange these sisters were.

Katarina laughed and Deara smirked. "Oh, dear me. No, darling, I don't intend to sacrifice you, if that's what is going through that pretty little head of yours. No. No. No. No. No." She smiled and looked at Deara. "It's just fortuitous is all I mean, that you should have been right there right when I needed you."

"Needed me for what?"

Deara was watching me intently now. There was a depth to her eyes that had me reeling.

"I need a pro-té-gé." She said the word in a chopping sing-song manner. She puffed. "Well, I *needed* a husband, but seeing as I don't believe in the institution of marriage and all the cultivating bloodlines nonsense, a protégé will just have to do." She said haughtily. "Now, I searched far and wide and found nothing. And where were you this whole time but on my very own little slice of land, just waiting to fall from the sky and into my lap." She gave me a wink at that. Something about the act unsettled me. "I was starting to think there wasn't anybody else out there suitable for me to snatch up."

"Not with a pulse, anyway," Deara said. She stood and the movement was a little too fluid. It had to be a trick of the light and my nerves playing against me.

"Don't scare the girl," Katarina chided her sister as she drifted closer to me.

My jaw set. I wasn't above boxing a little lady. Deara saw my hands ball into fists as she got closer and smiled. It was a smile that had my heart sinking.

"You're only making her more jittery by not being clear with her, Katarina." Deara was right in front of me now and it was like a wash of cold swam over me. Meeting her gaze was falling into the mists below. I felt trapped, flailing, sinking as I looked into her eyes. I had a feeling of otherworldliness.

Katarina prattled on, not seeing my sudden dip. "You are right, Deara. I am not being clear. I wasn't being entirely truthful to the young sergeant that came in here. I did leave my room for a moment today, just a peek. Happened to be when your poor soul was being beaten in the corridor. I will admit you caught my eye, and I got a little concerned those brutes would go too far."

The depth of Deara's eyes continued to hold me captive. "You looked at me in the corridor," Deara said, as though the words held all the answers.

Deara broke her gaze from mine. I gasped, realizing I had been holding my breath, then looked around the cabin. Unless the sisters had splurged for a second compartment, this one was only laid out for one. I understood why when I looked at Deara again. Her face was a mess of blood and gore. A hole in her cheek where a bullet had ripped through her face before exiting at the back of her skull.

I staggered back, knees hitting the bed behind me causing me to topple back. I stayed where I fell onto the bed, crushed awkwardly against the wall. Still, I didn't move. I couldn't. I couldn't do anything but stare silently at the woman standing in front of me. Her chest was a mass of tattered fabric and stab wounds.

Behind her Katarina continued chattering on. Whatever clarity she was bringing to the situation was lost on me, as entranced and horrified as I was by the sudden change in Deara's condition.

"I call it Moxie because I just think that's more fun than calling it Death Sight. Such a drab and boorish name for it. Anyway though, long story short, if you see my dear old Deara, then sure as sunrise, you've got it." She looked back over at me, a little frown crossing her features when she saw me huddled up on her bed. "My goodness, aren't you forward."

My jaw had dropped as I stared at the horror show that was Deara. There a moment and gone the next. The hole in her face, the gore, all of it vanished, replaced by the bottomless eyes and the smooth, rose petal skin.

"Oh dear. Deara, I thought you said I was scaring her, and you go and do that," Katarina chided.

Deara shrugged indelicately and returned to her chair and her reading. The book, I realized, only manifested when she reached for it.

"Did you hear anything I said?" Katarina asked with a pout.

"Specter … A specter." I stammered like a fool.

Katarina sighed and sat next to me. "That's not entirely true. Deara is fully manifested. She is here just like you and me. Except, only Death Sights can see her." She pulled me back up to sit properly on her bed. "Was it luck or divine intervention that brought you to me? I suppose it doesn't matter."

"What … What happened?" I said, too scared to look at Deara. Afraid she would show me her destroyed body once again. But I could see her out of the corner of my eye, calmly reading in the darkness of the cabin.

"To Deara?"

I nodded and Katarina looked at her sister. Deara gestured dismissively as if to say she didn't care if I knew or not.

"Well, it's likely important you understand; the Regulars aren't big fans of those of us with Moxie. Deara and I, well, we used to have a bit of a reputation for our *particular* craft. Only off Vale, mind you. Don't shit where you eat, as the saying goes," she said, her veneer chipping slightly. "What's the point of seeing the dead if you can't have a little fun with it?" Her words carried none of the lightness one would expect in conjunction with the statement. "A couple of the best conjures you ever did see. None of the smoke and mirror steam show nonsense you get with the charlatans. You can typically tell if somebody truly has the Death Sight or not. Sometimes all their hooting and hollering, calling the dead actually works, and you'll see the summoned on the edge of the stage trying to communicate through ears unable to hear their cries. The charlatans torture those passed with their games," she said, a bitter look crossing her face. "You really didn't realize it until now, what you are, I mean?"

I shook my head, but behind my eyes flashed images of friends lost in falls or beaten to death on the streets. We lived hard lives and few of us made it through childhood, much less to grow into adults.

Had those images, those tricks of the morning mists and pleadings of the mind been real, then? Had I been seeing the dead this whole time, only thinking myself in a depression of loss?

Katarina read the realization in my eyes and nodded. "Hmm. Yes. Plenty of folks with the Sight who don't understand it and can't handle what they see tend to slip into madness. It's hard to tell who is truly mad and who is plagued by the spirits of those they mistakenly draw to them." She looked at Deara again. "Anyway. Deara and I and our reputation found ourselves in a bit of trouble a couple years back. Deara had a nice young man ask her to speak with his departed mama. And when she obliged, I guess she fell into his sinister little trap. His mama gave him proof of her arrival at her side, and he took that proof and let it fuel his fear.

"He and his friends got hold of dear old Deara. I'm sure she showed you her wounds and that's why you are so pale. They beat her to a mess. Twenty-seven stab wounds in all before they put a bullet in her head and ended her life.

"The little bastards threw her body into the abyss, leaving behind not a speck of evidence, so everybody just says she ran off. Enough folk had seen her walk off with a young man that the rumors of her eloping with some devious wanderer became more prevalent than the rumors of her death. I only know because, of course, we found each other. But without proof, I would only be committing myself to a nut house or a similar fate if I tried to bring the facts up to the authorities. The Enforcers are worth less than ice water in the arctic."

"That's terrible," I said, looking at Deara. The woman gave another shrug and returned to her reading. "So ... We are aberrant?" I asked, returning to Katarina.

"Well, yes. I mean by the definition of the word. But the Abbies aren't like us. They can't see as we do, and we can't work magic through glyphs like they do. But we aren't *normal*, so I suppose we are aberrant." She released a deep sigh, then handed me a damp rag. "Keep getting that filth off of you; I need to see what I'm working with here."

I did as I was told, not knowing why, except that in the back of my mind I knew I was intimidated by this petite rich girl. She stood to bustle around the room and tutted at Deara, the ghost now perched awkwardly on the footlocker as she read. Deara allowed herself to be shooed away from the box, though I suspected that if she had chosen not to move, Katarina would not have been hindered in the slightest in opening the box, given the way Deara now stood in the bed, her hips rising from the covers in a sickeningly mind-bending manner.

I looked away from the distracted spirit and rose from the bed to stand as close to the wall as I could. "Why haven't I heard of Death Sights before?"

"Aside from being rare?" Katarina said, bustling about in the dark cabin. "The Abbies are the only Society-acknowledged magic conduits, but if the Death Sight isn't magic, I don't know what to call it. A gift, maybe, from some devious god. Either way, we are a bit rarer than the Aberrants. Either because those of us with the Moxie lose ourselves to our own minds or fearful Regulars find a way to off us on their own." She huffed, casting a disdainful glare at the small porthole and the hazy light filtering in before setting her hands on her hips and turning to me.

"I'll teach you all of this when we get to the estate, but it's not just Death Sights and those symbol-sketching Aberrants; there's all sorts of magic out there. Charmers, Channelers, Past Sights, Future Sights—though most of them are checked in for the long stay at the sanitariums—Present Sights—I don't recommend conversing with them, they are always so darn uncomfortable to talk to, see too much, you know—Deflectors, Reflectors, Breakers, Amplifiers, Sleuths, the list goes on. There are all sorts of types of Moxie out there. It is what makes the world go 'round, but nobody talks about it any aside from in the Abbies and Tinkerers. The symbol sketchers are the ones who are sought out and cultivated, thereby making them more visible. Less easy to push them to the shadows of Society."

"Why is that?"

Katarina took a seat on the footlocker. "It rather makes sense, doesn't it? They are the most versatile. There are thousands upon thousands of glyphs of power, all with different meanings and impacts. If an Aberrant really wanted to see the dead, I am sure they could find a way to do it with their magic. Even the misfires, the Tinkerers, can blend their weakened glyphs with invention." She frowned and looked toward the porthole again. "They are throwing your friends overboard." Her voice hollowed.

I was silent, my eyes following hers, but I didn't see anything. No bodies of vagabonds.

"How do you know?" I asked slowly.

She turned her eyes toward me slowly and extended her hand to me. "You really closed yourself off to your nature, didn't you?" Her voice was a little distant. I carefully set my hand on hers. "All the death on this ship, and you didn't feel it?" Her fingers closed tightly around mine. First, I felt a slight tug at the edges of my mind, a curious look on Katarina's face accompanying the sensation, then a subtle push.

A familiar feeling followed the woman's push. Lives ending. A sensation I had always noticed but chalked up to some dread at events witnessed, apprehension, fear.

"Oh, no, I see now that you know the feeling of death," Katarina said. "You just didn't know what to ascribe the feeling to." With Katarina's hand came an acute sense of the ending lives. Where it had once been a shade of a sense it was now pinpoint. The exact moment of loss brought a twitch to my eye.

She took her hand away, but the focus she had brought lingered. I felt another life end and knew that whether we had been friends or rivals, we had slept on the same floor and eaten the same paltry meals.

"How did you do that?" I asked quietly, half trying not to notice the deaths I could do nothing about and half feeling obligated to note each of their passings.

"She's a Channeler," Deara said, in her bored drawl. "Aberrants are Aberrants and they will never be anything more or less. It's not the same with the rest of us. All they do is pull from the fold, while we straddle its edges." For the briefest moment there was interest, but the ghost quickly wrangled it back into her constant detachment

"You will find blends of magics. My family made a point of cultivating beyond Death Sight, enough of a collection to almost ensure a double inheritance each generation. Deara, for example was both a Death Sight and a Past Sight—she saw memories. As she said, I am both a Death Sight and a Channeler. I can channel those special little differences in our abilities. Make them mine. I channeled a little bit of myself through you to help focus your abilities."

"So, what is she?" Deara asked her sister.

Katarina gave a delicate shrug. "As far as I can tell, a pure Death Sight, but ..." She frowned at me. "Sometimes the gods are devious." A buzz went through the ship before the lights flickered on in the cabin. Katarina clapped her hands together once and released an excited squeal. "Finally." She turned to me. "Well, you covered your face pretty well while the Enforcers were beating you, at least." She cupped my chin, turning my face from side to side. Her eyebrow cocked and a grin spread on her lips. "Not a terrible haul for the trip," she said appreciatively, causing me to swallow nervously. "I can work with this. You ever been to Junction?"

"I've never left Vale."

"Hmm … Well, have you heard their accent?"

I nodded.

"Think you can muster it?"

The streets had taught me more than sleight of hand and cutting purse strings.

"I think I might just," I said, mimicking the holier than thou tones and approximating the words.

Katarina beamed at Deara. "Look at that, a genuine mimic. We will work on your bearing but for now this will do. We just have to get you off this ship. Take that … ugh … whatever it is," she said, gesturing at my tattered jumpsuit, "off and let me assess the damage."

I hesitated in simply obliging to this woman's order without question, then bowed my head and did as she wished. I felt like pummeled beef, and if she could offer any assistance at all, I likely needed all the help I could get.

Katarina didn't offer me even a semblance of privacy as I struggled out of my clothes.

"The way I see it, you have a choice to make, Sade. You can come home with me. Let me train you. Let me pass my knowledge on to you. Or, once I get you off this ship, you can go back to the streets. I will admit, I tend to favor the idea of you coming on home. I imagine you would have to find a new gang after this mess, and you are getting a bit old for that now, aren't you?"

I swallowed. I had been planning on getting out; making my way on nothing more than a pocket watch, some rings, and a pitiful life of ferreting every spare copper away. It didn't sound like much of a plan now as it played in my mind, and it certainly didn't sound like much of a plan without so much as a landing pad after all of this. Sure, there were still some of my old gang around, but with Beater captured or dead the binding would snap and the remaining members would scatter to the winds. And for me, to have survived this fiasco, there would be suspicion. I would be labeled a snitch. Even if there was a doubt of my misdeeds, I would still be cast out. There wasn't enough room to risk a snitch in the ranks. Even if I wasn't, Katarina was right: I was getting too old to join another gang. If mine fell apart, I would be on my own.

"I'll go with you," I said, feeling cornered into the agreement and more desperate than I ever wanted to be. Another life slipped away somewhere on the ship. I shuddered.

"That is the right choice." She winked, then circled me. "My, my, you are well built, if maybe a little undernourished," Katarina said approvingly. I had never been ashamed of my body, never shy with it considering a life of tight quarters and communal living, but Katarina's scrutiny made my fingers itch for cover. "I'll make certain you are well fed, and we will train these muscles to do more than look pretty and threaten the wealthy. How does that sound?" It didn't matter how it sounded; Katarina was clearly formulating a plan with herself and only herself.

Deara peeked at me over her book and frowned before she noticed me watching her. The concerned look instantly vanished, and she turned back to her reading, her back now directed at me.

Katarina put a thoughtful little pout on her painted lips. "With all those cuts and bruises I don't know how in the heavens I will get you off this airship." She was talking to herself now. "But I do love a challenge. Maybe with enough makeup I'll be able to make you passable."

"You'll make her look like a Red Light Girl with how much makeup it will take to make her passable," Deara said.

Katarina tsked at her sister. "We both know the right dress is all it takes to throw the dogs off the scent."

"I don't have to be able to smell to know it would take quite the dress to cover up that particular scent," Deara said, peering at me over her book and wrinkling her nose.

"Don't be a boor." Katarina said, circling me, her hand poised under her chin, finger tapping thoughtfully against her cheek. "She's not wrong, though. Keep scrubbing. Good and hard now. I'll help you if you need, but a girl's got to have her dignity. Isn't that right? And stop all that whingeing. It's not attractive."

I couldn't help but scowl at the woman. She was assessing me like a slab of meat with no regard for my injuries, the peril waiting for me just outside the door, or the death I had witnessed that day.

My expression flattened again. How much death must this woman have seen? I had no idea what was going on, but I had a creeping dread that following this woman's orders was my only chance at not being thrown into the abyss. Death over capture.

Still, the drive to survive was stronger.

"Look at you," Katarina said appreciatively. "Here I was worried all the fight got beaten out of you. I'm glad you still seem to have a little left. You are going to need it."

"I have survived the streets for nineteen years."

"Different streets," Katarina hummed, her eyes flicking to Deara for a moment. "I think I can work with this," she announced ceremoniously. "Once you are cleaned up, anyway. So just … Keep scrubbing. Focus on your hands and face, nobody will be looking at your legs, at least not until we are off this airship." She broke her own prim image with a little smirk.

I did as I was told. There really was no other option. This woman was probably my best chance at getting off this airship.

Deara watched me silently for a time, a strange, remorseful look in her eye that I couldn't quite place.

"You're resilient, I'll give you that," Katarina said. "I thought for sure the Enforcers would beat you to death, but maybe when you went limp it took all the fun out of it for them." She prodded at my bruised ribs, arms, hips, shoulders; there were bruises everywhere. When it seemed she had touched just about every inch of my body, she nodded with satisfaction. "No breaks, at least. Good, because I want to get started as soon as we are off this gods-deprived airship." She turned and dug around in one of her boxes for a bit before producing a little blue pill. "This will help with the pain. Get some sleep. We will get up early to get you ready."

"Can I ask one more question?"

"Of course, dear."

"If you didn't leave this room except to pull me in, where did you get the beef?"

She grinned. "Now, that is a good question." Katarina laughed and looked to Deara. "I haven't left, but Deara has. I told you, she's fully manifested. Small things like slabs of beef are no challenge for her."

"You're welcome," Deara said dryly, without looking away from her book, her mouth taking on a nasty twist at being revealed in her good deed done to me.

"It was her idea, you know," Katarina whispered, as if Deara couldn't hear everything said between us in the small space. "Can't tell her to do anything. She's a pretty unhelpful haunt to have hanging around."

I had a hard time believing the surly specter in the corner had gone out of her way in even the slightest for me.

3:

Katarina settled in under her covers and fell deeply asleep. I huddled on the floor in the corner. Deara had taken her leave, disappearing through the wall at her back. The coy look in her eye when she did so was a clear sign she chose the route of departure entirely to unsettle me. One day, and everything in my life had changed.

I considered the little blue pill Katarina had given me. I drank my share, but always stayed away from drugs. Never knew what was really in them, and I had seen too many lives ruined too often. Still, this little painkiller didn't seem like a bridge too far. Katarina had popped two herself before bed, though I didn't know what pain she was trying to dull.

A small form materialized by the door. The boy from earlier. Marco. Of course he had been a ghost. How many had I unknowingly interacted with over the years? The boy was timid in his approach. His wounds had all vanished and he looked hale and hearty except for the fact that he was dead. I didn't move.

He lay down on the floor beside me, curling into a little ball. Scared. Confused. Needing comfort.

As uncomfortable as I was, I couldn't imagine what the ghost child was going through. I put my arm around him protectively and he settled back against my chest. He was cold. Like holding mist. But somehow I didn't mind.

He seemed to calm and drift off to sleep. I marveled at that. How could a specter sleep? Deara didn't seem to need such a thing, but maybe she was off sleeping somewhere by herself. Or maybe this child still had not fully come to understand what had happened to him.

I swallowed the painkiller and let its soothing cradle me to sleep.

4:

When I woke, the boy was gone, Deara still hadn't returned, but Katarina was in full swing. She bustled around the little cabin, tossing items in the footlocker on the floor beside me with the haphazardness of irreverence. I pressed back and away from her chaotic shuffling.

"Did you know these little windows opened? I can't imagine the foolish soul who would ever dare such a thing when a stray cloud could waft in at any time," Katarina said. "But who am I to speak?" She saw my nervous look at the window. "It was only open but a moment. Just long enough to toss your dirty rags out. I would hate for the Enforcers to find them stashed anywhere around my cabin and come knocking. We have enough troubles as it is without an investigation on our hands. Though, I do admit, I find this little device intriguing," she said, laying a careful finger on the talons she had left on her bed. "Terrifying, to be sure. I thought you might like to keep them."

"Those talons can be very dangerous," I warned, standing to check the lock on the spring mechanism before Katarina did something she regretted. My body ached from the dive, the beating, the night on the floor.

"Are they a weapon?"

"They are a lifeline," I said, shaking my head then stretching. "That's not to say they have never been used as a weapon before. But if you miss your landing on a dive, a sharp pair of talons may be the only thing that saves you." I resisted the urge to strap the device to my bare arm.

The woman looked at me appraisingly, then nodded some silent approval to herself.

"What?"

"I think you will do just fine under my tutelage. Maybe I can pass you as a cousin or some distant relation. I suppose we will see." She carefully set my talons in a small box that she then tucked away in the footlocker beside my dive pack. How the sergeant had not taken one look at the clothing all around the cabin and realized the footlocker had been empty, I didn't know, but it didn't matter. Somehow, I had evaded detection this long. "What skills do you have?" the woman said while I watched the array of clothing disappear item by item into the chest. "I mean, aside from dashingly boarding airships and robbing the masses."

"I ... I don't know."

Katarina straightened, turning her attention from packing to me. She handed me a dress, then turned to her box of makeup. "There must be something. As you said, you've survived the streets, so you must have some ability, even if it is just protecting your head. By the way," she produced the pocket watch and handful of rings, "I found these in your pack. I know the Darres, you know?" She must have seen my nervous twinge because she waved a dismissive hand. "I'm not going to turn you in for stealing the man's watch, but I am curious what you were planning to do with them?"

I shrugged. "Sell them off. I'm at the end of my time in the gangs unless I'm willing to make a few compromises that I am not."

"I think I understand. And what, pray tell, was your plan after selling these fine items off?"

I looked at the porthole wistfully. "Maybe leave Vale. Find a house willing to take me on or a seamstress so hard up for help they will take on a woman without a reference." It was sounding rather hopeless a plan now that I was saying it out loud.

"You wanted to go straight?"

I nodded.

"That's a little boring, but I suppose I have never had to risk my life trying to jump onto an airship to survive." She nodded toward the dress. "Well, hurry up now. We don't have all morning." She returned to her halfhearted packing. "Do you have any skill with a needle?"

"I do."

"More or less than your ability to mimic a Junction accent?"

"I dare say more," I said, feeling this was hardly the time or person to be modest around.

"Well, why didn't you say that when I asked? Either way." She turned, equipped with a set of brushes and powders. Her eyes went to the dress. "What are you waiting for?"

"Oh." I looked at the dress in my hands. The blue silk and extravagant billows of fabric held to form by an intricate weave of lace. I hesitated, but Katarina was waiting, her perfectly placid face chipping into a downturn curve each moment I balked.

I hurried to dress, wishing I could somehow keep any part of my body from touching the elegant fabrics. Katarina fussed around me, pulling here and lacing there to make the dress look as though it had been made for my body and not hers.

"You're a little taller and your build isn't quite right for this cut, but," she stepped back to assess, then finished with her adjustments, "I think this will work. Those boots of yours luckily don't have much lift, otherwise they may show under the hem. Any lady worth her passage on this airship would take notice of *those* in an instant. We can't do anything about that build of yours, so we will just have to accept a little less than perfect. We will work on getting a proper diet into you so you aren't all muscle and wire. It never hurts to have a little softness, you know." With a wink she spun me around so my back was to her, and set upon my hair.

Her brush slid over my greasy black hair and I felt another wave of shame at the idea of destroying yet another of this woman's nice things. Katarina was focused now, though, and seemed unbothered by my grime ruining her implements. While she worked, Deara drifted back into the room, looking at me disapprovingly before lingering behind her sister.

"We'll get you a proper bath when we get home, but this should do for now," she said, brushing and pulling and pinning my hair back in a tight braid and coil. "What do you think, Deara?"

"Hmph," Deara gave a bored grunt, but she was still appraising me.

"Sounds like a harumph of approval," Katarina said, spinning me around again.

"Dress her up all you want, but somebody is bound to notice her and get you caught, Kat," Deara said apprehensively from her corner.

"Not if we get you cleaned up and looking pretty," Katarina said with such conviction that I almost believed her. Then I remembered my black eye and split lip. As if she could read my thoughts, she said, "Now to see about those bruises." She set the brushes to my skin, brushing, powdering, assessing. "Don't want to go too thick. Don't want to go too light." She pursed her lips in a tight little pinch as she focused.

"You're forgetting about the Abbies," Deara muttered, sounding reluctant to help. "If they take any notice of her at all, they will prod."

"It warms my heart to hear a little concern from you, Deara," Katarina drawled, not seeming to feel the same threat in the air that I did at Deara's reminder. If the Aberrants so much as looked at me,

I was certain they would see a vagabond playing dress-up with a blackened eye, bruised cheeks, and a swollen lip.

Katarina held up a mirror and I was surprised at what I saw. A young lady stared back. The angular black eyes that I knew had to be mine reflected back at me. I was still a little swollen and the bruises still darkened my skin in some areas, but Katarina knew her craft and had worked to soften the bruising instead of simply trying to cake them away. She had pulled my sheafs of black hair back, hiding the grime and poor care with a tight braid and artistic coil just over my left shoulder. There was still function in the style, I couldn't help but notice. Artistically done up, but neatly out of the way. A woman could do a dive with her hair so finely tucked and woven.

My eyes went back to my face. Lips plump, if not a little swollen; sharp eyes; long lashes; a defined yet delicately round chin. This was not what I thought I looked like. I hadn't taken much time to look in the muddy puddles or distorted reflections on shop windows. I realized the last time I had really seen myself I had been a child with the round face of youth. Somewhere in the years I had lost all of that.

"A little vain, isn't she?" Deara said, and I realized I had been looking for too long.

"I'm sorry," I said, dropping my eyes. "I'm just not used to seeing my reflection so clearly."

"You poor dear," Katarina cooed. "Well, you are going to have to learn how to take care of yourself, so we will have to remedy that. For now, though, here." She set a dainty hat on my head. The short lace veil sweeping over the narrow brim cast just enough shadow over my eyes to hide the remains of the bruising, but not enough to be suspicious. It was the sort of attire no wealthy lady would be seen without on the streets of Vale. They wore their little hats like badges of honor. I had made fun of the foolish little frills in my youth. Now I was glad for them. "Deara?"

The specter didn't just glance at me this time, but instead stood and circled. "I think she will pass. If it's just the Regs she's trying to deceive. I still think you are not giving enough credit to the Aberrants. They aren't just bulls; they have sensitivity, too. They will notice her because she has magic. The moment they do, they will probe to see what she is, and the moment they do that, they will see exactly where she came from."

"I'll be with her, so as long as they probe me and not her, we will be fine. If Sade here can keep her head about her when we pass the Abbies, we won't have any trouble."

Deara shook her head. "I still think you are taking things too lightly. But it's not my head." Whether it was a loss of control fueled by her irritation or to drive her point home, the specter's gunshot wound took shape on her pale complexion. She shook her head and the wound disappeared again. She looked at me while Katarina returned to her chaotic packing. "Be careful," she said quietly. "My sister has a way about her that tends to disregard the safety of those around her. But she's still your best bet to get off this airship."

"You don't think this is going to work?"

Deara shook her head. "Not at all. By virtue of you being a Death Sight, you will attract their attention. There are Aberrants throughout the ship and I wouldn't be surprised if they are at the dock as well. The Enforcers don't want to let even one of you little rats scurry out from under their heels." Her sour tone softened, and she almost looked apologetic for the statement. "Look. Even if the Abbies don't pay you much mind the first or second time, my point is that one of them will. If only out of curiosity. They can sense us … you," she corrected, remembering she no longer fit with other Death Sights. "They can sense your connection to magic but not what you are. Inevitably, one of them is going to get curious and prod to figure it out. These Abbies are used to getting away with invading whoever they want whenever they want, and now they have the excuse of official police business. Unless you had a lot of friends in your gang who are still hanging around and looking out for you, being a Death Sight is only going to play against you here. And that puts Katarina in danger."

"It took me too long to find another Death Sight, and one I approve of, too," Katarina cut in. "I am not going to let some fool Aberrants sink their teeth into her. Don't you worry, Sade. And you, stop pumping fear into her, Deara. As if that will help us in any way." She put her foot down and set her hands stubbornly on her hips to stare down her sister. "Honestly, why do I keep you around?"

"If it's you keeping me here, I do wish you would stop," Deara drawled, then summoned her book to her hand with a swipe of her fingers. "Fine. I'll just be over here."

"Can I … Can I ask why you stay here?" I asked timidly.

Deara snorted. "Stay here? And where is it you recommend I go?" She sneered.

I shook my head, seeing I was going to get nowhere fast with the specter, but tried again. "What is keeping you here?"

Deara didn't respond right away, but glanced at me over the edge of her book.

Katarina darted from the room to grab a porter for her footlocker. With her sister gone, Deara sighed a long, deep sigh.

"It doesn't work like that," Deara said glumly. "There is no staying here or going there."

"What about moving on, though? The *great beyond* or whatever?"

"The *great beyond*?" She snorted. "A fantasy of the Regulars who fear the potential of nothingness at the end of their lives."

"But there must be something. I mean," I gestured toward her, "if you are here, then there is something?"

She gave me a coy look. A thoughtful grunt emitted from her throat before she remembered she hated me. "Does my existence evidence that?" she snarked.

"I mean, in a way, doesn't it? The dead must go somewhere. Otherwise, the streets would be filled with them."

"And how do you know they are not? You, who in all your years have never realized how many dead you were seeing in the streets? Thinking them living, thinking them walking around. Tune them out once and you will see just how possible it is. This concept of moving on, of going to a *great beyond*. I've seen nothing more than the dead simply disappearing. Fast, slow, it doesn't matter. They just stop being."

"Stop being?"

"Disappear."

"Isn't that moving on?"

"Moving on implies some peace. Some coming to terms. This is not that. This is simply an end. Days, weeks, years, millennia. The dead peel away until there is nothing left, then they are gone. Does that sound very appealing to you?"

I swallowed.

"I thought not. Hence the Regulars and their *great beyond*."

"But there must be something. An end state? Why would there be a transitional phase if it was just to nothingness?" I said, not comprehending. "I mean, what happens to the dead when they … you know …" I struggled for words, "are not here anymore?"

"Look. I don't know the answer. And I don't really feel like philosophizing with you right now." Deara growled. "All you need to know is there are dead who are here and then not. Some pass. Some stay. It's not a choice."

"If it was, would you go?"

"I don't know," Deara admitted. "Not even Albain knows what happens when we go. So, why rush toward that?" Albain, the God of Death. Was he now my deity? I hesitated at the prospect of simply casting aside Devton for this new god.

"Have you spoken with him?"

"Albain?" She laughed. "Have you ever tried speaking with one of the gods? Their representatives are mindless drones. I imagine a conversation with one of them would feel very much like a conversation with you."

I sighed and shook my head, turning back to the mirror to check that nothing had fallen into disarray during the discussion.

Behind me Deara sighed just as heavily and said, "I have never made an attempt to speak with Albain. I was never the most devoted Death Sight. Supposedly the gods are still on their isle should you ever wish to try. Maybe he does know what is beyond. Maybe he chooses not to say." I turned to look at the ghost. She was looking at the porthole with a wistful look. Tired. Her eyes shifted to me. "Anyway, you have more important concerns right now." She gave me a strange look, then with a flick of her wrist summoned her book back to her hand.

"How …" I started, then thought better of it.

The specter did not bother looking up from the pages. "I read this book cover to cover in life," she said. Her voice held none of the previous malice that had seemed to constantly float in her words before. "Three times I read it. Thankfully I have a good memory." She looked up at me with those deep eyes. "Seems that talent translated with me in some way. Even if it is a very small way." Before I could say anything else, she cut me off. "Don't think too hard on it. Besides, you have your whole life ahead of *you* to ponder such things."

I watched her return her eyes to the pages. It all looked so real.

The door opened and Katarina led the porter, a young man, in, gesturing at the footlocker.

"Ready?" Katarina asked, setting her hand on my arm to be escorted from the room.

Stepping from the cabin seemed a foolish venture, but staying inside was not an option. I swallowed and set out with Katarina.

"We have a watcher," Katarina commented, her eyes flicking to the specter boy tailing us down the corridor. Marco dodged expertly around the flowing skirts of the ladies and the rushing porters filling the hall even though I suspected he no longer had any need to be so careful. "He seems awfully intent on you. You didn't manifest him, did you?"

"I don't know how to do that."

"Did you tell him to do something? Give him an order? That sort of thing?"

I thought back and winced. "I told him to stay with me. I didn't realize …"

She looked at me out of the corner of her eye, amused. "One day as a realized Death Sight and you've already manifested a dead. Just ignore him. He will go away."

"Did I do something wrong? Did I trap him here?"

Katarina laughed in a sing-song manner. "No. If they manifest, they weren't going anywhere fast anyway. Some dead pass instantly and some linger; it's just the inexplicable way of it. All you did was add a crowd to your life. It is kind of creepy having a little kid follow you around, is all. And right now, it's rather distracting." This coming from the woman who saw dead on the regular and had her dead sister walking at her side at that very moment. Maybe it was different with family. "Like I said, ignore him and he will move along eventually. Try to stop looking at him."

Marco followed us at a distance, eyes fixed on the Enforcers and Aberrants lining the corridors. I did my best to keep my eyes forward as if the presence of the Aberrants didn't coil my insides. I pretended not to notice their eyes on me, picking apart my thin disguise at Katarina's side. Deara walked as though shielding me from the more intense gazes, stating that the interference of death could throw off the Aberrants. I wasn't certain the interference was enough as time and again eyes fell on us.

The light of the outside and the city beyond peeked in at us from the door to my escape, but first, immigration stood in our way. I tried to beat down the rising anxiety in my chest as we joined the line of well-to-dos as they moved closer to the inspection point.

"Madam, your papers." The sergeant from the day before smiled at Katarina, gloved hand extended to receive the damning documents.

Katarina cast him a winning and altogether too forward smile as she dug around for the requested travel documents.

An Aberrant stood close at our right, her eyes locked on us as Katarina produced the papers. "I'm still working on immigration documents for her," she said with a slight nod toward me, "but as you can see, her travel documents are in order."

"Reason for immigration?" he asked, looking over the paperwork.

"Well now, the best help a woman can find comes from Junction. Isn't that so, Sarah?"

"Yes, madam," I said in the bounce of a Junction citizen, trying to ignore the curious stare of the Aberrant.

The man looked up at me. Suspicious? I couldn't tell. Everybody seemed to be able to see through my act. "Got a little bit of a shiner there?" He noted, an apologetic tilt to his eyes.

I touched the bruise delicately and ducked my head so the hat hid it in shadow. "Yessir. I'm afraid I was in the halls when those ruffians came in." To my right the Aberrant was flicking a glyph into the air with a lazy finger. I swore the rings on her fingers hummed as the glyph burned into existence. I knew I was made. And if not, I was about to be. Deara had been right. Simply having ties to magic seemed to draw the interest of the Aberrants.

The Aberrant grinned, then straightened from the wall to come over.

"I am truly sorry you had to go through that," the sergeant was saying, but I had abandoned all pretense and turned my head in full toward the Aberrant who leaned close to whisper in my ear.

"How many dead do you see, Death Sight? I can feel them hovering around you like flies. I wonder why? What makes you so interesting to them?" Her voice was silk. Deadly silk. Thin lips pulled in a mirthless smile.

Deara shifted uncomfortably and Marco all but charged the woman.

"Excuse me?" I asked, taking an appalled step back from the woman who seemed ready to sketch another glyph into existence, something to dig deeper into my being maybe? Something to pull the tortured truth from my lips?

Behind me a man shouted and a woman screamed as Marco crashed unseen through the lot of them, sending papers flying and knocking purses from hands.

Deara vanished from my side, and in the next moment there was chaos on the docks ahead where the prisoners were being held for transport. I saw the links of chains binding the beaten vagabonds rattle and fall away. Deara flashed between them.

"Dear me," Katarina exclaimed and nearly fainted before I caught her, only adding to the sudden chaos.

The sergeant spun, shouting and brandishing Katarina's papers at his men. He turned back to us and shoved the documents back into Katarina's hands with a swift apology and a bow before running off to get the prisoners back in their bonds.

The panic of the crowd behind surged and a sea of well-to-do bodies suddenly dove between me and the Aberrant, seeking escape from the haunted airship.

Katarina grabbed my hand and pulled me along with the crowd, sinking gratefully into the panic.

"Maybe you should keep that little manifestation around," she said. "If nothing else, he seems protective of you."

I looked at the vagabonds. There were so few of them now. All looking worse for the wear, but their sudden hope for freedom kicking a little life into them. It was a futile thing that would only result in more pain for them. I didn't know how to feel at the faces I did not see among them. Death over capture had been the mantra, but they seemed a poor set of options as I walked free.

"Can't we do anything for them?" I asked, desperate.

"Would they have done anything for you?" Katarina said dryly and all I could picture was Twenty pushing me ahead of her like a shield. "Deara already did too much for them. Let's make the most of it."

"What about your trunk?" I said in a weak attempt at slowing her down a moment.

"I'll send a porter down to fetch it. I'm not going to change my mind. Now, come on."

We hurried from the shipyard and the rush of panicked citizens, armed Enforcers, and overeager Aberrants just waiting to be let off the leash.

I felt foolish striding openly in the overly bright port, playing dress-up in a borrowed dress and my black eye. I knew that even with the chaos behind us, people were looking at me. I was certain of it. Any moment a hand would grab my arm and pull me back with the rest of the vagabonds. My shoulders hunched protectively around me.

Katarina nudged me with her elbow, grabbing my arm as though we were the best of friends. "Stand up straight. No young lady would carry herself like that."

She was right. I had played the part on cons. I knew better than to let the act slip. I could picture the withering look that Deara would be giving me had she seen, eyes screaming her disapproval. I set my jaw, straightened my spine, and rolled my shoulders back. I hadn't survived as long as I had in the gangs to be outdone by these soft women.

At the edge of the docks Katarina gestured for a motorcarriage and we climbed in. For a moment I wondered how Marco would find me again, but the sight of the Aberrants organizing into ranks on the docks overpowered that concern. The boy would find his way, even if it wasn't to me.

"They have created quite the haunted airship with that little action," Katarina said, sounding almost amused as she settled back into the seat and the motorcarriage roared down the road. "That much concentrated death, it tends to create lingerers. The best thing they can do for it now is sink the ship into the abyss."

"What happens to the dead onboard if they sink it?"

Katarina looked at me like I was foolish. "They are dead." She sighed, remembering how new to this I was. "It is not as though they will die again. They will stay, go, or if they are lucky, move on." She leaned over and nudged me. "You're home free."

"Thank you."

"Thank me after you understand what you've gotten yourself into." She sat back and looked at the passing city.

The yellow of electric lamps kept the streets in a constant cover of sickly light. Near the docks, roughnecks moved between warehouses. The driver did well to avoid the rougher parts of town, but in the lowlands, as the port was, it was difficult to avoid all the dark and dank. I looked down familiar streets, a strange tightening in my chest. As we moved higher I could swear the lights became whiter and brighter, less sickly. One could almost feel the money in the hum of electricity.

"She knew I was a Death Sight," I said softly, though the rumble of the motor drowned out our voices before they could reach the driver. "That Abbie."

"Aberrants are pricks. They really don't like the rest of us. They will always get into our business, welcomed or not." Katarina opened her small case of pills and swallowed one back before returning them to the safety of her purse. I frowned, wondering again what pain the woman could be experiencing, then let it go.

"Why do they care?"

"I don't imagine they would if the Regulars didn't take such an issue with us. Aberrants are the little pets of the Society Chairs, so what the Regs don't like, they don't. The Regulars don't like those of us who can see what they cannot. They don't like the idea that we can chat with their dearly departed. They don't like that we can hear the truths of those passed."

"The dead can lie, though, surely?"

"They can indeed. Whispers, though, barely have the wherewithal to think, much less lie. They just enact events from their lives, so it really is only the vengeful dead who do. But you can tell a vengeful spirit easy enough. The need starts to overcome them and what they were in life is swept away by it. Those without the consuming fire of vengeance, their lies might be little things, but they aren't the sorts of things that lead to wrongful accusations. You see, the dead simply have no reason to lie. Not anymore. Not to those few of us who can see them. So, they often tell the truth. Their murders and misdeeds are brought to light, but too often there is no justice. The Death Sight who knows the truth just ends up accused of insanity. Still, the threat remains that the truth may be found out, and even if a Reg hasn't done anything wrong, at the very least, they don't like that we are different." Her eyes flicked to the driver, but the man was intent on the road and seemed to care nothing for our subdued conversation.

"So, Deara doesn't lie?"

Katarina laughed prettily, but heartily. Enough to draw a quick glance from the driver through the rearview mirror before his eyes returned to the road. "Oh, Deara lies a lot. I've been trying to get her to tell me who murdered her for years now, but I made the mistake of manifesting her before she gave me the name." She clicked her tongue. "Once the dead fully manifest, they are as close to life as they ever will be again. They are as they were, only on a transitional plane. You will start learning the nuances." She cast me a coy glance out of the side of her eye. "She's taken an interest in you, you know, dear? She may not act like it—she likes her little facade—but oh yes, she is intrigued. Maybe just because you are a Death Sight from outside any of the major families. Maybe because you were brought to us under such provenance. But," she looked at me in full now, "don't forget that she is dead and you are alive. And don't let her forget it either."

I frowned and shook my head. "I won't, madam."

"Good. You can forget the subservient nonsense, dear. I've decided, I need you to come from one of the lesser branches of my family. It will be easier for me to get the Society to accept you that way, and I *do* want you to be accepted. The Norwoods of Junction don't get out much and you are ever so good at that accent, it almost makes me swoon. Nobody will question it. I'll write my fool uncle to inform him of his darling daughter that he never knew he had. You look like you are half Junctionian, anyway. A thin cover, but enough for the right touch of intrigue and scandal needed to get you invited to parties." She grinned and swept a hand toward the window at the approaching estate. "Home sweet home."

I turned my attention to the manor as she gave the gate guards a small nod. We were higher above the cloudline than I had ever been invited before. It was dangerous territory to tread as a vagabond. Still, we were nowhere near the summit of Vale. On the worst days a stray cloud drift might still be a concern at this altitude, but it would be far less than what I had experienced in the lowland slums.

The manor itself was larger than any house I had ever seen, but I had a suspicion this mansion was considered small among the well-to-dos of the higher climes. Still, I gawked. The drive was long, the grounds well kept, the grass green. I had never seen green grass. Any tufts of it I had seen up close had been yellowed sprigs fighting for life between the bluestone slabs of footways of the low city. The lack of green in my visual palette had never been so apparent as it was now.

"Get that bad habit out now," Katarina warned, unamused by my staring.

I obediently turned off my amazement and sat serenely beside Katarina as though this arrival home were no different from any other.

A butler hurried from the house to open the door for Katarina. "Welcome home, madam," he said with a bow. He cast me a questioning look.

"My cousin."

He bowed again. "Your baggage?"

"Ah, yes, there was a bit of an incident at the port. Send somebody down to fetch my trunk, would you?"

"Of course, madam."

Katarina led me into the mansion. I had been in houses so grand before, but never as a welcomed guest. Two bronze statues of elk stood at the entryway, an imposing opulence.

"You can have Deara's room," Katarina said as we strode in.

"She absolutely cannot have Deara's room," the specter bristled, appearing at her sister's side.

"It is not as though you use it," Katarina said with a drab look at her sister.

"It is the principle of the thing," Deara said, giving me a dour glance.

"Fine. Fine." Katarina turned to the waiting maid. The woman clearly could not see the specter in the room with her, but seemed accustomed to seeing her mistress talking at the air. "My dear cousin will be staying with us. Please show her to one of the spare rooms and have a bath arranged for her."

"Yes, ma'am."

She curtsied to Katarina, then to me, then turned and started down the hall with all the expectation in the world that I would follow her.

"How long have you served here?" I asked casually as she led me through the halls. I did my best not to stare too long at any of the paintings or let my eyes linger on the vases that I was certain were worth more than the collective of everything I had ever held.

"My family has always served in the Norwood household, ma'am," she said in only half an answer. She opened the door to a bedroom and showed me in. "This will be your room during your stay." She eyed my clothing. "When your baggage arrives, I will have a dress set out for you. While we wait," she ushered me over to the wardrobe and withdrew a dressing gown. "And the bath is through here." She led me through the room to another chamber with indoor plumbing and a clawfoot bathtub. She was nothing if not efficient as she moved around the room, hanging up the dressing gown, starting the water in the bathtub, and arraying a selection of soaps and fragrances. "Will you need assistance disrobing?"

"If you don't mind undoing the first few laces, I should be

alright from there," I said, suddenly antsy for relief from the rigid structure of Katarina's dress.

"Of course," the woman said with a little bow before assisting me.

The release was almost more painful than the tension had been. Without the support, my ribs suddenly felt on the verge of collapse.

The maid pointedly took no notice of the bruises, seeming almost entirely unsurprised by them. She bustled to the water as I finished undressing and added the contents of a small jar of what looked to be salt, then collected the dress from me. "Shall I have this returned to the madam, or was this a gift to you, ma'am?" The look she gave me told me just how suspicious she was of my relation to Katarina.

I could only give her a look that said I wasn't entirely certain myself.

"I'll have it sorted out," she said with another little bow and took her leave.

The water was soothingly warm and I found myself relaxing into the tub against my better judgment. I had no doubt that I was still in hostile territory, even if Katarina was making every overture of kindness. Still, the water was nice, and it had been so long since I had experienced a warm bath. It was a luxury that had my eyes lulling closed.

A memory tugged at the edge of my mind. Two nights ago. A hand sliding into mine. The charm passing from my hand into Eda's. An unassuming bit of metal pressed with heads of wheat; I could not even remember when I had first found the charm. "For luck," I had said. The certainty that this would be our last dive. It all felt so long ago. My finger touched the hollow of my throat where the charm had always rested before I had given it to Eda.

"You might drown," Deara said, startling me back to my senses. "That's what mother always said anyway."

My eyes snapped open. I sank deeper into the tub in a thin attempt at obscuring her view. My cheeks were moist, but I hoped the steam would hide it.

"Don't get too comfortable here," Deara said, eyeing me. "Katarina will not let you. This is your warning, Sade. The moment Katarina decides that you are healed enough, she will start your training. She is not a forgiving person. It will be for your best, but you might not be happy to be here after that."

I couldn't tell if the specter was trying to scare me out of her home or being honest. I had the feeling it was the latter.

"Why does she need a protégé?" I asked instead.

Deara shrugged. "It's not that she needs one per se …" She looked hesitant to really dig into the subject, then sighed and sat on the edge of the tub as though I was not currently trying to find some semblance of privacy in the water. "The Norwoods are, as of late, a small and dwindling clan. And … this can be a big and lonely house," she said in a half answer.

"Since you died …"

She snorted and looked down at me. "Before I died." She shook her head. "The Norwoods used to be a much larger family, not so long ago. We used to be able to justify our branching out to Junction. It was ultimately a misstep. When we did, the College got it in their heads that having such a dense pocket of Death Sights so nearby might not be the best idea. Those Abbies are very secretive, after all."

"They sent Aberrants after your family?"

"More or less. It wasn't always so direct, you understand. The College likes its shadows and pretending that its Aberrants are under the heels of the Enforcers. It's not so. Not always, at least. As far as I can tell, the College answers only to the gods, and that's only when the gods decide they care enough about what the Society is scheming to stick their fingers into the pie. Anyway. That's likely discussing points well above the caliber of anything you have ever thought to concern your mind with." She stood, suddenly cold again.

I sat up in the tub, rankling at her sudden rebuff. "Why are you so negative toward me?"

Deara kept her back to me. "She could have found better. A street urchin. Really?" She shook her head, turning to look at me again with a glower. "There is better out there; there must be. Or have we really been so degraded?"

"You don't know anything about me."

"I don't," she acknowledged. "I don't know that there is much to know about you, if I'm honest, *Sade*." She said my name with a venomous slide. "You grew up picking pockets and threatening others for their *things*. And now you will benefit from my sister's wealth for nothing more than existing? For being a Death Sight. You don't even have a family name." Her eyes narrowed and her head tilted slightly. Her tone softened with thought. "Or you don't know your last name." Her voice grew quiet and exasperated. "Albain forgive me, I can't shake this feeling that you are not exactly what you seem."

"You mean a pickpocket? An unworthy benefactor?"

She glared at me, hardening again. "I mean a Death Sight. I mean …" She struggled for a moment as though trying to figure out exactly what she did mean. "I mean you have that damn look in your eyes that I see in the Aberrants and in their victims who don't even realize their minds have been jumbled up." She gave an exasperated growl. "What is it about you … Damn it all, if I could just …" She looked at her hands, then closed her eyes and disappeared.

I stared at the spot she had occupied moments before, uncertain if she would be reappearing any time soon, then swallowed. One moment warm, and the next suddenly so cold; the specter left me reeling.

I finished scrubbing myself clean, working the grease and grime from my hair with anxious fingers as I thought about Deara's words. What had she meant that I had the look of an Aberrant? Or that my mind was jumbled? The woman didn't make sense. Still, any enjoyment I had found in my bath was gone and I was soon drying off and draining the sullied water.

I secured the dressing gown around my body and padded into the bedroom that was to be mine.

The maid was arranging a dress on the bed for me, an old woman standing near the bookshelf behind her. The latter woman had a lost look to her eyes, her face slack even as her lips mumbled quietly to themselves.

"Don't mind her, ma'am," the maid said, straightening from her work.

"You can see her?" I asked cautiously. The old woman's dissociated gaze and the way she did not interact with the bookshelf, but instead moved as though at an unseen desk told me she was dead.

"No, ma'am, but I have been around long enough to know that the Norwoods can see things I cannot. I've heard the sisters mention the Widow Reese enough times to know she frequents this branch of the house. She's harmless, as far as they say." She turned her attention back to the dress. "Madam Norwood had this sent over for you, ma'am. It was one of Deara's. She was a bit taller than her sister, so the length should fit you well, but it will have to be brought in here and let out there, I am certain," she said, pinching the fabric of the waist and tugging at the hips with a thoughtful eye.

I looked at the dress apprehensively, knowing just how little Deara liked me. No doubt seeing me in her clothing would only make her hostility worse.

"I told her to give it to you," Deara said in a bored drawl from the corner. "Well, I told Katarina to give it to you."

I turned to her, startled at her sudden reappearance. She made a shooing gesture at me and rolled her eyes.

I turned back to the maid, who was watching me through slitted eyes. I could see the assessment she was conducting as she tried to determine where I had been dug up from. Maybe she could see through the Junction accent I had determined to keep even while in the house. When playing a part, I had learned it best never to break character. I had watched one of my friends slip during a con. It didn't matter how hard-handed Gan had been. That didn't stop the cleaver from falling on his wrist in punishment. I swallowed at the memory of him dragging himself back to the den after that.

"I'll assist you," the maid said, prompting me into action.

It wasn't long until I was subjected to another session of having my hair brushed and coiled.

"I can do my own hair," I complained when the maid's fussing over me grew to be too much.

"Very well, ma'am," she said, backing away a step with a dissatisfied frown. When I refused to apply any makeup, that frown only deepened. "But your eye," she said, hesitant to question my decision, but nervous that I would displease her employer.

"Will heal better without being poked and prodded. Are we expecting guests today?"

"No, but …"

"If Katarina takes issue with my decision, I will resolve it," I said, knowing that would likely not assuage the woman.

The maid put on her best conciliatory face and begrudgingly allowed me to leave my room.

Deara followed just behind me as we set off in search of Katarina.

"Oh, good," Katarina said, helping herself to a bottle of what looked to be whiskey. She poured a healthy splash into her teacup and beckoned for me to follow her. "I suppose I should give you the tour, dear cousin."

I wondered idly how much she had managed to drink during my bath. The look Deara cast me said it was no small amount, despite the day being only half done. I understood now the concern I had glimpsed in Deara at the thought of her sister being alone.

"I think your staff is suspicious of my relation to you," I commented when we were away from the prying ears of the aforementioned staff.

"They always think they know everything about everyone. Pay them no mind," Katarina said flippantly.

"Our uncle doesn't have any daughters," Deara said in explanation. "So, they likely know you are of no relation to us. But as long as my sister wants to play the game, so will they, and so should you."

One moment the specter seemed irate at my very existence and the next she seemed … not welcoming, but tolerant, at least. I didn't know what to make of her yet. Maybe that was what she wanted. To keep me on my toes. To make me trip up in some way.

"You have free range of the house," Katarina said with a yawn, a lot less attentive than she had seemed on the airship. "This is the library … assuming you can read?"

I nodded.

"Oh, good. I had no interest in teaching you," she admitted. "We have books on all variety of subjects: romance, drama, history, glyphs, blah blah blah. But Deara squirreled away the picks of the litter in her room and I just haven't gotten around to having them put away. If you are looking for a more refined selection, raid her room."

Deara's expression remained flat, which I could only interpret as annoyance at the idea of me rummaging through her stuff.

Katarina stopped at a window overlooking the gardens.

A fog was rolling through the lowlands around the port far in the distance, but no bells rang in warning, so I knew the drift was harmless. I caught myself thinking of my gang and then quickly dashed the thought away. The majority of them were dead now. Those who hadn't taken the dive that day would scatter to the winds the moment they heard about the debacle on the airship.

"The gardens," Katarina said with a sweeping gesture toward the well-tended greenery. A wall surrounded the estate, but a second wall of tall hedges marked the center of the gardens, blocking the space from view, even from our vantage on the second story. "You'll be well acquainted with the gardens when you are fit enough to start training." She turned from the window, but I lingered, taking in the amount of green this woman had so readily at her disposal. In the slums, days could pass without so much as seeing even a green shirt pass on the street.

I took one last look before following the woman as she continued her tour. A life in the slums made it difficult to remember the beauty of Vale. The half-valley that led to the ports and lowlands of the floating landmass, and the forested mountain that climbed away from the fall of the abyss only to drop off in cliffs on the northern edge.

Beyond the glass, I could see the Persephone drifting just beyond the Grand Cross Bridge and the port. The fate-filled airship that had brought me here was now floating out over the abyss, sinking toward the cloudline. Katarina was right. The airship had been condemned to the surface.

Katarina gave me an appraising look when I rejoined her. "You'll get used to it, my dear," she said with a subtly amused drawl. "The kitchens are down this way." She flicked a wrist toward a corridor. "Dining room," she said, bored. "My mother kept a sewing room," she said disinterestedly toward a door as we passed it, "as that seems to be one of your interests. I never really understood it since the servants can handle all that monotony for you." She perked up a bit as we came to a halt in front of a set of double doors. "This is the training room. Can't always be out in the cold."

"Training for what?"

She just gave me a wink and pulled me along on the rest of the tour. Deara didn't bother elaborating, either. A small pit formed in my stomach.

"We used to have a lot more family here," Katarina said, gesturing to the portraits hung along the hall. "I suppose we still do have some of them lingering about, but most moved on of their own accord. Don't be surprised if you run into one of our aunts or uncles in the hallways. They are dead, of course, but they do stop by from time to time. I'm only glad that our parents had the good graces to be quick burns when they died."

"Quick burns?"

She nodded and set her teacup at the base of a bust of some long-gone relation. "Here and gone. That's not usual for Death Sights or for very many of the folks with Moxie, mind you, but at least dear old Dad and Mama had a little sense. No need to hang around."

"How did they pass, if I can ask?"

"Oh, you certainly can. They were visiting my uncle—your very own papa," she said with a wink. "They had a bit of motorcarriage accident. Terrible thing. It had the signs of Aberrants all over it." She looked at Deara. "What was that? Five years back? Abbies can get away with anything most anywhere in the Society, but in Junction they run wild. They think themselves untouchable, so close to their beloved College." The young woman's scowl was a savage thing. "Yet another thing I cannot bring evidence forward on." Her scowl only deepened when an oblivious little girl wandered past, the feeling of death tied to her. The girl wore a devious grin on her face that seemed to be a Norwood trait, but she did not raise her eyes to us as I stepped aside for her. The stab wound decorating the girl's back set a heavy stone of dread on my chest. "A cousin of some sort who seems to refuse to move on," Katarina said dismissively. "At least she's not shouting and running through the halls today."

"Who did that to her?"

Katarina glanced at the girl in boredom. "One of the staff. When I tell you not to trust Regulars, that's just another example of why. The strange thing is her parents were killed in an airship explosion that wiped out half of our fine clan not months before. An awful coincidence, if you are to believe the tabloids." Katarina's features took on a bitter turn that spoke to her suspicion that the incident had been as much happenstance as her own parent's motorcarriage accident. She turned back to the tour.

Deara's eyes didn't even bother tracking the girl's movement.

"Can you see the other dead?" I asked, peeling my eyes from the absently wandering child and her wound to fall in behind Katarina.

The specter shrugged, eyeing the abandoned teacup disapprovingly, but not reprimanding her sister. "Some. If they are fully manifested. Some of the Whispers, the unmanifested, still come through to me, but it's a lot quieter now without all the quick burns clogging the streets."

"And your Past Sight? The memories?"

"Only my own." She shook her head. "Those abilities went with me, it seems."

"Well, maybe they didn't," Katarina chimed in. "It is just difficult to know unless she were to encounter another dead who happened to be on the same plane of the endless planes of the fold."

"What do you mean?"

Katarina yawned as she considered bothering with the explanation. "We have time for that later. Perhaps Deara will even grace you with some of her knowledge, since she was quite the aspiring scholar on the matter," she said, giving the specter a halfway disgusted, halfway bored look that told exactly how much interest Katarina had taken in the matter of the land of the dead. She sighed heavily and shook her head. "It is important that you understand the fold, but if I am being honest, the subject does bore me, and I would really prefer you read about it or talk to Deara." She gave the specter a pointed look.

Deara rolled her eyes but finally said, "Fine. I'll tutor her."

We passed a grandfather clock, its massive pendulum swinging, and its gears and chimes artfully displayed in a frame of wood and glass. Its opulence would be an impracticality for any other setting, but here in this house with its wealth, it only fit in.

"Now, I do have plans this evening, and matters to attend to beforehand. Scion of the family and all," Katarina said ruefully, casting an appraising look at me before grinning. "Deara. Be a dear and show her the rest of the estate."

The specter only grumbled as Katarina strode away.

"You can find your way on your own, I am certain," Deara said before disappearing. And suddenly I was left alone in a very big house.

5:

All I wanted was sleep and quiet, and time to think when evening came. I had started the morning trapped on an airship submerged in the failure and deaths of the day before. Only hours later I had been in this house filled with roaming ghosts, suspicious staff, and two sisters with intents I couldn't quite pin down. Abandoned by both Katarina and Deara, I had wandered for a time until I had found a familiar hall and my room to tuck myself away in.

The summons had come late while I had been studying the silhouette of the mountainside as the sun lowered. From my bedside table, a Tinkerer's device similar to my talker sounded with Katarina's voice. I had been tempted to ignore the woman's summons but instead found myself at her door.

"Katarina?" I called lightly, knocking on the woman's door before peeking in. "You called for me."

"Come here, Sade," Katarina said with a heady giggle that had me frowning. As I approached her bed, I spotted the cause of the woman's mirth. A man, handsome and well-muscled, and very naked. "I thought you may want to join us for a little fun," Katarina said with a feral wink as the man in her bed made his way around her body with his mouth. Fun that she seemed to be having, the drunken fuzz to her eyes and the bottle at her bedside didn't slip my attention.

I swallowed and backed away a step. "Oh. Um …"

"Come on, Sade. Don't be a prude. We will be gentle-ish." She cooed softly and I grimaced, trying not to see the cause.

"I'm … I'm tired. I'll let you two enjoy yourselves," I said graciously, then beat a hasty and very confused retreat.

Back in my room, I hurried into bed, uncertain what it was that had me so unsettled by Katarina's proposition. She certainly hadn't projected herself as shy, even in my short exposure to her.

"I'm sorry about her," Deara said, manifesting beside me as I stared at the ceiling. "Thank you for saying no, by the way."

"What in Devton's name was that about?" I asked, still reeling in my confusion. I pulled the sheets up tight to my chin. It wasn't like I had never had sex before, and it wasn't as though my friends had never gotten a little carried away in the act, but Katarina's offer had felt off, sodden with desperation and emptiness.

Deara sighed and sat on the edge of the bed. The fabric didn't shift around her and I couldn't help but wonder at that. She was able to interact with the physical world, going so far as stealing the steak for my eye, but only when she seemed intent on doing so.

"Katarina has been in a bit of a spiral," Deara admitted quietly. She lay down next to me, staring at the ceiling as I had been. I watched her, waiting for the swing between warm and cold in the ghost. She frowned thoughtfully. "I died when I was twenty-two."

Her eyes shifted to me. "That was over a year and a half ago. Katarina never thought she would be older than me, but now she is. It has been a … strange revelation for her. She was always the second sister. Everything was supposed to fall to me, leaving her free to do as she wished. I had to go and ruin her plans." Drawing in a spectral breath, she went on. "It took her a month to find me and manifest me. When she did, she was already different from the woman I remembered. She's vengeful, Sade. Watch out for that. There's a reason I never told her who killed me."

"You know?"

"Of course."

"And you won't tell her because …?"

"I know my sister. I know how she is now. It would become all-consuming for her. She would insist on bringing justice to the situation. It's not just the dead who turn vengeful. Katarina is just as dangerous, and she doesn't have much else holding her here."

"Shouldn't there be justice, though?" I asked, rolling to face the specter lying at my side.

She shook her head. "Not Katarina's justice. I don't have any way of proving what happened to me, so in court it would just be Katarina's word against theirs, and if I am being honest, the Society has already put us on the outside. This would just send the Norwoods further to the outskirts. And that's only if, somehow, I was able to keep Katarina from taking matters into her own hands." She snorted lightly and bit her lip before looking at me again. "It will be work for you to keep yourself from being pulled into Katarina's self-destructive spin, but do your best."

"Losing a sister is hard," I said. Having lost many of my closest friends, I could not imagine the loss of a true blood sibling.

Deara swallowed, her voice sinking to a whisper. "But she didn't really lose me, did she? I've been here every day tormenting her, keeping her as together as one can keep a fraying rope. But it doesn't really help because we both know that any day I could move on."

I shook my head. "I thought you didn't believe in 'moving on.'"

She sighed. "I was being spiteful toward you," she said in hushed tones. "There isn't hard and fast science on it, because how could there be, but … *moving on* … I believe it is a transition to a deeper level of the fold. Either way, it doesn't really matter, does it? One day you are here and the next you are gone, deeper in the fold or wiped from existence. It is not a conscious thing, as far as I can tell. Maybe it is a peeling away, or maybe it happens at compressions in the fold." She was thoughtful a moment. "Those of us with magic tend to create compressions in the layers. That's why Aberrants see us. Maybe that is also why Death Sights see so many dead pass on. Or it is all coincidence." She looked at me. "Do you even know what the fold is?"

"Where the dead go?" I felt foolish the moment the words left my lips, but before yesterday I had never put much thought to the matter. I always figured I would miss a dive or catch an Enforcer's bullet and that would be when I would learn what happened to the dead.

"It is so much more complex than that. It is the basis of all magic. The Death Sights have a sensitivity to it, but only enough to see what has passed into the transitional layers, ergo," she gestured at herself. "Hence why I believe moving on is just moving deeper. The dead pass into a layer a Death Sight cannot see into. The fold is like layers of existence all folded together, thus the name. Some layers are more transitional, some more persistent, some echo the past, and some seem to predict the future."

"So, the Sights, they are all sensitive to different layers of the fold?"

She smiled. "You catch on quick. Maybe I misjudged you."

I returned the smile, glad to be making any headway at all with this woman. "You said the fold is the basis of magic."

She nodded. "It is hard to explain, but ... it leaks over. I speculate that what the Aberrants have access to is just a fraction of the potential of the fold. They take from the fold while we merely access what is already there." She grew excited talking about this and I was glad that for once she wasn't casting me glares or pretending I didn't exist. "You see, the Aberrants are like little conduits for the magic that leaks to our side ... well, your side now, I suppose. They harness and manipulate it through the glyphs. Some Aberrants are better conductors than others, so that's why you see such disparity even among them." I didn't admit that I had seen no such disparity because I had always avoided all Aberrants. "Tinkerers are just Aberrants who can only harness a little of the magic. Just enough to enhance what they create. That's why the College doesn't bother yoking them. They don't have the raw potential."

"If the leak of energy from the fold is what fuels the Aberrants and the Tinkerers, what about Charmers or Sleuths? A sensitivity to the fold explains Sights, but I can't see the tie for manipulating emotions or detecting lies."

She smiled and propped her head up as she looked at me. "See, but that's the thing. We are all tied to the fold in some way. That is why we pass so seamlessly into it when we die. I think that is why Sights, Charmers, and so on tend to linger in transition, since they spent so long so close to the transitional layer, it is more difficult for us to resolve on the other side." She shook her head. "That's not what you asked, though."

"I think I understand all the same. Similar to how we have a sensitivity to see into the fold in some dimension, they have a sensitivity to the tie to the fold that connects us all to it. Through it they can either manipulate emotions or tell if a person is lying. Am I on the right track?"

She looked very impressed, a small smile playing on her lips, and nodded slowly. "Katarina never took an interest in any of this. She always said, *we can see the dead, why does it matter how we see them*," she said, mimicking her sister's voice. "I think the *why* is one of the most important things. Is it truly the gods who created these sensitivities? Do they really sit between us and the fold, dictating that you are a Death Sight and he is a Charmer? It's a fascinating prospect with a lot of implications." She sighed contentedly and laid back. "I don't even remember why we got onto this topic."

I didn't remind her of what her sister was up to in the other room and let the specter continue her dissertation on the fold. The woman could have been a scholar on the subject, had she lived long enough.

6:

The next morning found me at the edge of the gardens watching the fog roll across the lowlands. The grounds of Norwood Manor were expansive, with green swaths of grass surrounding the gardens edged in the tall hedge row. The stonework of the manor itself looked like it had withstood at least a thousand years and that it could easily withstand a thousand more. Still, looking further up the rise, it was now clear to me that as high up as the Norwoods were, they were far from the top of the Society. More estates with grander structures dotted the mountainside. I wondered if those at the top of the rise could even see the smog and grime of the industrial center of the low-alts anymore.

I had ferreted out some paper and a set of pencils and sat enjoying the morning with a sketch. I was idle and feeling guilty thinking that I was here while most of my gang had been thrown to the abyss, and that those who hadn't were in the hands of the Aberrants. Still, it was not as though I could do anything for them.

Katarina's trunk had arrived, confirming to the staff yet again that I was a play-acting stray and nothing more when none of my belongings arrived with it. Still, they bowed and curtsied and pretended like the best stage actors. When my talons appeared in my room, I knew the entire household would soon be able to guess at my origins.

"I found you." The child's voice drew my eyes up from my drawing.

"Marco." I beamed, standing. "I thought I had lost you at the port." I gave him a hug, his shoulders cold and misty but still comforting.

The boy stepped back, embarrassed. "For a li'l bit I thought these rich ladies had managed to steal you away. Then I saw that trunk with the big deer things carved into it and followed it here" he said, proud at his investigative skills. "You look like a lady," he said, a little bashfully.

"Are you implying I didn't look like one before?" I asked playfully, retaking my seat on the grass.

He shook his head emphatically. "No. That's not what I meant. It's just … It's different."

I had never been close with any of the younger members of the gang. So many of them got caught, killed, or run off that there was little reason to. I had never been close with Marco, but we had all looked out for each other and now we were all we had left of our past lives.

"It's good," he continued, sitting beside me with a smile. "The rich lady isn't treatin' you bad, right?"

"No."

"And they aren't makin' you do anything weird?"

My mind flashed to my unexpected evening, but I shook my head.

"No experiments or nothing?"

"Nothing like that."

"That's good," he said, looking down at the lowlands shrouded in fog and the abyss beyond. "I'm glad you got away," he said with a haunted edge. "Some of the others managed to hide till we landed, but it was like the Abbies was just toying with them. I didn't see a single one make it out of there. I couldn't help 'em. After helpin' you I was just so tired. Try as I might, I couldn't do anything but give some of them Enforcers a little shiver."

"I'm sorry, Marco."

"It's not your fault. That even one of us made it out …" He smiled, but it was a sad smile, and we lapsed into silence.

"You really shouldn't keep those things around," Deara commented from behind us. She gave Marco a suspicious look as she came around to stand before us. "You never know if they have something nefarious planned."

"One could say the same about you," I pointed out.

Deara shook her head, turning from the view to look down at us. "You can only trust a child as far as you can throw it, and seeing as that thing is dead, I don't suppose you can throw it very far at all."

It seemed the specter had decided to go back to being unpleasant.

"Deara. Stop," I chided.

"The College has spies. The Society has spies. You can't just befriend every ghost that comes around."

"I am not worried about Marco. We came from the same gang. He was on the airship. He helped when that Abbie got too close. Surely you saw him."

Deara narrowed her eyes at the boy and grimaced. "I don't always pay attention to the others," she admitted. "Still, children are always brutes. Even dead children." She raised her nose with a superior air, trying to cover her misstep. She looked down at my drawing, her lips pursing for a moment before she lifted her eyes back to my face. "That is nicely done," she said, as though it pained her to admit I had any skill at all.

I looked at the page and chuckled. "Thank you, Deara. I don't often have such a good vantage on Vale." I nodded to Marco and we stood. "Do you want to walk?"

"I don't particularly care one way or the other," Deara said, but fell in beside me as I circled the property. "Have you never left this rock?" she asked casually.

"Never. Except to dive."

"I rarely did until I died. After, it seemed I was always here or there with Kat. She liked doing the traveling mystic bit from time to time before, but now, well, she just hates Vale."

"She's lonely."

Deara tapped the tip of her nose with her finger. "She doesn't enjoy being a Death Sight anymore. I suppose I wouldn't either, in her shoes. My murder was a sign we needed to be more careful, though it came a little late for me, didn't it?"

Marco studied the specter from the protection of my left. He watched her as though she were a new species of carrion bird, but one he could learn from.

I looked at the specter striding wistfully beside me. When had she decided I was worth her time? She was as unpredictable in her temperament as the gale raging below the landmass. The only certainty was their intensity. Deara gave a heavy sigh, though she did not have any need to breathe. Still, I noted the activity in her chest, the rise and fall. Then I noticed her watching me just as keenly as I was watching her.

"You're breathing," I said, realizing the ease with which somebody could mistake my intentions in the study.

Deara rolled her eyes and waved her hand dismissively. "A lifetime of habits…"

"Why aren't you with your sister?" I asked.

"Is that your way of telling me to leave?" Deara said, suddenly very bitter.

"No," I said quickly. "That was not my intent. It's just that you two always seem to be together, and well, you don't seem to like me very much at all."

She harrumphed, but there was a conciliatory look in her eyes. "You are not as terrible as you seemed at first." She muttered the admission. "And as for my whereabouts. I have to exist somewhere and … I figured maybe you wanted some company on your walk. I didn't realize you would have *that*," she said, eyes flicking to Marco, "with you already." That seemed a half-truth only. Surely Deara would rather be tucked away somewhere with her book. My disbelief must have shown on my face because she said, "Fine. I was wondering if you read."

"I told your sister I know how."

"You told my sister you know how," Deara agreed. "But do you?"

"I cannot say that it was a pastime I engaged in often," I said, wondering what the specter wanted.

"I think you may enjoy it, were you to get into it as a pastime," she said with an innocence that seemed an act. She definitely wanted something.

"Hmm …"

She looked at me, a strange look in her eye that was both assessing and concerned. "If … If you don't actually know how to read and you were just saying it to gain my sister's approval, that is alright also," she said quickly. Then she suddenly turned hesitant, as if uncertain if the statement had touched on a sensitive topic. When my confusion at the question continued to slow my tongue, she went on. "I can teach you. It may be difficult considering the situation, but I am confident I could do it."

"I know how to read," I assured her. "I am more trying to figure out why the topic came up. I know you enjoy reading, but you don't seem to take much interest in what I enjoy. And if I am honest, recommending new hobbies seems out of character for you."

"Hmm. Yeah. You are right." Deara was displaying an odd emotion. Was she bashful? "I … I want to read a new book. The one that I can draw up from memory, it's … it's getting old. But I cannot exactly manipulate my surroundings easily enough to read anything new. I thought maybe if you read a book, you might allow me to read over your shoulder?"

"You really just need me to hold the book and turn the pages then?"

"I do not want you to feel like a book holder …" she said, surprising me with any concern for my wishes. "I thought it would be more fun if you could also read and then it would be like we were reading together. Sort of like a book club." Which was nothing I had ever had the opportunity to experience. Having two people share the same book sounded rather irritating, quite frankly, but Deara seemed excited by the prospect.

"Do you really want to spend your afterlife reading?" I asked.

"How else would you recommend I spend it?" Deara asked, almost defensive. "How would you spend it?"

I shrugged. "I don't know, I guess. I never actually thought about any of this until I met you. I always thought I would miss a landing and be lost to the planet, and everything would end in darkness. Just an end."

"Is knowing worse or better?"

I shrugged again. To drag around through an afterlife alone where only a small handful could even see you and you couldn't manipulate anything without immense effort seemed a boring existence.

"I may be a bit slower at reading than you."

Deara beamed, her excitement radiating. I stopped walking, so surprised by the specter's exuberance. "Practice will help us both. It's been a while for me."

"What do you want to read? I can run down to one of the bookstores in town, or if there's something in the house already ...."

"Anything you want. I'll go to the store with you. Let's find something new. But anything you want. I'll have Katarina give you the money." Her excitement drove rapidity into her speech. She grounded herself for a moment with a deep breath. "And since we really should start your education, I have some books in my room I want you to take. I was worried this tutoring would be pulling teeth with you. So far, I have been pleasantly surprised." She smiled at me. "And while we are out, you should get yourself proper supplies for drawing. It would be a shame to let that talent go to waste." She looked past me at Marco, a hint of reluctant warmth creeping into the specter. "What do you think, Marco?"

The boy was startled, looking from Deara to me and back to Deara. "Sade has always been a deft hand," he agreed.

"It came in handy for pickpocketing," I said, watching Deara for her reaction.

Instead of the expected glower and disapproving look, she snorted and shook her head. "I am sorry, Sade. For giving you grief. I just ... I worry about Katarina. I worry about the spiral she is on. I worry about the choices she makes. I worry what will happen when I am gone. Taking in a stray, a criminal who had just boarded our airship in order to rob its passengers, it felt desperate and poorly thought out. Though I shouldn't worry about her being able to protect herself. The bottom line is, you don't seem that bad." She looked at Marco. "While I don't necessarily approve of you keeping that kid," she said the word with enough discomfort that I had to grin, "around, it may be a good idea for me to teach him a few tricks."

If reading a few books meant the woman would play nice and I wouldn't be hung out to dry at every opportunity, I would gladly make the sacrifice.

7:

"We have a guest," Deara said, appearing at my side as I made to relax with a sketch after dinner.

After a week in residence at Norwood Manor, I was still getting used to the specter's sudden arrivals, and took a moment to calm my racing heart. "A guest?"

"Your father," she said with an ironic wink, urging me to stand up.

"My father?"

"Just come on," she said, leading me out into the hall.

Katarina's voice carried up to us, striving for a welcoming tone, but surprise and irritation ringing through instead. "We weren't expecting you, Uncle Olso."

"Pish posh, child, I got your letter about my daughter," the man's thick Junction accent boomed around the house. "I wasn't about to stay away."

"You could have sent word ahead of you," Katarina said, not bothering with a wholly soft tone any longer.

"A letter would have arrived on the same airship I did," the man said with a jolly laugh. "I didn't waste any time."

"I noticed," Katarina grumbled as we descended the stairs to meet the man and his luggage in the entryway. He turned at our approach and beamed.

"Oh my dear, darling, Sade," the mustachioed man proclaimed, wrapping his arms around me in a loving embrace as though I were actually his daughter. "I bought the airship ticket as soon as I heard you were here."

His blonde whiskers and bald head placed him in stark contrast with my darker features. That I was this man's daughter would be a hard sell on appearances alone. He was in his traveling clothes but even those spoke to his wealth. Thickly built and draped in a bright purple jacket edged in gold trim, the man's booming personality manifested itself in the loudness of his clothing.

I looked at Katarina quizzically over the man's shoulder as he tried to squeeze the life from me.

She just rolled her eyes and shrugged, then gave me a flutter of fingers I could only interpret as direction to just go with it.

I returned the embrace, a bit more halting and a lot more awkward in the action. "Father …"

"Dad, please," he said, sounding on the edge of a delighted sob.

"Dad," I said, trying and failing to banish my hesitant tone.

This time he did sob with delight, and his embrace returned in full force. "I always wanted a daughter and here you are. Oh, it is a gift from the gods for certain. Not that your brothers weren't just the best, but they always did favor their mother."

I could only nod against his delusion.

"Come, come, you must be hungry after your long journey," he said, offering me his arm and leading me through the manor as though I was the guest who had just arrived from across the abyss and not he. He stopped for a moment beside Deara and released a long and heartfelt sigh. "My dear. I am sorry for your loss," he said. Deara looked at her sister uncomfortably. "You really should visit your cousins before they move on. It is a might bit easier for you now, I suppose. No need for an airship these days, eh?"

"Thank you, Uncle," Deara said flatly. "I will consider it."

He nodded, patting my hand before continuing on.

"Uncle, exactly how long do you intend to stay?" Katarina asked, catching up to us on the way to the dining room.

He waved a hand, dismissing the question. "A few days is all," he said merrily, returning his hand to mine and pulling me along on in his quest for food.

8:

"What was that?" I asked, sitting heavily on my bed. Olso's insistence that I eat with him while I was still full from my own meal could not be refused. Two dinners in one evening was quite enough for me. I felt instantly ashamed at the thought as I remembered how many nights Eda, Gan, and I had gone without any food at all.

"There is never a halfway with Olso. It is either zero or one hundred percent with him." Katarina shrugged. "So, the man talked himself into thinking you are actually his child. It's better that he thinks it anyway, in case any Aberrants were to ever come knocking."

"What happened to his sons?"

Katarina sat beside me, looking up as Deara phased through the wall to join us. She fussed with her fingernail and sighed. "I've told you enough times that this world has a way of ferreting us Death Sights out when we aren't careful. Well, those boys were never known for being careful. They took their little act on the road. Like what Deara and I did from time to time, but with a lot more attention and a lot more frequently. They always needed to be the center of everybody's universe. There are enough charlatans out there claiming to talk to the dead and loved ones past, but I guess their act was a little too convincing since they actually were talking to the dead. I suppose one of their audience members got spooked and, well, matters were matters," she said with a glance at Deara. "What matters most is that man is fool enough to believe you are his daughter. The Junction Norwoods are not the most affluent branches of our family, but if he is going to help maintain you, I will not say no."

"I can get a job. I don't need to fleece your uncle for money."

"Oh, dear, you are going to have to do both. But for the time being, let's focus on getting you trained into a proper Death Sight. And while we do so, the money your darling dad supplies will ensure I can keep you fed and clothed in a manner befitting a woman of Vale."

"I've lived on Vale my whole life."

Katarina looked me up and down in my recently tailored outfit. Without a wealth of dresses, I had found a few abandoned sets of trousers and shirts and repurposed their fabric for myself. I always felt more comfortable in pants, and as long as I didn't leave the property, Katarina tolerated my deviance from her expectations. "Hmm. Well, charming as *that* is, past the midalts it is a different Vale. It might be time we start acting like we belong." She patted my hand and stood. "Get to know Olso. He's exhausting when he is on one, but that's better than him being boring, I suppose." She pursed her lips and set her hands on her hips. "Take a breather, then go find him in the study."

I knew an order, even softly delivered, when I heard one.

9:

I sat quietly, studying the man that was play-acting as my father as he twisted and swirled the ends of his greying mustache. He seemed content to stare off into space, listening to the newscast bleating out of the radio as he absently tended his whiskers.

"Sir," I said timidly, drawing his eyes and his overly wide smile.

"Dad," he corrected.

I bit my lip and looked into his eyes. "You do know I am not truly your daughter, right? Not even a bastard child of some long-lost mistress."

"You could be," he said as though in offer. His expression turned sad. "But you couldn't," he said inwardly. "I never once left the vows of my marriage." He looked at me with a clarity I hadn't expected. "I am alright with you using my name as your father's, Sade. I have already had my lawyer write up the paperwork for the acknowledgement, should you wish to sign it."

"The acknowledgement?"

"Of the lineage of my youngest child," he said with a slight cant of his head toward me.

"You cannot acknowledge me. I am not truly yours."

"If you don't wish it ..."

"It is not that I do not wish it," I said quickly, seeing his disappointment. "It is ... Why? Why would you do that for me? Did Katarina tell you how we met? Where I came from? Besides, this could be damaging for your good name."

"Bah. It does not matter." He spoke in a light boom, the deluded happiness returning at the renewed prospect of the adoption. "My nieces will already slander my name by touting you as their cousin. Besides, I ..." He lost some of his mirth. "I have nobody else. If you would allow me to be your dad, I could do nothing less than acknowledge you as my daughter." He smiled under his frivolous mustache. "Will you sign? You won't have to write or visit. Much, anyway." He said with a wink.

I returned the smile. "If you are willing to acknowledge me, then I will gladly visit."

10:

My newly adoptive father lingered, but after his pronounced entrance, he quickly seemed to retreat into himself, squirreling himself away in his room for days on end.

"He's not all there," Deara explained when I asked. "Not anymore. He used to be the happiest man you ever met. It was quite irritating, really. Then his sons were killed and his wife passed soon after. He changed, understandably, after that. Now he's rather prone to these large swings in his demeanor. Give him a few days and he will be back out terrorizing the household with his cheer."

"Was it a bad idea to let him adopt me?"

"Not at all. It should help him, if anything. As long as you don't also get yourself killed, I suppose." She looked at me for a breath. "Be a good daughter to him."

"I have never been a daughter."

"I am sure you will figure it out." She looked toward the window. "Now, come on, get dressed. Katarina wanted you to train with her today. Wear a dress you don't mind getting dirty."

"Should I just wear trousers, then?"

Deara cast an amused look at me. "I would wear a dress," she said. "Meet her at the center of the gardens, in the hedge circle."

I frowned at the spot the ghost had just faded from, wondering what exactly Katarina's training would consist of. Since arriving home the woman seemed only interested in drinking and her nearly nightly pleasures. Only her uncle's presence in the house, sparse as it was at the moment, seemed to keep her from spending the days in a light stupor and the evenings in bliss. I couldn't complain, though. I enjoyed the woman's company much more while she was sober, rather than in the despondent yet hungry state her drinking seemed to send her into. Sober or drunk, I had never seen the woman risk getting dirt under her nails.

I picked my dress, a simple cotton piece, and headed for the gardens.

I understood the high rise of the hedges around this particular section of the gardens now. Katarina moved in a flourish of skirts and fists that left me envious but that would leave any upper crust observer shaking their head in disgust. The man she faced off against was all muscles and fists. His dark skin shone with a light glisten of sweat that only served to accentuate the powerful coils of muscle.

"Finally," Katarina said, wiping her brow delicately and coming over to inspect me.

"Are you certain I shouldn't change into something more appropriate?" I asked, nervously tugging at my skirts.

"Oh? And what would that consist of? Trousers? You should train in what you will be wearing, and I don't expect you will be wearing trousers."

"I think she was," Deara commented.

"No lady of my house is going to go gallivanting around in trousers so long as a suitable dress can be found."

"But how am I supposed to move in this dress?" I complained, even though I had just witnessed Katarina's surprising ability to do so with such expertise.

"Do you think that the brutes on the street will give you the time to change into something else? No. So you will learn how to fend for yourself in whatever I say," Katarina said coldly. "Instructor."

I looked from Katarina to the approaching instructor with apprehension. He was thickly built but fast, and from my brief glimpse of their bout, seemed aware of not only his every step and swing, but also his opponent's. I felt uncomfortable in the skirts while walking. I couldn't imagine fighting in them.

"Try to hit him," Katarina ordered.

"What? I ..."

"Quiet. No doubt you have survived your fair share of fights to have made it as long as you have on the streets. Now, do as you are told or find yourself back on those streets."

I was starting to think that maybe returning to the grime would be preferable to this, but with a swallow, I raised my fists and edged toward the man.

I swung wide, a brawler's swing rather than with any skill behind the strike. The instructor caught my wrist, twisted me around, cranking on my arm to a point just before breaking my bones, then swept my legs out from under me. The man knelt on my chest while I struggled to suck in breath. His fist hovered threateningly. He glanced at Katarina, who gave a subtle nod, then brought his fist down hard against my check.

I saw stars. I lay in a daze, not even noticing when the man stood, giving me room to breathe once again. It was Katarina who stood over me when my eyes could focus.

"We still need you pretty, but that doesn't mean we don't have other ways of training you," she said. I couldn't understand what she meant at that moment, but it was quickly clear. This would be the last lesson taught to me in any visible means, but that wouldn't stop the brutal training technique.

I lay sprawled for several more breaths before Katarina stepped to the edge of the ring once again.

"Katarina," Deara said quietly to her sister.

Katarina waved the specter off with a dismissive flick of her wrist. "The world is hard on those who are soft," she said in a low growl.

Deara just shook her head and summoned her book to her hands.

Steadily, I picked myself back up and squared off against the instructor once again. His face was stone. I had no doubt the man would beat me to a pulp if Katarina told him to.

Deara sat by with her spectral book in hand, but her eyes were just over the edge of the pages, watching.

"I was hoping we would have a better foundation to start with," the instructor said. "Hopefully I don't have to break you of too many bad habits. Raise your hands."

There was no gentleness in the instruction. At times the lesson turned brutal if Katarina felt I wasn't being serious enough about my practice. The lesson only ended when I tripped on my skirts and was foolish enough to complain, if only just in one exasperated burst. That was when I learned just how hidden bruises could be. The beating only stopped when Deara stood over me, unable to intercede or even be noticed by the instructor, demanding her sister order the man to stop.

"That's enough," Katarina said flippantly while I curled in on myself at her feet. She crouched beside my head, gentle now. "The first day is the hardest," she cooed, stroking a hair back from my cheek to behind my ear. "A mob won't stop. A mob will not worry about your face. A mob will not care that you are as human as they are. They will tear you apart, and it will be so much worse than this."

11:

"She is not wrong," Deara said quietly beside me as I lay in bed. "Her means are a bit much, but Katarina is not wrong."

I had been beaten before. Still, I had thought maybe those days had ended when the sisters took me in. I looked away from Deara at the wall.

"One of our cousins had the Sight," Deara said. "He was just a child. A little boy. He didn't even realize the ghost he was talking to was a ghost."

I swallowed, knowing the boy had spoken to one of his spectral friends in view of the wrong person.

"We have seen a lot of loss. Our family is cut from its roots. That's why only Katarina and I really venture out anymore. The older members, those who have survived this long, have lost too much. She wants you to be able to protect yourself."

I groaned lightly and closed my eyes.

"I'm sorry," Deara said quietly and left me in peace.

12:

I felt a cold spot on my hand. Something soothing in my fever, and I wrapped my fingers around it. I lost myself to sleep again.

I don't know how long passed until I opened my eyes again. When I did, Deara sat unabashedly at my side, a speculative look in her eye.

"How are you doing that?" Deara asked. I had no idea what she meant, but I noticed her eyes had shifted to my hip, no, my hand. My hand wrapped around the cold.

Still in my haze, I craned my neck to see what she was seeing and there, clutched in my hand was Deara's.

"I don't ..." For a moment my haze lifted. "Am I not supposed to be able to?"

"No ... You shouldn't be able to reach across the fold. And so effortlessly ..." Deara said with wonder. "To my knowledge, no living is able to touch the dead or interact with our side of the fold."

"But you can touch our side." I had held Marco and thought nothing of it. "I've seen you move things before."

"I was once part of your side, Sade, and the effort it takes me is immense. Only that which is dead or has never been alive. Only that which is cold. Marco can tell you if you don't believe me." I had wondered why she insisted on reading over my shoulder, but that explained it. If she was not willing to put in the effort even for books, it must be difficult. "This …" She looked at me and shook her head again. "This should not be."

Deara continued to hold tight, her eyes locked on the contact. "You're warm." Her eyes closed. "Oh, I miss it. Feeling anything." She gave a covetous little groan. Her expression turned hungry, nearly making me wrench my hand away, but with a shake of her head she centered herself again and looked at me with a sadness. "I'm sorry. Maybe I've been here too long."

"Are you alright?" I asked after it was clear the ghost's momentary lapse toward the vengeful had abated.

The door opened, Katarina announcing her presence by saying. "I hear you talking so you must be back amongst the living."

Deara dropped my hand, but not before her sister took note, a confused tilt to her head and a curious look in her eye as she crossed to me. "I'm glad you are awake again," she said softly, but her eyes were on my hand. She looked between me and Deara. "Were you two touching?"

Deara didn't say anything. I didn't understand her hesitation in the matter, but I followed her lead. Our silence was enough of an answer.

"Give me your hand," Katarina said with an air of excitement.

It was Deara's subtle look of apprehension that slowed me in extending my hand to her sister. Katarina didn't seem to notice the slowness of my move as she snatched my hand up excitedly and then presented her free hand to her sister.

Deara frowned at the offered hand, then reached over me to press the tips of her fingers against her sister's hand.

"I thought you couldn't …" I started before Deara broke away from both my and Katarina's touch. The specter looked shaken, the years without contact having placed an unseen weight on her shoulders. Now she dropped under that weight.

"Now that is interesting," Katarina said, then took on a thoughtful quirk in her eyes before heading to my sewing table to grab a set of shears. "I wonder…"

Deara rounded the bed. From her stance I almost thought she

was putting herself between me and her sister. "What are you doing?" she asked with enough suspicion to set me on edge.

Katarina tsked and traipsed past her sister with a look of excitement. "Just a little experiment, Deara," she said, stopping at my side and taking a sheaf of my hair in her hand. She gave me a wink. "Don't worry, nobody will notice," she said as she picked a lock and raised the shears.

"I don't know ..." I resisted but didn't dare move with those excited shears so close to my head. With a snip, the lock of hair was cut free, and Katarina set my hair back in order.

She held the hank of black in her hand, then reached toward Deara.

I could see the resistance fighting with the curiosity in Deara face. Steadily she reached out and touched her sister's hand again.

Katarina grinned, holding the lock of hair triumphantly. "It works," she said. The foolishness of the grin turned suddenly wolfish, and the gentle touch of fingers switched, Katarina wrapping her fingers around Deara's wrist.

"Katarina," Deara gasped, jerking back, but Katarina held firm. A distant look crossed the living sister's face while Deara's slackened and shifted, revealing the marred flesh of a gunshot in her cheek, the beaten flesh, the stab wounds. "Don't." Her voice was slow, as if her mind were slogging through porridge.

It was the hint of pain that bled through the specter's slowed speech that had me struggling to sit up. "Madam," I said, reaching toward Katarina to break her hold on her sister's wrist, but the woman sidestepped smoothly, remaining out of reach. "Katarina."

"Rasczek ..." Katarina said, her face sour. "What were you doing with Rasczek?" She turned accusatory eyes on her sister. "No. I know what. There's no need to ask." Her voice was a bitter snipe.

Deara groaned. I had never seen the specter show any hint of pain or discomfort beyond boredom. The sound pulled at me. Deara seemed to be fading before my eyes. I edged closer.

"You were always so high and mighty, miss prude," Katarina said. "Always looking down on me, and there you were with Rasczek. And what did you get for it, dear old Deara?"

Healing body be dammed, I threw myself at the sisters, knocking loose Katarina's hold on Deara. Katarina and I hit the ground in a tangle of limbs while Deara spun away, eyes hollow as she rubbed at her wrist where her sister had held her.

Katarina seemed to wake from a dream as she worked to sit up.

I lay back, nursing my bruised ribs.

Beside me Katarina seemed to be clearing her head. She looked at me, then helped me back to my feet and to my bed once again. Deara stayed out of reach of her sister.

"Sade, I'm sorry. Are you alright?" Katarina asked, still slightly dazed.

I didn't answer, but looked at Deara. The marring of her fatal wounds had ebbed away but the darkness around her sallow eyes remained.

"Is she the one who killed you?" Katarina demanded.

A flash of fear played across Deara's face. "Emelia Rasczek did not kill me." Her voice was deep with warning. "Maybe you should have been less concerned with my private affairs during your little dive." Deara would not be allowing her sister to touch her again.

Katarina leveled her sister with a hard stare, then shrugged with a delicacy only she could muster.

A moment passed between the sisters before Deara disappeared through the wall.

"Well," Katarina huffed before her face smoothed as though nothing had just transpired. "That is an interesting little gift you have, but I don't know how much use you will really find in it. More of a parlor trick." She stuck her nose up and took her leave of the room, leaving me alone with my confusion and bruised ribs.

13:

I didn't see Deara for days after that. Wherever she was, I was sure it was not with her sister. Still, to have her avoid me now as well left a void. Without her, all I had was Katarina, who seemed more interested in her stream of young men and women than in her appointed protégé healing in the room beside her. When she did grace me with a visit between her parties and callers, neither of us spoke of Deara or what had transpired. I knew she still had my lock of hair squirreled away somewhere and I worried that as long as she did, Deara would stay away.

I had been left on my own since breakfast, and the hours of peace had been a kindness. Katarina had gone out to pay a social visit to one of the wealthy society women. For all she had said behind the woman's back, it was hard to imagine the two were truly friends, but I supposed the needs of station did not always coincide with true friendship.

With a sigh, I picked up the romance novel Deara and I had been reading. If she was never to return, I wouldn't be left wondering what happened to the overeager Mr. Reed and Ms. Pepper, at least. I made it three pages before I realized I wasn't alone.

With a start, I turned to face Deara's spectral form reading over my shoulder. "Next page," she said, ignoring my surprise.

"Where were you?"

"I have an entire afterlife to enjoy."

"Who is Emelia Rasczek?"

"I don't see how that is any of your business." Deara said shortly. "Now, I came back here to read. If you don't intend to do that, then I will leave."

I sighed and turned back to the book. I was a bit slower than Deara was with the words, but she waited patiently for me to turn the page. We continued on in silence like that for several pages. She read, then looked out the window until I turned the page. One day I hoped to be able to read as fast as she could, but I had not grown up with the pastime.

"Emelia and I were very close," Deara said while she was looking out the window after the fifth page.

"I take it you two were more than friends?"

Deara looked at me. "Depends on if you plan on chiding me like Katarina or not."

I gave her a smile then turned back to the book. "What does it concern me?" I turned the page.

Deara set her hand on my arm companionably and finished the page. "I did not think I would feel anything ever again," she said when she estimated me nearing the end of the page.

"Can you not feel the books or the clothes you wear or that chair beneath you?"

"It is a strange sensation that I hope you do not experience for a long time yet," she said, still with her hand on my arm. "Sade, I want you to be careful around Katarina. She has good intentions, and she will train you to the best of her abilities, but … We have lost a lot. We have seen the brutal edges of humanity. She let those brutal edges polish her into one herself, hiding it all under her prim exterior."

My body could attest to how brutal the woman could be when she got it in her.

14:

When I returned to training Katarina had a gentler hand, if not one that was wholly kind. She had made her point and beaten her message into me with Instructor's massive fists. I never thought of the man by his name; all he was to me was an instructor: a painful and unforgiving teacher. Even with Katarina he had a hard-handed way about him. The man had no qualms about striking a woman above his station. He almost seemed to see it as his duty, his responsibility to his student. Katarina seemed to relish the pain of her training. Still, the woman was skilled and gave as good as she got.

Conversely, I found myself often staring up at the sky with the man looming over me as I struggled to regain my breath. I was prone, gasping for air, when my new father made his appearance for the first time in what seemed like weeks.

"She's not wholly terrible, is she?" he commented to Katarina, who answered only with a delicate shrug.

I had no idea what delusion the man was seeing as he looked down at me lying flat on my back. Steadily I pulled in a little air, then rolled and slowly picked myself up. I dusted myself off and squared up against Instructor once again.

"She is getting better," Katarina finally acknowledged. "But let's not let her get an inflated ego," Katarina said with a nod toward Instructor.

For a moment I worried I was in for another beating, another lesson from Katarina. A gift from my oblivious new father. I was still, weeks later, feeling the last lesson.

The man gestured for me to strike at him, so I advanced. Trying to hit the man was like trying to strike wind. He dodged and stepped, his fist struck out like a viper, catching my ribs, but my stance held and I caught his wrist. He almost smiled when I made my grab, but then another moment later I was on my back wheezing once again.

"Does she have any idea?" Olso asked. I looked at him as my diaphragm finally remembered how to function, trying to discern what it was I was supposed to have any idea about. He was looking at Katarina, leaving me without any further enlightenment.

"I don't imagine she does," Katarina said ruefully, then louder. "Come on, Sade. That's enough for today. We can't have you unable to stand at the party tonight."

Instructor offered me his hand and I hesitantly took it. He pulled me to my feet and gave me a single nod. Approval?

"I'm sorry, what party?" I asked.

"Did I forget to tell you?" Katarina said thoughtfully. "Yes. Maybe. I don't have Deara's memory," she said with a pointed look at her sister. "The Norwoods received an invitation to a soiree at the Raszcek estate."

"I'll not be going," Deara said tightly.

"It is not as though anybody would notice if you did anyway." Katarina rolled her eyes, then looked at her uncle. "Will you be joining us this evening?"

He beamed at me. "I wouldn't miss my daughter's first soiree." For some reason that made me more apprehensive.

"Thanks ... Dad," I said, still awkward with the address. "I don't know that I have a suitable dress, though."

"You will wear one of mine," Deara said. "Get cleaned up, then meet me in my room."

I took my time in my bath, savoring the hot water and the soothing salts. My ribs were sore, but Instructor had a way of avoiding leaving bruises that were too noticeable.

The dress Deara directed me to was classic and certain to turn heads. There was something strange in the ghost's eyes as she watched me pin my hair and set her borrowed jewelry. A longing look and one of approval.

15:

"Miss Rasczek," Katarina said with a deep curtsy. She held her hand out delicately toward me. "My uncle, Lord Olso Norwood, and his daughter, Lady Sade Norwood." We each bowed graciously in turn.

The noblewoman looked at us all for only a moment before her gaze swept past us. I could almost feel her disappointment, thick as it was. Her eyes flicked to Katarina and she gave a slight bow, really just a light forward tip of her head. "Katarina," she said in what could almost be mistaken as a sigh. "Welcome. And welcome to you both," she said, not even looking at Olso or myself.

Katarina moved us onward and I leaned close.

"Does she know about Deara?" I asked.

"Why would she? It is not as though I told her." She said shortly, then sighed. "I don't know what she knows, Sade. I don't like playing all their games, and I especially don't like getting all that close with any of these people."

"Don't you risk making yourself an outsider, then?"

She laughed. "Dear. You are a Norwood. Others may call you 'Lady,' but an outsider is exactly what you are." She looked around the ballroom. "The only reason we get invited to these things is because we have money. *I* have money," she corrected. "Some of these families have a name and nothing else. If any of these eligible bachelors or bachelorettes show any interest in you at all, they are either looking at the size of your purse, or your tits. Nothing beyond that." She looked past me. "Uncle, would you mind terribly grabbing us a few drinks?"

He beamed. "Of course, my dears."

Katarina watched her uncle go, then looked at me. "Try not to sound like a rube when I introduce you to people, but at the end of the day, it doesn't really matter, does it?"

"Why even bother coming to these parties?" I asked the woman, who clearly had no interest in being at the soiree.

She winked at me. "A little knowledge of your enemies never hurt. Besides, since I failed to find a fitting Death Sight for a husband this last trip, this is a good opportunity to map out which eligible bachelor might be worth a bit of fun, at least."

"Is it that you didn't find a *fitting* Death Sight, or you didn't find any Death Sights?"

"Well, I found you, dear," she said coyly, knowing that was not what I meant.

I frowned and she just laughed and smiled. Those with magic were quiet and covert, but they seemed able to find each other. That she had failed to find any Death Sights aside from myself did not seem to bode well.

She sighed, throwing a little pity my way as I tried to sort out why the lack of Death Sights on her trip was so concerning.

"If the College isn't killing us, they are collecting us. Ask Deara about it later. This isn't the time."

I acknowledged with a nod and Katarina plastered a smile on her lips.

"Ah, Veruka," Katarina said ceremoniously, stopping a young woman with the proclamation. "What a pleasure it is to see you again." There was something wicked in Katarina's voice.

The woman looked from Katarina to me with a hint of discomfort. I recognized her from one of Katarina's evenings, the young man just behind her as well. The two had arrived at Norwood Manor together. I had made myself scarce well before they had left.

"Gaetan," Katarina bowed her head to the man.

"Miss Norwood," the man said, more at ease than the woman on his arm. He looked at me and gave me a small smile, knowing I knew about their many trysts. "And Miss Norwood. It is a pleasure. And my I say this is quite the look for you." He took my hand and kissed it. The subtle tongue running over his lips when he straightened again brought an unintended blush to my cheek. He returned his eyes back to Katarina with a questioning look.

"Maybe," she said playfully before looking around. "But there are a lot of fish in this particular sea. Let me at least cast my net for a time."

Olso returned with two flutes of champagne.

"You will let us know," Gaetan said to Katarina in quiet offer, then bowed low to Olso and retreated away with Veruka.

"Oh my, is that the Lady Thai there with Lord Jev? I haven't seen them in ages," Olso boomed, offering me his arm insistently. "Come, we must go meet them, my dear."

Katarina downed her champagne, then took my glass from my fingers and sent me off with a shooing gesture before setting off on her own hunt.

I followed Olso from wealthy cluster to wealthy cluster. Some were put off by his big presence with his booming voice but kept their peace due to his generally jovial nature. The man was met with condolences over his lost sons, and confusion when he introduced me as his darling daughter. Suspicious eyes turned toward me, and after the first few packs of well-to-dos, I excused myself from further introductions in favor of finding a quiet refuge for a short respite.

"I thought the Junction Norwoods only had boys," a woman said quietly as I passed, feeding the gossip. "What gutter do you suppose that one climbed out of, then?"

"Do you suppose dear Uncle Olso kept a mistress or a whore?" another sneered.

"They don't even look alike," the young man with them said. "Do you suppose the poor man is victim to a con?"

I moved away from the group, finding an alcove to take a few quiet moments away from all the fuss.

"Where is she?" The voice made me turn.

Emelia Rasczek seemed to have had a similar idea, tucked against the back wall. The woman had been drinking, but maintained all appearances of a noble woman. Away from the eyes of the crowd, she narrowed her eyes at me, a chip in her well-polished composure showing.

"Where is Deara?" Emelia asked, a small crease between her brows and her breath heavy. "Supposedly you are her cousin. You are wearing her dress. Her jewelry. So, you must know, right?"

"My lady, I don't ..." I looked back toward the party. For the time being, we were alone in the dimly lit alcove. "I don't know that this is the time or the place for this conversation."

Emelia glared at me. "Where did she go? You do know, don't you? I can see you do."

"My lady ..."

"Don't 'my lady' me," she growled. "Don't pretend you have any respect for me if you aren't willing to tell me the truth."

I swallowed, her despair palpable. "She's dead," I said softly.

"Dead?" The anger melted into confusion. The woman shook her head. "No. I don't believe you," she said firmly.

"Is it easier to believe that she just left without even a word to you, my lady?"

She frowned and I saw the denial flashing in her fluttering eyes. She blinked once, then again, and turned and walked away.

I slunk from the alcove and found Katarina. "I may have upset our hostess."

"Emelia needs to be knocked off her high horse more often, my dear," Katarina said with a bored sip of something that smelled much stronger than champagne. "What did you do?"

"I told her Deara was dead."

"Yes, that would upset her," Katarina rolled her eyes and sighed. "Well, she needed to know, I suppose. The way I see it, darling, you did our hostess a favor. She will get over it." She took my arm and pulled me on a stroll with her. "I may just take Gaetan and Veruka up on their offer. Sometimes it's just better to bet on the winning dog, don't you think?"

"Perhaps?"

She smiled and patted my hand. "I knew you would agree. I'm going to take the motorcarriage home. I will send it back around for you and Uncle Olso." She nodded toward her uncle. "He has been vehemently defending his honor and yours all evening, by the way. Seems to have come up with some cockamamie story about you and your adoption. Best for you to go and learn your history for yourself, maybe keep his lavish exaggerations under control." She gave me a nudge in his direction. "*You* are the one who has to live with his tall tales. *He* is just going to retreat back into hiding when he *finally* leaves."

I swallowed and returned to the fray.

"Her father was quite the accomplished scientist, you know," Olso was saying when I approached. "But studying the cloudline is quite the dangerous profession. My dear friend asked me, when we were just lads and Sade was just a wee thing, that if anything should happen to him would I take care of her as though she were my own. How could I not? We were practically brothers. But I do admit I could never have believed such a tragedy would actually befall him." He was solemn for a moment while his audience paid their obligatory moment of respectful silence. "The dear thing was always like a daughter to me anyway. I just wish it hadn't been tragedy that led to this gift." He beamed when he saw me and pulled me to his side tightly. "Ah, and here she is. I was just telling the others about how the gods brought you into my home, my dear."

I allowed myself to be swept into the consoling crowd of wealthy family heads as they fawned over Olso and his generosity, and me for my loss.

"And she is staying with Katarina?" an older woman said with clear disapproval. "Are you certain that is the best idea, dear man?" She didn't even bother trying to hide her dislike of the young woman. "Not to speak ill of your niece, of course. She just may not be the best influence for the dear child." She cast me a pitying look.

"I do appreciate your concern, my dear woman," Olso said with the most convincing pout, patting the woman's hand. "I know that my dear daughter can take care of herself. She wished to find her way in the world, and I cannot coddle her forever. Beside, I acknowledge that Vale does hold a bit more intrigue for a young woman than Junction."

The older woman took my hand. "If you ever need anything, dear."

"Thank you, madam. I appreciate your open and generous heart," I said in my most demure tone.

The woman smiled at her own perceived generosity.

And so it went for the rest of the evening until I could finally get Olso to the motorcarriage.

"How did you come up with such a fabrication?" I asked once we had some privacy.

He looked at me sadly. "The best lies have some truth to them, don't they? My best friend died during a research excursion. He did in fact ask me to look after his daughter after his wife passed years ago. Only ... his daughter was very much like him. The two of them were together in the balloon when the storm hit." He smiled at me. "I see the same spirit for discovery in you," he said, turning his attention to the window. "Please don't let it consume you, my dear. Some pursuits are not worth the cost." He got quiet, watching the night pass. "We are not expected to solve all the world's problems."

In the morning his bags were at the door.

"I've been here weeks already."

"Longer," Katarina drawled quietly.

Olso ignored her and went on. "It seems it is time I return home. If you need anything, my dear, please never hesitate. I do hope you will come visit me in Junction." He looked up at Deara and Katarina. "You two take care of my daughter." He looked at Katarina pointedly. "Katarina ..."

"Yes, Uncle. I will look after her," Katarina assured the man with an eyeroll.

He pulled me into one more rib-shattering embrace, then departed.

Katarina yawned and stretched. "I was wondering how long that brute would hang about. He did do us a favor, though, didn't he? There will still be some who are suspicious of you, but he did give quite the heartwarming story," she said, but she sounded nothing but bored. She yawned again, a deep yawn that showed me her molars. "Will you take her this morning, Deara? I'm not quite ready for my day."

"I thought she was your protégé," Deara said, but the ghost gave me a smile. "Though for what purpose, I can't even guess," she said under her spectral breath.

Katarina waved flippantly. "I was hoping she would be less tiresome than you," she said over her shoulder. "Can't have everything we want, though, can we?"

Deara shook her head at her sister's retreating back, then looked at me. "Did you see her?" She asked quietly.

"Who?"

"Emelia. How was she?"

"Deara …" I said gently. "She didn't know you are dead. I had to tell her. I don't know that she believed me."

Deara closed her eyes for a long moment, then nodded. "She will. She just needs time. Thank you for telling her, Sade." She let out a long breath. "Come on. Let's not waste the morning."

16:

"It is a strange thing," Deara said, watching me read that morning. "You are more educated than you should be."

I looked up from the pages, uncertain if I should be offended. "What do you mean?"

"I mean that, for a woman who grew up on the streets, you have a remarkable grasp of the complexities of language and, strangely, glyphs. Sometimes I swear you read glyphs as fluently as you do English." She looked at Marco and took a conciliatory tone. "Not to say that the streets do not teach their own lessons, but it's not usually book learning."

"I don't take offense, ma'am." Marco said. "Sade was always a weird one. I 'member Beater always saying she sounded too pompous for her own good."

I had heard similar frequently enough in my youth that I had, for the most part, trained myself out of speaking in any way that resembled the academics. Still, the speech patterns had made it easier for me when on the con.

"May I?" Deara asked, offering her hand.

"What are you hoping to find? I can just tell you."

She shook her head. "I don't know that you can, and that is what I am curious about," Deara said, still frowning at me.

"I think you are taking matters a bit out of proportion. I'm not even that fast at reading," I said, keeping my hand out of Deara's reach. She didn't try to snatch my hand up, and only dropped hers in a conciliatory way.

She shook her head. "You are out of practice, Sade. That is all. You don't struggle over a page the way I would expect. You have the habits of somebody who studied before," she said with a glance at my notebook. "If all you are lacking is practice, then that means you have a foundation. A foundation you don't seem to remember."

I swallowed and finally offered my hand. She wouldn't find anything, anyway. What was the point in resisting her desire to look? Her hand rested lightly on mine and she dove.

"A memory shared eases the burden," Deara said absently, her eyes far-seeing. Her words accompanied her memory. I saw through her eyes, a party, a ball, something frivolous and wealthy. A sweet smell in the air. A woman. The memory shifted, and it was mine. A man and his hands, a woman and hers.

"That's personal," I said tightly, remembering the evening in question. Eda and Gan and a night of foolishness between the three of us. The two of them were dead now: Gan before the Persephone, Eda during the failed raid. I didn't want to see them, and the memory faded. Now I saw Deara chasing a very young Katarina. The girl's genuine smile seemed a foreign thing to me, and I realized all I had ever seen of her was an act. My eyes refocused for a moment on the specter in front of me. She was deep in my memories, seeing far beyond what I could, far beyond what carried over to me. I allowed her the dive. She fed trickles of her memories over, greasing the depth of her prodding, her face twitching and shifting nearly imperceptibly as she worked through my past.

Finally, her eyes focused and she blinked. She took her hand back and frowned down at me. "You have gaps. I can't see into them. It is like there is a barrier."

"Maybe the memories are lost to time. You said so yourself that can happen. The details fade."

She shook her head. "Details may fade, the memory may become corrupted with your own ideals as you impose them upon it, but there is always some hint. Even back into the early years of life. Those memories may be nearly imperceptible and useless, but they exist." She frowned. "Yours end when you are maybe eleven or twelve. I couldn't quite pin it down. Don't you think that is odd?"

"No, I can remember before that."

She narrowed her eyes at me and shook her head once more slowly. "Hints of memories cobbled together without any detail, enough to keep you from wandering the streets helpless. Enough to make that Junction accent of yours come through so naturally when needed. I think you have more history on that float than you know. If I had to guess, that was a misstep of whatever Aberrant broke your mind. They didn't want you finding your way back."

"That doesn't make sense."

"No. It doesn't. I don't know, Sade. I thought I would find answers, and I guess I did." She didn't look satisfied. "Now I know why you have the look of somebody who has been tampered with. What I don't know is why. Aberrants don't normally rearrange children's memories just for kicks. At least, not so long as the Enforcers are around to keep them leashed." She sighed. "I'm sorry, Sade. Maybe," she looked at the book still open under my hands, "maybe we should be done for the day."

I nodded. "Alright," I said.

Deara yawned. "That was more exhausting than I thought it would be. I'm going to rest." She disappeared through the door with a stretch.

Marco was watching me. "Are you alright, sis?" he asked quietly, coming to my side.

"I'm confused, Marco." I looked at my hands, feeling suddenly like I could see the gaps in my memory. The lack of anything before one clear night on the streets. Deara's prodding seemed only to have formed holes in my mind. I patted the boy's shoulder, suddenly exhausted. "I need to sleep."

17:

The knocking turned insistent, barely pulling me back up from my drowsy daze. Marco shook my arm, his small cold fingers getting more frantic as I refused his beckoning to open my eyes.

The door opened and Katarina traipsed in as I cracked an eye.

"Sleeping, are you? I didn't expect that. Come on. Get dressed. I want to take you somewhere interesting. It's a real hot spot for dead."

She hauled me out of bed, and it was only a matter of minutes before we were in the motorcarriage, speeding across town. We stopped closer to the edge of the landmass than I liked to be. At least the slums were relatively close to the core, even bordering the abyss as they were. This park that Katarina had been so insistent on bringing me to was one of the distal regions, liable to fall away from the landmass with the slightest fluctuation in the core. While there hadn't been a fluctuation in the glyph core the gods had created to keep the landmasses viable in ages, I wasn't entirely comfortable trusting my continued existence to the old stone.

"We will be here a while," Katarina said to the driver, bounding out of the motorcarriage. I followed her begrudgingly.

"Iolde's Point," she said ceremoniously, looking out over the drop. The edge of the landmass. A few feet in front of us there was nothing but the cloudline, reflecting the orange and pink of the sun back up at us from hundreds of feet below. It almost looked inviting, except for the toxic fumes wafting up from the dead planet they shrouded.

In the distance, several airships dotted the horizon, their balloons and fins distinct against the endless abyss.

Katarina flounced to the very edge of the landmass, all the way to the railing meant to hold people on the ground. She breathed in and smiled as she leaned heavily on the railing, making me nervous the rusting metal would give and the woman would fall. It was rare, but fumes could rise even this high. Nor was it unheard of for there to be a variance in the landmass, a small tremor, and a distal region, much like the point, to break off and tumble into the abyss.

"Madam, maybe come back a little bit." I pleaded gently.

Katarina laughed. "Live a little, Sade. Come here." She beckoned me over.

I swallowed and then took a step toward the woman. What was I so scared of? I had leapt from bridges on the thin hope of landing on the backs of airships. I had braved climbs scarier than this. Had my time safe among the wealthy softened my edges? I met the woman at the railing.

She closed her eyes and inhaled deeply once again. "What do you feel? Why did I bring you here?"

I did as she did. I felt many dead. Not all seen, some too far out over the abyss, drifting where once the landmass had been, lost. Evidence that the point was indeed shorter than it once had been. I opened my eyes and the point was crawling with Whispers.

"Where did they come from?" I asked in surprise, looking at the droves.

"They have been here the whole time," Katarina said lightly.

"Why couldn't I see them?"

"You don't see every Whisper. It would drive you mad if you could, but that's not why. You know how the fold is layered. Some layers are easier to see than others, and the dead could be on any layer at any time. That is why hot spots like these make for interesting occurrences. It's like a dense knot of many layers of the fold coming within proximity. It softens the border. It creates leaks." She grinned. "There are a lot of jumpers here."

I didn't know why that made her grin, but maybe that morbid fact was appealing to Death Sights.

"Strange things can happen here on the right days. The layers of the fold line up just right and you can swear you can feel it passing through you. Swear you could touch the dead." She looked at me. "Maybe that's not impressive to you." She winked, then closed her eyes and took a deep breath. "There is a reason that Regulars claim areas of great death are haunted. When the layers compress and leak, even they can see the hints hidden in the fold." She opened her eyes and focused on a point just beyond the landmass. I watched the spot as well and saw the airship appear and dissolve once again.

"What …" I leaned against the railing to peer closer. "Can you predict the thinning?"

Katarina shrugged delicately. "Sometimes. Sometimes the sights are just like shooting stars: you have to be looking at the right place at the right time or you miss it." She turned to look back over the landmass. "Even on days of higher activity, actually being able to see into the fold is rare."

I looked down, below where the airship had passed. Superimposed upon the clouds was something that looked very much like a mountaintop. "What is that?"

She glanced down where I was looking. "Would you look at that?" she cooed. "I'm glad I brought you today. Normally, the point is just covered in Whispers and canoodling couples."

"It looks like a mountain …" Even as I spoke, the cloudline

started to overwhelm the view once again.

"It's possible it was a mountaintop, or will be a mountain, or is a mountain in some alternate layer of the fold. Maybe on some layer the planet is a habitable dirt ball rather than a fume-shrouded nightmare. I'm not the scholar that Deara is on the subject. All I know is that, if you bring a Sight here on a good day, you can drive them half mad with the things they can see." She looked around me and actually smiled. "I thought you might like it."

"I do."

She turned serious. "It's not all fun and games, though." She added a softening wink. "This is also an excellent place to train your sense."

We spent hours there, Katarina training me on how to focus on specific Whispers. I started to notice the patterns of their clothing. Started noticing the difference in behaviors. The differences of the ages. How long had some of these Whispers lingered in the transitional layers?

"With the right Whisper, you can learn almost anything, as long as you can keep them from manifesting under the attention. It is a fine line, but an essential one. Remember how I told you that the dead, as long as they are not manifested or vengeful, find no reason in lying?"

I nodded and she gave me a meaningful grin.

"Walking encyclopedias with no motivations or inhibitions, *if* you can find the right ones. Away from pinch points, it may be more difficult to find such a bountiful cornucopia of Whispers, but if you know what you are looking for, you can generally guess the correct locale to hang around. Just might take more time. Keep practicing." She gestured for me to go on. "Honestly, with how many Whispers there are here and the interference they cause, this is a supreme location to train your seeking. If you can pinpoint while wading through a sea of Whispers, you will be able to do it anywhere."

When she was away from drink and distracted from her sorrow, Katarina shone. I had only glimpsed this Katarina in Deara's memories. It was a refreshing change to see any true excitement in the woman, but it would only be a matter of time before she reverted back after we returned to the house. For a few hours, though, we were friends, and she taught me with the same fervor and enthusiasm that Deara did. Being a Death Sight was a burden and a joy to Katarina.

The driver was dozing when we returned. The sun was beginning to drop into the cloudline and, even with the constant glow of lights in the city, it wouldn't be smart to be out too late needlessly.

Katarina settled in the seat beside me with a smile. "I enjoyed this, Sade. Thank you."

"Thank *you*," I said emphatically. I realized I had needed the distraction as well. The work Deara had done in my memories had scared me. The revelation of the loss of my childhood had rocked me. I swallowed, glad that Katarina had turned her attention to the window during my momentary panic. She turned back to me and I managed to paste my smile back onto my face.

"I got you a position at Mrs. Sandfjord's dress shop," Katarina announced merrily, tucking her pillbox into her purse. Despite the good news, my smile slipped. "Considering your skill with a needle, it seemed a good fit. I don't know why you didn't pursue this sort of position sooner."

I didn't say anything, though she looked at me expectantly. Her eyebrow cocked and I understood. Gratitude was what she wanted. Had I not been distracted with my thoughts, gratitude would have been forthcoming. "Thank you, Katarina. Truly. It is all I wanted."

She rolled her eyes and patted my knee. "Well, you have a bit more than you asked for now, but I am glad I could help. And, well, I think you have progressed really well in your studies. It is time you have something you enjoy doing."

"I enjoy this, Katarina, I do," I assured her.

She laughed. "Seeing the dead isn't exactly the most joyous activity, dear. I know that well. Do try to do well at Mrs. Sandfjord's. She is rather the premier seamstress among the wealthy women, and her reference could take you far … If you do mean to continue this whole seamstress dream of yours." She turned away again and I was left to my thoughts. It was clear that the joy of the day had already been penetrated by cold despair in the both of us.

I could only hope that Deara had made more sense of my ruined memories than I had been able to. That she would have all my answers when we got home. But, of course, the specter was gone when we returned.

18:

A week passed, then two, and I started to wonder if Deara too had passed. That she had moved on without a word. I had started and finished one of her noir novels in that time, hoping that at any moment I would look up to find the woman silently reading over my shoulder. Even her guilty pleasure did not seem enough to draw her out. I had since turned to a textbook on botany, fascinated by the very idea of so much green space to allow for such growth.

When I got to my room, old Widow Reese was standing just inside the doorway. I couldn't help but wonder how many times I had entered and not even noticed the woman. I stared at her now as I sat on the edge of my bed. She wasn't manifested. Not even really aware of my presence. She was a shadow of the woman she had been in life, and likely of the specter she had been in death. How long had she been around? How much longer would she remain?

She drifted around the room while I continued to watch. How had I grown so accustomed to the woman's behavior that I had stopped even noticing her? That I could sleep even with the specter drifting nearby? I couldn't blame my time on the streets or with the gangs. If a living soul was ever doing what this dead woman was, I never would have been able to sleep.

Marco stepped through the door, casting a glance at the widow as he entered. The woman always made the boy uncomfortable, and why wouldn't she? I should have been uncomfortable too. She was harmless, though. Not manifested. Not malevolent. Sometimes there and sometimes not.

Marco climbed onto the bed beside me and huddled close, watching the ghost as she made her rounds. She stopped here and there where furniture must have been in her time, toying with objects of her memory, then moving on. Suddenly, I felt like an invader, an intruder in her space and her private moments.

"You're spoiling him," Deara said behind me. "The child is dead. He has to accept that. Cuddling and coddling him as if he were alive isn't going to do either of you any good." She paid the widow no mind. Today, it seemed, she had decided to ignore those not manifested. She followed my gaze and sighed. "Is the widow back?"

I nodded, mix of relief at seeing the specter's return and irritation at Deara's aloofness at having disappeared struggling for dominance. "Your sister has been looking for you. *I* have been looking for you."

Deara ignored me. "I always found her rather creepy. But," she shrugged, "the dead will do as they do." She settled by the window, looking out.

"Where have you been, Deara?" I tried again.

The specter just shrugged. "I had some things to think about." She gave me a strange look, as though considering her words.

"I missed you," I confessed.

She just gave me a half smile and a nod.

"Did you want to read this evening?" I asked.

"No. If you intend to stay up, you should use the time to study."

"What's the point of it? It is not as though I can do anything with these glyphs," I complained, but still I pulled the text down from the bookshelf and set it on my desk.

"It is important to know what an Aberrant is throwing at you."

So, I read, learning the curves and dashes of the glyphs with a familiarness that unsettled me. I had seen many glyphs in my life. They practically ran Vale, their dim glow plastered on walls and hidden in mortar, the hum of their magic a rhythm that played in my ears so constantly I barely even noticed it anymore.

"What glyph were you just studying?" Deara asked quietly.

I realized I had started to drift after the hours of study into the night, and blinked a few times to clear my mind. "Hmm." I looked at the page of my notebook. My fingers held a loose grip on my pen, the ink having splotched and drifted along the page with my drowsiness. I lifted the nib and looked at the origin of the drift. "*Fael* ..." I said the distorted glyph's name, cocking my head at it, then translated, "Ignite? I think that's it, anyway. I nearly drowned it," I said, frowning at the glyph swimming in ink. Deara looked over my shoulder and gave a tight nod. "Why?"

She only shrugged, but there was a depth to her eyes that had me concerned. "You should get some rest."

I obliged and moved toward the vanity, but watched the specter. "Why?" I asked again.

Deara watched me from the window. "Something in your memories. I think with my prodding, something from beyond the barrier broke free, and I just didn't realize it right away."

The specter turned to face the dark outside.

"I don't think you are a Death Sight," she said as though to herself.

I looked at the ghost. "What do you mean?"

"It is hard for me to explain, and I don't understand it." She kept her back to me. "I've been trying to figure this out, but it is slow going." She glanced back at me. "Get some sleep." She beckoned to Marco, who had been practicing rolling a pencil back and forth across my sketchbook. The boy looked confused at the invitation, but jumped up at the prospect of something, anything to do.

"Night, sis," he piped before following Deara out.

19:

Deara was in a much better mood when she came to me the next day while I enjoyed the morning air at the edge of the estate. She was nearly bouncing as she looked down at the pages under my fingers. "Botany. Interesting. You know, there is a glyphwork study that I would recommend you read, if that is of interest to you," she said with an excitement that completely distracted me. I set my book aside and looked up at her.

"Deara?"

"I should have asked Marco for help sooner. That boy has a talent for sniffing things out, doesn't he?"

"Deara," I prompted again. "What's going on?"

She sat on the bench beside me. "I was so trapped in the mindset that you were a Death Sight that I didn't see it. You're not like Kat or me. Not a mix of magics … Well, you are, but," she slowed down, trying to organize her thoughts, "you are not a Death Sight. Not naturally, at least."

"Deara, please, be clearer."

She looked down. "I didn't want to tell you this last night, but I think when that barrier on your memories chipped, I think I saw your mother. I think she was a Lock. I think you are one too."

"A what?"

"I also just heard of it." She bounded to her feet again. "Marco helped me find this …" She looked around expectantly, then sighed. "Hang on." She vanished for a long moment, then reappeared, glaring at the air beside her. "Oh, I hate dealing with the nonmanifested. One more time." She vanished again, and this time when she returned, it was with an old man at her side. His hollow eyes and slack face were an expression I had come to know all too well: the lost dead. How long had he lingered in the fold already? "That's better. Whatever you do, do not try to manifest him. These damn Aberrants are damn near impossible to get any information out of if they manifest." She turned to the man. "Tell me about Locks."

The man was slow to speak, his mouth working up to the action in slow quakes that steadily grew in size. "Locks ..." His voice was quiet and I took a step closer, but no more, not wanting to draw his attention. "Locks ... rare form of Channel ..." His mouth moved soundlessly a few times before returning to his recitation. "Unlike their cousins, they can only take from the dead. They are thought to be rare, but that may be due to the fact that their ability is useless if no dead reach across the fold to them, unless they also possess the abilities of a Death Sight. Once a Lock has been gifted the abilities of the dead, they appear to retain the abilities until their own death. This ability to wield the traits of all others with a natural connection to the fold made Locks a threat to the Society, leading to the hunt and destruction of their kind seven centuries ago. While it is suspected that some Locks may remain, they cannot become realized unless they also inherit the abilities of a Death Sight, or a dead Death Sight willingly passes their abilities to the Lock. If an Aberrant of the College suspects a citizen of being a Lock, they are to apprehend immediately. All Death Sights should be held in suspicion ..." The man's hollow eyes gazed through me, then started to sharpen.

"Go." Deara's order was clear and swift. The man's eyes drifted again, and he was gone. "A Whisper of a dead College Aberrant is the greatest gift the gods can give you, if you can keep them from manifesting or moving on long enough to get anything useful out of them. Another reason Abbies hate Death Sights, mind you. They normally keep a few pet Death Sights on hand to either manifest the lingerers or confirm the passing of the quick burns. We got lucky that one slipped through the cracks." She looked back toward the house where we could hear Katarina and Instructor working in the gardens.

"I don't know that I need to tell you this, but Katarina cannot know what you are. If you can, you should get your hair back from her. She usually has good intentions," she turned to me with a sadness in her eyes. "She just gets a little too absorbed, a little too greedy, a little too destructive. If she figures out she can take abilities from the dead ..." She shook her head. "You've seen it. You understand."

I nodded. I did.

I looked at Deara. "You said you saw my mother?"

She looked momentarily uncomfortable. "The only indicator was that she looked very much like you," she said. "But yes. I think so."

"Can you show me?"

She took my hand. "The memory is a fragment. Barely there, but it is more than we had before." She pushed and it was barely a glimpse. Sound seemed distorted, and the image itself was a faded and fractured thing.

A dark-haired woman extending her hand toward a man. A dead. Him taking hers. If there were words exchanged, they were as lost as the details. I barely looked at the man, the way he seemed to drift out of existence when he took my mother's hand.

Deara held the memory in place, frozen in the glimpse. Then it faded, and she gave me an apologetic smile. "I'm sorry, that's all I have."

"It is more than I had before," I said, looking at my hand in hers with a frown.

"I will keep trying," she promised.

- 91 -

PART 2:

ABERRATION

- 92 -

1:

Deara's hand rested on my shoulder while I worked, trying to focus on my sewing while the specter did her best to distract me with memories. For months, she had prodded at the edge of my missing memories, cautiously chipping away at the barrier. After so long, I thought I would be used to it.

"That is highly distracting," I growled quietly in case Mrs. Sandfjord was feeling nosey today. The older woman seemed to have few qualms about listening at doors if it meant gossip would be laid at her fingertips. Still, her shop was premier, and if I ever worked up her trust enough to dig myself out of the menial work, I would be able to hold this experience aloft elsewhere. Katarina seemed only to care that she no longer needed to spend her inheritance on my maintenance and could instead focus on more important vintages; the bottles collecting almost as quickly as her maid could clear the empties.

The memory in the back of my mind was recent. It was Deara's. The specter standing over me while I read. Her eyes drifting to the sketchbook left open beside me, then to the pages of notes I had compiled as I studied.

"Could you not at least show me something interesting?"

"I thought you were trying to focus. I figured this would be a less intrusive memory than anything else."

"Less intrusive? It's outright boring."

"Well, excuse me," she laughed, not worried in the slightest that

Mrs. Sandfjord would reveal herself a Death Sight. If she were one, the old woman was damn good at hiding it, with Deara and Marco's frequent and unexpected visits to the shop. "You should show some of your designs to Mrs. Sandfjord," Deara said in a distracted tone as she grabbed hold of whatever memory she had been seeking between my ears. "They are not half bad. That old woman likes you, even if she pretends she doesn't. It's fashionable to dislike Norwoods, is all."

"Mmhmm," I said, my hands stopping in their work at the specter's deeper intrusion. The last thing I needed was to sew my own fingers into the jacket I was mending.

My eyes half-lidded the way Deara's did as the memory hit us both. Massive walls lined with books. Blurs and fractures. Another broken memory.

Deara growled in frustration and let the memory slip away before risking me passing out. "It's a library, I am sure of it. If I could just catch a detail. Anything in the blurs, I could ground the memory. Maybe repair it enough to crack that barrier."

"Why does it matter so much, Deara?" I asked, not for the first time, as I returned to my work.

"I can't understand how little you seem to care, Sade. It's your memories. It's your life. You aren't even a little curious?"

"Whatever you are looking at is hardly my life. Even if I lived it, it's not what shaped me. It's not the experiences that molded me. It's all lost. Maybe it should stay that way."

"And what about what you are? You really don't want to know about being a Lock? How your family survived this long? Maybe the answer is in your hidden memories." She was reaching, knowing full well what my interest level was.

As far as I was concerned, a Death Sight or a Lock, it didn't matter. I was not about to start absorbing the dead for their power any time soon if I could help it. That I could see the dead and talk to Deara certainly proved interesting in academic pursuits, but I couldn't see much use for it beyond that. Katarina only ever shut down any hint of an idea at how the ability could be used. She had trained me to focus my magic and she had trained me to protect myself. That, it seemed, was the extent of what was due her protégé. Still, she didn't kick me out, and at times seemed to genuinely enjoy, if not my companionship, my presence in her home. That was enough for me, and I didn't need memories of some forgotten past to retain my position.

I sighed and shook my head at the specter. "Maybe it's best that the answer stays there."

Deara glowered. "You sound like Katarina." The ghost paced away from me, frustrated with not only my lack of curiosity, but also her lack of clarity. "You don't seem to understand, Sade. The memories are hidden. They are behind a barrier. If they were meant to be lost, they would have been destroyed. These, though, seem like they were kept intact. Preserved against the distortions of time. Protected from your own alterations."

"That doesn't mean anything, Deara," I said, my own frustration with the months of intrusion starting to bleed through. "Poke. Prod. Do what you want. But leave me to work." I turned my eyes back down to the jacket.

Menial work. Tedious work. But it was a steppingstone.

I was glad that Deara had resorted to sulking in the corner when my workshop door opened, drawing my eyes up from my sewing to find Mrs. Sandfjord chattering pleasantly with Emelia Rasczek.

"Sade will take care of you, darling," Mrs. Sandfjord said with a pleasant tone to the woman, casting a warning look at me. This would be my test to see if Katarina's referral had been based in truth. I had worked for Mrs. Sandfjord for three months already, but only on low-stakes projects. Nothing too risky for her business and her reputation, and nothing that showcased any real talent in me. Emelia Rasczek was not considered a menial project. "She has quite a good eye and deft hand. I am certain she will tend you well, my lady." To me, Mrs. Sandfjord said, "The young Lady Rasczek will be attending the Beford-Hummel wedding." As though I should know the lucky couple. And likely I should, but the Norwoods had not ranked high enough for an invitation. "She will need something befitting." She glanced at my sketchbook as though giving me permission to use my better judgment.

She probably questioned that instantly when I curtsied to Emelia Rasczek a little awkwardly, overtly aware of Deara staring from the corner. We had not expected this.

Mrs. Sandfjord gave me a withering look at the unbalanced nature of my curtsy, then took her leave.

"The wedding date, my lady?"

"Three weeks," Emelia said, her cheeks going pink. "I know that is short order, but I," she shook her head, "I seem to have been distracted and lost track of things."

I nodded, looking the woman over, trying my hardest to ignore Deara's intense stare.

"Do you have a dress in mind already?"

Again, Emelia blushed. "I admit, I am not very good at this sort of thing." I didn't believe that for a moment. The woman was immaculate to a fault. Her current attire at the peak of fashion. The soft yellow dress corseted and trimmed all in lace was one designed to catch and hold the eye, though I could not quite get past the silly little hat that current trends decreed she wear. The outfit would have done better with only the waves of her hair to accentuate it. "I usually have Imogen tell me what she thinks is best."

I didn't know who Imogen was, but I nodded, smiled, and opened my sketchbook. "Do you have a preference on color?" I asked as I worked, eyes going between the woman and my page. Avoiding Deara.

She circled the workshop, looking over the array of fabrics before stopping beside a deep red sheaf. I couldn't help but look at Deara now, the ghost standing just beside the fabric stand, fixated on Emelia. Quickly I looked back down, my pencilwork a little heavier than I would have liked. "Perhaps something like this. What do you think?"

I looked up from my sketch. "That color will be lively on you, madam," I said with a nod of approval as I appraised the woman's sun-darkened skin against the fabric.

"Emelia," Deara said from the corner, finally finding her voice. "Sade. That is her."

My eyes flicked to the specter nervously.

"Thank you," Emelia said, looking at me for the first time. "Do I know you?"

I swallowed, focusing on my sketching. "We have met, my lady." I didn't want to remind her of the circumstances of our meeting, but there was no avoiding it. "Sade Norwood. You invited my cousin and me to your party a few months back."

Her eyebrows knit together.

"I'm going to need your true measurements," I said in the hopes of distracting the woman. "Under your clothes," I elaborated.

For a moment the woman blushed, then nodded. "Of course."

"Do you need assistance in undressing?"

"Oh no. I can manage ..." she said, looking down at her

billowing skirts. "Well … maybe I ought to have you help me."

"Sade." Deara drew my eyes again. "I need you to speak for me."

I handed Emelia my sketch as I stepped to her side. "What do you think of something like this, perhaps, madam?"

Emelia looked at the drawing absently and nodded once, not having really seen the design. "Yes, that will be lovely," she said, her voice distant. She set the drawing down, and adjusted her eyes to focus on me. "Norwood …" Emelia said under her breath.

Deara closed the distance between us.

I pursed my lips and assisted the woman in relieving herself of the thick fabric of her winter dress while diligently trying to avoid Deara's pleading eyes.

"Sade," Deara said more insistently.

I cast her an exasperated look and, for a horrified moment, realized that Emelia was watching me in the mirror. I favored her with a smile before returning my full attention to unlacing her dress.

"She knew what I was," Deara said, almost begging. "She will not turn you in, Sade. Please. Do this for me."

"What is it?" Emelia asked finally.

I swallowed and looked up at her. She had definitely noticed my distraction.

"Nothing, madam. I apologize. I was just thinking about what would suit you best," I said, hoping I sounded convincing.

"Sade," Deara's voice went from insistent to something that had me on edge. I looked at the specter nervously then back at Emelia, knowing she had seen the glance. I tried to paste another smile on my face.

The woman looked down at me with a cocked eyebrow and pursed lips. "You are acting as though I have a third breast, woman. Look me in the eye."

Aside from Katarina, who seemed a far cry from any of the gentlewomen I had met since, I was not accustomed to such crassness from one of the well-to-dos and was shocked into looking at her.

"That's better. What is it?" The woman demanded. "Last time we met, you told me Deara was dead. A fact I have yet to be able to prove. So, what is it now? Hmm?" She seemed not at all slowed by being in only her underthings.

"Sade," Deara said, her frustration burning.

My eyes flicked to the side and Emelia followed my gaze with narrowed eyes.

"Damn you, Sade," Deara growled, stepping to my side in a blink and shoving me harshly. Her hands made contact, rocking me back. She wore a self-satisfied smirk while Emelia's confusion grew.

I set my jaw, then met Emelia's eyes. "Deara would like to speak with you." I said tightly, not liking having been forced into it.

"Deara ..." the woman said, spinning around to take in the entirety of my small workshop. "Where is she?" she asked in confusion that had melted from irritation to hope.

"I did not lie to you at your party," I said carefully.

Emelia either did not hear or did not care. She grasped my shoulders and shook me in a moment of frustration. "That is a cruel joke." She was fire now.

"It is not, my lady," I said quickly, looking at the ghost for her next words.

"Tell her what you are," Deara advised.

I swallowed. How many times had Katarina told me not to speak of the ability on Vale? How many times had she told me how dangerous it could be?

"I can see the dead," I said cautiously, ready to defend myself.

"The dead?" Her face twitched as though trying to push the thought aside. "Where is Deara?" Emelia asked, looking around once again.

I shook my head. "No ... Miss Rasczek." I said, drawing the woman's eyes to me. "Deara is among the dead. She is here with us now."

Emelia shook her head. "What?"

"It happened the night after the Darre's anniversary party," Deara said, setting her hand in mine for support in her memory. I repeated her words for her. I watched as Emelia's face folded in shock, denial, sorrow. "I must have slighted Alec Gao in my rejection of his advances at the party." I realized I was reciting a truth that Deara had kept from her sister for years. "He was angry already and flew off the handle when he realized I had slipped away with you. He knew there was somebody else, but he didn't know about us," I echoed Deara's reassuring tone, but the woman standing in front of me looked like reassurances of her own safety were the furthest thing from her mind. "He used the fact that I am a Death Sight to stir up a posse."

Emelia looked at my hand where it held Deara's unseen, then raised her eyes to mine, then to where she approximated Deara to be beside me.

"How?" Emelia's voice cracked. Her hand clutched at my free hand, finding support in a stranger. Something flashed in her eyes and I realized that she was staring at Deara. She could see her. "De … Deara."

"Sade …" Deara said anxiously.

"Can you …" I said.

Emelia cast aside my hand in favor of wrapping her arms around Deara. The moment our fingers separated, Deara vanished from Emelia's sight, her arms grasping only air, and the woman's face melted again. She rounded on me. "What sort of twisted trick is this?"

I backed up a step, eyes flicking to Deara, who gave a slow nod. "It's not a trick," I said carefully and extended my hand to the woman. "Take my hand again."

With a look of apprehension, Emelia set her hand lightly on mine, then turned toward Deara slowly, as though torn if she truly wanted to see the specter. Deara seemed equally uncertain. There was danger in this ability.

"Deara," Emelia said, confirming that she could see the specter once again. Her fingers wove with mine, grasping tight to prevent me from banishing the image. She looked at me. "Can she see me, hear me? How does this work?"

"Neither of us understands how this works," Deara said, and Emelia turned back to the specter. "All we know is that Sade is the key." Deara's hand tightened on mine, cold mist made solid. She swallowed nervously. "Emelia. I need you to accept that I am dead. And I need you to know I didn't just disappear. Not by choice."

Tentatively, Emelia lifted her hand to Deara, who equally hesitantly brought her hand to the living woman's. I felt like an intruder in their moment and turned my eyes to the side to allow them as much privacy as I could while holding both their hands. There was a little gasp and both their hands tightened on mine as the living touched the dead.

"Tell me," Emelia said.

Deara shook her head. "It may be better not to know the details."

"Tell me," Emelia said more firmly. "Alec Gao. What did he do to you?"

Deara shook my hand slightly to get me to look at her. "There's no need to pretend like you aren't here, Sade." She sighed, and I could see the reluctance in her to tell her story. "This does not get back to Katarina. If she tries to take on the Gaos, they will kill her too."

An image filled my mind, overwhelming, filling my senses, replacing them with a memory of the past. Of Deara's past.

The happy sensations of a body that had spent the evening in bliss made my stomach tingle as it had hers. Even the yellow of the constant beating of incandescent lights around Vale seemed pleasant. Deara had looked at her hands, fingers playing over fingers in a memory of touches. "Emelia," she had tasted the name on her lips.

Beside me I felt Emelia's knees weaken as the memory filled her as well. Without breaking contact with either specter or living woman, I managed to help settle the women to the workshop floor while the memory continued to swirl before us.

Deara stepped from the calming party into the crisp night air. She enjoyed the moment away from the expectations of the well-to-dos to bask in even so recent a memory.

"Where did you slip off to?" The voice was smooth cider behind her.

"Ah, Alec. I was wondering where you lit off to," Deara said, turning to a handsome young man with a smile.

"I could say the same about you," he said, eyes narrowing. I felt the nervousness that Deara had at that moment. His hand found her arm, gentle but with something restraining in it. "You know. I heard a rumor out of Bevilla," he said coolly. "Something unseemly, to be certain. That you claim to talk to the dead."

"I've never claimed that," Deara said, uneasy, taking a step back. Alec's hand tightened on her wrist and suddenly the bliss of the evening was replaced by terror. "Who would tell you such a nasty thing?" She asked, mustering all due shock and surprise in her voice.

"Daniel Vitan. Was it just a lie?"

"Assuredly." I could sense the nerves bubbling in Deara's chest. "I have never even been to Bevilla."

He smiled, but only one corner of his mouth lifted in the strained expression. His hand did not loosen. Deara's eyes drifted to his restraining fingers. "Of course not." He patted her hand gently, the second corner of his mouth finally struggling to join the first in rising. Malice. "It is a wretched place filled with transients. I can't imagine what an upstanding young woman of your cut would be doing on such a float." The smile was sickening.

Alec drew her along, further from the rest of the party goers, and she considered fighting the man. A little blackmail she could handle, though. She hadn't expected his true intent.

He looked down, shaking his head. "I wish I could wipe the memory of his running lips and distasteful rumors from my mind, but I don't think they were only nasty words." He drew a sharp breath in through his nose and glared down at her. "Maybe I could believe you if everything you say weren't a lie."

"Alec ..."

He growled, yanking her toward him. "Who were you with tonight?"

"With? I ... I don't know, Alec, I spoke with so many people this evening."

"You know what I mean. Who was it you slipped away with? Who was it who swept you off my arm and took what was due to me?"

Deara backed a step away from him, but his hand remained locked around her wrist. "What do you mean to imply with that?"

"Maybe you can still put my mind at ease," he said, and this time his voice held a sinister slide, like a knife waiting to be drawn. "Give me a kiss, my dear."

The memory faded and it was the three of us alone once again.

"You don't need to see the rest," Deara said grimly.

"Show me," Emelia said.

"It is not a memory you will want," Deara said pleadingly.

"Show me how you were taken from me. I don't want the memory, but I do need it."

Deara swallowed, her eyes flicking from Emelia to me, then my sight phased back into Deara's memory. The darkness. The men in varying states of misguided fear and anger. Alec goading the action on. The knives flashing. Three men, twenty-seven stab wounds. Deara had still been alive somehow after the beating. The stabbings. Everything that had come before. I felt her pain as my own. She held nothing back. Still, memories faded and warped. We saw the brutal flashes but not the details. Alec's face. Contorted, disgusted. The blood. The clouds. The darkness.

Deara slowly removed her hand from Emelia's, then from mine as she stood. Her haunted expression hid the brutal marks of her demise as she retreated a step. "Take care of her for me," she gave as a final direction before moving toward the wall.

2:

Deara departed, leaving me alone with Emelia crying into my shoulder. I was just glad that, through all this, Mrs. Sandfjord had refrained from poking her head in.

"I … perhaps should have gotten your measurements beforehand," I murmured when her sobs had slowed, rubbing the woman's back.

She laughed in a deep choke and pulled back enough to look at me. Taking a long breath in, she steadied herself, still holding my arms as I held hers. "Yes. Perhaps." She wiped away the tears and I could see her sorrow had morphed in that moment into something other. "I don't want you to get in trouble. Let us get this done quickly."

I nodded and grabbed my measuring tape.

While I worked diligently, Emelia seemed to study me. "You are not related to them."

"I would have thought you heard my dad's tale." I said, making a quick jot in my sketchbook before returning to measure her hips.

The conversation was a forced, awkward thing now, Emelia still struggling with a gamut of emotions from witnessing Deara's death.

"But you *are* a Death Sight," Emelia said. "Where did they find you?" There was something in her eyes now. She was distracting herself, but in a way that set me on edge. There was suspicion there. "Deara trusts you?"

I gestured for the woman to lift her arms so I could run the tape around her chest, all the while avoiding those dissecting eyes. "Out of necessity, perhaps."

"It was Katarina who brought you on, then."

I straightened from my work. "She did."

"From Junction."

"Hmm," I acknowledged tightly, moving quickly now.

"Where did they elevate you from?"

"I am finished with your measurements," I said, stepping back. "My lady." I bowed my head. "I will need a week before we can do the first fitting. Do you need any assistance with your dress?"

Emelia looked me over, then nodded. "I will, actually." She wouldn't let me dismiss myself that easily.

"Of course," I said, moving to retrieve the woman's garments.

"You know you are a noblewoman now, right?" Emelia asked

with a subtly aggressive tone. "No need for all the subservience."

I gave her a thin smile. "While that is true, it does not hurt to show others a little courtesy," I said tensely.

"Hmph." Her mouth pinched to the side as she studied me. "Your hands are rough. Scarred. Lean. Muscular. Accustomed to hard work. A hard living. You have scars one would not expect to see on a researcher's daughter." Observations only. I knew better than to acknowledge them, but I did.

"You know many researcher's daughters, then?"

I held the dress while Emelia took her time to get into it, ignoring my comment.

"Common, that's certain. Maybe lower than common. Not from one of the major families. They elevated you because you are a Death Sight. They *are* getting rather rare these days." She watched me in the reflection of the mirror. It seemed Katarina's training had paid off, because my face gave away nothing as I worked on the woman's laces. "Did they find you in one of the Dove Cages? They certainly seem a place Katarina would find appropriate for ... *talent acquisition.*"

"I'm flattered you think I'm refined enough to be an entertainer in the Cages." Regarded as little more than pleasure houses by the more prudish citizens, the Dove Cages were home to some of the top performers in the Society, though their talents were often dismissed for the sultry nature of their performances.

She gave a dismissive snort at my sarcastic tone. "Perhaps I am giving you too much credit. But, there must be something to you to have caught Katarina's eye. Drunken mess that she is, she is still shrewd. She wouldn't be so desperate as to take you in solely because you are a Death Sight, surely.

I glanced over the woman's shoulder to meet her eye in the reflection of the mirror. "Why does it matter to you, my lady?" I finished her lacing and held up her coat for her.

She turned to face me. "Because Deara trusts you. You owe your loyalty to Katarina for elevating you from whatever ill repute you were destined for, yet Deara shared with you something she does not want Katarina to see."

"Without me, she and you could not touch," I reminded the woman. "I was incidental."

"That is what I am concerned about. Deara is not your benefactor." She looked at me, hard. "Will you tell Katarina what was shared with you?"

"Not if Deara does not want it told."

The woman grabbed her handbag, considering its contents a moment before turning narrowed eyes on me. "Deara is not wrong. If Katarina finds out about Alec, if she tries to challenge the Gaos, they will kill her. If it turns out that all you truly are is her dog, and you report this back to your master, Katarina will die." This aggression in the woman had me backing away a step. How quickly she had swung from intense sorrow and pain to this.

I said nothing and turned to the swathes of fabric that I would be pulling together into a dress for this woman.

She made a contemplative noise, then took her leave.

I looked at the fabric running between my fingers with a pit in my stomach. Deara had said that memories could leak. Had Emelia seen something? A memory of mine that had somehow slipped through the background of the others? Something that had set her on edge and made her suspicious of me? Something that would bring trouble for Katarina and me?

I wished Deara would return. That she would give me advice, or some semblance of comfort, but her need for space after the visceral memories was understandable. Even as I ran my hand over the fabric, all I could see was the blood that had coated Deara's hands. Her blood. The way she had raised them weakly in her final moment in the vain attempt at defense.

3:

Katarina took a seat on the bench to the side of the training mats. I flopped down on the mats themselves to recover.

The woman mopped the sweat from her brow, then smiled down at me. "You seem rather more motivated than usual."

I let my head roll to the side to look at her. "I'm just having fun, is all. I enjoy these moments, Kat." And I clung to the distraction.

She leaned back against the wall. "Should I call in the instructor, then? Make this even more fun?"

I laughed. "I think I have gotten my ass handed to me thoroughly enough today. Thank you, though."

"Perhaps I should call him in here for myself, then," she said playfully.

"You have more in you?" I asked in surprise. How long already had we been sparring?

She chuckled and returned her eyes to me. "Dear, I always have more in me." With a sigh, she joined me on the mats and we stared at the ceiling. "But this is nice too, I suppose." She closed her eyes.

"Why is Instructor so good?" I asked, watching the woman relax.

"Instructor …" She laughed. "I love how you call him that. You do know he has a name, right?"

"Tomas. Yes. I know he has a name." I would still just call him Instructor.

Her eyes cracked for a second, but drowsiness started overtaking her again and they closed slowly.

"He used to be an Enforcer in Dorado." The float was notorious for its high crime rate. A rate I had always suspected was inflated by their desire for independence from the Society, or at least equal representation. They did not have the surnames that garnered positions as Society leadership, so little consideration was ever given to their wishes. Dorado was relatively flat, with enough farmlands to support themselves and a handful of smaller floats in their vicinity. Their ample food production was essential for many of the more industrialized floats of the Society, though, so there was no chance they would ever break free.

"Tough streets, from what I hear," I said.

"Yeah," she said, her voice growing more distant as she settled in. "He's a Future Sight. What we call a near-sighted Future Sight. He can see just ahead. It makes him good in a fight, but he's never been very good at seeing well down the road. Sight or no. It's charming, in a way," she said with a subtle half-smile as she drifted closer to sleep.

"And you are only telling me this now?" I asked playfully.

She gave a small shrug. "I didn't want you to get in your head, dear."

I chuckled and joined her in closing my eyes. It had been a hard day, and the mats beneath us were starting to feel terribly comfortable.

4:

The door to my workroom opened.

"I will be with you in a moment," I said cordially, my attention fixed on the fabric between my hands.

A wash of despair and fear and then a hollowness overwhelmed me, trapping my breath in my throat. The abruptness and force had me toppling back, collapsing to the floor as I reeled. I pressed back until I found the wall for whatever support it could give me.

"Who are you?"

I looked up, and Emelia was standing over me. She reached down, her hand touched my cheek, and the emptiness intensified until I felt like nothing but a shell.

"You are not who Katarina claims. You are not who Lord Olso says. What is your name?" she demanded quietly, crouching in front of me. The hollowness was replaced by fear, all consuming. My heart raced and tears welled in my eyes. Then it was gone again, and I was nothing.

"Sade Norwood." I said, my voice that of a mindless husk. I didn't care that my eternal grasp on the Junction accent that I had diligently held onto for nearly a year slipped away.

"No. You are not. You are not a Norwood. Not a balloon scientist's daughter. Not a Dove. So what are you? I saw your memories. They certainly were not mine, and there is no way they were Deara's." Her brutal hold on my emotions lessened somewhat, and I felt a welling of sadness in my gut. Her sadness. She wasn't used to wielding her dominion over emotions as a weapon, I understood in the moment of freedom. Her eyes widened as she realized her slip and with heart-stopping abruptness I was empty again. "You grew up in the College of Aberrants. Who the fuck are you?" she asked slowly, enunciating every word.

"College …" I said, and even with the mind-numbing press of her magic, a hint of my own confusion managed to wedge itself in. Deara's prying had broken something loose, only for it to slip away into Emelia's head.

Her narrowed eyes widened and her hand snapped back from my face, freeing me from the void. I gasped and sputtered at the rapid return of sensation, confusion and fear that were all my own rushing to fill the void left open by the Charmer. Overwhelming in their suddenness.

"You didn't know ..." Emelia said to herself. She looked at her hand and clenched the fingers, pulling the fist back against her stomach as though to hide the offending digits. "Shit." She leaned back, confusion and shame in her eyes as she looked down at me. "You didn't know."

I began sobbing on the floor as my emotions tried to right themselves. The woman was powerful. Without even touching me she had exerted such dominance over my mind that it had sent me to the floor. "The ... College ...?" I said through chattering teeth.

Emelia looked around. "Is Deara here? She can show you ..."

"No ..." I rolled to my hands and knees, panting, my heart still trying to right itself after the assault. "I haven't seen ... seen her for days ..." I looked at the woman, who still held her clenched hand against her stomach. "The Norwoods adopted me. Legally adopted me. Their uncle willingly adopted me. Because I am a Death Sight. Whatever it may have been before, my name *is* Sade Norwood." I groaned. Not knowing what emotions belonged to me anymore, nor which to ascribe to Emelia's power. "They didn't find me in the Dove Cages, I am not a Red Light Girl, it was just coincidence that brought me to them." I looked down at my hands, the fingers trying to dig into the floor for support, strained and arched like spider legs.

She frowned at me. "Are you an Aberrant?"

My head swung. "No. I'm not an Aberrant. It is not possible to be an Aberrant and a Death Sight." There was no reason to correct her assumption about why I could see the dead. Locks were more hated than Death Sights. I grabbed the unadorned dress form in front of me and used it to pull myself back to my feet. "I would think you would have known that, Charmer." I said, not looking at her, but instead draping myself over the dress form for support, my chin resting on its shoulder. "Ugh," I groaned. "I suspected there was something to you, but I didn't expect it to be so powerful."

"I'm sorry," she said, picking herself up off the floor. "I thought ... I don't know ..."

"The College," I prompted her, turning my head against the headless shoulders in front of me to look at the woman. "What did you see in my memory?"

She backed away from me, pulling both her hands tight against her, but we both knew she didn't need physical contact to overwhelm me again if she wanted to. She was afraid of what she had done.

"It's alright," I said, managing to straighten my back and stand with only the power of my legs. "But please. The memory?"

"It is your memory; how do you not know it?"

I rubbed my temple and shook my head. "Deara says I have holes. Bound areas. All she has been able to pry loose was a library. How do you know what you saw was the College?" I didn't wait for an answer, my mind reeling at the implications. Was the College lurking behind it all? I shook my head. "None of this makes sense. My earliest memories are of ..." I stopped, trying to pinpoint my earliest memory. I remembered nothing but being on the streets. I shook my head again, a wave of despair that was all my own sweeping over me.

"You were a child," the woman said quickly, feeling my desperate emotions swelling. "I think. The perspective was that of a child. It was confusing. You were in a classroom. Not a library. There were Aberrants, young Aberrants. I recognized their robes. You were watching a lesson. In the seats with the Aberrants, a desk in front of you. A ... a professor." She narrowed her eyes, studying me. "She looked very much like you, if I am remembering correctly. She was teaching the Aberrants." She frowned. "If you are not an Aberrant, why would you have been at the College?"

I closed my eyes and tried to picture this memory of mine that this woman could so vividly recollect, but there was nothing. I wanted very much for Deara to return, but she was nowhere to be found. "Damn it," I growled. "I don't remember it. I remember my childhood, but I don't remember that. At least, I think I remember my childhood."

"I saw others," she said slowly. "Falling through the sky, an airship, playing dice in an alley. Those were yours also."

I nodded, closing my eyes. I had not expected my memories to bleed to Emelia.

"What will you do with this?" I asked quietly.

She frowned, not certain herself. "Tell me who you are," she said softly.

"Why does it matter who I am?"

"What did you see of my life?"

I shook my head. "I didn't see anything, my lady."

She gave a derisive laugh. "Exactly." She shook her head. "Shit. What am I doing here?" She rubbed her eyes. "I shouldn't have come." And with that she departed.

Mrs. Sandfjord poked her head in. "Was that Lady Rasczek I saw leaving just now?" The concern in her voice was that of a woman who thought she had bet on a losing horse.

"Yes, madam. She was just checking on my progress."

"And?"

"She seemed a little distracted, but otherwise content with the work, madam," I lied, not certain which emotions Emelia had been displaying on her journey out the door. Not certain which now lived on my face.

Mrs. Sandfjord's mouth was fixed in a subtle frown, but she nodded. "Good." Her fingers tapped anxiously on my workroom door before she nodded again. "Good."

5:

I dreaded the woman's fitting, but the time had come. The dress was made, and I needed her to try it on so I could finalize the project and be done with it all. With halting fingers, I lifted the shop's talker from where it hung on the wall and called the Rasczek residence.

Emelia arrived late in the day, looking equally uncertain about our meeting. I met her at the front of the shop, hoping Mrs. Sandfjord did not sense the tension between us as I led her back into my workshop. Emilia was immaculately tended as always, except for a small amount of dirt under her manicured fingernails, which she quickly cleaned away when she saw me looking.

The woman looked around my workspace with apprehensive eyes. "Is she here?"

"No. She hasn't been around in over a week. Is that what you are hoping to gain in this exchange?" I flicked my eyes to the side to look at the woman. She was richly garbed, but in a wool dress much less formal than what I was sewing for her. Her everyday wear was worth more than all the dresses Katarina had sent me to purchase for myself combined.

"No," Emelia said slowly. "If she is gone, she is gone. I cannot see her as you can, and I must accept that. It is a dangerous ability that you have. A person could get addicted to that. I just wondered if she was nearby." She sounded genuine. Her mouth pulled to the side and she looked around the space awkwardly. "Where does she go?" she asked casually. It was a forced attempt at small talk.

"I would rather say that is her business," I said with a slight shrug, then nodded toward the dress.

"It is beautiful," Emelia said with a distracted smile. The smiled crumpled and she looked at me. "The way that I treated you after ... It is not enough, but I must apologize. I was in a strange headspace after what we saw and, well, Katarina and I have never seen eye to eye. I ... I was jumping at shadows, letting my suspicious nature get the better of me."

"It is good to have a healthy suspicion," I muttered, then looked around. Deara hadn't appeared since sharing her memory. I was glad she didn't choose this moment to return.

"Still, what I did ... I've never done anything like that before. I was just so angry. I was angry at Alec, but you were the only one available for my abuses. My only outlet for my rage. And when I realized what I was seeing in your memories, I ... I lost it a little."

"I might have reacted similarly," I admitted softly. "You are taking this all very well, all things considered."

She looked down. "I wouldn't say well." Her eyes raised to mine. "You gave me months to mourn, yet I was in denial in my grief." She frowned. "And before that ... I knew she was gone in some form. I knew I wouldn't be seeing her again." She glanced around uncomfortably, uncertain if she could trust my assurances that the specter did not linger nearby. "It has been over two years since she disappeared. I loved her and I have grieved her."

I nodded my understanding. She gave me a wan smile.

6:

The last week had been spent with shears in hand and fabric under my fingers as I worked diligently to meet Emelia's tight deadline. I stood back while Mrs. Sandfjord assessed my work. I still had much to do, but she seemed content in her scrutiny.

"I was worried when Mistress Norwood could not provide any references of previous employment for you. But you do have the deft hand she touted you for." She nodded to herself. "And on a rushed order, too." She turned to me with approval. "You'll have to get used to that, I suppose. The high ladies tend to forget how long their gowns take to create. They may wear them once, but we spend weeks on them." She shook her head. "The young Lady Raszcek is usually good about that, but she did seem distracted this time." She patted my hand, approval radiating off her. "She was happy with the work at her fitting?"

"Indeed."

Mrs. Sandfjord looked at the dress once more, a little smile on her lips. "I'll leave you to it."

It was late when I finally finished my work for the day. The sun had set and my colleagues had all taken their leave long before. Still, I wasn't alone when I left the dressmaker's shop that evening. I felt acutely aware of the shadow approaching while I locked the door. My hands readied themselves for defense.

I turned, fists up, but dropped them with a heavy breath when I saw it was Emelia.

"I wanted to make it up to you, for being so very unpleasant," Emelia said shyly, not noticing I had been ready to strike only moments before.

"By ambushing me from the shadows?" I asked, my fists loosening.

She drew in a breath and shook her head. Her lips pursed and she stepped fully into the yellow lights. "I didn't think it would be so late when you left," she said, seemingly embarrassed now. "The other tailors all left a while ago."

"I have a high-priority order this week." I turned toward Katarina's estate.

"I suppose that would be mine," Emelia said, her mouth pulling to the side before she sighed and chased after me.

I stopped. "My lady, is your motorcarriage nearby? I don't know that you should be walking alone at night."

"And you should?"

I rolled my eyes. "It is not something I am unaccustomed to."

"I would like ..." She looked uncertain. "I would like to know more about that. If you would allow me. Do you drink? I'll get you a drink. If you want." She was flustered.

I narrowed my eyes at her. "And then there would be two women walking alone at night after having a drink. I think I will escort you home instead. My career as a dressmaker is dependent on you being satisfied at the end of next week."

She frowned with thought. "You'll spend the night, then. We

have many rooms. Or I'll send you in our coach."

I looked around. It was getting dark, even with the constant burn of the yellow lamps. I had spent too many nights on the streets not to know the dangers. Maybe these streets of the higher alts were a touch safer than the ones of my youth, but I wasn't about to get complacent. "Alright." Anything to get this woman moving toward safety.

"And you will have a drink with me at the estate." She said it with renewed authority.

"Fine. If you will lead the way, madam."

"Emelia."

I shook my head. "Do you really want to know about my past so badly? Why?"

Emelia started walking, silent with her thoughts. A small crease between her brows. Her boots clicked along the cobblestones, and I sent a quick look around to ensure that the two of us were alone. A few passersby hurried home across the street, but the area was quiet. Alone, I could make my way mostly unseen, but this woman did not seem to have the same ability. Every step and sway had been trained into her for the very intention of drawing the eye. Even without the fold, she was a charmer. I found myself wondering where her chaperone was as I hurried to catch up with her.

"Could you stop that?" I complained as I slowed to walk just a step behind her.

She glanced back at me. "Stop what?"

"Everything you are doing. Every single movement. Can you stop trying to draw everybody's attention?"

Emelia rolled her eyes and gestured delicately around at the empty streets. "And whose attention, pray tell, do you think I am drawing?" Still, her walking seemed to stiffen and her natural sway suddenly became awkwardly choppy. "Is that better?" she asked, tightly. It seemed she was putting in a genuine effort now and the act was causing her pain.

"That is so much worse. Just go back to how you were."

She pinched her lips and I saw that even in the sour little expression, there was an appeal. The woman couldn't help herself. Still, the awkwardness retreated once again and she relaxed back into a slightly subdued stride.

"Deara trusts you," Emelia said. "That's why I want to know about you. The two of you are not friends simply out of necessity."

"She never would have looked at me if I couldn't *see*. I wouldn't be alive if I couldn't *see*. And I can see in more ways than one. You aren't asking about my past simply because Deara trusts me."

She swallowed, and I could read a little pulse of shame in her expression.

"Fine," I relented, not wanting to face the words from her lips. "What do you want to know?"

"You are from the gangs, right? You were one of the boarders of the Persephone?"

My jaw tensed, and I looked at the road ahead with trepidation. A little cluster of Enforcers and their dogs lazily patrolled the corner ahead.

"I saw the airship before they sunk it," Emelia said quietly. "The one that I saw in your memories was the very same."

I increased the distance between me and the noble. If she called out, I would make it only steps before the dogs got me.

Emelia closed her eyes and shook her head, then laughed. I frowned at the innocence of the laughter. "Of course you are from the gangs," she said, looking at me with a new light. "And of course you were one of the boarders." I couldn't read her, and that made my feet falter. "I knew you were more interesting than you were letting on." She frowned at the space between us, then spotted the Enforcers lazing ahead. "I'm not going to call the Enforcers on you, Sade," she assured me, then offered her hand as if to tow me along behind her.

I eyed the Enforcers once more, then continued walking with the woman.

"I was raised in the street gangs," I said when we had passed the Enforcers and their smiling dogs. "I boarded the Persephone. The only reason Katarina bothered to hide me was because it was Deara I turned to for help when I was being beaten to death during the heist. I could have looked in any direction. Everything was a smear of blood and blurred bodies. But I happened to look at Deara."

"They threw all of your companions overboard," she said remorsefully.

"I am well aware. I was ferreted away in Katarina's footlocker while they all made their final dives."

"I am sorry."

I looked at her. "Why?"

"Those were your friends, weren't they?"

"I am used to the loss," I said tightly, trying not to think of who I had lost that day.

"But you can still see them?"

I looked to our right at a passing group, my eyes lingering on an old man sitting silently against the house at his back. The group passed without noticing him in the slightest. The man was in death as he had been in life.

Half a block ahead another specter stood, unaware of the small cluster of dead that massed around them. This wasn't the first cluster I had seen. The oddity was one that Katarina had told me not to dwell on. The Whispers could not see each other, yet they managed to flock. Or was it that this block was a particular hot spot of death? Perhaps. The thought did not invite me to linger.

I hurried Emelia along past the group.

"I don't exactly look for my former acquaintances, living or dead."

"Why is that?" She slowed a step to bring me even with her.

I looked at her and, in response, slowed to set myself a step behind once again. It would not be appropriate for me to set myself as this high woman's equal. "Because, madam, I was the only survivor of an Enforcer ambush. It tends to look suspicious. It looks very much like I was a rat."

"Were you?"

I gave a dry laugh before catching myself. There had been so much death that day and she so casually asked if I had caused it. "Was I the rat? No."

"Then it was purely circumstance that preserved you. Surely your friends would be able to understand that, were you to explain."

"And what would I tell them? That a rich lady took pity on me? Or honesty? That I see dead people and, because of that, I am now a rich lady's pet protégé?"

Emelia's face pinched, and even the unpleasant expression found its way into being beguiling. "You can't be her pet *and* her protégé."

I snorted. "You would think that, wouldn't you, but Katarina manages."

"You and Katarina do not get along."

"We do and we don't. Depends on her mood, mostly." I shrugged.

"Did you prefer your life before?"

"You wouldn't ask that if you had lived my life before," I said quietly. "I spent nearly every day looking for a way out of it. Knowing that I probably never would claw my way out. It is so difficult. To have nothing. To come from nothing and think that somehow I would find that one person who was willing to take the chance and give me a jumping point to escape the gangs. It is why I started drawing. An escape, I suppose. It is why I threw myself into sewing, even just mending the other kids' clothing. It was a bit of hope. I wasn't exactly cultivating a lucrative life skill jumping off of bridges. So, no. I would not say I preferred that life."

"You could have gone to another float? Started fresh. Bevilla doesn't place the same credence in one's past and family name as we do on Vale."

"Bevilla," I said with a shake of my head. The isle was not exactly the shining gem in the Society's crown. "Trust me. I thought about it. The Persephone was supposed to be my way out. My last dive. Eda and I, we were going to get ours and get out." I closed my eyes a moment, thinking how foolish it had all been. Thinking of my pitiful life savings. We would have blown it all on the travel document fees and airship tickets.

"You had somebody, then?"

"I did. For a time. You avoid getting too close to anybody because, sooner or later, everybody misses a dive. You avoid setting yourself too far apart, because then nobody watches your back, and it's easier to prey on an outsider even within your own gang. And sometimes, no matter how well you manage your proximity, you still become prey ..." I shook my head, realizing that I had slipped into a fog of memories I had done well to push back. Emelia was watching me with assessing eyes. She had dropped back a step once again and I hadn't noticed in time to return to my respectful distance. She hooked my arm in hers so that I could not drop back again. "I understand well why Katarina does not get close to anybody. Why she does her best to enforce a divide." I blinked. "I don't know why I told you that."

"Do you worry about crossing paths with anybody from your past?"

"They wouldn't even recognize me," I said, gesturing at the fine dress. It was simple enough for work, but far beyond the cheap scraps of cotton I would have found myself in on the streets. "They wouldn't expect to see me as I am. They wouldn't expect to see me at all. As far as they know, I missed my dive that day on the Persephone."

Emelia couldn't understand the full meaning of my words, but she nodded. "I am sorry, Sade."

I looked at her suspiciously. "Why am I telling you this? Are you Charming me?"

Her eyes turned apologetic, but there was a hint of amusement on her lips. "No … I don't … I don't typically use my magic unless I have to. I was wrong to before." That hint of a smile bloomed a little. "I suppose you are sharing because you want to."

I tried to ignore that and instead surveyed the streets. "Is it much further?"

"Not much, no."

"Good. Then perhaps we should hurry."

Emelia frowned, but followed my eyes toward one of the shadows lurking between a stand of buildings. The shadow straightened from where he had been leaning against the brick wall and approached. A young man still by many measures, but the streets had aged him into hardened leather with a malicious sneer. Behind him, a small cluster of thugs materialized from where they had been hidden in the alley.

"Step aside, Bots." The man flicked his knife at me, using the slang for those born on the streets. The term had become all-encompassing for anybody born low, regardless of whether that birth happened on the cobbles or in a house. We were all low and we would all remain low. Dressed simply for work as I was, this man would never guess the wealth I had accidentally found tied to my adopted name. "We ain't need anything from you. Just your little miss."

"Don't even think about touching her," I warned, putting myself in front of Emelia.

"Loyal little snipe. Fine." The man brandished his knife at me. "You try to look out for one of your own and this is how they answer. So be it. Nobody gonna look twice at the body of a bots and we will still walk away with your little miss tonight. Last chance, girlie."

"Walk away," I said again, running through a quick inventory of my assets. There weren't many. I stayed between the thugs and Emelia. The woman moved to stand beside me, though I doubted she had any skill in a scrap. I shoved her back and kept an eye on the knives approaching.

The man spat, then lunged. I caught his wrist, twisted, then brought the man's arm down on my lifting knee, feeling bones break. The knife clattered to the cobblestones in conjunction with the man's scream. Two more men jumped to fill the void left by their leader, and I said silent praise for Katarina's foresight in making me train in skirts, brutal as her lessons had been. I kicked one man back with a strong boot to the chest. The heel crunched against his sternum and he fell backward. He scuttled back, gasping while I turned to deal with the third man. He was fast and his knife came close to carving my nose from my face more than once while I dodged and blocked. I kicked with a low chop that landed against the side of his leg, forcing his knee to buckle, then brought my elbow up hard into his chin sending him to the ground in a daze. The two grunts shrunk back in fear.

I swept a knife from the ground and crouched over the leader. "Walk. Away," I growled, knife poised.

He looked at me, the knife, his men, and the damage I had wrought, then nodded. "We're gone."

I straightened, stepping back while the men pulled each other to their feet.

I scanned the area, then tossed the knife to the side.

"Let's get inside, shall we?" I said, ushering Emelia on.

"How ... how do you know how to do that?" Emelia said, letting me goad her onward.

"Katarina."

"How does Katarina know how to do that?"

"And why shouldn't she?"

Emelia grabbed my hand and stepped quickly, drawing me along. She was shaken, but not so much as to lose all bearing.

"You saved my life."

"Well, I don't know that they intended to kill you so much as ..." I trailed off, not wanting to go further down the line of speculation.

She stopped, pulling me into a tight embrace that made my ribs groan before letting out a jet of breath and rushing us along again. She was right; we hadn't been far from her estate. The closer we drew, the busier the streets became. The rich enjoying the night as though there was no work to be done in the morning. Enforcers strolling casually by to keep the ruffians at bay. Emelia didn't slow, but I marveled at her continued grace while I felt like I was a disheveled mess being tugged along behind her.

"Miss Rasczek," the gate guard acknowledged, looking at me curiously.

"Good evening, Mikael."

The gatehouse behind the man would have been large enough to house an entire gang comfortably. I had to check that my jaw had not dropped looking at it.

She slowed once we were inside the walls.

"I think I have had enough excitement for the evening, my lady," I said, looking up at the expansive mansion where it crouched before the black pines of its own private forest. Jutting chimneys, prominent towers, the soaring columns of the entryway, and swaths of carved stone adorning the exterior made for an imposing sight. The Rasczek estate made Norwood manor appear puny in contrast.

"I really do wish you would call me Emelia."

I continued as though she had not spoken. "Maybe next time for the drink, and perhaps if you are going to be out late, consider a motorcarriage next time."

The woman pouted, then gestured toward one of the waiting servants. "Bring the coach round. Have my friend brought to the Norwood residence."

"Yes, my lady." The man bowed low, but I could see the judgmental look when he saw I was just as common as he was.

7:

"You were out late," Katarina greeted me. "Was that the Rasczek's motorcarriage?"

I should have known she would recognize the vehicle.

"It was." There was no point in lying. "The young lady commissioned a dress and came by to check on its progress."

"Which daughter?"

"Emma?" I said with a thoughtful cock of my head.

"Emelia."

I shrugged as though I didn't care one way or the other and unlaced my boots.

Katarina sat beside me. "Have you seen Deara?" There was a sadness in her that she didn't bother hiding behind a bitter attitude or sweet voice.

I frowned, straightening to look at her. "Not recently, no. Has she not been around?" I felt a genuine surge of concern flutter in my chest seeing Katarina like this. Surely her sister could feel if something was wrong. What if Deara had passed on and I had seen the last of her already? What would Katarina do if her sister was well and truly gone?

Katarina shook her head. There wasn't any suspicion in her, just worry. Her hands knotted together in her lap.

I finished removing my boots quickly, feet sliding gratefully into a pair of slippers, then offered her my arm.

"When did you see her last?" I asked as she took my arm. I led her toward her room.

"When she left with you for work, over a week ago."

"I haven't seen her since I took the Rasczek commission. I assumed she was with you."

"She probably saw Emelia coming and made herself scarce for a time." Katarina's mouth pulled as though she were chewing on the very thought. "Dry old Deara could be very sentimental," she said with a nod. "I'm certain she will resurface when your business is concluded with the young Lady Rasczek."

I opened the door to Katarina's room for her. "I will let you know if I see her. Though she will probably come to you first."

Katarina shook her head, looking me up and down. "I am not so certain she will. She seems to favor you these days."

"It's only because I am new and she has known you your whole life. You are still her sister, Kat."

She gave me a little smile that said she wasn't so certain Deara still saw it that way, but patted my arm. "Sleep well. And do try to be home earlier tomorrow. You make me worry when you are out so late."

"I'll try." I gave a slight bow and closed the door with her tucked neatly behind.

8:

I had been so focused on my sewing I didn't notice the specter standing in the room with me.

"Sade."

I jumped and swore. "Deara?" I stood and wrapped my arms around her. "Where have you been? I wasn't certain you would come back."

Deara looked at the door to my workroom, then at me. "Can we go for a walk?"

I glanced at the window, then back to the ghost. "Can you give me ten minutes to wrap up? Then we can walk home."

With a small, distracted smile, Deara nodded and sat on the stool at the edge of the room.

"I tried to get into the College, but they can keep even the dead out. There are not many places with wards strong enough to level across the fold, even if it is just the transitional layers. The cores. The College. The Isle of the Gods. It took a lot of searching to find out anything useful," Deara said as she waited.

"Anything useful?"

She leaned forward, balancing precariously on the stool with her elbows on her knees. She had done away with her usual skirts in favor of a pair of high-waisted trousers and shirt that looked very familiar.

She saw me looking with curiosity and rather than answering my question, said, "I thought I would try something new. See what all the fuss was about." She picked at the trousers.

"How ..." I shook my head, turning my attention back to my work.

"Understanding would take an entire lifetime, and then some," Deara said with a chuckle. "Focus on your work. What I have to tell you is important."

I glanced up at her then nodded. "It is good to see you, Deara."

"It is good to see you too, Sade."

When the work was done, I grabbed my coat and gestured toward the door. Deara didn't bother waiting for me to open the door for her and instead stepped through it.

I met the specter on the street and we started walking. I had gotten used to taking the less-trafficked routes home. Better for talking to the unseen.

"You are an anomaly, you know that?" Deara said, following me down the streets. "A real enigma. But I cracked the code. Once again, I was limiting myself by my own lack of imagination. Which, when it comes to you, is a mistake."

I cast the specter a quick questioning look, wondering what she was on about. Then I bobbed my head to the gentleman passing on the street. Deara walked through the man without any regard, passing unnoticed. It still upset my stomach watching her do that.

"It was limiting me in realizing that you are something that has never been before. At least, something that has never been documented."

I turned into a shady park where we were momentarily alone and finally said in hushed tones, "What are you getting at? Why were you trying to get into the College?"

"Because I saw more of your memories."

"You and Emelia both."

Deara looked intrigued. "What did she see?"

"The College. A classroom. A lesson, it seemed."

"She told you that? Interesting …" Deara thought about that for a moment. "I saw something different, but that's promising. Maybe the barrier on your memories is breaking down."

"Breaking down for others. I haven't seen anything but that one glimpse you showed me."

"You have told me repeatedly how little interest you have in knowing. Maybe you are getting in your own way with that attitude, Sade. We step on our own toes more often than we like to admit." She gave me a coy look. "Maybe this will get you to want to look deeper," she said thoughtfully, as though to herself. "I watch you while you study glyphs, you know."

I flicked my eyes toward her in acknowledgment as a motorcarriage passed on the street in front of us.

"Have you ever noticed anything happen while you are really focusing on one? Or, better yet, when you are getting tired?" Deara said.

"Like what?" I asked, confused.

"Like a candle flickering to life while you draw *Fear*? The glyph for ignite," she said, giving me a pointed look. I remembered the night she was talking about. I hadn't noticed the candle. I had assumed I lit it prior to starting my studies and had just forgotten as I grew more and more tired. "You are an Aberrant," Deara said.

"No. I'm a Lock." I was forced to seal my lips again as we stepped out of the park to cross a boulevard.

She shook her head emphatically. "No. Well, yes. But not because you were born with that magic. No. Your mother somehow gave it to you. You, my dear, are an Aberrant. A Natural, if I'm not mistaken. It is in your memories, Sade. Buried. Warped with time, perhaps." We stepped off the main boulevard once again and finally my lips were free to move.

"What do you mean, 'gave it to me'? Aberrant?" I sputtered in my confusion. "It's not possible."

She took my hand, drawing me into an alley for a moment away from eyes.

"Transferring one's connection to fold, their ability ... It's theoretical only, but ..." Deara gestured at me. "Clearly it is possible. You are evidence of that. I just don't entirely understand how you did it. It would take an immense amount of power, and a very impressively designed set of glyphs."

My mind flashed to what Emelia said she had seen in my memories. Being at the College as a child did not mean I was an Aberrant. Then the Persephone played in my mind. The Aberrant carving his glyph into the air, only to have it backfire. The pull and release I had felt.

"I'm not an Aberrant," I said quietly, my denial squeezing my voice to barely a whisper.

"Look," Deara said gently, lifting my hand. I felt her magic rise in me.

Her words guided the memory that played in my eyes. *A woman with her greasy black hair pulled back tight, her clothes dingy with grime, young still, a perpetually devious look in her eyes. I had grown accustomed to seeing her face in my mirror. We were somewhere I didn't recognize. A dark tunnel. Glyph-lined. The underworking, maybe? She wiped her grimy hands on her trousers and glanced around before tracing a symbol into the air in front of my eyes.*

I felt the memory as though it were my reality standing in the overly bright streets of Vale. The draining in my chest a shadow from the past as the glyph bled from my mind and flared into being between us. My mother's hands found mine, and a moment later we were in the quiet darkness of a small house. Modest but well kept.

"What is this?" I asked quietly, my mouth struggling to work under the flood of the memory Deara dredged up.

"Your mother. When I showed you my life, I got pieces of yours in exchange," Deara murmured, though nobody else could hear her. "I didn't understand what I was seeing, but," she shook her head as the memory continued.

My mother moved unsteadily around the house, and I saw now that she was bleeding. A gunshot through her hip merely seemed to slow her down. Under the scraps of her now tattered clothes, the glyph burns on her back and legs were in full view as she rummaged hurriedly. She slowed and tumbled to her knees, her hands failing to support her against the counter.

I hurried to her side and crouched. She was silent as she looked up at me, then pressed her hand to my cheek and held my gaze tight to hers. She spoke the intent with only her hands, and I understood. With a few deft flicks she sketched a glyph in the air, my eyes following the complex tangle of lines and dots as though the symbol were my creation, not hers. Her free hand took mine as the drain started and I felt my magic reserves swell, a deep, heady thing as moment by moment the glyph stole from me and my mother replaced.

"Amplifiers," Deara said, her voice distant, taking me out of the memory with intention while the glyph struggled into existence. "Somehow, she figured out how to amplify your magic. I don't know if it was through the glyph because she does use the amplifiers in its construction, but it feels more like a pairing than simply glyphwork. Her own natural magic, maybe? If she was a Lock, then maybe she was gifted the ability of an Amp or a Channeler." She was quiet as the memory caused a tightening in my chest. "Do you feel it?"

I couldn't speak, and only let out a small groan. I was glad for our seclusion on the side street. I knew what the glyph was doing. I knew what my mother was doing. I knew what was playing before my eyes and ripping through the heart in my chest. I knew it then, too. I knew I would be killing a dying woman. My mother.

Deara took her hand away, the memory swirling away like mist.

"Are you alright?" Deara asked, worried.

I pulled in a tight breath. "Yes. She ... I ... I took her magic."

"She gave it to you."

"It killed her."

"She was already dying." Her hand extended toward me, palm open again. "May I?"

I took another steadying breath, and confirmed our continued seclusion with a flick of my eyes to the left and right, then lightly set my fingers on hers.

My mother stood before me, and she lay at my feet. She smiled down at me, her ghostly hand touching my cheek, then she was gone.

"A quick burn ..." I said, etching her face into my memory. The final sight as she departed this world.

"Not entirely. It took me a while to understand what I was seeing. She released herself. By giving to you." Deara sounded wistful, and I yanked my hand away, afraid the specter would do something irreversible.

"Don't worry. I'm not quite ready to go yet. It doesn't make sense. It doesn't feel whole. Do you understand? I think I'm missing something, and I need to sort it out still. She passed something to you. Once you had her ability as a Lock, I think maybe she made you a Death Sight. The glyph could only do so much, even with how impressive a feat it was. She was intimidatingly well versed in glyphs for a woman who could not use them herself." She had a hint of longing in her admiration. "But glyphs like that have been attempted before. They always fail, to the detriment of the Aberrant and the unwilling test subject. She was willing, though, and you are a Natural."

"What does that even mean?"

A pinch of thought formed between her brows. "Think of rain. Think of rain and watch my fingers." She took an Aberrant's casting stance and started drawing a symbol in the air in front of me. Even with my doubt, I found my eyes following her hand, the glyph etching in my mind with the thought of rain. The symbol fixed, then released with my breath, and was lost from my mind.

Deara dropped her hand with an expectant look.

I looked at her. "What were you hoping would happen?"

The specter waited, looking up.

"I had wondered how those flames came into existence while you were studying glyphs," the specter said, eyes on the sky, waiting. "You were drifting off while reading, then, poof, a set of candles on the table flickered into flame. I was certain you had gotten Marco to play some trick on me. It was you."

As she spoke, raindrops started falling around us. She looked at me excitedly. I hurried to cover under the thin awning of a shop, no interest in the acid that sometimes found itself in rain.

"I told you so," she said. "That is not an easy glyph to manifest, either. At least, that's what I read. And you didn't even have to draw the symbol."

"Well, you drew it," I said quietly, looking out at the falling rain from the paltry cover of the storefront.

"Come on," she said with an eye roll. "That's not how glyphs work, and you know it. Aberrants need the gesture. The intent. They can't just read a glyph. They can't watch somebody draw it. The magic channels in the action. Unless they are Naturals. And Naturals are very rare indeed. Very. Very. Rare." She looked up at the falling rain, a moment of excitement leading to her full manifestation, the cold drops rolling down her face and wetting her shoulders. She allowed the fold to take her again, not wanting any passerby to see the distortion of the falling drops. "It is clean. It should be, anyway. The three dots on the lefthand side purified."

"It should be ..." I drawled, not ready to risk my skin on *it should be*. Well-dressed and a hint respectable-looking, I hadn't been chased from the doorway yet, but I suspected that would only last so long if I was seen talking to myself. "Fine." I stepped out into the rain, knowing I needed to keep moving, to stay ahead of this conversation as it drifted out further and further over the abyss.

Deara walked beside me, beaming. "A Natural. Ha. A Natural in the guise of a Death Sight. Your mother was a clever one. She hid you. Maybe it led to you having a difficult life on the streets, but it kept you from being warped into a tool of the Society."

My jaw clenched, partly against the cold drops and partly against the thought of my mother's decisions for me. It had been a risk. Any number of dives could have ended in disaster. Any number of fights could have gone in the fatal favor of my rival. Any number of harms could have befallen me.

"Why ... why would she hide me?"

Deara shook her head. "I cannot say. I do know that the College leashes their Aberrants with bindings. Turns them into better tools to be manipulated by the Society or the gods. Maybe she wanted to protect you from that? I only glimpsed your memories, and the abilities of a Past Sight are something she never collected, or never shared with you. Or that I never saw in your mind. I ..." she sighed. "I'm sorry I don't have a better answer for you, Sade. You really have not remembered anything more?"

"No," I whispered, head ducked to hide my moving lips, though the rain had driven all other pedestrians indoors in a hurry. "Only what you have shown me ..." Deara's infectious curiosity was starting to get the better of me, and I found myself actually wanting to find some glimpse of my past.

"That potentially makes sense. The glyph your mother had you use was distorting," she explained. "Within itself, it makes itself unmemorable. It's an embedded protection to prevent Aberrant prodding. What we saw seems crisp, clear, but it was distorted. The problem with distortion is that it can be difficult to control. It's likely that everything from before your mother and you brought that glyph into existence was caught up in it. You told me you don't have many memories from before the gangs. That all you could dredge up was darkness, a body, the streets alone. Maybe it was a protection of its own. With the knowledge your mother seemed to have of glyphs, I wouldn't be surprised if the amnesia, all of this," she said with a general gesture at my face, "was intentional."

"How do you know so much about this?"

"A dead Aberrant on the drift can be a wealth of uninhibited knowledge." She smiled. "And I just so happen to know where one is now."

A motorcarriage rumbled past and I took several side steps away from the roadway to avoid the oily splash.

"Why does any of this matter, Deara?" I asked the woman, flicking my eyes toward her.

"You are an Aberrant. An unleashed Natural. You could have so much more than my sister can give you."

I stopped and looked at the specter. "I don't want anything, Deara."

"Sade? Is that you, Sade?" Emelia's voice drew both Deara's and my eyes. The woman peered out at me from the stopped motorcarriage. "What are you doing out there? Let me give you a ride."

Deara looked toward the carriage, then at me. "You are one of a kind. You may not want anything, but you should be ready for anything." Deara smiled and nodded toward the motorcarriage. "Take the ride." She spread her arms and looked up again, the rain once again dripping onto her skin. "I'll see you."

"Your sister needs you."

Deara acknowledged with a soft mumble, her face still to the rain.

"Don't get sick," I said with a little smile, and walked toward Emelia's offered transport with Deara's laugh following me.

"You are soaked," Emelia chided, sliding over to admit me into the seat beside her, welcoming me with a thick blanket. "Absolutely soaked." In the mirror I could see her driver's silent disapproval as he brought the motorcarriage back to life. The woman sat close, regardless of the impropriety and my wet hem brushing against hers. "And chilled to the bone." Her arms wrapped warmly around my shoulders and rubbed.

"You will ruin your dress, madam," I commented.

She smiled. "Then I will have an excuse to get another. Where were you off to?"

"I was just enjoying the day."

"This rain was rather sudden, wasn't it?" She gestured to the driver. "Home then? And maybe you will invite me in for tea?"

"I don't know that Katarina will like that," I smiled, "but would you like to come in for some tea?"

Why was I inviting this woman in? Why did I feel light when she favored me with another brilliant smile? This venture was dangerous and foolish. Noble as the Norwoods were, they didn't hold a candle to the Rasczeks. And I was only a Norwood on paper.

Still, I couldn't deny that Emilia intrigued me. The little flecks of dirt at the edges of her nails, the only deviance from her otherwise immaculate appearance, intrigued me. The budding calluses I saw on her fingers now, and her sun-darkened skin, intrigued me. This was a woman who was walking in two worlds. I just couldn't tell which two they were.

She must have seen me looking at the tiny fleck of dirt, because she wiped it away a moment later with a hint of a blush, as though I would pass high judgment against her for a little grime on her fingers.

"I was at work," Emelia said with an embarrassed laugh.

"Work?"

"Well, it's not work in the traditional sense. I don't get paid for it. I just ..." Her sudden awkwardness with a hint of defensiveness on the topic had me confused.

"I didn't peg you for somebody who works," I said. "I'm sorry if you didn't want me to ask about it. I was just surprised."

"Oh. I didn't mean to get defensive about it. I suppose I am used to my friends giving me strange looks at the way I choose to occupy my time."

"And how do you choose to occupy your time?"

She smiled, but looked ahead, out the rain-covered windshield of the Rasczek's coach.

The motorcarriage pulled up to the Norwood estate.

The butler met us with an umbrella, which was far too late for me, but sheltered Emelia as we climbed to the door.

I was glad when we made it to my room without running into Katarina.

"Tea?" I said to the butler, and he gave me a small bow before setting to the task.

I turned to Emelia. "I'll just be a moment," I said, then ducked away to remove my soaking dress.

I could hear Emelia flipping through the books on my table while I stripped off my wet dress and replaced it with my dressing gown.

"You are quite well studied," Emelia said.

"You are assuming I read all those," I commented lightly, letting down my hair and toweling it dry.

"Did you?"

I chuckled. "Yes. Deara can be quite insistent." I stood beside her, looking down at the pages while I continued to dry my hair, conscious of the small drops of water that could go rogue and damage the delicate paper. Texts on glyphs lay interspersed with tailoring guides, sketch references, and the occasional sordid romance—Deara's guilty pleasure when it came her turn to pick the novel we read together. I hoped Emelia would not take note of those particular titles as she looked through my small collection. "I do actually enjoy it, though."

"Did you read this?" Emelia asked, lovingly thumbing through my botany reference book.

I nodded, intrigued by the excitement I saw flashing in her eyes.

"Maybe I don't need to be embarrassed by my interests, then," she said, rueful.

"You should never be embarrassed by your interests. Unless they are very strange, indeed," I added with a joking wink.

She laughed, then lifted the book from the desk. "No stranger than the fact a dressmaker studies glyphs," she said with a pointed look at me and a little grin before looking back down at the pages.

"Well, I do make more than dresses. Fine suits, shirts, skirts, and such."

She laughed. "Oh yes, how careless of me." She beamed and we made way as the butler came in, setting down a tray with tea and a small arrangement of biscuits before retreating once again. The tea went untouched.

"Naila Green is an expert in the field," Emelia said as she flipped through the pages of the book cradled on her arm. "Her work with crop hardiness and production has led us to being able to support a larger population than ever before. Have you ever visited her Conservatory?"

"I can't say that I have," I said.

"I'll have to take you sometime. It is not so far outside of town. I am there nearly every day I have time. I can't believe you've never gone." Her face fell for a moment, and she looked up from the pages as she remembered where I came from. "Right ... I suppose that truly was thoughtless of me."

I shook my head. "No. It's alright," I said, coming to stand beside her. "You really love this, don't you?"

She glowed. "Botany is a passion of mine. My mother thinks it is a foolish pursuit, but I've been working with Naila for nearly half my life now. Her knowledge is insurmountable, having spent her entire life devoted to the study." She sighed wistfully.

"From what I have heard, you are on track for a political career," I commented.

"That is the case," Emelia said a little flatly.

"If this is your passion, then why do you pursue politics?"

Her expression took on a confused tilt, as though trying to reason through that very question herself. "Because it is what is expected of me, perhaps. My father is a Society Chair and my mother was a representative until just recently, when my sister took up the mantle." She shrugged, fingers resting on the meticulously painted image of a genetic manipulation study. "We already have one black sheep in the family, with my brother running off to become a doctor."

I couldn't help but laugh. "That's all it takes to become a black sheep in your family? I can't imagine what your parents would think of me."

Her eyes drifted from the page to me with a thoughtful look before she leaned over and kissed me lightly. "I don't really care what they think, I suppose. At least, in that regard." Her eyes returned to the pages while I felt an unbidden flutter of excitement in my stomach. "So much of Naila's work is sidelined by the Society. Without a strong voice within the political system, we have gone without the significant and essential funding that the industrialists have. She has scientists and field botanists, people who have actually attended the academy for the study," she said with a hint of regret in her voice. "They assist in her studies. What she is lacking is a politician in her corner. Sooner or later the Society will have to realize that we *cannot* survive without crops, and that the glyph cores can only do so much for us if we continue industrializing without regard for the natural world. At some point, even the gifts of the gods won't be able to sustain us." She was getting heated just thinking about it and took a steadying breath.

"That is where you find your purpose in politics, then?"

She closed the book and turned to face me. "That, and other things," she said slowly. I had heard about Emelia's calls for social reform. The dangerous positions she put herself in with the industrialists and the idle wealthy. Still, the woman was a product of her upbringing and played within those bounds. "You are not what I expected," Emelia admitted.

"I can't imagine what you expected from your seamstress?"

"I don't know, just not ..." Her eyes drifted to the books and my notebook. "It is not a comment on your upbringing. Most of my friends have no interest in doing more than taking over the family business or squandering the family money. You ..." Her hand touched mine. "I feel like I can actually have a conversation with you and genuinely say I am interested in what we discuss." Emelia turned me to face her, a small hungry look forming in her eyes. "I am glad I came across you before you spent too long out in the rain."

I smiled and backed away, aware of the distance closing between me and the bed. There was no denying what was happening here, and no reason to stop it this one time. "Are you sure you don't want some tea first?"

"Hmm," she hummed instead of answered, in pursuit. She reached out, catching my hand and pulling me to her. "I prefer after," she murmured against my lips.

"Sade," Katarina pushed into my room without knocking. "Have you seen Deara? She came home finally, only to disappear again. The witch has barely given me the time of day recent—" Her voice cut off instantly when she saw Emelia hurrying to sit on the chaise. A small panic played in Katarina's eyes.

"I dare say she knows you are a Death Sight," I said, pulling my dressing robe tight around my body and moving to the mirror to brush out my hair. Letting the fire that had formed in my gut abate. Emelia, for her part, was the very vision of composure.

"She knows …" Katarina echoed in a small, choked voice, then her panic abated to be replaced by rage. She slammed the door closed behind her. "Between you and Deara, I swear to the gods, you two are determined to get us dragged through the streets and burned." She closed the distance to me in long strides. "I don't care how close you think you are with young *Lady Rasczek*," she said with a bitter glare at Emelia. "How many times have I told you, you cannot trust anybody?"

Emelia stood. "Katarina. I am not going to tell anybody you are a Death Sight," she said soothingly, but Katarina was not about to be appeased by this woman's reassurances.

"Is that what you told Deara before you got her killed, too?" Katarina snapped, rounding on the woman. Emelia stepped back as though struck.

I grabbed Katarina's arm before she could do anything too drastic. "Katarina. That was not Emelia's fault."

"Emelia?" Katarina said, allowing herself to be turned back toward me. She laughed bitterly. "You two are fucking, aren't you?" she said with anger-fueled realization. "Stupid, Sade. And I thought you had so much promise."

The venom melted from her features, and she softened. A confused expression came to her face, until she looked down and saw Emelia's hand on hers. Katarina yanked her hand away, but the heat was gone from her. "You're a fucking Charmer. Of course you are." She rolled her eyes. "I suppose I should be appreciative of your exchange, but you know how the masses treat those of us who see their dearly departed. It is hardly mutually assured destruction revealing you as a Charmer. If I could even prove it."

"Maybe you wouldn't be able to. Maybe I wouldn't be dragged through the streets. At least, not right away. But you know the power of a rumor, and you know how the other families will lash out if they can blame our success on our magic. My destruction will not be as swift as yours in this exchange, but it will be as certain."

Katarina stuck her nose up, drawing in a long inhale. She turned from Emelia back to me and shook her head with disappointment. "Don't be a fool, Sade. You cannot trust Charmers. You never know if your emotions are your own or *hers*." She turned on her heels and left.

Emelia sat heavily on the chaise, watching the door close behind Katarina's retreat. "She is right, you know. You cannot trust a Charmer. Sometimes I don't even realize I am doing it."

"You have more control than you think," I said, turning back to the mirror to continue brushing my hair. "Not all of your charm comes from your magic."

She chuckled contentedly. "I appreciate you saying as much, even if it's not true." She stood behind me, her fingers gently gliding over my shoulder to my hand to take the brush and set it aside. "Sade, will you tell me what is wrong? You have had this look in your eye, and, well, I can feel your uncertainty in the air like a thousand needles. Is it me? Is it this?"

I frowned at her reflection. "It is not you. Though, if I am honest, you make me confused. But it is not you." I sighed. "I'm sorry."

"No," she smiled, turning me to face her. "I don't want an apology for it. I just want to help, if I can."

"I don't know that you can. But, thank you. I just have some things I need to think on."

"I won't press. Just know I'm here."

"Do you think maybe you are too good of a person, Emelia?" I asked lightly.

"It's darling that you think that, but don't get me wrong: I *am* burning with curiosity." She took my hands and kissed my cheek, then retreated a step to give me space.

I closed the distance, bringing my lips back to hers, intent on finishing what Katarina had interrupted. Movement out of the corner of my eye drew my attention, only to find the Widow Reese making her circuit of my room.

"Gods, I really should change rooms," I grumbled.

"What is it?" Emelia asked, glancing where I looked, but intent on me once again, mouth on my neck.

"We have a visitor. An old woman."

"Ah." Emelia straightened, suddenly uncomfortable and uninterested. "Perhaps it's a sign we really should just start with the tea."

9:

"I have a delivery for Lady Emelia Rasczek," I said, holding the dress bag as though in offering for the butler to evidence my claim.

"Yes, very good. This way, ma'am."

I looked back, signaling for the driver to take his leave. I hoped I would not see Emelia, and I hoped I would. What had started the day I had made it rain would not burn down until it had found its resolution, I was certain, but I was growing less sure that pursuit was such an innocent idea. Listening to the prattle of the other dressmakers at Mrs. Sandfjord's made me worry what the wrong gossip may do to Emelia. As Deara had pointed out, hating Norwoods was in fashion.

Not to mention, I had seen precious little of Deara in the last few days, and I was a little worried that the specter did not approve of my activities with her love. It would certainly be easier if I did not see the noblewoman.

"My Lady," the butler announced me, and I knew I would have no such luck.

"Ah, Miss Norwood. I was starting to worry I had asked too much of your skill," Emelia said, standing from where she had been writing at her desk with a welcoming smile.

The butler departed and I felt suddenly very awkward alone with the Charmer.

"Shall I try it on?"

"If you wish, my lady."

"Are we back to 'my lady' now?" Emelia laughed. "I thought maybe we were beyond that. Especially since you are nobility yourself."

I shook my head, unbagging the dress carefully. "A much lesser form of it, and one with much more humble beginnings."

"Still, can't we do away with all the 'my lady's, please? For my sanity. Simply being born should not grant me that respect." She stripped away her dress without bothering with her privacy screen.

"You don't hear many nobles say that." I held her new gown for her to step into and helped her dress.

"It's an easy thing to say from our vantage, isn't it?" she said with a sigh as I worked the laces. "Still, I don't feel it is right." She looked back at me, biting her lip. "A family with my status is likely to get me a Society Chair. A life of politics doesn't seem very exciting, does it?"

"Do you enjoy it, though?"

"The politics?" She frowned, then looked embarrassed. "Yes," she admitted slowly.

"Then it is right for you."

She grimaced. "I didn't earn it. Nepotism should not be the basis of our political system."

"Work with what you have," I said with a shrug. "You will only effect change from the inside. If you want the Society to take notice of Doctor Green's work, on the impact of industrialization, you have to be able to steer its eyes."

Emelia's eyes narrowed and she smiled. "An interesting, and valid, point from a woman who grew up on the streets. Wherever did you come from?"

"You've seen more of my childhood than I have, potentially," I pointed out, then nodded toward the mirror.

"You haven't been able to remember any more?" She stepped away from me to look at the mirror. I watched her walk, checking the hem and drape, but admittedly enjoying the sight of the woman in the gown I had made for her.

She looked back at me, and I realized I hadn't answered her, utterly distracted by the cut and fall and accentuations of the gown. I shrugged. "Some. It doesn't matter much."

"I don't believe you for a second," she said with narrowed eyes before turning to the mirror. "You do amazing work, Sade." She turned to me. "What do you think?"

I met her eyes. "I am certain you already know what I think."

She grinned. "You are that proud of your own work?" She turned back to the mirror, her hands running over the fabric with an appreciative stroke. "Are you content?"

"I'm content."

She smiled at me through the mirror's reflection. "Help me out?"

She stepped out of the dress, and I swept its length up and away to hang it. I turned my full attention to her dress, setting the fabric to hang to avoid any wrinkles or a poor drape when the day to wear it came. While I fiddled, she watched, settling only a dressing gown back over her shoulders behind me.

"It is a beautiful dress," Emelia said quietly, closer behind me than I had thought. "The silhouette cuts quite the figure." Her hand settled on my shoulder. "I still owe you a drink. The tea didn't quite hit the spot." Her voice was light, but her tone had dropped low. There was uncertainty and hunger in her pitch as she pulled lightly on my shoulder to turn me. "Leave the dress, Sade."

I looked back at her. "I don't know. I thought the tea was pretty good." I let her turn me to face her.

There was a headiness in her hooded eyes as she took in a deep breath, focused entirely on me. I felt a little pull in my gut at her stare alone. She hesitated only a moment more before leaning forward to press her mouth to mine. I was a statue of uncertainty for only a moment before the stone of me melted against her heat, her longing desire. It was like a dive. One moment, all the security of ground under your feet, and the next, nothing but open air cradling you. The winds pulling and whipping. No idea if it would be the clouds of a fall welcoming you or the solidity of success when you landed.

The two of us met, clashed, vying for control, mouths and hands asserting themselves, softening, pressing and pulling in a war between tenderness and need. I felt a wall, the floor, the wardrobe, and finally the bed behind me as we tumbled from surface to surface in our dive. Emelia nipped and moaned and kissed. I caressed and sighed and found myself utterly at a loss.

10:

It was dark when I opened my eyes. The yellow lights of the city filtered vaguely through the drawn curtains of Emelia's room. Emelia was tight in my embrace, her hands holding my arms to her, her ankle tucked neatly between my legs, completely immersing herself in me. Keeping me locked to her with no chance of slipping away without waking her. Unable to leave, I allowed myself to relax against her, to take in the fresh scent of her hair and savor the way her body managed to conform perfectly to mine. For a moment, a woman could forget the disparity between us and foolishness of what we had just done. For only a moment.

Beside the window, a silhouette that cast no shadow stood. Deara. She crossed to me, touching my shoulder for only a moment before withdrawing her hand, not wanting to wake Emelia.

"You are a good person, Sade. Better than I think you realize. Emelia is a good person. Better than she realizes, as well." It was her way of blessing the events that had transpired that evening. "Look after each other." She spoke as though this hadn't just been a single lust-driven evening. Deara looked up, over my shoulder, and a thousand miles away. "I have something I need to talk to you about when you return to the estate." Her eyes drifted back to me, a little smile on her lips. "Take your time. Enjoy your morning." She leaned down and kissed my forehead, then carefully touched Emelia's cheek for just a moment before backing away and fading.

The touch had been light, but it stirred Emelia enough for me to tighten my arms around her. To turn her head and bring her sleepy lips to mine. To make me forget for a while longer the finality I had seen in Deara's eyes.

11:

When the morning came, Emelia released me from her restraining hold, but I found myself lingering for a moment, two. Then I shook myself clear of the foolish haze holding me in place and made to dress.

She watched me with a curious look on her face but said nothing.

Fully clothed once again, I checked myself in the mirror, then gave her a low bow. "I hope your dress satisfies."

She laughed. "It will do more than satisfy, Sade. Come here."

"I think I should go, my lady," I said instead with another bow.

She rolled from the bed and crossed the room with a litheness that surprised me. She held my chin in her hands, eyes burning intensely into mine. "This is not the last we will see of each other, Sade."

"It probably should be," I said quietly and with effort. The woman had a way about her that made me want to agree.

"There is no reason it needs to be."

"When you need another dress, you know where to find me."

"That's not what I mean."

I was overtly aware of her bare hips, her nudity, her intensity, and a drive to stay with her. I wanted to kiss her, but I knew if I did that would be the end of my resolve. Instead, I stepped back, bowed once again, and took my leave.

Without bothering to cover up, Emelia peeked out the door and called after me. "I still owe you a drink."

I smiled, and was glad the hall was empty. The house was grand, grander than Katarina's. The wealth older and more refined. There were none of the verging on desperate attempts to display wealth I had seen in some of the industrialist's homes. Just an inherent knowledge of the wealth possessed, and it was immense. I turned a corner and nearly collided with several maids setting about their days. They tactfully pretended not to see me pass. They had apparently been briefed by the night shift on their mistress's evening guest. A woman waited for me at the end of the corridor. With a discrete nod she directed me out of the main halls and to the servants' way. She fell in beside me, directing me with quiet nods.

She escorted me all the way to the servants' gate at the estate wall, casting small smiles and acknowledgements to the delivery carriers and workers passing through before turning to me.

"You will be discreet, I am certain." There was no question in her words, just an affirmation.

"Of course," I said with a nod. I realized that it didn't matter to these people if in fact I was now a noblewoman; I would never be as noble as their master and mistresses.

She gave a nod of her own, an eyebrow raising slightly as her lips pursed. "Don't let me hear otherwise." She turned and returned to work.

I was not worried about what the woman would do if I was indiscreet. I was more concerned what Katarina would do when I returned home.

When I got home, though, Katarina was either still drunk, or nursing a bad hangover.

She was sprawled with a leg tossed over the arm of the chair she lounged in. A teacup rested precariously in her hand. For a moment, I wasn't certain if the woman had dozed off. The nervous maid standing in the corner, ready to lunge to rescue a falling teacup, seemed to think that, if the woman wasn't asleep now, she would be soon. Katarina's head canted slightly so she could see me.

"That's yesterday's dress," Katarina tutted, then cast me a playful smile. Her voice was strained even in its light-heartedness.

"Get cleaned up. I wanted to go out today. If you aren't too tired ..." She winked.

I smiled. "I'll be quick."

"Take your time. By the way, Deara has been floating around. Being dreadful as always." She returned her attention to her tea. Or her nap; I couldn't be certain which.

Deara materialized beside me as I ascended the steps to my room.

"She's just glad you seem to be following in her footsteps," Deara drawled.

"I'm sorry, Deara," I said quietly, aware of how acute Katarina's hearing could be when potential gossip was involved.

Deara smiled and followed me into my room. "I meant what I said last night. Don't be sorry. My time has passed."

"It doesn't have to, though. I could give you a lock of my hair. It works for Katarina's channeling. It could work for you."

Deara swallowed, a hint of longing in the action, then she shook her head. "No. When I say my time has passed, I think it well and truly has."

I didn't like the meaningful way she said that.

"Deara?" My hand stopped on the dress I had been considering for the day, and I turned to face the specter.

"I don't have anything more to show you in your memories, Sade. The barrier is broken. You just have to be willing to look beyond it now. I think you were why I remained." Her hand trailed over the books arrayed on my desk. She raised her eyes to me. They were hollower than usual. Maybe she *was* reaching the end of her time. Maybe she could tell. "You need to be willing to look."

I shook my head. The woman seemed to be fading. "I don't ..." My hands fell from the dress, all attention on Deara. "Deara ... What are you getting at?"

She sat at the window, looking out as she always did. "Your mother made you a Lock. She made you a Death Sight," she said as though that were an answer. And maybe it was. One I didn't want to hear. "I have a last gift for you, as well." I shook my head and she pressed on. "You take a part of the dead. It becomes part of you. My ability to read memories of others, for example. I could pass it to you. You could take it from me."

My head swung more vigorously. "No."

"You don't understand, Sade. I want to pass it to you."

"What will that do to you?"

"I don't know." For all her uncertainty, the specter sounded hopeful. "I don't know," she repeated and smiled. "Maybe I'll move on from here. Maybe I'll end. I don't know what follows. I am ready for it."

"No, Deara. I will not be the vehicle for this."

"You need to be. I feel such certainty in this. I need this, Sade."

"Does Katarina know?"

Deara's pleading instantly flattened. "No. No, Sade. Never tell her. If Katarina can take this from you, she will."

I swallowed, knowing that was exactly what Katarina would do. The woman had a need to collect, to own.

"What if you regret this decision?" I asked feebly.

Deara grew rueful. "If I'm lucky, I won't be able to regret it." She stood, crossing to stand before me. "Sade. I want this. I want you to have my abilities. I want what comes next." She gripped my hands in hers. "What am I supposed to do here? Keep reading over your shoulder for the rest of your life? No." She shook her head adamantly. "No. It is time. Sade. Please. I'm having a hard time keeping myself together. Retaining who I was. Not hunting for vengeance. Not being consumed by my own murder." She looked at her hands, then at me with despair. I had seen her slips. So many slips. Recently more. "And ... Sade. I love you, but you make me long for life. Being able to touch you—being able to touch life—it makes me *hunger*."

Reluctantly, I nodded, then wrapped my arms around the specter. "What am I supposed to tell your sister?"

"Just tell her you saw me disappear. That there was something resolute about it. We have seen it before. She'll understand. She cannot know that this was my decision. It is best she believe I moved on like the rest, without the pomp and farewells. It is safer this way." She returned my embrace with a content hum. "I've missed this, Sade. I don't know if I would be able to continue, knowing all I am missing in even just the simplest of touches." She dropped her hands back to mine and I felt a pressing on my mind, a second awareness. Deara's memories. Her abilities. Her life.

I gasped at the onrushing, taking it all in, accepting Deara into myself and feeling her fade. Images flashed and a swell of energy rocked me back, but Deara's hands were tight on mine as mine were tight on hers. The transfer came to me naturally, my core knowing how to accept and accommodate all that Deara passed to me. I felt Deara fade, saw her memories flash past, saw her lose substance before me.

"You look best in green," she said with a smile, then she was gone.

The swirl of energy faded, leaving me on my knees, panting.

I looked up. Deara was gone, nothing left in her place except the memories she had passed to me. All of her. I closed my eyes against the torrent of images. Her memories, the memories of those she touched, who had stood out to her. Reading over my shoulder. Emelia's smile. Her death. Deaths. There were so many deaths in her family.

You look best in green.

I snapped back to myself. Katarina was waiting. I couldn't keep her waiting.

Standing, my knees felt shaky for a moment before I could steady myself. One moment I was myself, the next I was Deara. She had handed me a power I didn't understand, and a lifetime of memories filled with memories. It was overwhelming, suffocating. I found myself once again and managed to wrangle the rest into the background.

"Deara," I whispered, hoping the specter would step through the wall. Hoping she hadn't truly pushed the last of herself into me. She didn't manifest.

I waited. I scrubbed my face and cleaned myself as best I could. Still, she didn't manifest. I dressed in green, and still no Deara. I knew that this time she was gone. Truly gone. I had only known her a year, but the loss felt like a hole.

I'd had friends, but had never gotten so close. We had always had the understanding that one day one of us would miss a landing or catch a bullet. There were so many ways to die on the streets. And if we didn't, we would have likely become rivals. The streets bred a different sort of friendship than the quiet company of Deara reading over my shoulder. Of her instruction. Of her quiet acceptance of me.

I found Katarina where I had left her. The woman had given up any attempt at hiding her hangover and was sloppily dozing in her chair. The maid shot me a disparaging look, hoping I would sweep the woman away from the room so she could set it back in order.

"Katarina," I said, stooping beside the dozing heiress.

She started awake, blinking away her exhaustion. "Sade. Took you long enough."

"I think Deara is gone," I said softly, aware of the maid listening in the corner.

Katarina blinked once, then nodded. "I'm not surprised." She knew exactly what I meant. She stood, straightening her dress and gave another curt nod. "I'm not surprised." She repeated. She hooked her arm in mine, holding me tight to her side. "Come on."

For a moment I thought maybe it was denial, then her hand clasped mine and I knew there was no denial. Katarina felt the loss of her sister deeply, but was fighting to hold her composure.

"We can stay in today," I offered.

Katarina shook her head and laughed, a forced, barking sound. "Why would we do that? I'm fine, Sade," her voice chipped with a bitter edge. "It's not like Deara was ever going to not be dead. Let's go."

12:

I spent weeks watching Katarina, prepared for a spiral, but the woman seemed stuck at baseline. That almost had me more nervous than if she had spiraled. I found myself relying more and more on Marco to keep me apprised of the woman's activities while I wasn't around, which was increasingly often following the Beford-Hummel wedding. I had never expected these two men I had never met to be such a boon.

It seemed Emelia's dress had drawn the interest of more than a few of the wealthy and now, if I wasn't sewing, I was being invited to tea as no Norwood had been in ages. The attention was not something I was used to, but I managed not to draw more ire upon my adoptive family. I knew the attention was all in the hopes of acquiring their very own piece of attire from my workroom.

The door chimes jingled. Mrs. Sandfjord was already up front, so I kept my attention on my work.

"She's in the back, my lady," Sandfjords's gravelly voice reached my ears.

"Thank you." Emelia.

I frowned and finished my work before looking up.

Emelia stood silently by, letting me finish, her purse held delicately in her perfectly manicured fingers as she watched. The woman was primmed for an outing. She always dressed her best, but today not a hair was out of place. No dirt under her nails.

"You can't possibly need another dress," I said, aware of Sandfjord's prying ears.

She pouted. "If that's what it takes to see you."

"And why would you want to see me, my lady?" I asked, folding my hands in my lap.

"Emelia," she prompted softly with a despondent frown.

"Emelia … why are you here?"

"I was just on my way home and saw the storefront. I just. I didn't want you to think it was just the night." Her eyes were soft and pleading.

I looked up at her. "And why can't it just be the one night, my lady? There's—" I stopped, looking toward where Sandfjord was working. "Emelia. There don't have to be feelings in this. We had fun. Got carried away, maybe. It would be better if we leave feelings out of it."

"But there are already. I felt it in you, too. Can we just … Can we just go for a walk or something? Please?"

I hesitated. "I don't know if that is best," I said quietly.

This time Emelia looked to where Mrs. Sandfjord would no doubt be standing and shook her head. "Can we go for a walk?" she asked again.

I gave a heavy sigh and stood. "Do you want to borrow a coat?"

She smiled at my concern for her comfort but there was a sadness in the expression. "I'll be fine."

I pursed my lips but held the door for her.

"I will be out for a few minutes," I said to Mrs. Sandfjord, who just gave me a knowing look and a nod. How much had she overheard? How quickly would my gossipy coworkers spread this news?

I allowed Emelia to lead as we strolled in silence for a few blocks before she said, "Are you enjoying your work?"

I chuckled, knowing full well that was not what she wanted to ask. "Yes. I am. It has been busy the last few weeks. Since the Beford-Hummel wedding. It seems somebody had quite the dress there?"

She laughed. "Dear me, yes. And that somebody sang your praises too. I hope Mrs. Sandfjord gave you a raise."

"I don't exactly *need* the money," I said, surprising myself. I had never thought those would be words that ever left my lips.

"But you enjoy the work?" Emelia asked, steering us away from the bustle of the boulevard in favor of a quiet park.

"As I said, yes. Not quite as thrilling as throwing myself off bridges, but it is a nice change of pace. My other clients haven't been quite as intriguing as you were." I smiled, then looked at the ground. When I raised my eyes again Emelia was watching me closely. "Fine. You are right. There are already feelings. Of course you know, because you can feel it."

"It's not fair, I know that," Emelia said.

I shrugged. "It is also not fair that you saw my memories, and they excited you. If you hadn't, maybe you wouldn't have taken the same interest you did. We both came into this with an unfair advantage. So, I suppose we end up even."

She looked down, then her eyes fluttered back up to mine and I felt a strange pull in my gut. "I'm not going to lie, Sade. Your memories did excite me. What you've done. What you've lived through. But you have been given an opportunity to play the role of lady. To let Katarina or Lord Olso take care of you for the rest of your life. You've been given an opportunity to become one of the many idle lords and ladies and you haven't taken it."

"I work in a dress shop. I wouldn't say I am the most exciting person anymore."

"Just because you don't jump off of bridges does not mean you aren't exciting." She cast me her winning smile and I buried my hands in my coat pockets to distract myself.

"Any discussion on this is purely academic," I said. "I don't know what you want from me at the end, Em. You need the freedom of being able to leverage a relationship with somebody with much more political clout than a Norwood. It would be better if you leave yourself open to those higher pursuits." With that I took the lead and turned us back toward Mrs. Sandfjord's. "I shouldn't be away from the shop too long," I said, meeting her eyes for just a moment. I could see her sadness and indecision.

"Sade … I cannot help but want to see you," she said in a final attempt.

"I am a novelty, is all."

"You are not …" She frowned, and I knew she was thinking that maybe I was. "You are," she admitted finally, "you are different. I spend days at these stuffy outings, pasting a smile on my face and making small and very useless talk, playing a game of words with everybody I meet. In the one glimpse of your life that I saw, you gave me more excitement than I have ever had before."

"That's not true," I said. "You haven't seen yourself talk about your work at the Conservatory." I gave her a sad smile, then looked around at the quiet street we occupied. "Whether you realize it or not, Em, you have been avoiding being seen with me this whole walk," I commented. "Even if we were cautious, you know better than I what that game of words can do."

She frowned, a little glimpse of shame showing in her eyes. "I didn't mean to do that, Sade. I'm sorry."

"I know. It's alright. I do need to get back to work, though."

Emelia grabbed my hand before I could walk away. She looked pained. "Wait. Please just wait a moment. Let me think."

I took her hand. "I know I can never be anything more than a mistress to you, Em. I understand that. But do you? Would you be able to live like that? Your secret on the side, and all the whispers."

"Maybe it doesn't have to be like that."

I laughed sadly. "I am not the one who falls in that instance." I kissed her fingers and stepped back. "You know where to find me."

13:

"Sis," Marco shouted excitedly, knowing none of the many passersby on the street could hear him. "Watch this!" He knocked over a bundle of wood where it had been left leaning against a building. It toppled, causing a young man to jump and shriek in fear.

Marco laughed heartily and bounded to my side. "I'm getting good at that, aren't I?" he said, full of pride.

I gave him an acknowledging half smile and he beamed. My eyes drifted past him to a beggar crouched against the front of one of the port warehouses. Mrs. Sandfjord had sent me to ensure the arrival of a shipment of summer textiles, more and more in demand as the weather started its climb out of the cold and damp winter months. The weather was never really too terrible on the isles. Vale being one of the more temperate floats, I had rarely seen snow except on the highest heights of the mountain to the north, where its peaks climbed beyond the protection of the glyph core. Still, those who could afford to have new clothing to fit the season, did.

My eyes slid away from the woman to the warehouse. The port was crowded with the impoverished and vagabonds. Still, my eyes returned to the same one woman. I looked at her, trying to understand why she was familiar.

"Reeva," Marco said beside me. I had trained myself not to glance at the specter, and certainly not to acknowledge him when in view of others. "She was in our gang," he went on, used to my lack of response on the street.

Twenty. Older now, I supposed. We both were.

She was alive, though she looked only half-there. The year since the Persephone had not been kind to this woman. Her usual gold-dusted skin and dark waves of hair hid under layers of grime.

Marco drifted toward her. There was no way she could see his approach—I felt no aberration from her—yet her sunken eyes lifted from the street, seeing through the child and finding me. I kept walking, pretending not to notice the furrow in the woman's brow and her confused, considering look. Her grey eyes were piercing.

"S ... Sade?" The woman's voice rang out beside me, strong despite her wretched state. "Is that you?"

I swallowed and faced the woman in the shadows.

"That was your name, wasn't it? Sade?" Reeva asked, straightening against her wall. Squatting on the ground as she had been, she had looked much diminished, but now I could see she had managed to keep herself relatively fed and maintained. If there was one thing I remembered about her, she did what she needed to survive.

I nodded, uncertain at the situation. I couldn't help but look around at the street, eyes scanning for the woman's gang.

"I'm alone," Reeva said, knowing exactly what was going through my head. "I don't have somebody waiting to jump you." She narrowed her eyes at me. "I didn't expect to see a familiar face out here. Not one from that day, anyway."

"Neither did I," I said, feeling suddenly very rude at my need to hurry. She saw my anxious look at the warehouse. "I'm sorry. I'm working."

She chuckled, taking in my dress and my locale. She had only ever seen me in trousers and grime. That I was on the docks, freshly bathed and in a simple dress for the errand, I knew what she thought. There weren't many ways out of the gangs that didn't involve a compromise. "Wouldn't want to keep the boys waiting."

"I'm not working in that capacity," I said awkwardly. "Look, Reeva, if I gave you money, would you be able to buy a meal?" She knew what I was asking: if the money given to her would only be ripped away by whatever gang she was beholden to now.

"I'm on my own," she said, shaking her head.

"Would you accept it?"

She grinned. "I'm begging on the streets, love. Do you think I'm going to turn down some money?"

I was covert in handing her the bills. It wouldn't do to make her a target by others more desperate. She held my hand for a moment as the bills changed owners. "Maybe when you are not working," she said with a meaningful look. She saw my hesitation and shrugged, then gave me a curious look. "Do you see any of them? From the Persephone?"

I frowned, not completely comprehending. "They all died …" I said, shaking my head in confusion.

She grinned. "Oh, I know. Better hurry along."

Reeva was gone when I left the warehouse, porters loading the many crates of fabrics into a motorized lorry behind me. I looked where the woman had been, then up and down the street.

"Marco. Do you think you can find her?" I asked him quietly.

The boy looked uncertain. "She's strange but ... Yeah. I don't see why not."

I gave the boy a small smile, then turned back to the porters and their work. The boy could find dead Aberrants, rare as they were, but he seemed apprehensive of his abilities to find one woman. Without knowing her usual haunts, the woman seemed to elude him, and when he returned to me at the end of the workday, it was without success.

Perhaps it was for the best.

14:

"I'm surprised I never thought to come out here myself," Katarina said, hands behind her back as she stared up at the twisting trunk of a mottled tree. "I've only seen trees like this in warmer climes. I didn't know they could be grown on Vale."

The Naila Green Conservatory was a marvel. The sprawling campus boasted an arboretum the likes of which I could never have imagined during my life in the slums, with gardens of brilliant flowers from around the world and a massive glass building at its heart.

Children darted here and there while parents and happy couples strolled idly through.

"How much magic they must need to maintain this place," Katarina mused.

I shook my head. "It feels surprisingly light, considering. Tinkerers' crafts only for general maintenance, it seems."

Katarina snorted at me. "It feels light? And when did you become so attuned to the fold that you can just say whether or not a place is covered in magic or not?" She wandered on down the path as it wound past the research center.

I wondered about that. How could the woman not feel the absence of magic? The quiet without the constant hum of the glyphs that powered the city, pushing water and illuminating the streets. I followed her, ignoring when she reached in her purse for another of her little blue pills. The woman had endured a savage bout with Instructor just the day before and must have been feeling it in her bones.

"It is important for us to maintain biodiversity on all the Isles. I am sad to say that much of the plant life that you can find here can only be found within this conservatory, these days." I balked at the voice of the speaker, not wanting to round the corner. I hadn't realized how involved Emelia was at the conservatory and had allowed my curiosity about the place to get the better of me. At the very least, I had hoped that in all the acres, we wouldn't run into each other.

"Is that Emelia Rasczek I hear?" Katarina asked with a playfully suspicious look at me. "Now I see why you wanted to come here."

"I didn't realize she would be here," I said tightly.

"And is there a problem with that? I thought you two were

rather close," Katarina said with a smirk.

"I don't think she wants to see me."

Katarina grinned and pulled me forward. "Well, let's just get this over with, then."

Emelia's eyes lit on me, but she didn't falter in her words to the small crowd. Katarina's arm locked around mine, holding me tight at her side while we listened to Emelia's speech. I did my best to pay attention, but lost focus as Emelia's eyes found me again.

Her speech was impassioned, but still rang with the tone of a politician seeking support.

"I had no idea she was so fervent about preserving green spaces," Katarina said with an eyeroll as the speech came to a close.

Emelia's eyes found mine again as she shook a few hands, telling me not to leave with a look.

"And you feel we should have fewer green spaces and less biodiversity?" I asked Katarina, strangely defensive.

"Well, now, I didn't say that, dear," Katarina huffed. "She's coming over." She relinquished my arm finally. "I'm going to be anywhere else," she said with a devious wink before wandering away, looking up at the trees.

"It was a good speech," I said when Emelia came over.

"I am speaking to people who already agree with me," Emelia said with a sigh. "What do I gain by doing that?"

"You gain a base and help establish a platform and trust among your supporters," I said, and she gave me a coy look and a smile. "I didn't realize you would be here today."

"I've been meaning to stop by Norwood Manor, anyway." She wandered away from the trail and the passing families and lovers.

"Why haven't you, then?" I asked, following her. It had been weeks since we last spoke.

She bit her lip and looked up at the sky. "Well, I suppose I thought maybe you didn't want to see me. That maybe it would be easier for us both not to pretend we could be only friends and nothing more."

"So, you made your decision, then?"

She frowned and tapped her foot. "If it were just a matter of me making a decision, then this would all be easier," she growled. "Unfortunately, you are right that I need to keep my political avenues open. And that is not fair to you."

"I told you that the decision is yours. If nothing more, I will value you as a friend. I understand if that means I have to stay away. But it does seem likely that you and I will cross paths, either at some misguided soirée or on the street, so we should at least agree on where we stand. The circles of Vale do not seem very big at all, once you are in them."

She shook her head. "They are not. Would you really be able to handle being in the shadows with me?"

"Would you be able to handle the rumors? The whispers? The sideways looks?"

She looked down for a moment with a sigh, then leaned forward and kissed me. "We will see what happens." She smiled. "I don't want to stay away from you." She looked back toward the park visitors. "Will Katarina be irritated if I join you both on your walk?"

"She is always a little bit irritated."

Emelia laughed. "Oh, it's not just directed at me, then?"

"I dare say not. Though I am not going to lie. You draw much of her ire. I think it is your name more than you, though," I said as we meandered back toward the main way.

Emelia nodded. "Well, I understand that. I cannot say that the name Norwood rings well in my household."

"Why the contention?"

Emelia looked up at the trees in thought before returning her eyes to me. "That is a long and confusing story. You can pick at the knot of the hatred and never really understand its cause, but my best guess at it is that the Norwoods used to hold a Society Chair. It was my family that tipped the vote to eject Chairwoman Leeta Norwood."

"Which very suspiciously preluded the mass slaughter of my family," Katarina said darkly, joining us. "It makes a woman wonder what exactly the Society Chairs voted on once the Norwoods were closed out."

"I don't think you can ascribe your family's misfortunes to the Society," Emelia said defensively.

"Maybe it is not the Chairs directly ordering hits on my family, but they certainly have played a part. There was no reason for Leeta to have been ousted. Before the vote that removed her, she was well-liked. So maybe it wasn't the Society directly, but who has the power to manipulate such a large body of minds? The College, maybe? The ..." Katarina frowned, her features taking on a confused look, as though she had lost her train of thought. "The

...." She shook her head and her mouth closed.

"Don't you think you may be reaching a little, Katarina?" Emelia asked softly. "I do not deny the misfortune that has befallen your family. The move to Junction should have been a golden opportunity for your family's growth, if it had not been for a string of tragedies. I am sorry for all you have lost, but you cannot possibly blame so much circumstance on the Society."

"Do you deny that Leeta was well-liked?" Katarina asked, still looking as though she were hunting down her lost thoughts.

"Well-liked does not equal a competent decision maker," Emelia said cautiously. "I was not there, so I cannot say what happened, Katarina." She sighed heavily, her eyes turning pleading. "Are we just going to perpetuate the animosity that our parents held for each other?"

Katarina scowled and strolled just a little ahead of us. "We will see. See what you do with the Chair that will be handed to you."

Emelia frowned, but rose to Katarina's ire. "Need I remind you that if you have any interest in being a Chairwoman, you can always run? Try to reclaim what Leeta lost."

"Oh, the target that would paint on my back," Katarina mused humorlessly. Her eyes drifted to me. "I will try to be nice. For Sade's sanity."

"I didn't know that preserving my sanity was ever one of your concerns," I joked.

Katarina rolled her eyes, then smiled and took my arm. Even with her pasted smile, I could feel her tension in the tightness of her fingers digging into my arm. "I wouldn't have wasted all my time training you if it weren't." She looked past me to Emelia. "Are you going to give us the grand tour of this place, or what?"

15:

It took Marco a week to track down Reeva once again.

"I told you, she's a weird one, sis. Like your eyes just fall off her when you're lookin' at her," the ghost said. Strangely, I knew what he meant. It was why I hadn't even remembered her name.

I looked at the sky as I followed the ghost down toward the port. It would be dark soon. I had lost track of time while at Mrs.

Sandfjord's, my attention fixated on the detailed work of the coat and tails I had been commissioned for. Even with the constant glow of the streetlights I had burned too much of the day to be venturing deep into the slums.

"Maybe we should leave this until tomorrow," Marco said, following my train of thought with a nervous air.

For a moment I slowed, then continued on. "I'll rent a motorcarriage if it gets too late," I assured him. "We should at least try to find Reeva though."

His misgivings only stopped him for a moment before he rushed ahead, preferring to get this all over with faster.

"I should be flattered that you are willing to risk your life to visit me," Reeva said, stepping out of the shadows of the alley beside Mrs. Sandfjord's shop. She nodded toward where Marco was standing. "And who's that with you?"

"You can see him?" I asked.

"No, love. But either you are a high-functioning loon, or you are a Death Sight with a ghost following you around. And I know you are a Death Sight. So, do I know them?"

I looked at Marco, then at the pedestrians on the street. "Maybe we should take this inside." I flagged a motorcarriage down.

"If you have an inside to take us to, I am not going to say no," Reeva commented, watching the driver pull to the edge of the road.

I climbed into the back of the cab, sliding over to make room for Reeva.

"No, ma'am. Not her. I'll be cleaning the filth out for days if I let her back there," the driver said. "You, I'll take. Not her."

I looked at Reeva, her street filth and ragged clothing, then lifted a couple extra bills from my purse and passed them to the driver. "The Norwood Estate."

He considered the money, then with a grumble, paid no heed to the woman climbing into the backseat beside me. I glanced at Marco, and he nodded before disappearing.

"He has a point," Reeva said. "I am disgusting."

"You can use my bath when we get to the estate."

She chuckled. "I don't even know where to start with that comment. Was it a year ago we were sleeping on the same floor? Now you have an estate? And your very own bath?"

"It is not where I thought I would be, either," I said quietly. "How did you know where I worked?"

She shrugged. "I watched you at the warehouses. I got curious. I wouldn't have bothered you had you not been clearly coming to find me. In the slums. At night. Dressed like that."

"I sometimes forget that I cannot pass as unnoticed down there as I once did."

"There is no reason for you to go down there, as far as I'm concerned. Especially if you have an estate now. Some of the old gang are still on the streets. If they saw you like this, I think they might think you made a deal. I know there's no way you would have been stupid enough to make a deal and stay on this float after what happened on the Persephone. The others, though, they don't always think." She looked out the window as we pulled up to the Norwood estate. "Nice work, Sade."

I paid the driver while he grumbled some more about the filth staining his seats.

"That is not coming in my house," Katarina said as we entered, setting her glass of whiskey down with a definitive thump.

"Don't mind her," I said, walking past Katarina toward my room.

Katarina growled, but didn't bother following us. "She's not staying here, Sade," she called after me. "And if anything goes missing while she's here, you are responsible."

"Yes, yes. Good evening to you too, Katarina."

"We are not running a gods-damned halfway house," Katarina continued to yell. "As though Marco wasn't bad enough. This is the last time, Sade."

"Very welcoming," Reeva commented. "But, once again, her complaint is not without merit. I wouldn't want me in this nice house," she said, taking in the paintings and busts with a covetous look. "Don't worry. I'm not going to nick anything. I wouldn't be able to fence anything this fine without finding myself a hand short in lock-up." She looked at me. "You did well for yourself. At least somebody got out. Out of the slums. Out of the Persephone. How did you, by the way?"

"Katarina," I said with a glance back the way we had come, then directed her into my room. "We will talk after you get cleaned up. I'll have a meal brought around for us."

I had to admit that the woman was much more palatable after she had cleaned weeks, if not months, of grime from her body. She had helped herself to my clothes by the time I returned with dinner, foregoing even the simplest dresses for a shirt and trousers.

"Take however many pairs you need," I said, setting the tray of food down on my desk.

"You're being overly generous, especially considering you barely knew my name before." Still, she grabbed one of my bags and stuffed a couple changes of clothes into it before sitting down to eat. "Didn't you ever learn not to feed the strays? They always come 'round begging after they find the handouts."

"How long have you been on the street?" I asked, sitting across from her. I glanced at Marco as he walked in and made himself comfortable on the chaise behind Reeva.

"This time … A few weeks. I had a place for a little bit, but then the Snakes rolled through the building. Didn't have any use for me, it seemed, so I got kicked. It's happened more than a few times this last year. I always find somewhere to land after a time." She dug into the meal with the fervor of the starving. "I won't go to the homes," she said between bites. "Untamed brothels is all they are. And I won't go to the brothels. Beater was bad enough, but at least he wasn't a stranger." The name of our old ringleader felt so detached from the me of now.

She saw my discomfort at the thought of the man and sat back from her food.

"I'm not going to try to move in here, don't worry," Reeva said. "That being said …" She looked uncertain about her next words. "Do you think you might be able to help me out with a job? You've got this house; any room on the staff?"

"Katarina is very particular about her staff," I said cautiously. "Most of them have been part of the household for generations."

"I get it. You don't want me eating the pie you've cut yourself such a nice slice of," she said, misunderstanding my qualms. "I don't hold that against you. I wouldn't want some ghost of my past hanging around me all the time, if I could help it."

Marco glanced up at me, and this time I acknowledged him with a small upturn of my lips to reassure him. To Reeva I said, "If I'm honest, I didn't expect to see you or anybody else from the airship again. I thought you all died. So, how did you escape?"

"You first," she said with a small swallow.

"Katarina was one of the passengers. She snuck me off. Kept me hidden from the Abbies."

She nodded and bit her lip, a flash of consideration in her eyes.

"You got lucky. I don't think anybody else got off. Except for me, of course. I guess we could always be wrong. The Aberrants swept the ship thoroughly after the passengers left. They were all over the thing. And the docks and the warehouses. They were everywhere. I saw a few of the smaller kids get flushed and killed. I think some of the older kids were dragged off alive. If they are still alive, I'm sure they are at the work camps by now, wishing they were dead." She frowned, then looked at me. "Beater I know is dead. I saw his body. They tortured him. He had to have been dead." Her voice dropped for a moment, then hardened again. "He was an asshole, but ... well, he was our asshole, wasn't he? Nobody should go that way." She shook her head. "I guess this is all a long way of saying: I shouldn't have escaped. But ..." She hesitated again. "You see ... I am a little bit aberrant. Not in any useful kind of way."

"You're aberrant? I don't ..." I didn't sense any magic on her, but I stopped myself from saying as much.

"Yeah. Don't get all excited about it. Like I said, I'm not any sort of useful kind. I can't draw glyphs or see the future or anything so palpable. I'm a Breaker."

"A what?"

"We are not well known because we are dead zones. I block magic. It sounds useful. It's not. I'd have to get real fucking close to an Aberrant to stop them from burning me alive with some glyph or some such. I can only block it at its source, you see. There are other Breakers that can project it. Or so I'm told. But I am not one of those lucky fuckers. All it really does for me is hide me. An Aberrant could damn near be staring me in the eyes and not even see me, as focused on their magic as they are. The Regs could have found me on the Persephone, but they were so reliant on the Abbies that they didn't bother opening the crate I had squeezed myself into."

"It sounds like a pretty useful ability."

"It doesn't come with the glamor of being a Charmer or a Death Sight, does it? Though I suppose it comes with less of the murder, too. Us Breakers tend to go very unnoticed by the rest of our little community of magic."

"You knew I was a Death Sight?"

"Oh, love, you are a powerful one. Weird thing about Breakers, we can't do anything with magic, but oh, can we see it. Like the Aberrants can. And let me tell you, any Aberrant would see you like a beacon. You aren't any regular Death Sight, either. I can tell you that. It's one of the reasons I stuck so damn close to you on the airship. Part to hide behind you, and part to hide you. When I saw we were well and truly fucked, I let you go and you flared like a little beacon of magic for the Aberrants to be dazzled by."

"That's why the Aberrants hesitated when you let go of me and ran," I said, almost to myself.

"Like a flash of Death Sight light," Reeva said, wiggling her fingers like the flare of fireworks then shrugged. "Gave me some pretty good cover, I'll be honest. Thought you got killed." She frowned at me. "Whoever is training you is doing pretty well at getting your footprint a little more controlled. Not that it was terrible before, just noticeable. And once you notice that in a person, you can't stop noticing it."

"I don't understand. From what I've been told, even Aberrants can't tell a person's magic without prodding; all they can sense is proximity to the fold. How did you know I was a Death Sight?"

"Like I said on the street: You are either high-functioning, or there is a dead behind me," she said, jerking her thumb back toward where Marco sat. "See, you can tell, but it ain't a magical way. You always looked at spaces as though somebody was standing there with us. It doesn't take a genius to crack that one. Though you could have just been a loon, I suppose. But crazy mixed with magic, that generally equals some sort of Sight. I've been doing this a long time and I like knowing what sort of person I'm sitting across from." She glanced behind her. "When I said 'dead,' your eyes flicked to the side. Barely noticeable, but those reflexes can be hard to hide. There's somebody here with us, isn't there?"

My jaw tensed and I nodded, looking at the boy. "Marco. He was on the airship."

"One of ours, then?"

I nodded.

"One of the little ones?"

I nodded again.

"I told Beater something felt off about the ship. That his little shit lieutenant, Vik, was acting strange before the heist," Reeva grumbled. "The fool man never saw me as anything more than a plaything." She shook her head and looked where my eyes led her. "I am sorry, Marco. It was probably me who sent you to your death, and I take responsibility for that."

We lapsed into silence.

I gave in and said, "I know a few of the families in the mid and upper alts. I can see about getting you a position in a household. If you can clean yourself up and promise not to make me regret helping you."

She perked up. "I can get myself cleaned up, and you aren't going to regret it."

"Do you have anything better to wear?"

"I do not. So, it's a good thing I know a dressmaker," she said with a wink.

"I can't make you a dress."

"It doesn't have to be nice. Just nice enough. And I will pay to for it, just not right away."

I frowned, not wanting to say no, but also not wanting to add yet another dress to my already full list.

"Now, I can get a dress. Don't get me wrong, love. But you want me to walk the straight and narrow, and frankly I want to, too. I can't do that without a little trust and a little help. You take care of me, and I'll take care of you. Sometimes having a Breaker around has its uses. Even if it's a pathetic little thing, you're part of my family."

"Now you are just pandering."

"No. I'm not, Sade. I mean, yes, I am. But not entirely. We ran together."

"If I'm honest, I can't really say I took notice of you."

She nodded. "I know. That was by design. And yes. A year ago I would have thrown you in front of a fireball if it meant saving my skin, but it's a shit life on the streets and it's a shit life outside a gang. Maybe I've had a couple come to Ralti moments," she said, referring to the god of compassion. "I thought I lost my entire gang. Then you popped up." She met my eye and held it. "If you are willing to take the risk I know it is to recommend me to one of your sparkly friends, I will do what I can to protect you too, Sade."

I closed my eyes and released a long breath through my nose.

"She's being honest, I think," Marco said quietly.

I nodded and opened my eyes. "You'll take one of my dresses. I'll even tailor it down for you. It is going to be difficult for me to explain how I know you, but I may have one friend willing to consider you without too much question."

"Thank you."

16:

"Miss Razcek will see you," the maid said, looking me over with a curious and slightly disapproving glance. Did I have a reputation already in the house? "Follow me."

Once again I was brought along the servant corridors, away from the eyes of the madam and master of the house, away from an errant glance by one of their guests.

The maid showed me to Emelia's rooms, then bowed, stepping back and away.

"I was excited to hear you had come by, Sade," Emelia said, greeting me at the door. Her hands found mine and she drew me deeper into her room. "I am exhausted from talking politics with these people."

"I didn't realize you had guests. I apologize for interrupting."

"They are friends of my parents," she said dismissively, sitting on the lounge set under her window and pulling me down to sit beside her. "Besides, from spring to fall we always have guests. You would never be allowed over if having guests precluded your visits." She took my hands in hers and smiled. "I am so pleased to see you."

I hesitated, seeing her hopefulness. It had been foolish to go to Emelia first, but I trusted her more with the matter of Reeva than any of the other mid- to upper-alt families.

"I'm going to ask a favor that you have no reason to grant," I said.

"Out with it, Sade. Just tell me what it is."

"I was wondering if you had any positions open on your staff?"

"I am not going to hire you onto my staff," she said with a laugh, then her face melted to concern. "Did Katarina kick you out? Are you alright?"

"Not for me. One of my friends."

"Oh." She frowned. "From before?"

I nodded.

She sighed. "I don't suppose she has references."

I shook my head and Emelia bit her lip. "Katarina won't hire her?"

"She does not let anybody from outside in anymore."

"I suppose she has good reason not to trust anybody," Emelia said quietly.

The last time an outsider had been hired on, the man had

stabbed Katarina's young cousin. According to Katarina's gossiping maids, he had seemed steady enough until finally he had snapped while watching the girl chatter merrily with the air. Or, listening to the counterpoints of the butler, the man had been part of the conspiracy against the Norwood family and had accepted a payment from the College. His family had, after all disappeared to the winds as soon as the murder had occurred. Either way, the result was the same: Katarina never hired outside the families of her current staff.

"Well. Tell me about her," Emelia prompted

"She's from Dorado." I started.

"That's not much of a selling point, Sade. It is rare that anything good comes out of Dorado, especially the people." Emelia said with a frown.

"I know, but I'm not going to lie to you, and I want you to have proper expectations."

She pursed her lips and nodded. "Best you set my expectations, then."

"She will work hard in whatever role you give her, but I would not say she has refined any of her many edges."

"I can deal with rough edges. I just don't know where I would put her. I don't know how I would explain the addition to my parents, considering they are the ones who pay our staff. You haven't even told me what her skills are." She frowned, trying to figure a solution.

"Aside from being good at climbing, I actually don't know. She claims she is up for any task assigned to her, and I do not necessarily doubt that is true, but everything with a grain of salt." I sighed and met Emelia's eyes. "If I'm honest, I don't know much about her, even though we came from the same gang. I know she will do good work. She has basically been living on the street for the last year, since the Persephone, and I don't think she will be quick to squander an opportunity to change that situation."

Emelia clicked her tongue a few times in thought as she looked toward the window. She squeezed my hands. "Can she hide the fact she's from Dorado?"

"I doubt it."

She looked at me. "You have to understand, if she's from Dorado, if anything goes missing from this house—"

"She won't steal from you."

"That's not what I'm saying. But if anything were to go

missing—to be even misplaced for a time—I cannot guarantee that my mother won't come down on her, guilty or not. Simply because she is from Dorado."

I nodded. "I understand." Standing, I let her hands fall from mine. "I guess I should head out, then."

"I didn't say no, Sade." Emelia looked up at me. "I just think it is important that you and she understand that."

"She's from Dorado. I think she knows exactly how the people of Vale feel about her the moment she opens her mouth. Frankly, I don't think she cares. And, honestly, I was hoping you wouldn't either."

She frowned, struggling with her Society deep prejudices. Her concerns weren't without validity. Reeva did come from the gangs. Still, so had I. I couldn't help but wonder, had I had a Doradian accent and not one from Junction, would Emelia have looked twice at me?

"I should let you get back to your guests, Em. Have a good evening." I bent and kissed her, then straightened to leave, but she grabbed my hand.

"Don't be disappointed in me, please. I am just trying to figure out how to get her past my mother. If she can climb, maybe there is a position for her at the Conservatory, but I would need to talk to Naila about the funding. We just don't have an open position on our staff, so it will be difficult to sell this to my mother without her asking too many questions. Questions I would not be able to answer easily. I don't care that she is from Dorado, but …"

"Your mother will. I understand."

Her eyes turned pleading and she pulled lightly on my hand. "Sit with me, just for a little bit longer. Please?"

I sighed and sat. We had seen each other several times over the weeks, but not much. I had to admit, it was nice just to be with her. There was a reason I had come to her first, instead of anyone else. "Your guests won't be looking for you?"

"No. As I said, they are not here for me, but my parents." She smiled and kicked her feet up into my lap. "You are a welcome break from discussing politics with old armchairs who will never find a modicum of flexibility in their way of thinking, no matter how many times they see that things are changing."

"I thought you said you didn't want to talk politics," I commented lightly, setting a hand on her ankle.

A memory broke free: my hand on Eda's ankle. Instead of the chaise supporting Emelia, there had been Gan with Eda pulled up against him as we laughed. Both their faces were so clear in my mind even though the memory was years old.

I snapped my hand back from Emelia's leg, fingers clenching closed.

"What was that?" Emelia said, sitting up with as much surprise. "Was that a memory? Was that your memory? Is …" She looked around.

"She's gone. Moved on," I said quietly, looking at my clenched fist and berating myself for my accidental slip.

"Then, how?" Emelia asked, looking at me expectantly. "You did that?"

I looked at the waiting woman and sighed. "There's no getting out of an explanation, is there?"

She shook her head. "Not a chance."

I returned my eyes to my balled fists. "When Deara moved on, she gave me her Sight."

"How is that possible?"

"How can I touch the dead?" I said with a shrug. "Some things are not supposed to be. I happen to be one of those things. I'm a Lock. Gifted the ability of a Death Sight. Gifted the ability of a Past Sight."

"A Lock?"

"Don't worry about what I am, exactly. Just know that it is possible. And that the College put a moratorium on the existence of Locks, so it's best not to speak about it openly."

"Why would you trust me with such dangerous information?"

"Because I know I can." My fingers steadily unfurled, and I set my hand back on her ankle.

"Who were they? The two I saw." She asked.

"Eda and Gan. I used to run with them."

She could see there was more to it than that, but she let it rest.

Settling back once again, she gave another small shake of her head. Her eyes lingered on me. We were silent, just enjoying each other's company. She gave me a wan smile and grabbed her book. I wouldn't be going anywhere fast. I drew my sketchbook from my bag and settled in.

Bells rang outside. The sound tinny, the pattern unmistakable. A cloud was drifting onto Vale.

I leapt up and sealed the window behind us, pulling the drapes for the added protection. Emelia was just a moment behind me. I drew her away from the pane of glass. Even sealed, I didn't trust the opening.

"It is unlikely a cloud could even reach us here, Sade," Emelia said soothingly, pulling me now toward the bed to sit. "We are too high for the gasses to reach even on the worst days. The number of wards it would have to overcome to climb this far is immense. But it is best you stay until we get the all-clear." She held my hands in her lap, holding my eyes.

I balked. "No, Emelia. I should go. You have guests you need to get back to. You are right, the cloud won't reach this alt. I should go home."

"Just because the cloud is unlikely to reach us here doesn't mean it won't reach Katarina's estate. It's too dangerous." Her grip tightened with a touch of fear. Her sudden change of positions a clear sign she had no desire for me to leave, and my switch evidence that I knew I ought to.

"I've survived cloud drifts before," I started, then felt the now-familiar pangs of death from the south. I stilled and Emelia stilled with me, seeing my sudden unease. "Marco. Are you near?"

It took a moment, but the boy materialized at the door. He hadn't wanted to intrude, but he also was never far.

"Check on Katarina? Please. Make certain she is taking this seriously? She will have felt that right now, so she should be, unless she's drunk. And tell her I'm staying in shelter until the alarm passes."

The boy nodded vigorously. "She's going to ask where you are ..."

"That's fine. You can tell her."

He started to fade.

"Wait. And ... Reeva. She'll be harder to find. But she can't feel what just happened."

"I'll find her," he said, sharpening with his nod before fading away.

Emelia waited, having only been able to see me talking at open air. She looked uncomfortable but not afraid.

"He's gone," I said.

She nodded slowly. "Who is Marco?"

"A boy. He died on the Persephone," I said absently, staring toward the curtained window. The cloud was rolling through the slums. Only the poor lived in such a low-lying spot. Still, there should have been more warning than this.

Emelia frowned. "How old was he?"

I realized I had never asked. "Ten or eleven, perhaps?"

"That young? He was one of the boarders?" Her face fell and I could see the thought hurt her. "Why do we have children risking their lives in such a manner just to survive …"

"You are a good person, Emelia."

My jaw tensed and I shuddered as another wave of death struck. My eyes drifted back toward the window.

Emelia followed my eyes. "What's going on?"

I blinked, clearing my mind of the loss. "It's the slums, I think. I can only really guess, but it's south of here." The ringing of the bells took on a sinister pitch with the ebb of life in the back of my mind. I forgot about Emelia for a moment as the bells pulled me in.

"Sade?" Emelia's hand gently touched my shoulder, her voice nervous. I had drifted closer to the window. Her fingers tightened, pulling me back. "Sade." Her voice was commanding now and broke me free of my daze. She spun me to face her, eyes locking on mine.

"I'm okay," I said, but my voice was hollow as another creeping slip of death pulled at my mind. The cloud was rising.

Jaw tensing, Emelia glanced behind her at the door. "Maybe we should move deeper into the house? A room without windows, perhaps?"

"It won't reach this high. These deaths are the people caught in the streets. The undergrounds. The alarms never come fast enough for the lowlands. For the slums." My voice was weak and haunted. It did nothing to set Emelia at ease. "I can't do anything for them, but I can't not feel their passings." Katarina's training had been a double-edged sword. I could control and harness my ability, but along with it, my sense of magic and of death was only stronger now. Try as I might, there was too much to push away this night.

Marco manifested at my side. "Katarina is … she's busy … but she's safe at home," he said with an awkwardness that told me how the Death Sight was choosing to distract herself from the mass passings. My eyes fell on Emelia. Similar pursuits could do me well, but I banished the thought quickly.

"Reeva?" I asked, turning my attention back to the child.

"Found her in the old den. It's the Jun Jun Gang's now, but they don't seem to be forcin' her out. She's not exactly welcome, either, but I think she will be alright until the cloud passes. They got a few outsiders hunkerin' down with 'em." A big enough cloud could stop even the deadliest rivalry on the streets for a little while. "I'm going to stay with her, if that's okay with you? Make sure they don't force her out before the cloud clears."

I wasn't certain what the specter thought he could do to prevent that, but I nodded. "Of course."

Marco disappeared again, and I lifted my eyes from where he had been to Emelia. The woman was waiting patiently, aware that we had a visitor and, at my look, aware he had left. She took my hand, and for a moment when our skin touched, I felt a sensation like falling. *Reeling, the scent of cloud vapor, darkness, a dive. My last dive. The dread the moment I had missed my landing. The pain in my wrist as my talons snapped forward, tearing into the fabric of the airship.*

Something different. *My fingers gently working into soft soil. Emelia's hands. Lovingly setting rows of seeds.* The calm of the scene brought me back down.

I snapped myself out of the spiral of the memory. The glut of death was making it more difficult to control Deara's gifted abilities. Emelia's eyes were wide. She had seen my memory as well.

"I'm sorry," I said, pulling my hand back slowly.

"Was that ... was that what you did before Katarina took you in? Is that how you boarded airships?" She sounded almost excited.

"Well ... that wasn't a particularly good boarding," I admitted. "I almost made the final dive that day."

"That was the Persephone."

I nodded again.

"That was an important boarding for you, wasn't it? Your mind seems to go to it a lot."

"It changed my life. So, it only makes sense."

She grabbed my hand again and pulled me over to the bed, all fear of the cloud rolling through the lowlands lost from her mind. She sat on the edge of the mattress and pulled me down beside her excitedly. "Can you show me another?"

I found myself distracted in her enthusiasm. "I suppose. I'm not very good at this yet. Let me focus for a moment."

She was silent, both her hands wrapped tightly around mine. Her anticipation flowed between us, the Charmer's control slipping.

The drive of the woman's emotions drew another memory to the surface unbidden, and a moment later my gut tightened. *Her lips on mine. The soft commanding presence. The feel of her skin under my fingers.*

I broke the memory off with an embarrassed shake of my head. "Oh," I said.

She laughed. "Oh indeed," she said deeply, and I knew that once again she had shared the memory. "I'll try to get myself under control," she said, knowing her anticipation had snapped the memory free. Instead of getting her magic in line, she smirked and sent another little thrill up my spine.

I groaned and looked at her. "That's not fair."

She grinned and kissed me, her magic receding but the thrill remaining. "No, maybe not. But I got to see how you felt, so I wanted you to know how it felt for me." She brushed her nose against mine. "Now, are you going to show me one of these dives or what?"

"If I'm honest, I preferred the memory you shared with me," I said with a smile. "But alright."

The distraction was working. I closed my eyes and found a smile on my face.

"This was my first one," I said, and my voice sounded distant as the wind pulled at my clothes and howled in my ears. *The hands of my memories looked so small to me now as they clutched at the rope, my lifeline. The small rise of excitement flared in my chest, roiling uncomfortably with the anxiety of what I was about to do. A small ship, just a commuter ferry really, approached the bridge. This would be a small affair, just a couple of us kids making the dive. There was no expectation that I would make the landing, and I knew that. How many first dives turned to final dives. Still, you had to start with one.*

I swallowed and held my lifeline tight. I knew I would have to release my grip; holding too tight would cause me to miss. I knew all the tricks of the older kids, but that didn't stand for much.

The ringing of the bells was just a distant thing now.

I dropped. Freefall greeted me with open arms, nothing but wind wrapping itself around me. I wheeled, trying to get a feel for the dive, trying not to fall into a panic, drawing ever closer to the surface of the ferry balloon.

Emelia's breath was warm on my face as her forehead pressed against mine.

I understood the theory behind a landing. I knew how to hit, how to roll. How to set myself. Theory was a long shot from action. Excitement and terror vied.

Emelia's lips were on mine now. Our hands stayed locked together, but my free fingers leapt to exploration. Hers twined in my hair and pulled me closer.

The confusing web of emotions from the memory and my reality shattered in a disorienting crash. An urgent knocking sounded on Emelia's door.

"My lady," the maid's insistent voice called through the door.

Emelia and I were caught reeling.

The door opened and the maid slipped in before closing it tight once again. "I'm sorry, my lady, but your mother is coming."

Emelia looked up at me, the two of us somehow having found ourselves tumbled on the bed. I quickly found my feet, setting myself back in order. She groaned and rolled to her feet, checking herself in the mirror. She looked at me and, with a wink, ran a tongue-dampened finger over the corner of my mouth to clean away the smudge of her lipstick.

The maid stood with her back pressed against the door, pretending not to see.

Emelia cast a look at the woman and gave her a nod. She had her back to me now, her attention on her wardrobe.

"Emelia," the staccato of her mother's voice sounded as the maid pulled the door open. "Baron Tonson was wondering where you had run off to. Awash with concern he was that you had gone out for a stroll when the bells started sounding. I told him we had nothing to fear here, of course," the woman said, striding into the room. "But whatever are you doing, child?"

"Ah, mother," Emelia said, a pique of irritation in her voice. "This is Katarina Norwood's cousin. She made my gown for the Beford-Hummel wedding. I asked her here to help liven up a few of these drab things," she said with a fresh, petulant note and a sweeping gesture toward the wardrobe.

"Hm. I thought I had heard something about another Norwood in town," Lady Razscek said, casting a disdainful eye toward me. "It was a lovely dress. If not a little too daring."

"Thank you, my lady," I said with a demure bob. I hoped in vain that Emelia had inherited her Charmer's ability from her father, because my emotions were running high.

Emelia cast an apologetic glance at me before her mother turned back to her. A little wave of calm soothing away the tumult in my gut.

"I can't imagine why my daughter would have asked you here in the evening," she said with a suspicious pith at her daughter and a glance out of the corner of her eye at me. She was definitely a Charmer.

"That is my fault, my lady. I was working at the shop today and could only come by after."

Lady Rasczek's lips pinched. "Well, at least one of the members of that family is a contributing member of our society," she chirped.

"It is not as though either of us have actual jobs, Mother," Emelia said derisively as she turned back to her wardrobe. "So isn't it unjust to hold the Norwoods to that standard?"

"It is not as though you do not work, Emelia," Lady Rasczek said, with a hint of softness in that cutting voice. "You just have higher pursuits." She flicked her wrist dismissively. "Besides, you know what I mean. Their family used to be tasteful. Since they had those girls though …" She shook her head. My presence was completely forgotten. Emelia did nothing to remind her mother of me standing behind her. I moved away a step, sinking further from the woman's mind with distance.

A man appeared in the hall behind the maid, then slipped away. A ghost. Here and gone. He had been dressed for work outdoors. No doubt one of the house staff who lived in the lowlands. His body would be found when the cloud moved on.

The two ladies bristled and snapped at each other, unaware of the presence of death even in their home. The initial wave of loss had abated as those caught out passed and those who had found shelter remained safely tucked away. The maid made an uncomfortable move toward the door, and I considered following her.

One step, two. Lady Rasczek either took no notice of me or paid me no mind as she lambasted Katarina and her good-for-nothing relations. Emelia pointedly kept her eyes off me as I moved.

I was about to slip past the maid when Lady Rasczek said, "Well, I suppose you are here now, and it's not as though we can turn you out with a cloud alarm active." I knew the words were directed at me and turned to face the lady of the house before she could take full notice of my attempted departure. "I don't imagine the devil of a cloud will move off until the sun burns it away. Imogen will show you to one of the spare rooms."

"Thank you, my lady," I said, bowing low.

While it was not typically frowned upon for women to bow, it seemed quite frowned upon by this particular lady. Still, I had all but given up on my curtsies, as their awkwardness only ever seemed to draw more unwanted attention.

After another peeved look, she turned to Emelia. "The young Lord Gao is taking shelter with us this evening, as well." She said his name with much more warmth than she did any of the Norwoods'. "We are all in the study. You will join us."

"Ah, well. If we are entertaining, then Sade will join us as well," Emelia proclaimed.

I cast her a long look that told her exactly how much I wanted to be entertained, and she merely grinned when her mother turned her back.

Lady Rasczek strode past me without any further acknowledgement.

Emelia waited until her mother was well on her way down the hall before joining me at the door to peek out at the woman's retreating back. She ducked back into her room and pulled me against her once again, regardless of the waiting Imogen.

"I'm sorry about her," Emelia said when she finally let me breathe.

"I would have been perfectly content in my room by myself this evening," I complained.

"I'm sure you would have been. But I would have been bored. And I would have been thinking about you alone in your room."

I glanced at Imogen, who was once again pretending we didn't exist.

"The young Lord Gao." I said quietly.

Emelia frowned and nodded. "Alec. Yes. I know." She glanced at Imogen. "But I can't exactly cast him out into the cloud. And I can't go shouting for the Enforcers. The only evidence we have is your knowledge, and unless you are planning on subjecting yourself to the Aberrants, that does not count for much."

"So, we grin and bear it and pretend he didn't brutally murder our friend?"

"Well, you won't be grinning. He is an ass."

I grumbled and she took my hand. I felt the soothing in her touch and cast an unamused look at her.

17:

Alec looked at me with a sneer when Emelia led me into the study. "Katarina's cousin, aren't you?"

Deara's memories of her death played in the back of my mind while I pasted a forced smile on my face and brought myself to curtsy, aware of Lady Rasczek's eyes on me.

"Shouldn't you be getting home?" he scowled.

"We will not be sending her outside," Emelia said firmly. "All have refuge during a cloud breach. Not only is it law; it is common decency. Decency that you yourself are the benefactor of."

"Well, then I suppose, lucky you." His voice dripped with disdain and suspicion. "It's not every day that somebody like you gets to enjoy such hospitality."

"You make it very tempting to forget what common decency is, Alec," Emelia warned.

"Emelia. Behave yourself," Lady Rasczek chided.

Emelia cast Alec a bitter glare, then assumed a face that conveyed nothing but serenity. "Very well. Perhaps the evening can still be salvaged." She gave him a subtle bow of her head, then turned her back on him.

The young man looked peeved, then made his way to the bar cart.

Emelia drew me over to the couch and sat me down next to her, disregarding the disapproving look from her mother, instead casting her a disdainful look of her own, then cracked her book once again. Her leg rested against mine, and I felt Lady Rasczek's judgmental gaze. I didn't think I would be as intimidated by Emelia's mother as I found myself now. I sought refuge in my drawing.

"Wine?" Emelia asked me quietly once Alec had moved away from the bar cart. "Might help you loosen up."

I gave her a nod and she stood, leaving me alone.

Lady Rasczek filled the void quickly. "I don't know what your game is, Miss Norwood, but if my daughter moors her ship to your dock, you will drag her down into the abyss with the rest of your family." Her voice was deep and hushed.

I swallowed, uncertain if the woman's words were a threat or warning. Looking at the noblewoman brought no clarity to the situation. I narrowed my eyes. "You seem to imply that the

Norwoods are destined to fall," I said just as quietly.

"Isn't that obvious enough?" Lady Rasczek said tersely. "It seems they are already there, with only Katarina left to hold them above the cloudline."

"Mother," Emelia cut in, standing behind us. "The Baroness was hoping to bend your ear some more." I had seen Baroness Tonson at a handful of parties and always avoided her. The woman had a prattling way about her that kept me always a safe distance away. With the men otherwise occupied with their drinks, she was quickly finding herself in need of attention.

Lady Rasczek looked me over once more, her nose wrinkling ever so slightly as she did, then stood.

"Don't mind her," Emelia said, setting a glass of wine on the end table beside me.

"I'll try not to," I said, uncertain how I was supposed to not mind the woman's words.

"Why are you sketching our groundskeeper?" Emelia asked, an odd look on her face as she peered over my shoulder.

"Your groundskeeper?" I said, looking at the half-done sketch. I set down my pencil and looked up at her. "I was trying to figure out why I recognized him."

"I was unaware you two had ever crossed paths. Did you remember?"

Her hand was on my shoulder. I set mine on hers and focused the memory. The man from my memory was younger. The details of his face lost to the inattentiveness of youth and the fading of time. He had volunteered at the orphanage before I had turned to the gangs. I remembered him serving food, helping the small children, but there was nothing distinct about the man in my memories. I let my hand slip away from hers, not wanting to prolong the touch that would only bring disdain from her family and guests.

"He's a good man," Emelia said. "Why did he come to mind?"

I gave her a look and her eyes widened, then softened with remorse. "Oh." She frowned, then came around the couch to sit beside me, regardless of the ire her mother continued throwing her way in glances and glares. "I just saw him today."

I patted her knee and then closed my sketchbook, resting my hand on its cover.

The lamp on the wall flickered lightly, and Alec and the Baron laughed drunkenly at some joke behind us. Emelia's father began regaling them with some exploit of youth that was no doubt a majority fabrication by this point. I found myself watching Alec Gao out of the corner of my eye before Emelia refocused me. Still, I felt another handful of lives slip away below.

"Can I see another of your drawings?" Emelia said after a time. I was grateful for any distraction the woman could afford me.

"Mostly just sketches," I said shyly, a nervous habit to make excuses for any lack of skill.

"I would like to see them, still. If you are willing to show me." She smiled warmly, her hand lightly touching mine.

"Yes. Sorry." I smiled and shook my head at myself. "I'm used to keeping these things to myself. Only Deara ever really took an interest."

Emelia's smile turned sad at the woman's name, her eyes drifting toward the drinking men.

I redirected her by opening my sketchbook. "Like I said, sketches." I felt a wave of uncertainty as I let her take the book from me, but I shook the feeling away.

Lady Razscek's face only took on a deeper disdain as she looked at us, Emelia's shoulder resting against mine now. I kept my eyes off the mistress of the house and watched Emelia as she slowly turned the pages.

"It's beautiful work," Emelia said, stopping for a moment on a sketch of Deara reading at the Norwood estate. Her hand brushed mine and I felt her sadness and the flicker of her anger as Alec laughed once again. She turned the page and found a study of hands and smiled. "Those are yours," she said looking over the array.

"They are the most available to me."

The next page showed her the underside of a bridge, the interlocking beams of metal above and the gentle waft of planetary gas floating beneath. She grinned. "The Grand Cross?"

"I still have dreams of it."

"What are you ladies up to over here?" Alec asked, hands gripping the back of the couch as he looked over our shoulders. I hated his handsomeness. His smug self-confidence. The entitled cant to his dark eyes. I hated that this was the man who had killed Deara simply for rejecting his advances and that he was walking free as though he had never done anything wrong in his life.

"What, we've got a little artist here?" Alec asked with a smirk.

He snatched at the sketchbook, but Emelia kept it out of his reach. "Oh, come on." He reached for the book again, seizing it from Emelia. He flipped through the pages, a frown forming on his lips as he saw the drawings of Deara. He tossed the book back to me, narrowing his eyes. He sneered and turned his attention to Emelia. "I don't know why you take such an interest in these Norwoods. Leave the chaff to her doodles." He took her wrist and pulled her to her feet.

I was on him in an instant.

This was the man who had savagely murdered Deara for spurning him, for being a Death Sight. I knocked his hand away from Emelia's wrist with a backhand strike. With a turn of my hand, I had his wrist trapped and twisted up behind his back.

"Did the lady ask to be touched?" I growled in his ear. Even with her surprised gasp, Lady Rasczek said nothing at the sudden change to the room. The man had gone too far, and even she was willing to acknowledge that. "Perhaps it's time you go to bed."

"Aren't you a bit beneath giving me orders, Norwood?" he said with a disdainful drunken slur.

Deara's destroyed face danced in my eyes as my anger surged at the man. He instantly paled, and I knew he had seen the memory. Hopefully he would not realize what I was from the slip and he would instead chalk the image up to a moment of guilt at his actions. It was a thin hope.

I released his wrist and he slid away, a haunted look on his face.

"Perhaps it's time you go to bed," I repeated slowly.

His lips quivered in a mix of anger and fear, and he turned and strode from the room.

I looked at Emelia. "Sorry," I breathed.

She shook her head slowly. "He was out of line. But maybe it's time we all go to bed. Imogen, can you make sure that Sade finds her room, and have Darus make sure the young Lord Gao does not leave his?"

"Emelia," Lady Rasczek started to chide, but quieted when she saw her daughter's smoldering rage. "Yes. It is late. We should all retire," she said instead.

18:

My door cracked and Emelia slipped in.

"What happened?" she asked quietly, sitting on the edge of my bed.

I sighed, shaking my head. "I sort of pushed a memory on him. Deara didn't leave me with a manual when she gave me this. I'm doing a terrible job at controlling it."

"What was the memory?"

"Deara. But after."

"He should be confronted with his sins," Emelia said righteously, but I could see a nervousness in her. "He knows what you are now, then?"

"I don't know. It was just an image. Only a flash. It's possible he will not realize ... I won't count on that, though."

"You may want to warn Katarina. Alec may draw his own conclusions about what she is."

"I'll warn her." I said, though I didn't know how I would explain without telling her what my abilities truly were. What Deara had done. I patted her hand. "You should go back to bed."

She laid down beside me. "I intend to stay here tonight, if that's alright?"

"I don't think your mother would be happy to find out."

Emelia chuckled lightly. "Likely not, but I don't suppose I really care right now."

19:

"Sade," Marco's soft whisper stirred me from my sleep.

Emelia shifted behind me, her arm still draped over my waist. "Marco?"

"The cloud is movin' off. Should be gone by the time the sun is fully up."

I gave a sleepy nod of acknowledgement.

"I don't know how she knew I was there, but Reeva told me to go away."

"Sounds like her."

"Can I stay here?" His usual chipper demeanor seemed sunken

after the night of death.

I shifted, making a little room on the bed for the boy. Emelia continued to sleep soundly against my back, even when the boy lay beside me, huddling close.

20:

"You must be Marco," Emelia said, her palm curled around my hip to keep in contact with my skin so she wouldn't lose sight of the boy. "I recognize you. Sade is quite good at drawing, isn't she?"

The boy nodded. "She can see me?" he said, looking at me.

"I can see you."

"She can hear me?"

"And hear you," Emelia said with a smile. "As long as we are touching Sade." Emelia's fingers were warm against my hip.

Marco looked between us excitedly as he slid from the bed, his cold fingers gripping mine tightly. "Miss Emelia, Marco Heartcove," he said with a bow and a flourish of his free hand.

"He's a charming one, isn't he?" Emelia whispered in my ear. "It is a pleasure to meet you, Marco."

"Can you check on Katarina?" I asked the boy.

His nose wrinkled in a grimace, and he groused. "I would rather not."

"Oh, stop whingeing, you don't have to look, just make sure she hasn't left the house. Then, maybe find where Reeva slunk off to. I want to call on her today. I'll meet you at the house."

Marco frowned, but his eyes found Emelia's hand sliding a little higher up my side, and he nodded quickly and ran off.

"He seems nice."

"I could have manifested a worse kid, I suppose, especially given the options."

"Mhm," Emelia hummed, already distracted by our isolation. Her hand continued its climb.

I exhaled, long and heady, ready to let myself be won over by Emelia's touch. Her fingers slipped away, and she backed away enough to be clear of any contact with me. She didn't want me thinking she was working her magic. With her, I knew it was a gesture only.

"What is it?" she asked quietly.

I shook my head. "Nothing."

"I'm rather attuned to emotions, or did you forget?"

I looked at her, thinking. What was it that was bothering me? I shook my head, eyes stuck on the woman in front of me. "Something feels off. In the air. I don't know. The night might just be getting to me a little. That much activity passing into the fold and all."

She swallowed and nodded. "I know what you mean." Her hand settled back on my hip.

"Are you going to try to distract me again, my lady?"

She smirked. "Only if you keep calling me *my lady*."

I looked at the window and the rising sun, slightly dimmed by the fog in the air. "I suppose we still have time before I trust the air completely again, *my lady*."

At the phrase, she pulled a heavy breath of annoyance in through her nose, her finger trailing an absent circle on my hip. Then she gave a small laugh and smile. "This is a terrible time to ask it, but when things have calmed down, show me little bit of where you came from? Take me under the Grand Cross."

I chuckled. "Sure. Why not? Just bring my lady under the Grand Cross."

"Why does it sound like you think I'm joking?" Emelia said.

Her distraction worked. I completely forgot about the sickly feeling in the air. Instead, I propped myself up on my elbows to look at her with a little rush of fear in my chest. The Grand Cross Bridge was a five-mile climb over open air if you traversed from land to land, and even staying close to the rock face, it was over two miles wide. The bridge had become a replacement for land itself, with a full town built on its wide swath. Both the mechanical and the magical supports for that large a bridge struggled to maintain its stability with so much activity above. I shook my head at her slowly.

"Because you must be. I am not bringing you under the Grand Cross. Do you have any idea how many vagabonds have fallen? There is a reason we call those who have made the crossing Hard Hands." I turned her hand palm up. "These are not exactly the hardest of hands." My fingers lingered where they rested.

She closed her hand around mine and met my eyes. "I can do it."

I closed my eyes with a sigh. "You are right; your timing is terrible. There was just a cloud drift last night. What if there is another while we are under the damn thing?"

"We will pick a nice day to go," she said lightly.

"There are no nice days under the bridge. It is a two-and-a-half-mile climb with ripping winds."

"I'll have an expert with me."

"I'm not bringing you down there in skirts. The winds will catch them like a sail, and you will pull me right along with you, sending us spiraling into the abyss," I tried again.

"As much as that may be a deterrent for Katarina, it is not for me. For some reason, I have a feeling you can outfit me with the right gear."

I said nothing for a long time.

"Will you at least acknowledge that I can do this?"

My mouth pulled into a tight line, but I gave a little nod, the barest of agreements that maybe she would not get us both killed on this expedition.

"Then you will take me under?"

I flopped back down to the bed in defeat, frowning, and sucked air in through my teeth. "Fine."

She smiled, rolling up onto an elbow to look down at me. "I'm going to hold you to that."

I just shook my head and wished she would forget the notion after the morning. I looked at the window again. The brightening sun. The fog was already burning off and the idea of bringing Emelia under the Grand Cross Bridge wiped any careless feelings from me. "I should really go check on Katarina. I have a feeling that drift reached higher than we think it did."

She let me off the hook, her eyes lifting from me to the window as well. "It shouldn't have reached anywhere at all," Emelia said quietly. "Not with the barriers in place."

I bit back the desire to tell the woman just how common those glyph barriers failed for the lowland slums, and instead sat up.

"Thank you for hosting me overnight," I said cordially.

She laughed, grabbing my arm and turning me to look at her. "Are we going back to pretending there are no feelings here? Am I going to have to get a new dress made just to see you again?"

I leaned down and kissed her. "No. I'm sorry, Em. I fell back on habit."

She pulled me back down to her and I lingered, tempted.

"Can I call on you tomorrow?" She asked.

I just smiled and stood.

"I will take that as a yes," Emelia said, lying back, content.

21:

"Miss Norwood," Alec's voice sounded behind me. He had been waiting for me just beyond the walls of the Rasczek estate, far enough to keep the curious eyes of the estate's guards from spotting us. "It seems we should have a little talk."

"A talk? Whatever about?" I asked, trying, and no doubt failing, at innocence.

"About Emelia. About the fact that she is mine. About whatever you did to me last night." He still looked a little pale from the images that had flashed in his mind.

"And what exactly are you accusing me of doing to you last night?"

He glowered. "I think you know. So, let's talk." He grabbed my arm.

"If you think this talk is going to go the same way your last talk with Deara went, you are mistaken," I growled, freeing my arm from his hold and putting a little distance between us.

"You *are* one of them." He snarled, drawing a pistol from inside his coat.

The glyph was fast to my mind, paralyzing him where he stood. I closed the distance, grabbing the man's gun—the same one that he had used on Deara—and breaking it from his hold.

"I am so much more," I said quietly, my touch pressing him down to his knees.

His eyes were on the pistol now in my hand. "Abomination," he ground out with his loosening muscles.

"*That*, you are right about," I conceded. "And *you* are a sniveling little shit."

I set my hand on his cheek and pushed Deara's memory of her own death into him. I made him relive it from her perspective time and again until he was a sobbing mess. "I shouldn't let you live," I whispered in his ear. "But I am merciful." I tapped the pistol lightly against his frozen cheek once, and I saw the fear spike in him, the memory of the gunshot echoing in his mind. "Merciful, but I can change my mind quickly. Don't give me reason to."

22:

Katarina dismissed me without so much as a hello.

"Your fucking little ghost already checked on me," she groused, throwing a pillow at me when I dared to peek my head in. She would be nursing her hangover for much of the morning.

Instead of waiting for her to recover, I set off in search of Reeva. Marco had gotten used to the woman's strange ability to hide from even so skilled a tracker as himself, and had found her holed up in a new hovel in the lowlands.

"She wants me to bring her under the Grand Cross," I complained to Marco, shaking my head as we strode from the Norwood estate. Keeping my eyes on the move had become a constant habit. Always watching for an observer. Always cautious that I would be seen talking to the air. I was doubly aware of how dangerous a position I had put myself in with Alec, and hoped the man was too nervous to take action right away.

"So, bring her under," Marco shrugged.

"What if she falls?" I said, seeing the fool boy couldn't understand how ridiculous an idea it was. Children.

"She won't fall. You'll make sure she doesn't. And if she does, you can always just," he waved his hand in a mimic of an Aberrant's glyphwork.

"It's not that easy," I grumbled. "I'm not that good at glyphs yet, and Emelia ..." I shook my head again. "She's not like us."

"Eh, maybe you don't give her 'nough credit, sis. She's not like all the other rich folk you go 'round. I think she can do it."

"Damnit, Marco. You were supposed to agree with me," I groaned, but now we were on the road and the conversation became one-sided. It was for the better, because clearly the ghost didn't share my fears at going under the Grand Cross Bridge ever again. It wasn't long before the conversation ended entirely.

It was a hard walk through the midalts. The lower I walked, the worse the situation got. The loss of life had been immense. Family members cried in the streets. Some houses remained silent, and I tried not to think too hard on the cause, but the feeling of death was thick all around. Whispers and quick burns clogged the streets in wandering masses. Reeva had made it, though. Marco said that she had. Traveling through the midalts, it was hard to see how.

Still, the people of the slums—those with a home to escape to—were more accustomed to the fight to survive a drift, while the midalters had rarely had to make use of their drills in real-world applications. I was surprised at how high the drift had reached, but we all knew it was a possibility with a big enough storm below, even with the protective glyphs around the landmass.

"It's me," I announced, entering Reeva's squat. The lock was broken, and the door barely seemed to hold shut, but it was shelter. I held the door closed and drew up a quick glyph of repair for the lock. I didn't know why I trusted Reeva with the knowledge of just how tangled up in the fold I was, but I did.

"Thanks," she said distractedly from around the corner. She had sensed the magic and hadn't questioned it in the slightest. "Can you bolt it?"

I did so. "How did you find this place?"

"A little old woman used to live here," she said as I came around the corner. "I scoped it out a few times. You know, just to know who was around." She was staring hard at a man hunched on the floor in front of her, babbling. "Saw her dead in the street this morning."

"Is that ... Is that Beater?" I asked in confusion.

She nodded. "Looks like."

I watched the man scuttle from spot to spot on the floor, pressing his ear to the ground time and again. Reeva watched me watch him.

"I thought you saw his body."

"So did I, but here he is. I found him on the streets. The fumes seemed to avoid him like everybody else avoided him," Reeva said, her eyes returning to the erratic man. "He was a piece of shit, but nobody deserves this."

The ringleader had been tortured to breaking by the Aberrants. I could see the scars left on his flesh, but the assaults had gone deeper, snapping his mind. There was no sense behind it. Torturing the man this far could only have been for their fun. He scuttled to the next spot, then looked up at us expectantly as he repeated, "The Breaker brings our salvation. The Landbringer: our fall. Our fall ..."

He looked around with terror. "Our fall. We are falling. Falling. Falling."

"What is that he is saying?" I asked, with a pit forming in my stomach at his words.

Reeva shrugged. "The proclamations of a lunatic, I assume. He's been at it all morning and gods know how long before that."

His ear returned to the floor. "Can't you hear it? Can't you feel it? The sickness? The fall? The ground approaching. The snapping." He looked at us again, as though pleading. "The savior. The seals breaking. The … The Breaker brings our salvation. The Landbringer: our fall." His babbling bubbled down to inaudible mumbles as he moved from spot to spot.

"He thinks we are falling?" I asked. "What is the sickness he is talking about?"

Reeva looked from the man to me. "Sade. Look at him. He's insane. They snapped his brain. For kicks."

"Why would they release him, though?"

Reeva shrugged. "A cautionary tale?" She eyed the man uncomfortably as he continued around the hovel with his babbling. "I couldn't just leave him in the street, but this level of chaos is not within my capacity for tending."

Marco hid behind me nervously. I patted his shoulder, then dropped to a crouch before the man, watching his erratic behavior.

He listened to the ground at my feet, then pushed up to all fours and stared at me. There was no recognition. No sense in his eyes. "We're sinking. Sinking. Can't you hear us sinking? Listen." His ear returned to the ground.

"What will you do with him?" I asked, eyes returning to Reeva.

"I'm tempted to throw him into the abyss," she said with not even the slightest reaction from the man. "But it just doesn't seem right." She frowned. "You got me a posting, right? So I don't need to stay here watching this disaster all day?"

I nodded. "If you know anything about groundskeeping, you have a job."

"I'll learn."

I didn't think it would be as easy as Reeva thought just to learn the skill, but the woman was resourceful. I nodded.

"Hayden," I said to the man, but he didn't respond. Just moved here and there on his quest to press his ear to every inch of the hovel's floor. "Beater," I tried once more, and still no response.

"What are you listening to?"

This time he looked up. "The planet."

"That doesn't make any sense. It's not as though we are actually connected to the planet up here," I said, trying inexplicably to reason with a madman.

"We were once. Vale didn't rise from nowhere," he sounded surprisingly lucid for a moment. "We will return once again. The bindings are failing. We are sinking." His ear returned to the floor.

I straightened and looked at Reeva. "Do you think what he is saying is true? Do you think the landmasses are sinking into the abyss? We haven't had a drift like last night's in as long as I can remember."

Reeva shrugged. "I think he's lost it, Sade. I think he's rambling and raving. I think the Aberrants fried his brain just to see that they could. They made him think things that could drive anybody mad. Then I think they threw him out onto the streets to die."

I frowned, but nodded agreement. The woman was right. There was no denying that the ringleader had snapped.

Reeva cast Hayden a last look before turning to me, doing her best to pretend the man wasn't quietly babbling to himself behind her.

"If I'm taking on groundskeeping work, I don't suppose I still need a dress," she said.

"I don't suppose so."

"Do I need a funny accent like you?" She nudged me with her elbow playfully.

I smiled. "Only if you think it will add to your mystery."

"I intend to go as unnoticed as possible around your Charmer's family." Her smile faded into a grimace as she watched Hayden move about the floor. "Do you suppose they would have turned us into that, or just raped and killed us?"

I squeezed her hand. "Best not to think about it."

"I think I'm going to choose not to think about a lot of things." She was looking at the door now, and I was certain she was failing not to think of the bodies in the streets. Those who hadn't been able to find shelter.

23:

Katarina was in a better mood when I returned to the house. Better being only a relative term. She was still in a piss-poor mood. Still, she sought me out, joining me in my room with a little box under her arm. She hadn't bothered with getting dressed or putting on any makeup as she usually did, and that made me look at her with concern.

She gave me a tired little look and an eyeroll as she flopped down on my bed with a sigh. "I don't know how you got any sleep last night," she groaned, pulling my pillows over her face. "Even with the most attentive of distractions …"

I grinned. "I don't think I'm as strong a Death Sight as you."

She only groaned again, then threw a pillow aside so she could breathe unhindered by down. "What a useless ability to be strong in."

"Who were you with?"

She cast me a disparaging look. "You don't want to know." It had to be somebody who knew she was a Death Sight and was close at hand. "Fine," she growled. "Tomas."

"I always suspected you two were up to no good," I teased her.

She glared at me. "It is a very complicated relationship," she said dryly. I could only imagine.

She rolled to her side and unlatched her little wooden box. Lifting the lid, she poked around for a bit, then picked up a string and threw it at me before flopping back down.

I looked at the braid she had tossed my way. Hair.

"It's yours," Katarina said. "I don't want it. And I didn't ask you if I could have it."

I lifted the thin braid.

"Katarina," I said quietly.

"What?" She groused, turning her head to look at me.

"Thank you."

She scowled at me, but I could see a softening at the edges of her eyes. I considered the strand, then allowed the glyph to form in my mind and ignited the braid on the release.

Katarina frowned at me, not moving from where she lay. "What's that? Another one of your little vagabond tricks? Some sort of sleight of hand?"

I shook my head slowly and drew the glyph for revitalization in the air with my finger, then released its intent into Katarina.

She perked up a little with several blinks, but didn't move from where she lay.

"You mean to say that you could have been curing my hangovers all this time?" she growled.

I smiled. "For some reason, I thought you would be more upset."

"Oh, don't get me wrong, dear, I am right pissed. I'm just too tired to do much about it. Did Deara know?"

"She was the one who figured it out."

"Of course she was. And you are just so damn unaware of yourself, you never even knew you were an Aberrant," she said disparagingly. "You know I hate Aberrants?"

I nodded. "Does that mean you hate me now?"

"Oh honey, I have despised you from the day we met," she said with a smile. "You didn't have to tell me what you are, Sade," she said with an unexpected gentleness. "In your shoes I never would have. But you did, and I suppose that is endearing, or sweet, or overly trusting. Now, can you give me another shot of whatever that was? I still feel dog-tired."

I laughed and joined her on the bed. "I'll consider it. If you tell me what all you have in that box."

She rolled onto her back, pulling the box up onto her chest and fingering through her small collection of braids. "Amplifier, Charmer, Sleuth," her finger paused, and she grinned. "If I'm entirely honest, this particular donation was not made entirely willingly, either. Sleuths don't really like when others can tell if they are lying, and this man did nothing but, it seemed." She chuckled.

"How do you find all these people?"

She shrugged. "It's not like there's a secret society of those of us with Moxie or anything, but you start to notice the signs of it on folks. Somehow, we always seem to gravitate to each other. I'm sure Deara would have had some theory on that." She sighed and lifted one of the braids from her box. "I know you two were trying to figure out why your memories are so fractured. Did you ever learn why?" She looked at me. "I could try to help you if you needed, still."

"I did it to myself. With a glyph." I sighed. "I honestly don't really want to keep poking at it."

She nodded with an understanding look in her eye, set the braid back down, and relatched the box, setting it aside. She sighed and curled up against my side in an unexpected display of affection. "I miss Deara," Katarina said, her voice barely a whisper.

I rubbed her back. "I know."

She was quiet with her thoughts for long enough that I wondered if she had nodded off.

"Did she tell you who killed her?" she asked quietly.

"I know," I admitted.

Katarina nodded into my shoulder. "Would I have gotten myself killed?"

"Very possibly."

She sighed and shifted to look up at me. "Did you do anything about it?"

"Only when pushed."

"I don't imagine you skinned him alive, as I may have, so what did you do?"

"Deara gave me her memories of that night. I gave them to him. Made him relive them from her eyes, feel her pain, experience her fear time and again."

She swallowed and settled back against my side. "Without retaliation?"

I didn't think it wise to tell her how recently this had all occurred and said, "Just because he hasn't retaliated yet doesn't mean he won't."

She sighed again, deeper this time. "I'll protect you." She looked at me with narrowed eyes. "Though I suppose you *are* a gods-damned Aberrant." She laid her head back down. "I don't really understand how that all works, but honestly, I don't rightly care either."

"I really thought you would be more upset."

"I'm surprised you told me. You and Deara liked your little secrets." She shrugged. "So did we, though." She took my hand. "I hate the College, Sade. I hate the Society. I don't hate you. That you are an Aberrant doesn't matter as long as you don't start acting like one of those beasts from the College."

"I don't intend to go through a complete personality change," I assured her.

"You would be surprised how quickly a drop of power can corrupt," she said softly. "How thoroughly it can change a person."

"You will watch out for me."

24:

"I'm here to see Lady Rasczek," I said to the butler when he greeted me at the massive wooden doors to Rasczek Manor.

"The young lady is currently on an expedition with Doctor Green."

"I am not here to see Emelia." I felt a little guilt for coming when I knew she would be away.

The butler's mouth pinched, but he bowed and retreated to deliver the message. I was left alone in the entryway to look up at the vaulted ceiling and grand staircases.

The *clack-clack* of the woman's heels clicking down the hall brought my eyes back forward. The butler strode just behind his mistress, looking ready to eject me from the house at the woman's slightest hint.

Lady Rasczek stopped in front of me, putting her hands on her hips. I felt a familiar waft of intimidation strike me and straightened my spine a touch more to resist it. The woman was not large by any means, our eyes meeting on equal level, but she cut an imposing figure, only made more so by her meticulous attention to her appearance. Not a hair out of place, not a wrinkle of fabric to be seen on her clothing. Even the subtle signs of age seemed by design.

"Make it quick," she said in her deep staccato.

I looked once at the butler, then squared up against the woman. "Leeta Norwood. You know why she was ejected from her Chair."

For a moment the woman faltered, clearly not having expected that. "You want to know about Leeta?" she said slowly. She raised a perfectly manicured hand and dismissed the butler while studying me. "And here I thought you were going to try to blackmail our family." She turned on her heels and started into the house.

I stared after her, uncertain if she wanted me to follow or not, then decided to pursue her.

She didn't say anything until we were in the study.

"Leeta Norwood," Lady Rasczek said, sitting at the massive wooden desk. The carved lions only made the piece more imposing. She gestured at the seat across from her and steepled her fingers.

"You do know something, then."

Lady Rasczek's eyebrow raised as she considered me. Here, behind her desk, the woman seemed less imposing, but I still felt nervous in her presence.

"Why do you care? Thinking of running for a Chair?" Her mouth lifted at the corner in an amused smirk. "You do know there are no available positions for representatives from Vale, don't you? Not to mention the extensive background check."

"That's not my interest."

"Katarina then?"

"Not hers either." I shook my head. "No. We don't want the Chair. But there is a connection there. Once Leeta lost the Chair, the Norwood clan was verily destroyed. Just enough of it remaining to let the tabloids call it a sequence of unfortunate events rather than wholesale murder."

She studied me, her lips pinching into a tight line. "From what I understand, you don't come from their family. So, why do you care?"

"I have their name now, don't I?"

She drew a long breath in through her nose as she looked down it at me. "I wonder how much they have told you ..."

She knew what the Norwoods were. "It had something to do with them being Death Sights?"

"A dangerous admission," Lady Rasczek said, but with an air of approval. "So, you are one too. You are not from one of the major families, though, and as far as I know, the College has all but locked down stray Death Sights. Somehow, you seem to have slipped through the cracks ... Interesting."

"More or less interesting than you being a Charmer, my lady?"

Her eyes narrowed. "Emelia ..." she growled.

"I can feel it on you. You are subtle, but I know you are trying to keep me intimidated."

She laughed. "If I'm able to intimidate you, it is because you are at least a little bit intimidated. I don't have quite the skill that my daughter has."

I sniffed. "I suppose I inadvertently tipped my hand, then."

She gave a small smile, a tight little thing, but one that had a true hint of amusement in it.

"Where do you come from?" Lady Rasczek asked.

"Your daughter knows. Isn't that enough?"

"Hm. So, not a researcher's daughter."

"I didn't say that. Just maybe not the researcher everybody thinks." I folded my hands in my lap. "Leeta," I said, steering the conversation back to the topic of interest.

Lady Rasczek sat pensively. "Leeta," she agreed. "If you know she was a Death Sight, that should be enough for you to draw your conclusions as to what happened."

I shook my head. "I wonder though, how many of the Society Chairs would actually care that she was a Death Sight, as opposed to, say, a Charmer."

She looked a little intrigued. "I'm not going to pretend you are not smart enough to have figured out that a significant number of the Society Chairs have some tie to the fold. So, your question is, who in particular wants the Death Sights removed from the equation?"

"And your answer is?"

She raised an eyebrow. "Who has the power to change the mindsets of that many Society leaders?"

"I understand the College likes keeping their pet Death Sights, that they take the 'strays,' as you call them, but that doesn't explain the ejection from the Society."

"Maybe not, but who runs the College?"

"I assume you don't mean the Chancellor. So, you must mean …" My voice drifted as I almost lost my thought, but with a breath, I found it again. "You must mean the gods … Jespair," the God of the Aberrants and leader of all the gods. It wasn't unheard of for the gods to meddle in the political affairs of the Society, but to take aim on one family in particular seemed an extreme. Still, surely Jespair had sanctioned the extermination of the Locks. Maybe now her eyes were set on the Death Sights. Lady Rasczek said nothing, so I continued on. "You mean to imply that Jespair killed the Norwoods?"

She looked surprised. "You were able to say it? And here I was, ready for this conversation to go nowhere but in circles." She looked momentarily impressed. "In that case, perhaps this is not a useless endeavor and complete waste of my time and breath."

"I am glad that I inspire so much confidence in you, my lady."

She sat forward. "Oh, it is not confidence you inspire in me. But fear. For my daughter. Because if you are able to pursue this, as I know you will, you risk dragging her down with you. If the gods wanted Leeta out of the picture, succeeded in doing so, and hamstrung her family so thoroughly they could never reclaim their position in the Society, do you really think I want my daughter associated with somebody who might go poking and prodding into an issue years dead? The Norwoods were not just some industrialist house." I read the comparison she didn't want to voice between the Norwoods and her own house. If the gods could tear down one old family, what was to stop them from taking down another?

"I won't ask questions if you give me the answers. Why would the gods want Leeta removed from her authority?"

"Believe it or not, I do not have all the answers, Miss Norwood. Towards the end, Leeta had interesting friends with interesting thoughts. Perhaps it had something to do with that, but if you were to ask any of the Chairs who participated in the vote, they would not be able to tell you clearly why they ousted her. So don't go asking. It won't only get you in trouble; it would be pointless."

"Is your husband included in the mass amnesia?"

She gave a small and very tight nod. "I trust this is enough information for you to see that the matter with Leeta Norwood is best left unprodded, unless you have ambitions to end up as she did. In which case, you will leave my daughter out of it."

I contemplated my hands a moment. That the gods were behind the destruction of the Norwoods was a bridge beyond what I had expected. I had come to Lady Rasczek seeking only a confirmation that the deaths of the Death Sights had not all been happenstance. I raised my eyes to the woman. "You will not tell Emelia I was here, I expect?"

She acknowledged with only a look.

I stood. "Thank you, my lady."

Studying me, she exhaled through her nose. "This proved more intriguing a conversation than I had anticipated, Miss Norwood," she admitted. "I've told Emelia time and again that she can keep whatever lovers she wants. I will protect her and our family from the rumors and scandal. As long as she takes a suitable spouse."

"And in this scenario, I am only ever the mistress on the side."

"As a Norwood, be happy you are at least that." She gave me a knowing look, then nodded toward the door, lifting her pen. "You know your way out."

I set my hand on the door handle, then stopped. "Last question. Why did you leave politics?"

She looked up from her correspondence. "Because I know how to protect my family, Miss Norwood. Sometimes it is better to just let things run their course. There is no sense in tying your own noose." She returned her eyes to her paper and pen. I took my leave.

25:

"Did you know any of Leeta's associates?" I asked Katarina cautiously as we got ready for yet another soiree one evening. I had let the matter rest for weeks after speaking with Lady Rasczek, but curiosity got the better of me.

She thought for a moment. "No. My great aunt was already getting old when I was born, so I can't say I took much of an interest in who she passed her time with. Besides, she was always busy with matters of the Society and all that hubbub. I assume most of her acquaintances were of a political nature. Then she died pretty much as soon as she got ousted from her position." She looked at me curiously. "Why do you ask?"

"No reason, I guess. I was just curious." It didn't seem a matter that Katarina had any interest in dissecting, nor did she seem to have any knowledge on the matter.

"Are you wondering why she was ousted?"

I shrugged, but nodded. "Do you know why?"

"No. But if I had to guess, she was starting to slip with her age. Maybe she talked to too many dead, but I remember her being a bit of a squirrely one. She made claims that the …" Katarina's expression fell as she seemed to forget what it was that her great aunt had been proclaiming. "That … the … hmm …"

I watched Katarina struggle with her words with interest. This wasn't the first time this had happened.

"That the what?" I prompted.

Katarina looked at me dumbly. "That the what what? What were we talking about?"

"Your Great Aunt Leeta. What claims was she making before she died?"

Katarina cocked her head at me with a pitying look. "My dear, I don't know why you would ask such a strange question."

I gave her a quizzical look. "That's what we were talking about. You said Leeta was making claims that got her ousted from her Chair."

Katarina raised a dainty eyebrow at me and then shrugged. "I have no idea what you are talking about, dear." She turned back to her mirror and her makeup. "You'd better hurry up now."

Apprehensively I returned to my preparations. I looked over Katarina's shoulder at the mirror as I wove my hair back. "Is Leeta still around?”

“She was a quick burn.” Katarina said as she outlined her eyes. She straightened and lifted a pin from her vanity. Turning to me to slide the pin into my hair, she said, “Don’t ask about Leeta, Sade. I’ve gone down that rabbit hole and it leads nowhere.” She took her hands away from fussing over my hair and met my eyes.

I gave her a small, dissatisfied nod.

“Leave it, Sade.”

“I’ll leave it,” I promised.

Katarina’s lips pinched. She brushed a stray hair from my forehead, then nodded with approval. “Let’s try to have some fun tonight. The only reason we were invited to this was because of you, you know.”

The Rasczek’s anniversary party was not one I was entirely excited to attend. Even though the invitation had boasted Lord and Lady Rasczek’s names, I knew it was Emelia who had forced the issue with her parents. Comfort levels be damned, it was not exactly an invitation that could be rejected.

26:

Katarina found me watching the party from the balcony above the ballroom. Below, Emelia’s sister, Lynn, in from her time politicking on Junction, was drawing quite the crowd. She knew how to bend the ears of the mass of well-to-dos; a skill she used as a representative of Vale. Across the ballroom, Emelia’s black sheep doctor of a brother had ferreted himself away into a dark corner with a young woman. My eyes continued their scan, finding Emelia laughing with a small cluster of her own. The woman was hot on the heels of her sister for currying favor.

I couldn’t help but notice Alec Gao’s absence from this and the last several parties. Rumor was he had suffered a psychological break and was now quietly tucked away somewhere far from the flashbulbs of the press. I cooed my regrets along with the tittering masses.

“You’re not very good at these still, are you?” Katarina said, joining me in leaning against the banister.

“Well, somebody keeps abandoning me at them, so how am I

to learn?" I said lightly.

Her mouth pulled to the side thoughtfully. "I suppose that somebody would be me. It was rude of me to do so," she admitted, nudging me with her elbow. "Here's a hint. At social gatherings you should socialize." She grinned.

"I am just taking a breath. All I ever hear about is my father's research, which I know nothing about, or greedy comments about Emelia's gowns."

"They know you make them," Katarina said with a dainty shrug.

"I also designed three of the suits down there," I said, spotting the attire in question, "and the very dress on your body."

"All of which have received compliments," Katarina pointed out. "You have a name for yourself now, Sade."

"Making rich people clothing," I said, uncertain how I felt about that.

"Isn't that what you wanted?"

"It is," I assured her. "And I still love it. I just," I groaned. "I'm just so tired of all the side-eye compliments and covetous little remarks that seem to accompany Emelia's dresses in particular."

"You've been in the game long enough to know rumors are currency. You and Emelia are not the most discreet," Katarina said, trying to keep her disdain for the woman out of her voice.

I sighed.

Katarina joined me in the sigh and then gave me a commiserating half smile. "Look at it this way, dear. Emelia only stands to lose going with you, with a Norwood. She doesn't need our money, and our status will only be an anchor to her. That she's willing to be so open with you in spite of that reality ..." She gave me a coy look. "I would take it as a good thing."

"She needs to leave herself open to political arrangements," I said. "If she's not careful, our indiscretion and those rumors will close those potential arrangements off."

"Oh, and you two have already discussed this, then?" Katarina asked in surprise. "You *are* open with each other, aren't you? And you, what, agreed to be her not-so-secret mistress?"

I pursed my lips and Katarina sighed again, knowing that was a yes. "I may not like her or her uppity family very much, but she likes you, Sade. A lot, it seems," she said, as though it pained her to admit.

We watched the party goers below. The Lord and Lady Rasczek merrily accepting congratulations and toasts to their health and prosperity at the head of the room. The clusters of gossipers and those who chose to dance the night away. The knots formed and shifted, some couples breaking away. The gossip shifting as the groups did.

"Deara and I always used to come up here when we needed a break from all the claptrap and judgment," Katarina said quietly. "We used to watch the crowd, like we are now, and make up stories. Like Lady Thai and her salacious youth. Mister Ketz and his twenty cats. Just nonsense stories really. I miss it." She frowned, her eyes turning to me. "I miss my sister, Sade." She swallowed and closed her eyes. "I miss who I was before. I miss who she was." She looked at me. "You brought her back a little bit, you know? Back to what she was like before. Made her happy. It can be so hard keeping them from turning or from peeling away." She shook her head. "She was tired, Sade. I knew it. I knew she felt like she couldn't leave me alone and that only exhausted her more. I could tell she was about to move on before she did. I ... I miss her, but I ... I'm glad she's gone." She frowned at the admission. "Am I a terrible person for that?"

"No, Katarina. No."

She smiled weakly. "Sade. Will you promise me something? Promise you won't do anything stupid and get yourself killed? I can't have another sister die. I can't. The Rasczeks. They have enemies. They have rivals. They have targets on their backs. More than we do. If you and Emelia are really going to be tying your airships together, I just want you to be careful. In the great game of the Society and their Chairs, we Norwoods aren't anything but expendable."

I set my hand on hers and nodded. "I'll be careful."

She smiled thinly, setting her other hand on top of mine. Something slipped from her to me. A memory of Deara standing in my very spot. I kept my face still, careful not to give away that I had seen what currently seemed to be playing in the woman's mind.

Katarina shook her head, then patted my hand and straightened. "Well, we'd best get back to it," she said with her usual facade of joy as she pulled me from the railing. "You know Emelia had the audacity to ask me where you had slunk away to?"

"And my suspicions on where that was seem to have been correct," Emelia said, coming up the steps to join us.

"And with that, I am going to retire for the night," Katarina said.

"Alone?" I asked.

Katarina sneered at me. "Sometimes, I do enjoy my alone time. Now, the real question is, should I expect you home tonight?" Katarina asked with a surreptitious look at Emelia.

"I'll find a motorcarriage if needed," I said.

Katarina nodded. "Have a good night, you two."

Emelia took her spot at the railing without a word.

I settled beside her, waiting. There was something bothering the woman. I didn't need to be a Charmer to know that.

"My mother has stopped speaking ill of you these last couple weeks," Emelia said casually. She was definitely peeved.

"Your mother was speaking ill of me?"

Emelia cast me a look that was less than amused. "Imogen says she saw you visiting with my mother while I was away."

"Ah. That's what this is about. I thought your mother would have kept your staff tight-lipped about that."

"So, it is true?"

"I'm not going to lie about that."

"And your conversation with my mother consisted of …?"

I cast her an amused glance. "Do you think I tried to blackmail her, or threaten her into liking me?"

Emelia's lips pinched and she looked back down at the ballroom. "I didn't say she likes you."

I sniffed. "Yes. That may have been a reach." I turned Emelia's face to look at me. "I went to her to ask about Leeta. She said something on the night of the cloud drift that made me think. Wonder if she knew more than she was letting on."

Emelia laughed. "You went behind my back to ask her about a political maneuver at the Society Chair level? Maybe she does like you." She shook her head and turned to lean her back against the railing as she considered me. "She will still never approve of you."

"Oh, I know. Don't get me wrong, we talked about that too." I took her hand for only a moment. "I'm sorry I didn't tell you. Are you mad at me?"

"I was peeved when Imogen told me," she admitted. "Especially since it has been weeks that I had no idea, and I have seen you more than a few times." She narrowed her eyes at me playfully. "Now that I know what you talked to my mother about, I'm not mad." She sighed. "It's refreshing not having to listen to her pointed remarks. I was surprised when she actually agreed to invite you and Katarina tonight. I'm glad she did." She kissed my cheek.

"Don't you worry when you do that?"

"Not in the slightest. The gossip has already taken root." She kissed my other cheek. "I am not ashamed of you, Sade." She kissed me once more, lips soft against mine, then smiled. "Tomorrow?"

"Tomorrow what?"

She just winked. "I'll stop by."

I didn't trust that devious wink at all.

27:

Katarina said nothing when Emilia showed herself into the house. The two women exchanged looks and nothing else. The ice between them still seemed to be in the early stages of thawing.

"I don't know why she hates me so much," Emelia grumbled as we walked toward my room. "I thought we were past all this."

She was wearing a very sensible pair of trousers and a simple shirt, but still managed to make the clothing look elegant. Still, the change in her usual attire had my eyebrow raising. Trousers and a shirt: the bane of Katarina's existence. The heiress's disapproval could have stemmed from Emelia's wardrobe alone.

I dodged around the little ghost girl who liked to run up and down the halls. She had been at it for hours already, much to Katarina's ire.

"I don't think she hates you," I said, tsking at the reckless dead. She may not be hurt in a collision with my legs, but I could still break my neck. "She just likes being difficult. I wouldn't think too much on it."

"You two better not get too comfortable," Katarina called after us in a bitter snipe.

Emelia raised an eyebrow at me as though I had been proven wrong.

"She has guests this evening," I said dismissively.

"So, I'm to take it she's looking out for me and my reputation?"

"More likely mine, but yes." I took her hand with a smile. "I am glad you came by."

"I don't know that you will be happy that I did in a moment," she said as we entered my room. She closed the door soundly behind us.

"Why? Did you fire Reeva?"

"No. It's nothing like that. She's been doing a wonderful job. Wouldn't label her as the most personable, and she's good at making herself scarce, but the work is getting done." She shook her head, and I spotted the hint of nervousness in her as she intertwined her fingers. "No. That's not why I came … I thought you might agree to take me under the Grand Cross."

My face fell. I had hoped that, with time, the fancy had faded for the woman. That maybe she had come to her senses. Here I had been hoping that her choice of trousers over skirts had been driven by recent changes in fashion trends of the young ladies who came to Mrs. Sandfjord's. That my little campaign among the well-to-dos had started to tip the scales. Or that maybe the woman wanted to visit the Conservatory. Really, anything but going under the Grand Cross Bridge. I swallowed.

"Today?"

"Why not? The weather is clear. There are no drifts anticipated." She shrugged and smiled nervously.

"Why do you want to do this so badly?" I asked.

"I have never done anything in my entire life half as exciting as what you have," she said, admitting a truth I know pained her. "I go to balls. I host parties. I curry favor and collect debts. I talk and talk and talk. I want to do something other than that, just once. I need to know if I'm making the wrong choices for my life."

"And you think making a crossing that only the Hardest Hands and the most desperate make will tell you if you are on the wrong path in life?"

"It will tell me *something* about myself, I am sure."

"It is incredibly dangerous, Em."

"I trust you."

"The weather could change at any moment."

"I trust you," she repeated.

"If you fall, there's nothing but the abyss to greet you."

She swallowed nervously.

"Would you like to reconsider?" I asked softly, hoping she would.

"No."

It had been too much to hope for, anyway.

"That explains your choice of attire," I sighed. "It is still not enough."

Her eyes drifted to the jumpsuit hanging in my open wardrobe.

"For some reason, I think you may have something more suitable for me to wear if this will not do."

I groaned. If the woman had a death wish, who was I to stop her? She smiled, knowing she had won.

"Have you ever climbed before?"

"I've been practicing on the northern edge. Katarina is not the only one who enjoys a little physical activity," she said pridefully. "Just because I don't punch people in the face doesn't mean I don't have the strength for this."

"I never implied anything like that," I said, taking my two jumpsuits from my wardrobe. Somewhere in the back of my mind I had known that she would follow through with this request. Still, I had told myself the jumpsuits had been a craft of nostalgia. The tight yet unrestricting fabric a comfort for me. "I've never taken Katarina under the Grand Cross either," I pointed out, handing a jumpsuit to Emelia. "That should be nice and tight."

"Not too tight, I hope."

"Exactly as tight as it needs to be to keep you from being swept away into the abyss and dragging me with you."

She looked it over with another nervous swallow, then started to change.

"I wish you would reconsider this." I set out a leather jacket and a pair of gloves.

"I'm not going to."

"Fine. Then you will want those. The gale only gets stronger under the bridge. And it is not as though the Enforcers just let anybody climb under the bridge. We are going to have to slip past their patrols just to get to the underside. They are likely to shoot first and ask questions later. It won't matter if you are a high lady or a gutter rat when they pull the trigger. Life is cheap in the slums, and you are going to have to look like you belong when we go down there. Are you certain you want to do this today?"

She sniffed, pulling on the jumpsuit. "Yes. And trying to get in my head isn't going to stop me."

With a heavy sigh and a shake of my head, I gave in and started changing. "Fine. But we are not going the length. The width is a hard enough journey, and I don't want to be caught without the rock face to shelter against if a storm does kick up."

"I'll agree to that."

"I hate this," I said, pulling on my jumpsuit.

She kissed my cheek. "I know. But you are going to keep me safe."

28:

"This is amazing," Emelia said, clinging to the support beams as she looked down at the abyss.

"No. It is horribly dangerous," I corrected, yelling over the winds and feeling very foolish indeed for agreeing to this noblewoman's request. I fixed the cloth over her mouth and nose nervously. With my luck, a stray fume drift would find us. With my luck, I would be found responsible for the death of a high lady seeking a thrill I never should have agreed to bring her on. With my luck, we would both be swept into the abyss before the day was out.

I watched her as she braved the winds and I knew that if she fell, I would follow. I looked down at the cloudline. It looked closer and more ominous than I remembered. I had been out of the game for a while, and already my days on the rise had made me soft-bellied at the sight of the big drop. Had I lost my hard hands so quickly?

I took Emelia's hand and led her along the beams, the rope tied around our waists a lifeline that would kill us both if one of us were to slip. The winds raged, but my feet at least were still sure. I managed to get her into a pocket, a small refuge from the roaring winds of the constant storm raging below.

"Amazing," she said again in the semi-calm as she looked down at the flashes of lightning ripping through the clouds.

I watched her with a roil of apprehension. One misstep on her part and we could both fall. An overly forceful gust of wind. An errant planetary fume. But the excitement behind her goggles fed an excitement in myself that vied for supremacy over the fear.

She looked up at me, holding tight to the support beam beside her.

"I know you won't let anything happen to me, and I will not let anything happen to you." Even with the grand distraction of the abyss, she could still sense my anxiety.

I smiled behind the cover of the cloth over my mouth and nose and nodded. "I know. Are you ready for another stretch?"

She looked down, then nodded quickly. I didn't need to be a Charmer to see her building her courage to go back out into the winds.

I held her hand tight as we moved from beam to beam. I had practically grown up on the underbelly of the landmass and its bridges, but even for me, this maneuver was dangerous. We reached one pocket, then another before I got us to the cave. The small nook was the perfect resting place for those desperate enough to make this climb. It was a risk bringing Emelia here; I wasn't the only one who knew about the spot, but even in the midst of a gang war, vagabonds on the climb made room for each other at the cave. There was a respect in having made it so far and an understanding that those who came here often had nowhere else to go. We were making progress faster than I had expected, but still the going was slow, and already the day was coming swiftly to an end. We could only rest for a few moments, but we needed the reprieve.

I checked the spot before pulling her in behind me.

Outside, the clouds below were taking on a savage tint that I knew all too well. There was a storm below, and that meant that soon the weather would turn up here. It would not be impossible to continue the climb, but getting caught on the underside of the bridge when the weather turned with an inexperienced climber set my heart racing.

There was sound at the back of the cave, another group already occupying the space. I leaned close to Emelia to talk as quietly as the winds allowed. "If we encounter anybody else, try not to get noticed. Just let me do the talking, alright?" I said, dropping the Junction accent that had become my truth in the last year. That had apparently been my truth in my childhood. "We should rest here before continuing on." I eyed the cloudline again and knew that moving on would not happen for some time yet.

I looked toward the sound of laughter. The space had changed in the time I had been away. There was still the small alcove for those on the climb to rest and move on. But beyond, it appeared a tunnel had been carved. At the other end of the tunnel came sounds suspiciously reminiscent of a bar.

"What's over there?" Emelia asked, taking her goggles from over her eyes and peering down the tunnel.

"Something new," I said apprehensively.

"Can we look?"

In the subtle glow, we could see the tunnel bloom into a room. Not a room, a fully formed tavern.

"What in the abyss …" I muttered as Emelia excitedly pulled me toward the space.

We were halted at the entry by a thickly built woman and her poised fingers pointing at our faces.

"Why are you down here?" the woman asked, her finger dancing in a glyph that enforced the truth.

"I wanted to impress her," I said against my own volition.

"I wanted to impress her," Emelia said, looking equally put off at the forced confession.

The two of us looked at each other and the Aberrant laughed. "Well, I'll leave you two to work that one out between yourselves, but first: rules. If you drink, you don't climb until I say you do. I've got rooms in the back if needed. Which brings me to rule two: respect your fellow traveler. If you don't, you get thrown. If you are going to have a fight, you have two minutes to sort it out before I sort it for you. This is a safe haven. Everybody here made the climb for some reason. Which brings me to the final rule: no Aberrants. No Enforcers. No snitches."

I looked at her quizzically. "You are an Aberrant, though."

"Non-affiliated," she said gruffly. "Which is to say that if the College were to find me, I would be put down. So. No Aberrants. Any more questions, or can I get you ladies something warm to eat?"

"Something warm would be nice," Emelia said sweetly. "But I don't suppose you brought any money?" she asked me.

"No bother, ladies. Welcome to Rhoda's Rest." She stepped aside to admit us to her humble hole in the wall.

"You are Rhoda, I take it?" I asked, still not wholly come to terms with a bar existing in such a locale.

"Astute. And this is an inn for the desperate souls forced out onto this climb. Or, as it turns out, foolish young women trying to dazzle each other for a thrill." She gave us both a piercing look and Emelia looked a touch shame-faced at having demanded such an expedition. "Go and have a seat. Chat about how you don't need to endanger each other's lives to impress one another, and I'll bring something 'round." The woman gave us both an amused look before letting us enter her establishment.

Emelia took my hand and pulled me to a table in the back. I would have preferred staying closer to the exit in case we needed to make a hasty escape, but allowed her to lead.

"Thank you for bringing me here, Sade," Emelia said, looking around. "Though I know *this* was a surprise for you."

"Did you really ask for this to impress me?" I asked.

"Did you really agree to impress me?" she asked with a smirk.

"If you will remember, Em, I only agreed after a lot of hinting and haranguing."

She shrugged and winked. "Yes. Maybe I did put some pressure on you." She smiled as she looked around at the dimly lit lodging house. "This is strange, right?"

"You mean the underground inn that you have to risk your life climbing across the underside of Vale to get to? Yes. It is very strange."

"As long as I haven't been missing out on this my entire life," she said playfully, looking at the other occupants of the resting point. A young man sat in the corner, looking jittery with nerves. A man on the run. A woman hunched protectively over her plate, watching the rest of us. A boy held tight to the pack on his front, not touching the food set before him. A small handful of scruffy vagabonds, the source of the previous laughter, sat gathered around a table and dice. They were the only ones who seemed in high spirits, fueled by drink as they were.

"I am glad you have had a safe life," I said quietly, watching the others continue their gambling. "I am glad you don't know the exhilaration or terror of a dive, nor the uncertainty of a heist that could go wrong at any moment and lead to an Aberrant's torture. I am glad that we all have you working with Doctor Green to feed more families. I am glad that you are doing work that matters. That can save lives and take away some of the pain of growing up without."

"Sade ..."

I looked her in the eye. "I mean it, Emelia. My memories may feel exhilarating, but I have felt that same thing in yours when you work at what you love. I could feel the same rise in you when you had that breakthrough with that little red flower. I couldn't tell you what in the abyss any of that was, but I could tell it meant something to you."

For a moment she smiled at the memory. "We were researching

cold hardiness in certain strains of plants to aid in crop…" she shook her head, looking embarrassed as she cut herself off. "I didn't realize you saw that memory."

I cringed. "It was an accident. It just sort of slipped over a few weeks ago while I was doing your fitting for last night's dress." I took her hand in mine. "My point is that, at the end of every one of those exciting and dangerous dives, all I have done is hurt people or taken from them. Not you."

"You will be disappointed in me, then, for pursuing politics."

I shook my head with a smile. "No. As you said, your scientists need somebody in their corner. You have the voice and the drive for it. You can bring about change. If it is what you want to do."

She closed her eyes and, with a heavy sigh, folded forward until her forehead was pressed against our hands.

"Is she alright?" Rhoda asked, setting down a couple bowls of stew and a pair of mugs.

"She's fine," Emelia said for herself, straightening once again. She looked at me long and hard.

"Well, the storm is picking up out there," the innkeeper said, setting her hands on her hips. "You two picked a bad night to play chicken over the abyss. You will weather it here."

"I didn't agree to that," I said, uneasy with the Aberrant's proclamations. If Emelia was not returned home, I didn't know what would transpire. I could not imagine the chaos of Lady Rasczek kicking down the doors of Norwood Manor with a posse of Enforcers at her back.

"When you stepped into my home, you agreed to my rules. You two will stay the night and if the storm is abated enough in the morning, you can carry on in your little escapade. The door is sealed already," she added, gesturing toward the entryway. It looked no different than it had when we entered, but now I could feel the hum of additional magic emitting from the entry.

"Thank you for your hospitality," Emelia said graciously before I could put forth any further argument.

Rhoda smiled broadly at her. "I'm nothing if not a good hostess." She looked at me curiously, then left.

"What was that about?" I grumbled at the woman's back, a touch nervous she had sensed something in me I didn't want her to.

"Well, we may as well get comfortable then," Emelia said excitedly, taking a long drink from her mug. "It's not bad." She looked toward the group of gamblers. "From your memories you seemed pretty well-versed at dice. You want to go play?"

"I don't know that we should be drawing attention to ourselves, Em."

She grabbed my hand and pulled me to my feet. "Let's have fun tonight, Sade. Please." And, of course, I relented.

29:

I woke, content with Emelia at my side in our strange little lodge for the night. Already I could tell the air wasn't as charged as it had been the day before. The storm below had calmed as much as it ever truly did.

Emelia hummed serenely in my arms. I held her tight then lightly brushed my lips over her neck and down her shoulder to the faint scar I had been studying before she woke.

"What's this?" I asked, kissing the scar then resting my chin on her shoulder.

"A remnant of childhood," she said after a brief hesitation. "A memory of a fall."

"It looks more like an incision than an accident," I commented, feeling she was hiding something but only wanting to press lightly. The straight precision of the scar was what had caught my eye. The intention in the cut.

She turned in my arms, facing the scar away from me with a smile on her lips.

"We are alone without concern of being interrupted and all you want to do is ask me about some silly scar?" She asked with a twinkle in her eye.

She didn't want to tell me, so I let the matter drop and instead allowed her to draw me in.

"It is certainly not *all* I want to do." I answered her smile with a kiss. Her hips pressed closer and for a moment I was tempted. Our locale set a nervous thread in me that had me halting. A monk's cell of a room carved into the underside of Vale was not the most comforting of dens. "We should really continue our climb while we are well rested."

She chuckled, her mouth on my throat. "I need a few minutes

to wake up still." Her lips were unrelenting in their exploration, and I gave in.

It was only when we both lay still, content with her head on my chest and my hand on her back, that I tried again.

"Are you ready?" I asked her. "With calm enough air, it shouldn't take long for us to get back up."

She shifted to smile down at me. "I would rather spend the entire day underground with you than have to return home. But you are right, we should go."

I kissed her cheek and pulled her to her feet.

In the main room, the dice players from the night before continued to slumber in snoring heaps. The anxious young man had disappeared, either still in bed or out on the climb. Rhoda gave us a nod as we passed.

"Be careful out there, ladies," she warned. "The winds have died down, but you know how bad the fumes can get after a storm."

Emelia waited until we were back at the cave entrance, lifeline secured between us, cloth tied over noses and mouths, and goggles fast over our eyes to ask, "Do the fumes reach up here often?"

"Don't think too hard about it," I said, checking and rechecking the lifeline. "If you start feeling strange, lightheaded, anything, you will let me know."

She nodded.

"Good. And I'll do the same." I stepped out onto the hatchwork of beams, checking the winds and the security of our footing before holding my hand back to Emelia.

The morning air was relatively calm compared to the sudden storm of the day before. Below us the cloudline glowed in welcoming shades of red and orange. At least if I fell today, I would have a nice view.

I climbed ahead of Emelia. We were getting close to the end of the crossing. I didn't like coming up from underneath during the day. Too much chance of being spotted and questioned by Enforcers. Too easy to have innocent intent appear less-than in their eyes.

Waiting for Emelia as she crossed another support beam, I smiled. Her feet were already well adjusted to the work and her hands harder than I had thought they would be.

"You are a quick study," I called over the winds. "You could have been a Hard-Handed vagabond in another life."

She grabbed my arm and took a rest against the vertical beside me. "I told you, I climb," she said. "There are some technicals on the mountain that you need to be able to climb to get to some of the rarer varieties of wildflowers that Naila and I have studied."

"Ah, context," I laughed. "Now I believe you. I believe you would figure out how to do nearly anything if there was a plant you wanted access to."

She laughed and nudged me back out toward the beams to make the next section.

I obliged, stepping out over the clouds once again. She followed behind, and we made our precarious way with the winds ripping at every inch of our bodies.

"Sa ..." Emelia's tongue loosened in her mouth like a drunk. I'd heard the effects of a fume drift enough times to know Emelia only had moments before passing out.

I instantly reached back and grabbed for her, but out of sorts as she was, she stepped back and away, her eyelids fluttering.

She started to fall, but I caught the rope tied around her waist. To keep myself from being dragged with her, I wrapped my free arm around the beam at my right and held tight to both the dazed woman and the cold metal. On instinct I had held my breath the moment I realized that fumes had reached us, but there was only so long I could hold out that way.

I struggled to haul Emelia back up, but I didn't have the leverage or the strength with only one arm available and a waning breath. If I lost consciousness inhaling fumes, it would leave Emelia dangling and more than likely we would both fall.

Hands grabbed my waist.

"Pull her up."

The voice was familiar, but I didn't have time to think about why as I released the beam and trusted the newcomer with both our lives. I grabbed hold of Emelia and heaved, leaning back enough to leverage her back up onto the crosswork. I sat against the upright, pulling her tight against me while I panted. If I was going to lose consciousness, at least we would be on the beams. We would have a chance.

The fumes had passed though. I drew in clean air, or clean enough.

"Tarry lungs and hard hands," Eda said, crouching on the beam in front of us. "Doesn't look like your friend has either of those."

She smiled. "I didn't think I would see you again, Sade."

"Eda …" I could tell she was dead. The wind that tore at Emelia and me didn't even muss the woman's hair.

Her eyes were on her fingers where she had touched me. There was surprise and confusion in the specter as she struggled to understand how she had managed to prevent my fall. Then something darker crossed her eyes that set me on edge. She reached forward, her misty fingers brushed my cheek curiously. "So warm …" She shook her head, the covetous groan of the dead touching life abating in her throat. "It took me a while to realize what had happened. Spent a lot of confused time on that damn airship. You know they sunk it into the cloudline?" She looked out over the drop.

"Eda, I'm so sorry."

"Why would you need to be sorry?" she asked, but there was a flash in her eyes that made me nervous. She touched my cheek again, and again stared longingly at her fingertips.

I pinched Emelia's hand, trying to rouse her.

The ghost's eyes raised to mine. "You almost look nervous, Sade. Like you don't trust me. Like maybe you are guilty of something? Why did you survive, Sade?" The ghost's voice pitched to a snarl. "Why did you survive? Did you betray us? Is that why I'm dead? Was it you?" A gory streak of red dashed across her gut, her fatal wounds exposed now.

"Eda. Don't give in to the anger. Please. Eda. It's me. I did not betray you. I promise."

The ghost stood over us while I continued to try to rouse Emelia. Nowhere was ideal to come across a vengeful dead, but over the abyss with an unconscious woman tied to me was especially bad.

"Your promises are worth dirt," Eda growled. She reached down, her hand wrapping around my throat. The usual cool mist of the dead was instead an intense cold in this vengeful spirit. She hefted me up while I struggled with her hand, an unnatural strength in her fingers.

"You survived where all the rest of us died. You. And you alone." I wasn't about to correct her about Reeva. Her face contorted with anger into something I barely recognized as human. "Did you betray Gan, too? Oh, I'll bet you did."

My struggle against her hold was in vain. The cold felt as though it was spreading down into my chest. The frost superseded all. At a touch, she was pulling me into the fold with her.

"E ... Eda ..."

"What was it for? What, Sade, did you betray us for? You wanted out. At the cost of your friends. Us? We loved you." She swung me out over the abyss. "We loved you," she growled again, giving me a little shake. My heart sputtered, an icy spike driving slowly through it.

A hand grasped my ankle and an essence, calming and warm, wrapped around both me and Eda.

The specter released me, her uncontrolled vengeance flooding out of her in a sudden wash. I just managed to grab hold of the support beam in time to keep me and Emelia from falling to the void.

Eda backed away from us, unconcerned with the potential of falling. Unconcerned with us as she stared at her hands in confusion.

I hauled myself up, checking on Emelia, who still looked dazed, but aware enough now.

"I'm ... I'm dead." Eda looked from her hands to me. "Sade ... It's you. I didn't mean to. I'm so sorry. I just ... A thought hit me, and I couldn't control it. I couldn't stop the cold hatred."

I held Emelia tight against me and watched the ghost. A single thought could set her off. We couldn't be on these beams any longer.

"I've had just about enough of this adventure," I said with my frozen throat. The secret wasn't worth our lives. I brought the glyph into the center of my mind and released. A moment later, Emelia and I were on her floor.

"What ..." Emelia said, her shock registering in my tight hold. "How?"

I released her and fell back, clutching my chest. "I ... I'm an Aberrant," I said through the lingering pain.

Still dazed from the fumes, the woman only looked at me in confusion. "Aberrant? You are a Death Sight."

"Aberrant, Sight, Lock," I felt exhaustion overtaking me. "Whatever else my mother managed to push into me when she died." My tongue was heavy, leaden with cold. "I should go."

"You are in no condition. What if that ghost comes back? Sade, I don't care what you are. You are not leaving. That thing almost killed you."

"Eda," I said, trying to roll to all fours, only to fail.

"Eda almost killed you," Emelia said, gently. She pulled me into her lap. "I've never felt something so cold."

My head lolled against her, her warming touch soothing. Even if I wanted to leave, I wasn't certain I could. My mind couldn't focus enough to draw intent and my legs did not have the strength to stand.

"What if she finds us again?" Emelia asked, holding me tight.

"She will," I slurred. "She's grown vengeful." I could no longer fight the droop in my eyelids and lost consciousness in Emelia's embrace.

30:

Emelia was still beside me when I opened my eyes. Outside, the sun had yet to dip below the horizon so I could only hope I hadn't been out too long. Her hand rested on mine, eyes watchful and waiting. My chest still felt cold, but not with the same oppressive grip that had my heart freezing. My eyes darted to the vagabond standing in the corner, out of reach.

"She's here," I said, voice low, getting to my feet to stand between the ghost and Emelia.

"I could have killed you while you slept," Eda said matter-of-factly. "Even with the Charmer." She was different now, hovering on the edge of manifestation. "I don't want to kill you. Not right now."

"Why are you here?" I asked, seeing that Eda was little more than a Whisper now. The rush of vengeance and then the crippling warmth must have ravaged her being.

Her eyes watched me with indifference. "You came here." She blinked several times and for a moment looked as though she was about to manifest again. "Gan is dead. He has moved on. I will move on." She faded again, her eyes slackening as she looked at me. "You are a gateway."

She walked closer to me, and the lost look in her eyes froze my heart in a different way.

"We loved you," she said again with a frown, middling in her manifestation before she pressed her lips to mine and the icy spear of her existence ending lanced me.

It was different from Deara's passing, gentler without the flood of magic and stored memories, but still the rush of Eda's energy wasn't enough to keep me on my feet.

Emelia just barely caught me, helping me to the floor. I was surprised by my sobs. I had known Eda was dead, yet seeing her and confirming it rocked me, even after so long.

I swore, trying to get control over my emotions. Trying to stop the tears and the pain in my chest.

Emelia put her hands on my shoulders, holding me tight. "Cry, Sade. It's alright," she whispered.

I did. I cried until I had no more tears, curled in on myself, my arms wrapped tight around my knees. When finally I could catch my breath, I leaned into Emelia's shoulder.

"You must have really loved her," Emelia said remorsefully. "I'm sorry, Sade."

I shook my head against her shoulder. "I did. She was my best friend. Eda. Gan. They were more than friends. But ... it's not just that." I looked up at her. "It's everything. All of it. This life. My gang. My closest friends, dead. Deara is gone. Katarina puts on a good show, but she is little more than a shadow now. It's all so much, and constantly, at the back of my mind I keep thinking about ..." I broke off, realizing what I was about to say. I didn't need Emelia worrying about the landmasses sinking under our feet. There was no need to put my fear into her.

"Thinking about what, Sade?" Emelia asked cautiously.

I shook my head. "No. It's nothing."

She frowned but continued to hold me close. We sat in silence a while longer.

"Sade." The voice was timid.

My head snapped up at Marco's unexpected entrance.

"I'm sorry. I didn't mean to interrupt, sis, but Reeva wants you." He looked scared of a rebuke.

"Sade?" Emelia asked, following my eyes. Nervousness quavered in her voice and her arm tightened around me.

"It's Marco," I assured her. To him I said, "Reeva wants me? Right now?"

"I guess. I don't know how long she's been trying to get me to get you, but when I stopped in to check on her, she was just talking at the air. Can only assume she was hopin' I would pop in. Or she's as batty as the ringleader," the ghost said with an awkward shrug, eyes on the floor, speaking fast with his discomfort at my tears.

"Any idea what this is about?" I asked.

Again, Marco shrugged. "Looked like Beater's acting weird. But he's always strange, these days."

"Hmm," I said, not feeling entirely ready to face whatever Reeva had for me. "Alright. I'll meet you there," I promised, and the ghost disappeared, happy to be gone. I looked up at Emelia. "I have to see Reeva."

"I'll go with you."

"Haven't you had enough excitement for the day?"

"I'm going with you," she said firmly.

I relented. The vengeful spirit of a past lover hadn't tried to kill her today, I supposed. I let her help me to my feet, a thin golden chain falling from my leg to the floor. Stooping to pick up the necklace, I held it up so I could see the unassuming charm dangling from it. The thin metal and heads of wheat were familiar.

"Where did that come from?" Emelia asked.

I swallowed. "Eda," I said, frowning at the necklace. "I thought it was lost to the abyss ... Eda must have brought it back when she ..." I shook my head. "I gave it to her before the heist." I stuffed the chain in my pocket and turned to Emelia. For a moment, at least, I didn't want to think about any of it.

"Are you certain you want to go see Reeva right now?"

"No. But it will be a good distraction."

Emelia frowned, uncertain how to proceed. "Perhaps you rely too heavily on distractions, Sade. I can still feel your pain."

"And I can see your worry. I was not ready for today, and I never really took a moment just to mourn everything and everybody. That is all. If Reeva has been trying to get my attention, I should probably go."

Still she hesitated, then finally sighed. "Alright," she said, still holding me tight against her. I let her warmth comfort me as the icy pick of Eda's attack still worked to thaw itself.

"Are you ready?" I asked quietly.

She nodded, her arms tightening around me, but when I felt for the glyphs they slipped from my mind into a pool of exhaustion.

"On second thought, could we, maybe, use your motorcarriage," I asked with a swallow of defeat.

"Of course," she said, and instead helped me to my feet. "Are you certain this can't wait until you've had more rest?"

"I'm ready now."

She swallowed, clearly not in agreement, but nodded.

The motorcarriage roared and rumbled and I hated how much attention it would garner on the dingy streets that Reeva called home, but it couldn't be helped. I set my head on Emelia's shoulder, allowing my eyes to close while we set off for the lower alts. It seemed only a moment before the driver had brought us to a stop on a quiet side street, his eyes looking at Emelia with apprehension in the rear-view mirror.

"You'll be alright here, madam?" He asked, unable to hide his frown.

"We will be just fine, William. See you back at the house," she said, climbing down onto the grime covered streets.

Emelia looked only the more apprehensive about her decision to join me as I led her the rest of the way to Reeva's home. She knew Reeva only as an employer. This was maybe getting too close to the reality of the woman. "Do you have any guess at what she wants?"

"No doubt this has to do with Beater and his doomsday proclamations."

"What? Who?" Emelia asked, following me around the corner.

"Our former ringleader. He's, um … he's insane. He got captured on the Persephone and the Abbies … They went too far, or maybe not far enough with him."

I set my hand on the door to Reeva's squat, and with a long exhale, stepped inside.

"Damnit, Marco. Get Sade. I need to talk to her," Reeva was cursing the air when I walked in. "Oh. You're here," she said, turning. "I knew you were sending that ghost to keep tabs on me." She cast her eyes around the room suspiciously. "I guess it has its uses."

"What did you want, Reeva?"

"Did you pass the port? The College sent an airship of Aberrants over from Junction," she raged. "We don't need any more Abbies walking around pretending to protect us. No offense to you, of course."

"They were sent to refortify the cloud barriers after that last drift," Emelia said, following me into Reeva's squat and closing the door.

Reeva spun, realizing I wasn't alone. "What in the abyss, Sade! I invited you, not your high-and-mighty girlfriend."

"Your employer," I reminded the woman with a low growl. "You didn't spend Devton knows how long cursing at the air in the hopes it would get my attention to talk about an airship of Abbies. What's going on?"

"Who shit in your cereal today?" Reeva grumbled at my annoyed tone. Her eyes lit on Emelia, then narrowed at me. "I would think you would be a bit more concerned about the Aberrants than me. They won't even see me. You will draw their attention like a fucking firefly on a clear night." It was evident she had no intention of cleaning up her speech, even around Emelia.

"I'll manage. What's going on?"

Once again, she looked at Emelia, then her eyes went to the man sitting over his bowl. No longer raving, Hayden was quiet, his mutterings abated. He moved in a slow methodical way as he spooned whatever gruel Reeva had concocted for him into his mouth.

"He's calm. What happened?"

"Look, I should have told you this sooner, but I don't just air everybody's secrets on a whim. He's a …" Reeva hesitated with a glance at Emelia. "He's a Present Sight. I silenced the external stimulus," Reeva said, nodding at the braided bracelet around his wrist, the same brown as Reeva's hair. "It took a few days to really settle things in his mind, but without the Sight I think he is managing to sort out what was the Aberrants' torture and what was his Sight."

"And?"

"And I am starting to wonder if maybe it wasn't just the torture that broke him. That maybe that little prophecy of his wasn't some nightmare put there by the Abbies. Maybe he saw something. Something very real and very concerning," Reeva said anxiously.

"You think something is wrong with the cores?"

Reeva cast a helpless look at me. Beside me, Emelia shifted nervously. The glyph cores were the only things keeping the landmasses aloft. The only things keeping them survivable.

I swallowed, not liking the idea that had formed in my head. "I'll look."

"Look at what?"

"His memories of his capture."

"No, Sade. That was not what I was asking for," Reeva said quickly, her voice edged with fear.

"What exactly was he saying was happening?" Emelia asked in a small voice that drew both Reeva's and my eyes.

"You shouldn't have brought her here," Reeva repeated her misgivings.

"But I did, so put up with it." I looked at Emelia. "He wasn't exactly stringing together the most coherent of thoughts ... He says we are falling. That all the landmasses are falling. That the bindings are breaking and the cores are sick." She took a shuddering breath. I took her hands. "If it is true, it is slow."

"For now," Reeva said, staring at Hayden with deep-sunk eyes.

"How long has this been in the back of your mind?" Emelia asked, squeezing my hands to comfort me, though I could see troubling thoughts brewing behind her eyes.

"Since the cloud drift. That was when Reeva found him. I have had quite a number of things happen since then that have taken much of my capacity for worry. This seemed like the ravings of a tortured mind. It was easy to push this aside with everything else." I met her eye. "What's going on?"

"Ah," she looked at a loss for words. "This isn't the first time I've heard this. Maybe ... maybe you *should* look at his memories."

"No," Reeva cut in. "No. I'm not letting you do that, Sade. It's not happening." She shook her head. "You don't want to look at that. I won't let you. I don't need you turning into ..." She looked at Hayden.

"It's my choice."

"Are you sure? How do you know it's not your rich girlfriend influencing you?" Reeva spat, eyes narrowed at Emelia, not caring if the woman fired her on the spot.

"Reeva," I growled at the Breaker, but took a calming breath. "If you think she's influencing me, then take her hand." I looked at Emelia, who frowned in confusion but offered Reeva her hand as a gesture of goodwill.

With a scowl, Reeva set her hand on Emelia's. Emelia's eyes widened as Reeva took away her ability.

"Oh ... it's so ... calm?" Emelia said with an awed look at Reeva. "You're a Breaker?"

Reeva shrugged. She waited, then looked at me. "Are you sure you want to do this?"

"I think I have to," I said in a thin voice. "We have to know if it was the torture or his Sight."

Reeva grumbled and paced and finally took the small, braided bracelet from the man's wrist, then backed away. "I don't know what you are hoping to find in there, but have at it. If you turn yourself into a raving maniac, my generous nature is maxed out keeping that bastard alive."

"I understand."

"And don't ... don't look at anything personal," Reeva said uncomfortably.

"I will try not to."

"Hmm," Reeva growled and backed into the corner with her arms tightly crossed. Her foot tapped rapidly with her nerves. "If it starts looking bad, I am breaking it."

"Thank you, Reeva." I turned to Hayden, sitting in front of him. His spoon moved absently around his bowl as he muttered, unaware of my eyes. "Beater? Hayden? Do you remember me? I was in your gang ... with Reeva ... Do you remember any of that? Do you remember the Persephone?" He just continued to mumble to himself, staring deeply into the bowl of mush. "This will be a lot easier for both of us if you think about the Persephone." I hoped the name of the airship would trigger something in the man. Still, his eyes remained down.

I sighed and looked at the hand he left resting on the table beside his bowl, and set mine on top of his. I really did not want to do this.

The initial dive was a horrifying spiral of pain and terror and darkness. Under it all I could hear the mumbling abate and the man's prophecy begin again in the hovel.

I pushed a memory, something grounding, I hoped. A simple card game with Eda and the rest of the older members of the gang gathered around the table. Hayden responded in kind with a memory of just before the Persephone. His eyes roving over the sleeping members of his gang as he strategized with his lieutenants.

"That's a big heist, Beater; are you sure we can pull it off?" Benson was saying, the young man's broad chin coated in an uneven stubble he thought was more charming than it was.

Hayden's eyes flicked from the thin braid of brown hair around his wrist to rove over the gang again as he considered. His eyes fell on where the older members clustered. Me. Eda. Skylar not far off from us. Reeva waiting patiently for Hayden to be finished with his discussion just beyond us. A sea of youngers all around. "We have the numbers. Especially the desperate numbers. We have some of the hardest hands and tarriest-lunged divers on Vale. They are aging out and they know it. They need a big heist to break off. They know they are at the end of their lifecycle here."

"Then they will take their cut and they will run."

Hayden stared at Benson. "That doesn't matter. A heist so grand, there's enough to share. What matters is we get on that ship." He looked from Benson to Vik. "What do you think?"

Vik scowled into his thinking face, then nodded. "Yeah. Why not?"

The memory swirled away as I centered myself in the timeline, then moved forward.

Hayden's voice penetrated my dive, the prophecy ringing in my ears, spinning me through another sickening wave of memories.

*The control room of the Persephone. Eda was curled in around herself on the floor, still, with a spill of blood around her, an Aberrant standing over her—*the same who had identified me as a Death Sight during my escape—*and more just behind. The rest of Hayden's boarding party dead or dying as he succumbed to the onslaught of Enforcers.*

"What the fuck is this?" one of the Aberrants growled, grabbing Hayden's broken arm and holding it up before his swelling eyes. The braid was cut away and the Aberrant grinned maliciously. "Clever. Not clever enough. Looks like I've got full access now."

Another spiral and my hands clenched, one around Hayden's and the other around the edge of the table as my teeth ground. Searing pain. Torture. Bones breaking and mending. Mind warping. But something else. A beginning, an end, the future, the past. A brutal cross-sectioning of the fold. It hit me in nauseating knots of chaos, so entwined it was nearly impossible to pick it apart. The physical pain was nothing compared to the mental agony I was experiencing through Hayden's memories. I focused, trying to see past the pain. What had the Aberrants said, what had they done, when had the prophecy bleeding from the man's lips started?

"I'm going to stop this," Reeva growled behind me.

"No. Wait. Give her more time. She's strong," Emelia tried to stop the woman.

"Sade is not just meat for your fucking whims," Reeva snarled.

The future, the past, no. No. Something else. The present? So many layers. The fold. Not the future or the past, the present. The gods on their isle. Me buying my drawing materials with Deara. So many images so difficult to tease apart. A dark spot. That darling, soothing dark spot. The Breaker, it had to be. The promise of peace from this madness broken loose.

I watched events on a farm unfold on a landmass I had never seen before. I watched a crime that could have happened only steps away. I saw into layers of the fold where life existed on the planet's surface below, and layers where the land was scorched and blackened. I saw a baby born and a life end. I felt an Aberrant's magic tear through me while I saw images of fire forced into Hayden's mind. Then I saw what he had.

Suddenly it made sense. The prophecy. But now I was stuck, spiraling through the man's memories of the past as he saw into the present of the time.

A hand set on my and Hayden's locked digits so suddenly I jumped, throwing myself back from the table and the man. The torture he endured not just to his body, but his mind. I toppled, landing on my back on the floor and pressing away from the man as he stared at me and chanted his prophecy one last time before calming.

"F… fu … fuck," I stammered out, Emelia yanking me back against her to lend her support for the second time that day. Her hand brushed over my sweating brow.

"Sade? Sade? I was wrong. I am sorry," Emelia said, pleading with me.

I realized my lips were still moving, a repetition of Hayden's prophecy. With effort I made them still.

"Fuck," I said again, voice still shaky, but far steadier. Looking up at Reeva as she fastened the bracelet back around Hayden's wrist, I shook my head. "I didn't realize … They see across the fold."

"There's a reason Present Sights tend to find Breakers. It is not an easy ability to endure," Reeva said darkly, trying to soothe Hayden back out of his ravings. "He always wore a Breaker's charm on him. That's the only thing that kept him from turning to a gibbering mess like so many Present Sights." She frowned and her voice dropped. "At least, until the Aberrants found it. Then it all must have rushed in. I don't know. I'm not a fucking Sight," she said, her voice rising in frustration as she spoke. "You shouldn't have done that."

I panted, my head rocking against Emelia as she unabashedly stroked calming fingers up and down my arm. I breathed deeply, accepting the woman's charm to bring my heart rate back to baseline once again. "I needed to, Reeva. Hayden's prophecy. He saw it. The cores are breaking." I pressed my hand to my forehead, feeling a memory already slipping away. An important aspect. The Isle of the Gods. The gods in conversation.

"Did they know?" I said in a thin voice. "Were they trying to mend the cores? Had they ..." The thought started to slip away, but I managed to wrestle it back into existence. Had they caused the fissures in the glyph cores? I closed my eyes and shook my head. The thought was a foolish one. It had to be. The gods protected the Society and those within it. Even the vagabonds and slum dwellers. Devton looked after us.

Reeva looked up from tending Hayden. "'They' who?"

"What?"

"Did *who* know?" she pressed, leaving Hayden's side to squat in front of me with her eyes narrowed. "The gods?" At my confusion, she nodded. "Of fucking course," she laughed. "Well, you got further than most do. Looks like you can even bind a Natural. If only just a little."

"What are you talking about?"

Reeva took my hand. "You were about to question the gods. Weren't you?"

My head cleared and I saw that was exactly what I was doing. The gods had the power to help. Why weren't they? Their purpose was to protect us. Even the lowly slum dwellers. So they had sent Aberrants when what was needed was real power.

Reeva nodded, seeing the thoughts returning to me. "There we go. That's better. Looks like you just confirmed my theory."

"Which is?"

"You can't question the gods. There's a binding. A strong one. Slow exposure. You know the kind. It doesn't work on Breakers."

"It's Society-wide, isn't it?" I asked slowly. I remembered Katarina whenever she tried to tell me her theory on Leeta's expulsion from the senate. The way she constantly seemed to forget. "I've seen it in Katarina. It was different, though. You prompted me and I remembered. She seemed to have completely forgotten the conversation."

Reeva looked at me and shrugged. "The binding on you must be weaker for some reason." She looked at Emelia with narrowed eyes. "Like it seems to be on Charmer."

"How can you tell?" I asked, looking back at Emelia, who bit her lip, clearly knowing exactly what Reeva was talking about.

"None of that mind-numbing confusion that you just had. She knew exactly who you were talking about," Reeva said appraisingly. "How did you avoid the binding? A perk of being rich?" Reeva had let go of any sense for keeping her employment, given her attitude toward her benefactor, but Emelia did not look bothered in the least by the treatment.

"Not exactly …"

Emelia helped me to my feet, then with a sigh, pulled the collar of her jumpsuit away from her neck slightly to reveal the thin scar on the back of her shoulder. "It's a glyph ward. We have some of the best Tinkerers on our books," she said, setting her clothing back in a semblance of order. With the night underground and our adventure on the underside of the bridge, order was a relative thing. "It's a sub-dermal. Very effective against passive glyphs. It can be hit or miss with glyphs of a more direct nature. My mother always seemed a bit paranoid to me, but if there is a Society-wide thought binding, then maybe she wasn't too far off."

"Perk of being rich," Reeva grumbled her confirmation.

"I don't know that me having a glyph ward is the biggest issue here," Emelia said, redirecting the Breaker back to the point of our visit. "Even the fact that there is a Society-wide thought binding has to fall to second." She looked at Hayden. "He is a Present Sight and he saw us falling how long ago?"

Reeva returned to Hayden, studying the man. "I only found him after the cloud drift. I don't know how long ago he saw what he did." She glanced at me, looking for the answer.

I just shook my head. "I'm not going back in there unless I absolutely have to, and honestly, I don't know that I would be able to sort through that much chaos and keep my sanity."

"I don't see a need," Reeva said. "I mean, on the short end it's been a couple weeks, and on the long, over a year. We haven't plummeted into the cloudline yet. The descent is barely noticeable. Sooner or later the scientists and engineers should realize, right?"

"If the gods are involved, I'm not so certain," I said grimly. I looked at Emelia, who had affixed a frown to her face. "You said this isn't the first time you have heard of this possibility. When you said I should look at Hayden's memories, did you know what I would find already, Em?" The nervous insistence I had seen in her eyes before now turned to fear.

"I didn't know," she said quickly. "It's just … I did something

I know I shouldn't have. After running into you and Katarina at the Conservatory, I may have asked a few questions about Leeta Norwood's expulsion. My father, who was a sitting Chairman during the vote, could barely tell me anything about that day. He seemed to barely even remember Leeta. But, before that, the two of them used to talk. Generally about politics, generally with one or the other trying to buy a vote even as they stood across the aisle from each other."

"What does this have to do with anything?" Reeva griped.

I held a hand up to the woman and gave a nod to Emelia. "What did you find?"

She frowned. "I know asking about Leeta is a bad idea. That it draws the wrong attention. But the woman was in our house when I was a child. I didn't remember her, really. I was too young. My sister did, though. She said that the woman was off her rocker by the end. That she would come over trying to convince my father that they needed to force the College to investigate the cores. That there was something … I don't know what … but something about the cores that was keeping us prisoners, and that she thought they may one day fail. My sister was young, but she remembers the argument they had. Leeta had even brought some professor with her to back her theory. If you ask my father, he has no recollection of this."

"Does he have a glyph ward like you do?" I asked.

She shook her head.

"Does your sister?" Reeva asked.

"My sister and brother both, yes."

"That would explain why she can remember, and your father cannot."

I took Emelia's hands in mine, a sinking feeling in my chest. "Don't ask about this anymore. Don't ask about Leeta. Please. Promise me."

"Maybe that's exactly what we need to be doing, Sade. She clearly knew something."

"And the gods clearly didn't want it known. It is a powerful binding that can wipe so prominent a woman as Leeta from the collective memory of the Society. It's imperfect, yes, but people who do remember her barely do. I don't want that to happen to you. I don't want anything to happen to you."

"So, what, we just ignore this? We could be sinking into the cloudline. We could all die. Everybody."

I looked between Emelia and Reeva, then at Hayden muttering in the corner.

"What are we supposed to do?" I asked, at a loss.

We all fell into a despondent silence. Each thinking of our lack of ability to do anything to stop what we were slowly coming to terms with as reality.

Reeva swallowed, then looked at us both quizzically. "Why are you two dressed like that? You look like you are getting ready for a dive. You aren't planning on doing something stupid, are you?" She almost looked hopeful that we were.

"We went under the Grand Cross," I said, grasping for the distraction.

"The Grand Cross? Really? With her? And next you are going to tell me you took her on an airship heist," Reeva scoffed.

"Just the bridge," I said tightly. "A landside crossing."

"You went the whole way?" Reeva asked, realizing we weren't lying to her. She looked at Emelia with a new appreciation now.

"Near enough. We had a run-in with some fumes and a vengeful spirit, and I had to port us out from below," I said, still feeling the icy sting of Eda's touch.

"Who was it? Anybody I know?" Reeva asked, taking a seat at her small table. She was desperate to discuss anything normal, and apparently the attacks of vengeful dead counted as such these days.

"Eda."

"Eda?" Reeva said, thinking back to the gang. "Eda ... Oh. Yeah. You and her and what was his name? You were all a little too close, right? *That* Eda?"

I nodded.

"I don't know what you did to piss her off, but, well," she shook her head. "I am sorry she is gone, Sade."

"I knew she was dead well before she found us." My hand found the chain in my pocket, and I drew it out, letting it rest in my palm.

Reeva eyed the piece. "What's that?"

"Something I thought was lost. Eda brought it back from the abyss. I don't remember where it came from or when I got it. I've just always had it."

"A Tinkerer made it," Reeva said absently.

"How can you tell?"

Reeva just shrugged. "I just can. What does it do?"

I shook my head. "I've never noticed it do anything." I studied it closer now, feeling the inexplicable glyphwork melded with the metal. The etched glyphs had been hidden; the magic so subtle that I only recognized its existence with the charm pinched between my fingers. Whatever it was, the Tinkerer had not made the intent of the charm clear. I tucked the chain back into my pocket and sank down against the wall. "Whatever it does, it certainly does not seem to bring any sort of good luck."

31:

"Hayden knew you were a Breaker," I said, seeking any distraction from the day. I had returned to Reeva after seeing Emelia safely away in a motorcarriage bound for her estate. We had debated most of the day on what, if anything, our poor little trio could actually do. If we dared do anything.

"He found me pretty much as soon as I set foot on this float. Present Sights tend to find us," Reeva said, her knees tucked up against her chest. She was as glad for any distraction as I was. "Past and Future Sights can't see us unless we are the focus of the moment they are seeing, but to Present Sights we are like gaps."

"Beautiful dark spots."

She nodded. "A little bit of serenity. My position in the gang was always secure as long as Beater maintained control."

"Was that what you wanted?"

"I never expected much. A roof over my head, food on the table, and people looking out for me. In exchange for keeping a Sight from losing his mind, that seemed a pretty solid deal to me. Better than laying on my back for strangers, at least." She bit her lip. "He's not that bad a man. Cocky when he had his head on straight. Overambitious at times. But I've had worse, as I am sure you have."

"There's a reason I jumped gangs as many times as I did." I nodded. It had always been just a matter of time before the beatings grew too heavy, or the expectations for certain members of the gang too steep. "You two were closer than either of you let on, weren't you?"

"I can't exactly deny whatever you saw while you were poking around in there. I don't want to say we did exactly what Breakers and Present Sights tend to do when they find each other. But we did exactly what Breakers and Present Sights do when they find each other."

We lapsed into silence.

"We can't keep pretending this isn't happening, can we?" Reeva said into her knees.

"I guess not." I looked at Marco, who sat equally despondent against the far wall. "Do you think you can get to the core?"

He shook his head. "I tried with Deara a while back, but I s'pose I could try again. I don't know what I'm lookin' for, though, sis. I don't know all them glyphs like you do."

I nodded and looked at Reeva. "Even if Marco is able to get to the core, it doesn't gain us anything."

"The Landbringer brings our fall," Hayden muttered on repeat in the background.

I looked at the man, then looked at Reeva. "You'll be alright?"

"I don't know that I will be alright. But I'll be here." She looked at where Marco was. "Marco, if you are still here. Thank you. I know this doesn't impact you as it does us."

"We are family," I relayed for the boy and stood.

"Family," Reeva laughed. "What a sad, sorry family. But yeah. Family."

The ghost gave me a nod, then disappeared. I gave Reeva a nod and took my leave.

I didn't go far, though. I found myself at the edge of the Grand Cross Bridge, looking out over the abyss. Another storm seemed to be raging to the east, the clouds having turned sinister and dark, shocks of lightning racing through the sky.

This day had not ended up where I had thought it would, waking up beside Emelia in the calm of the underground.

"Move it along, bots. This ain't no place for loitering," an Enforcer said, thumping his club in his palm for emphasis.

I looked at the man, the small patrol behind him, and moved on. I could have headed toward Katarina's. I certainly needed the rest from the day, but instead I walked through streets from my past. Streets I knew I shouldn't walk. Knowing the inevitable only brought its small torture to the back of my mind. If we were sinking toward the noxious layer of clouds, I could do nothing about it.

"I recognize you." The voice was a hushed slither over my

shoulders.

"My word." I jumped as anybody would when confronted in such a manner and placed my hand over my racing heart to calm it. I turned to face the woman who was watching me like a cat with a mouse.

"Death Sight," she said. I had known before I turned that this woman was from the Persephone. The same I had seen standing over Eda in Hayden's memory.

"Aberrant. Where's your Enforcer?" I glanced about casually. In my heart I hoped, for the first time in my life, that an Enforcer was around.

The woman smiled, too toothy. Too certain of herself. "Don't worry, I don't have any of my pets around, *madam*." She snorted the word. "We can speak in private."

"What would I want to speak with you about, Aberrant?"

"Lea."

"What?"

"My name, *Death Sight*," she said pointedly.

I shook my head. "No. I'm not getting familiar with you." I turned on my heels and started walking.

"Like you get familiar with that Charmer of yours?" Lea said, pursuing me. Her robes dusted the filthy streets in a dignified swish as she stepped. This was a woman who thought herself above all others, and maybe she was a skilled enough Aberrant for that to be justified.

I swallowed, casting a sideways look at her. "Have you been following me?"

"You work at Mrs. Sandfjord's dress shop."

"You don't have to keep telling me about myself."

She grinned. "You are not who you say you are."

"My name is Sade. Is that what you wanted?" She could have prodded for that information anyway, and I wanted nothing less than for her to prod.

The grin spread wider in an unsettling manner and once again I looked around for her Enforcer, to no avail.

"Nor are you what you seem, *Sade*. You don't feel right." Her sharp eyes narrowed on me. "Do you even know what you are, I wonder ...?" Her eyes turned quizzical and her grin lost some of its malice as she considered. She started to raise her hand.

I stopped, catching her fingers in a tight grip. "No," I growled.

"No prodding. No doodling any of your gods-forsaken glyphs."

She looked at my hand, my grip firm and threatening. "As though you could stop me?" Her grin turned lopsided, a cold wash in her eyes. I recognized a challenge when I saw one.

I shook my head slowly, seeing the eyes of passersby flicking surreptitiously our way.

"What have you learned since the airship, I wonder?" She leaned close. "From my glimpse, I could see everything in there was so fuddled," she said, her free hand tapping my forehead and poising to draw a swift glyph. "Maybe it's been straightened out after this long year."

I caught her fingers and brought both of her hands down with a painful twist.

"I will break your hands," I threatened.

She laughed a barking laugh that drew more eyes than I wanted.

"I don't need them to cast. There are always other means. I am no novice." Though she maintained her even pacing and unconcerned eyes, I could see the sweat start beading on her forehead as I torqued her fingers. She sighed. "I am used to getting what I want through the simplest means possible. Glyphs. In your instance, maybe that gets me nothing." She was throwing in the towel. Carefully, I released my hold and she quickly withdrew her fingers protectively into her sleeves. The large sweeps of fabric her hands now hid within were designed to conceal the glyph being cast, but at the moment, at least, the Aberrant seemed to have decided against their use.

"What do you want?" I asked again, gesturing for her to walk.

"I have an insatiable curiosity. I will admit, it tends to get me in trouble. I want to see what's in that brain of yours." She held her hands up as if in surrender, the rings on her fingers strangely menacing. "I'm not going to prod. I've been told the genteel don't like it. Find it rude. I find it efficient, is all. More efficient than this prattling on and on with words, but I will play your game today. Street urchin. Hard Hand. Tarry Lung. Death Sight. Survivor. Lady Norwood. Sade Amsel." She grinned when I frowned. "Did you not even know your own last name?" She shook her head. "It was right there in your head and you couldn't even see it? I don't know if taking a peek back in your mind would tell me much. Somebody did some work on you when you were young. I could tell that from a glimpse only. A brief peek on the airship."

"How long have you been following me?"

"I only saw you a few days ago. I don't spend all my time on Vale. Nor do I typically waste that time wandering the streets, as you seem to enjoy doing."

"Garnet. Garnet. Garnet. Garnet. Garnet." A dead muttered as we walked by. Typically, I would have ignored the lost Whisper, but the man's eyes were on the Aberrant.

"Garnet?" I repeated quietly.

Lea looked at me, then at the space beside me. "One of your dead friends?" She asked, venom in her silky voice.

I looked at the man, realizing he was familiar. The lost Aberrant Deara had ferreted out to explain what a Lock was. The memory of the exchange felt like so long ago.

"A simple wanderer," I said, watching the woman closely. She was unsettled.

"Manifest them," she ordered me, as though I would acknowledge such a demand.

I shook my head. "No."

"Do it," she growled, forgetting her assurance not to use glyphs and bringing her hands up. I caught the one hand, but she moved with more fluidity and intent now. Still, I felt the crunch of her bones snapping in my hand as I made good on my promise to break her fingers if she tried a glyph. The pain barely phased her, and in a deft gesture I felt the sear of a torture glyph sink into my skin.

"Do it," she hissed as my knees lost their strength and my throat begged to release a burning scream. It was like acid flowing in my veins.

Before I realized what I was doing, an echo of the glyph formed in my mind and bled from my chest into her. Her hand tightened against mine as she felt the glyph tear into her. If my cover was blown, it was blown, and I allowed a well of magic to form in my gut and release in a savage prodding into her mind. I didn't have the skill of a College-trained Aberrant, nor the cunning with glyphs my mother had shown, but my months of poring through glyphs with Deara came into use as I dove. Using Deara's Sight risked memory bleed; glyphs done correctly avoided that.

Her eyes sharpened on mine, but her lips trembled and her broken hand shook in mine as the acid flowed under both our skins.

Sade Amsel. My name ricocheted around in her head like a mantra. She was searching for the meaning in it, too. There was something, but the haze of memories warped and turned me away. *Sade Amsel.* I pushed and she groaned, some of the fight in her going out, held on her feet by only our connected hands and the rigidity of her tortured muscles. *Doctor Amsel.* There it was, the edge of a memory ripping free. Deara's Sight grabbed hold of it. I really needed to get a handle on her Past Sight before the untrained ability dug me into a hole I couldn't climb back out of.

This woman knew my past already. I let that which was safe swim away from me. A dive, another night on the hideout floor, and I took what she concealed from herself.

"Doctor Amsel." Lea's voice was young, that of a child.

The woman in front of her turned, my face, only years older. My mother.

"Why do you bother learning about glyphs if you cannot use them?"

The woman smiled kindly. "So I can help you. So I can help our society. So I can ensure my daughter has a future." Her eyes went to the young girl playing idly in the corner of her classroom. Me, barely more than a toddler. "There is power in knowledge, Lea, even if you are not the one using the magic."

"Lock." The word was a sharp gasp from Lea's pained lips as she saw something in me I had not intended. "You are a Lock … Doctor Amsel … She was a Lock. No. No. No. You were nothing. The College never would have suffered Locks. You were nothing." Her free hand came up as a new resolve settled on her struggling features.

I read the intention in the movement of her body and swiftly threw her back against the bricks behind her, jarring her only momentarily. I knew what a Garnet was now. High level. As close to unbound as the College Aberrants ever got. She was a threat.

I stooped, drawing my knife from my boot and, as I rose, sank the blade between her ribs. Her hand faltered in its tracing of a glyph and she grunted against the punch of the knife. My hand fell away from the knife handle and I stepped back while she sagged.

"You have to finish her off," Marco was saying beside me. I didn't know when he had appeared. It didn't matter.

"No, Marco."

"She will heal herself. You know she will."

I could feel her drawing the magic in herself for the glyphs needed already, but for the time being her attention was off me.

"She knows what you are," he pleaded.

"She thinks she knows."

"She's not going to let this go, sis. She knows who you are. You gotta."

"Marco. No. I'm not going to kill her."

The woman chuckled. "I can't ... imagine ... I would be ... your first." Her eyes were losing focus as she sank deeper into a slump. Her lips curled in a mirthless sneer. "Or would I?" Her voice slurred with the effort of speaking.

I knelt beside her, grabbing the knife handle again. She watched me closely, her unbroken hand raising in defense.

"I'm going to pull this out, and you are going to use the last moments of your life before you drown on your own blood to heal yourself. You are not going to try to kill me again, or I will put this knife right back in you, but two inches to the left. Do you understand?"

She glared, but the fight was going out of her. Her head rocked in a nod and I counted down while she readied the glyph, the symbol hanging half-done on the ends of her fingers. As the glyph flared into existence, I pulled the blade.

She gasped and rolled to her hands and knees, coughing blood.

"Are you in a better headspace now?" I asked, the knife still ready in my hand.

"You're stupid to keep me alive," she said weakly, her hands shaking. I doubted she could cast much right now.

"Maybe. Now, I'm not claiming to be the best at this ... You may still die today if I mess this up," I said, drawing on the pages of glyphs I had learned over the months, forming a complex string of intent that manifested in magic rising and releasing. I watched her eyelids flutter and her pupils dilate as I jumbled her mind. "Forget my mother. Forget me. Forget everything that happened today. Sade Amsel does not exist." Her eyes closed and she slumped back.

I checked her pulse, then retreated into the darkness of the alley.

"She will forget all of it?" Marco said with amazement as he followed me.

"I don't know, Marco. I hope so." I doubted it, though. Maybe if I had more training. The woman wasn't a Natural, but she was strong, and no doubt the College would expend their fullest to get such an Aberrant back into fighting shape. "Could you get to the core?"

He shook his head. "No. I'll keep trying, though. I got closer than last time."

I found something about that very upsetting indeed.

32:

"Will you come with me to Junction?" Katarina asked out of the blue while we both sat in silence. We had occupied the parlor for hours, not saying anything to one another, just stewing in our individual thoughts. Katarina rolling one of her little blue pills between her fingers absently, but not swallowing it. For my part, I did nothing to break the despondent air in the room.

"Junction? You want to visit Olso?"

She laughed mirthlessly. "No. Dear me, no."

"Then why?"

"I want to pay the College a visit." I didn't like her tone or the empty look in her eye.

"I don't know if that is the best idea, Katarina," I said slowly.

"It most certainly is the best idea. You are a Natural. There must be some use to you," she said bitterly. "The Aberrants can't kill your girlfriend without repercussions. Bring her with. She would be a good shield."

"I have neither agreed, nor am I going to use Emelia as a 'shield.' What is this about?"

She looked at the pill in her hand, and then set it on the table beside her. "Those fucking Aberrants think they can take everything. They think they can do everything. They think that we are just meat to be butchered whenever we are no longer useful to them. It's only a matter of time before they come for us. Either to leash us or to kill us. Not just Death Sights. Everybody with a little Moxie. Better to take our fight to them."

"And what fight is that, exactly?"

"They killed my family, Sade. They killed my *entire* family. I won't let them take you, and I will not just let all they have done go quietly."

I pulled in a long inhale through my nose and released it on a sigh. "And what do you propose? Kill all the Abbies at the College? That can't really be your plan here."

Katarina pouted. "I don't imagine we would get through *all* of them," she grumbled.

"I'm not going to assist you in this, Katarina. I'm not going to let you charge off on a pointless suicide mission." I looked hard at the woman. "I know that is exactly what this is, Katarina." With a sigh and a shake of my head I tried another tactic. "Have you ever even killed anybody?"

"Have you?" she shot back, and I could see the answer was a no.

"Never on purpose," I said, remembering the Aberrant whose glyph I had hijacked on the Persephone.

"I see dead people all day long. This can't be that much worse."

"You listen to Whispers tell you who murdered them all day long. Do you want to be the subject of one of those ramblings?"

She pouted. "Fuck, Sade. Fuck you." Her grand plan was crumbling beneath her kicked-up feet.

"How much have you had to drink today?"

She laughed bitterly. "Don't ask questions you don't want the answer to."

I conceded that point and set my elbows on my knees.

"I just thought you may like to spar," I said. "Work off a little steam. But if you've been drinking ..."

She groaned. "I haven't. Surprising, I know. I've just been sitting here trying to figure out what it is you are not telling me this time. Don't try to play it off. You've been despondent for days. If it's not the College, then ... Did you and Emelia call it off?" She was unusually gentle in her asking.

"No." I shook my head.

She nodded, her eyes narrowing at me as she tried to see what it was.

"I don't want to trouble you."

"You trouble me every day. Why make this one any different?"

I snorted and rolled my eyes. "Oh, Kat. Are you sure you wouldn't rather just spar?"

She stood. "I would always rather just spar," she said flippantly. But her expression softened. "Sade. I hope you trust me."

I followed her toward the training room. "I do. Why would you doubt it?"

"Because you keep things from me," she said with a glance back at me. "Things that seem to deeply trouble you."

"I told you, I don't want it on your mind."

"Well, instead of whatever it is troubling you troubling me, I am now troubled trying to figure out what it is that has you so out of sorts."

My lips puckered and I considered. "Fine. You want to know? Alright. What if I told you the landmasses were sinking toward the cloudline?”

She stopped and turned. Her eyes scanned me for the joke and, seeing none, she laughed anyway. “Of fucking course they are. Oh. How could it be any other way. By the gods.” She laughed again, a small hysterical hint in the tone. “Well. It’s not like there’s anything we can do about it, so get over it, Sade. May as well enjoy our time while we have it.” She started walking once again.

“Really? That’s it?” I asked, jogging a few steps to catch up to her again.

She shrugged. “What does any of it matter?”

The maid looked shaken as she hurried to intercept us and silently curtsied to Katarina and me. She was hesitant in her words, but finally found them.

“Madam,” the woman said to me. “Lady Rasczek is on the talker.”

“Emelia?” I asked, coming to a stop.

“No, madam.”

Katarina perked up at that, intrigued. She grinned, excited at the prospect of Emelia’s mother calling for me and whatever fresh hell I was walking into. I cast her a nervous glance, then followed the unnerved maid. Katarina followed me giddily and pressed her ear close to the talker to eavesdrop as I answered.

“Lady Rasczek—”

“I told you to stop asking questions. Didn’t I? I told you not to pull my daughter down with you!” the woman raged through the receiver.

Terror raced up my spine, images of all the Aberrant-tortured bodies of street kids dancing behind my eyes. No. It wouldn’t have been so obvious. There would be a cover story. A motorcarriage accident, maybe. My mind was racing beyond my control.

“What happened?” I managed to say in a small voice.

“They took Emelia.”

“Who?”

Lady Rasczek actually sobbed, a broken, frustrated sound. “I don’t know. I …”

I could hear the fracturing of her thoughts even through the line.

“I’ll be right there,” I said coldly, anger flaring in my chest, and silenced the receiver.

“Emelia?” Katarina asked quietly, a profound level of concern in her voice, all her giddiness replaced. "Somebody took her?"

I nodded.

"I'm going with you," Katarina said firmly. "Tomas!"

I looked at the woman with my jaw tensed.

"You are going to go running pell-mell into gods-knows-what like a fool. Somebody has to make sure you don't get yourself killed," Katarina sniped. The contrast between this and the start of our conversation, I was certain, was lost on her.

Tomas jogged up, dropping into a low bow before Katarina. "Madam?"

"It never hurts to have a Future Sight on hand, either," Katarina said.

I just growled and quickly drew the glyph to transport us to Lady Rasczek's study. It was foolish to reveal myself an Aberrant to the woman, but knowing Emelia had been taken, I threw discretion to the wind in favor of speed.

Lady Rasczek shrieked when we materialized in front of her. Her composure was cracked and she looked worse for wear. At a glance, I could see the manor had been burglarized. Or made to look so.

"Were you with Emelia when they took her?" I asked, not giving the noble a breath to recover from her shock.

"I ... I think so."

I could feel the hum of recently released magic in the air. "How long ago?"

Lady Rasczek rubbed her temples. "Not long ... I ... Emelia. They took her."

"I'm going to get her back." I grabbed the woman's hand, seeing she was reeling from whatever botched glyph was fighting her glyph ward for dominion.

The memory was forthcoming, given its recent occurrence. *I stood beside Lady Rasczek's desk looking over a room being ransacked. Her body wouldn't move. I could feel the terror of that paralysis in her as she watched the Aberrants invade her home.*

"She's asking questions she ought not. Find her." The voice was familiar to me, though it had not been for Lady Rasczek. The woman who appeared in the doorway entered with a sweep of robes and an imposing air of authority. Lea stepped over a body at the doorway and turned to survey the books lining the walls of the study. She paid no mind to the trapped lady of the house while her minions worked. Steadily she made her way to stand before Lady Rasczek with

a considering look.

In the hallway I heard the echo of a statement carried through the over-loud speaker of a talker.

"Marco," I called the boy, trying not to break from the memory. A cold spot touched my hand and I knew he was there. "Warehouses."

"She's not supposed to be awake," Lea said, dissatisfied with whichever Aberrant had botched the job.

"The Representative is not here," a man reported behind Lea's back. "That bastard gave us bad intel."

Lea scowled, her eyes leveling with Lady Rasczek's. She stepped away, looking at the piled heap on the floor. Emelia.

"We put too much into this already. Take the girl. She's destined to be a Chairwoman, anyway. May as well get our hold established now. I'll retrieve Lynn Raszcek myself. Wipe the mother's memory. Do your job correctly this time."

An Aberrant drew a glyph in front of Lady Rasczek, only to have the glyph flitter away. "She has a glyph ward. A good one. That's why I couldn't put her to sleep fully," the man muttered. "Should I try to break it?"

"Leave it intact. I'll handle this," Lea growled. She looked like she was still recovering from the wound I had delivered her days before, and was reluctant to put much effort into anything, but there was no denying the certainty with which she approached Lady Rasczek.

The stiffness that held Lady Rasczek where she was abated and she managed to take a step back from the approaching Aberrant. Her hand set on her desk.

"Leave her. Please," Lady Rasczek barely managed to move her jaw enough to say.

Lea raised her hand. "She will be back. And this will all be an unpleasant dream." Her pointer and middle fingers poised and carved the air before Lady Rasczek's eyes. I read the intent in the glyph. Its magic was still wending its way into Lady Rasczek's mind as I held her hand. A memory that never happened. The memory went black as Lady Rasczek collapsed under the crushing force of Lea's magic. I knew the only reason I had gotten away from the Aberrant before was that I had surprised her.

I took my hand away from Lady Rasczek's and, with a quick glyph, tipped the scales for Lady Rasczek's memory in favor of her glyph ward.

"You weren't supposed to even know they took Emelia. The

Aberrants didn't account for the connections you would draw between this and Leeta," I said to Lady Rasczek. "They do intend to return Emelia, but not intact. I'm not going to let them do anything to her." I looked at Katarina. "We have time. But not much. Whatever they are planning, I don't like it. I don't like its implications. I think they are going to try to change her somehow. Are you intent on coming with me, still?"

"How many Abbies?" Katarina asked, sharing a look with Tomas.

"Five that passed this room, as far as Lady Rasczek saw."

"Five Aberrants is a lot, Sade, and we don't know how many more there could have been," Tomas pointed out gently.

"I'm going with or without you." I looked at Katarina, knowing she was the voice for both of them.

"We didn't say we are not going. I'm just saying this is stupid." Katarina looked past me at Lady Rasczek. "If we survive this, I expect a little more civility from your family." She turned to Tomas, who gave a nod of acknowledgement.

I drew up the magic in my gut, and a moment later Katarina, Tomas, and I were at the port. Familiar streets made for easy intent, at least. Transporting so many was getting exhausting.

I looked up at Tomas while we watched the roads from our alley. "Can your Sight tell us anything?"

He shook his head. "If I were a Present Sight, maybe. You wouldn't happen to know one of those?"

"Not one who is sane enough to help."

There was so much interference from the rise of cloud barrier glyphs that had been established by the shipload of Aberrants that I couldn't tell what was new and what was old magic floating in the air.

"Come on, Marco." I murmured as we took to the street.

The ghost never was one to disappoint.

"Sis! I got her. This way!"

Katarina and I both started after the boy instantly, while Tomas, who had not heard his shout, was caught stumbling after us.

"For a Future Sight, not very impressive," Katarina chided when he caught up to us.

"I can't anticipate everything you ladies do on a whim," he grumbled defensively.

"How many Abbies?" I asked Marco quietly.

"The scary one isn't there right now." I could only guess he meant Lea. "With the lady there were two or three, but there's a bunch around the docks."

"Well, let's hope they are getting hit with as much interference as I am." Going against trained Aberrants, I wasn't certain we would be so lucky. They could probably sense the trio of fold-sensitive marching toward them.

If the guards watching Emelia could sense us approaching, they certainly were not the cream of the crop, as Marco was able to lead us past the ones patrolling the exterior of the warehouse.

"There's a lot of magic in there," I said, eyeing the warehouse Marco pointed to. It looked like all the rest of the metal structures littering the port, surrounded by wooden crates yet to be stored and with porters milling about. Only, the air felt different around the building, crowded with glyphwork defenses as it was. We tucked ourselves behind a stand of crates and watched for our opening.

"How can you tell?" Tomas asked.

"Can't you hear the hum of the glyphs?"

"Glyphs don't hum," Tomas said with a frown.

"They do if you are an Aberrant," Katarina said tightly. "Can you tell what we are facing?"

I hesitated, not wanting to tip our hand with a glyph of my own, but decided the risk was necessary. I could guess there were magical detectors in place, but I didn't want to risk us stepping into a flaming trap if we could avoid it.

I focused and brought the glyph to mind. With its release, the defensive glyphs around the warehouse seemed to shine, I hoped only to me.

"Somebody might have felt that release. We are going to want to move fast now," I said. "Stay close to me."

I led Tomas and Katarina around the exterior, avoiding the traps with their deadly intent gleaming at me as we moved.

Tomas slowed me with a hand on my shoulder as we made to enter the designated warehouse. He had a look in his eye I was all too familiar with. One that had always meant I was about to be taken down, hard. I made way for him. Katarina moved in behind him as guards approached. The two of them wielded their fists and kicks with such an understanding of each other that I was sure I would only be in their way. I ducked behind crates as they silently took down the guards posted around the space.

"Wow." Marco said beside me, watching the two work. I stepped past the boy, bringing an Aberrant down with a sleep glyph before she could shout an alarm.

"Where is she?" I prompted the boy.

He dashed off ahead and I followed. Katarina and Tomas joined me at the door to the warehouse office, only lightly out of breath from their foray. Years of pummeling each other paying off.

"We'd better hurry," Katarina said quietly.

I looked at Tomas. He grimaced. There would be no hints from the fold on this step.

"There's four of them now," Marco said, stepping back through the door. "They are on alert, but I don't think they know what's going on."

"Alright, dear. We will follow you in this round," Katarina said.

I was overwhelmingly aware of how little I knew of glyphs, compared to these Aberrants. They were reliant on their gestures, though, and that would be my window.

I brought a glyph for paralysis to mind as I threw the door open. Two of the Aberrants turned toward us, only to be caught by the release of magic and fall frozen to the floor. My intent hadn't been far-reaching enough, and my grasp on the glyph only tentative. Katarina stepped forward, taking down the third in a flourish of skirts, but the last Aberrant raised her hands. A glyph etched and released.

I dove forward, swinging Katarina out of the way of the bolt of electricity that emitted from the glyph, the two of us hitting the floor hard.

A moment later, the female Aberrant cried out and collapsed in desolate sobs on her knees. Emelia's straining fingertips slipped from her wrist as the Aberrant fell out of reach of the restrained woman once again. I released a quick glyph of sleep, quieting the Aberrant before picking myself up.

I knelt beside the chair Emelia was cuffed to, years of habit taking over as I set to work picking the locks of her cuffs.

"Just," Katarina waved her hand irritably at the cuffs, pantomiming a glyph, "them off."

I realized what I was doing as the first cuff fell away and instead turned to the second with a glyph. It fell away instantly and I stood, hauling Emelia with me.

"What in Jespair's name is going on in there?" The Aberrant's shout was certain to draw attention.

Tomas met the raging Aberrant with a solid strike to the jaw that sent him sprawling.

I felt the surge of magic fill the room, and a moment later Lea stood before us with an unconscious woman at her feet.

"Lynn," Emelia said weakly, and I realized the heap was her sister.

Katarina saw my eyes on the unconscious form and dove for her, dragging the politician back to us.

Lea's eyes were filled with confusion before they fixed on me. I could practically see her damaged memories righting themselves behind her eyes.

I wasted no time, pulling Emelia tight against me as the others pressed close. I dredged up the magic, forcing intent into my fingers as I transported the lot of us back to the Rasczek estate.

"Sade? Sade!" Katarina cried out, just barely catching me before I hit the ground.

33:

When I opened my eyes, it was to Lady Rasczek sitting beside me.

As far as Aberrants were concerned, I was a sorry excuse for one. The amount of magic drawn through me with each glyph was absolutely draining, while the College Aberrants barely seemed to break a sweat. Once again, I had caught Lea off guard, and only for that reason had we survived.

I took a moment before meeting Lady Rasczek's hard stare.

"You saved my daughters, but in doing so, you declared war with the College. They won't just let this stand," she said darkly. "That you are an unleashed Aberrant only makes this worse."

"Would you have preferred if I let them alter your daughters? Make them puppets? Like your husband?" I growled weakly.

She answered with a scowl.

"The Society is a farce," Emelia said from where she had been standing silently in the doorway. "It's all a lie. And you knew, didn't you, Mother?"

Lady Rasczek turned from me to her daughter with tight lips.

"Is it declaring war to try to keep some semblance of autonomy? To keep my mind mine?" Emelia scoffed. "Have the Aberrants been working in the shadows this whole time, dictating who becomes a Chairwoman and who is ejected? Why bother pretending that we have any say in our lives? If the gods wanted to, they could drop us into the abyss at any moment." Her voice broke in a sob, pulling even my exhausted body upright. Emelia's eyes fell on me, the imminent break abating for a moment. "Sade saved me. She saved Lynn. Give her a little fucking credit, Mother." Her voice turned bitter.

Lady Rasczek gave a dissatisfied growl and stood. She looked about to say something, but instead took her leave.

Emelia lingered.

I watched her, making room for her beside me, but not pressing in any way.

She looked down at me with a shake of her head and crumpling features.

I saw it in her now. She loved her plants and her botany, but she also loved the Society and its potential, only to see the lie in it all.

She sat beside me heavily. "It's been a shit few days, hasn't it?" She said glumly. She leaned over, her head resting against my shoulder. I wrapped an arm around her shoulders and just held her. "I'm surprised Katarina made such an effort over me," she said, trying to add some levity to her voice and failing. Her forced laugh only carried the tones of a spent woman.

"Don't inflate your ego too much. She tagged along to protect me," I said softly.

Emelia laughed and then closed her eyes, pulling in a long, shaking breath. "How many people have they done this to?"

I didn't have an answer so I didn't try. "I don't know how to keep you safe now," I said quietly.

She shook her head. "It is not your responsibility, Sade. My mother has already upped the security around the manor, and we have a few measures we can take." She shifted to look at me. "You don't look so good."

"I'm not the one who got kidnapped," I said, dismissing her concern.

She cupped my cheek and sighed. There were so many thoughts in her eyes, but instead she just laid down, pulling me with her.

My exhaustion wrapped itself around me as quickly as Emelia folded me in her embrace.

34:

"Wake up."

The order was accompanied by a firm hand grabbing the collar of my shirt as my eyes snapped open. A second later and I was no longer in Emelia's arms, and instead laying on my back, sunk a foot deep in freezing snow. My senses faltered under the brutal slap of bitterly cold wind and blinding whiteness. The air was thin, barely breathable, and the wind seemed to catch whatever oxygen there was and freeze it in my lungs.

Lea stood as though the wind barely even touched her, her robes only slightly flicking as if in a breeze. The wind tore at my clothes as though I were on a dive, and my hands and face felt suddenly numb with cold. I was certain that if I didn't act fast, I would die.

I floundered with the glyphs in my repertoire. I could read them, but I didn't have a solid understanding of building magical intent. I fumbled with the glyphs that kept the landmasses survivable—Deara had made me study them enough that they should have been at the forefront of my mind. Breathable oxygen, shelter from the fumes, control over the turbulent weather of high altitudes, survivable climates. I cut out what I didn't need at this moment and wrangled the rest into a haphazard string in my mind.

The winds seemed to calm, if only slightly, and the cold seemed to ebb, if only by degrees. But the air became breathable, and I pulled in a stinging breath.

"Just because you are a Natural does not mean you can completely disregard the intent of the gesture," Lea said over the winds.

My teeth chattered and I swallowed cold saliva as I brought my freezing fingers up and drew my intent into the air.

Lea looked around, surprised and perhaps impressed, as the howl of the wind died with my release.

"Wh— what in the abyss?" I panted, trying to will my blood to thaw.

She crouched over me like a predator over its meal.

"That was a nasty glyph you used on me the other day, little sister." Her silky voice dropped to a growl. She glared hard at me, her hand poised menacingly, the flare of a glyph half-drawn, hanging in the air at the tips of her fingers. "An unleashed, untamed Daughter of Jespair." I watched her finger continue its slow movement, the glyph etching menacingly toward completion. "You could have killed me with that little trick of yours."

"I could have killed you with the knife in your chest as well," I said, hoping my nervousness did not add a quaver to my voice as I looked up at this woman and the deadly intent slowly being carved into existence above me. Still, I couldn't keep the chattering from my teeth.

She smirked, her finger stopping just short of completing a glyph that was sure to kill me. "Everything in my mind is telling me to kill you," she said quietly, poised and ready to release the glyph. "I want to. You are a Lock. You are an unleashed Natural. You are a threat. To the College. To the Society. To the gods."

I dredged up my own magical defenses, hoping they would be enough, but certain I would not leave this mountainside unscathed.

Her eyes were locked on me, cold and lethal. With a swipe to the side, she dashed the glyph from existence and growled.

"A Natural," she snarled. "The greatest gift Jespair can give any of her daughters and she gives it to you." She scoffed. "Of course she gave it to you. Only your mother could have made you what you are. Only your mother could have gifted you the knowledge and skill … but …" Her anger faded and she went to her knees. "But she died." She shook her head, uncertainty and sadness taking the place of her rage. When she looked at me, her hatred was gone, replaced by a deep-seated confusion. "There is a reason you exist," she said almost pleadingly. "Jespair would not have created you without a reason. You need to be trained."

"What?"

"We can't exactly have an untrained Natural running around."

"I will not go to the College."

"It would be better if you did." She frowned, chuckling dryly as she looked down at me. "You are going to be stubborn on that point, I already know. I will train you." She absently drew a glyph that brought warmth to my freezing bones. Hopefully it would keep the imminent frostbite from setting in, as well.

I was without words for a moment, and the Aberrant gave a grunt as she stood. Looking around at the calmed mountainside, she said, "You did this with a core glyph." She closed her eyes and shook her head, as though struggling with a memory. "It doesn't make sense. You should not know core glyphs; they are restricted. I don't imagine some vagabond just happened upon them in a book."

I frowned. Hadn't I, though? Hadn't Deara drilled me on them? I shook my head. No. Not Deara. The barrier was crumbling and hidden knowledge was pushing to the surface. My mother.

"It doesn't matter," Lea said quietly, suddenly subdued. She looked around. The entire snowy peak had calmed. She offered me her hand, but rather than take it, I pushed myself to my feet.

"I don't buy it. You wanted to kill me. Now you are saying you want to train me?"

Lea met my eye. "Last time, I found out you were a Lock, and maybe I overreacted a little." It was like a switch had flipped, and I wondered if maybe she was conditioned by yet another unseen binding to kill all Locks. "You are not supposed to exist." Once again, her eyes closed in a wince. There was definitely a memory breaking free in her mind, one she was not supposed to remember. I recognized the discomfort of a magical barrier breaking down. "Your mother trusted me, Sade. I didn't know she was a Lock," she said tightly, eyes still closed, "but I trusted her too. It was rare to see a non-Aberrant with so much knowledge of the glyphs … She was an impressive scholar." She opened her eyes, looking more exhausted than I thought she would have wanted me to see. "You need to learn economy. You are already breathing hard from something that should have been easy."

I was, in fact, breathing hard. I looked around us. "I wasn't exactly ready to be dropped on a mountain top."

She carved a glyph into the air, and suddenly my clothes were dry. My bare feet were still freezing, though, and I was less than pleased at our current locale.

"You won't be ready for a lot of things in life. Your reaction is what needs to be trained. You cannot just use core glyphs whenever you need something done. You need to learn practical glyphs, and you need to be able to draw upon them without thought."

"I have not agreed to be your student."

She laughed and gestured around. "And what will you do then, if I leave you here? Do you even know where you are? I can tell that the magical expense you have forced upon your untrained body has left you tapped and exhausted. You are not exactly in the best position for negotiation. And, frankly, my only other option than training you is to kill you."

I knew she was right, yet I squared my shoulders against this Aberrant. "Why not just kill me?"

"It would be a waste of the gifts that Jespair has given the Society in you."

"I don't think that is it."

Lea blinked several times.

"Leave the Rasczeks be."

"The Rasczeks?" Lea looked confused, as though the events of the day before were entirely forgotten. "Oh, yes. Your girlfriend. The future Chairwoman." She scoffed. "That was just business, and as far as I am concerned, beneath me, anyway. As far as the Chancellor needs to know, yesterday was a success. I will take care of my end. But that does not mean there won't come a day that a representative of the College knocks on your Charmer's door and asks for something. Best let the Rasczeks know. Is that enough for you, or need I remind you just how poor your positioning is for bargaining at this moment? I cannot have an errant Natural running amok."

There was something more to all of this. "Tell me why you are putting yourself through this."

She pursed her lips, then nodded. "The touch of your magic on my mind, it broke free memories I don't think I was ever supposed to see again, little sister. Memories of a person I was meant to forget."

She reached forward, setting her hand on my cheek, and I felt the memories pushed into me. For a second I fought, not wanting whatever this Aberrant was trying to show me, but quickly relented. For a moment, at least, she didn't seem to be trying to kill me.

There was me, a child once again. And standing over Lea and me as we played: my mother. "I need to get you back to the College before your prefect notices," my mother said quietly, patting Lea's head.

"No!" My child-self declared, wrapping her arms tightly around Lea's body. I was confused by this memory. By the child version of Lea putting her arms around my shoulders in an embrace.

"I'll see you tomorrow, Sade. Don't worry," Lea assured me. I could feel

her longing to stay. The remorse at being forced to return to the College. But also the fear of being found out. Of endangering the girl in her arms or the mother standing over us.

Lea glanced at the table. The work piled neatly there. Dangerous work, but important.

"I know she was using me because I am a powerful conduit," Lea said on the snowy mountain. "She would have known I was Garnet potential, even then."

In the memory, she looked up at my mother, and I felt the same swell of affection that Lea felt toward the girl still stalwartly holding tight to keep her exactly where she was.

"When my parents knew what I was, they practically threw me in chains and shipped me away," Lea said bitterly. "Your mother might have been using me, but I thought of you as family." The memory faded away, and I saw the strained look on her features, as though she was struggling with an emotion she was unfamiliar with. "You don't remember me at all?"

For a moment I wanted to remember this woman. The girl I had seen myself throw so much love to. This woman was not that girl, though, and I saw nothing in my memories when I looked at Lea.

"I broke my memories after my mother's death," I said carefully, seeing that my memories mattered to this woman, for whatever reason.

Lea frowned, her lips pulling into a dissatisfied line. "You didn't just break your memories. You cleaved Professor Amsel from the minds of everybody at the College. She's nothing but a faint memory, even though it's been barely a decade since her death." She sighed and shook her head. "That must have been her intention. Only she could have designed a glyph so flawlessly that you could manage such a feat." She looked at me, then looked at the sky. "I don't have time for all this. Do you accept or not?"

"I thought you had no leash."

"I may not have an Enforcer following my every step, but I do have appointments to keep." She looked at me pointedly, and I knew that refusing her offer for training made me a threat she could not endure. I was confident neither in my ability to defend myself against this woman, nor in my ability to get off this mountainside.

"Fine," I said, as though I really had any choice. I knew this woman could and would kill me. I knew I needed training. Slowly,

I extended my hand. She took it and, with a grin, shook.

"A Natural. Do you even have an inkling of how rare Naturals are? Almost as rare as Locks." She shook her head. With a quick gesture, we were standing in front of the Rasczek's manor. "Get some rest. I will find you when I have time to start your training." A moment later, she was gone in another flare of magic.

"Sade!" Emelia's arms wrapped around me. "Are you alright? You're freezing. That was the Garnet from yesterday."

"She wanted to talk."

"Talk? That's all?"

"Well, there was a bit more to it, but yes." I looked at the guards posted around the estate. "Your family will not have to worry about her anymore."

"How are you so certain?"

A memory of my arms around a girl I thought of as my sister played in the back of my mind. The barrier was shattering.

"I agreed to be her student."

35:

It was Emelia's opinion that returning to a semblance of normalcy would do me well. After everything that had happened, I had no interest in normalcy. Katarina had returned to the Norwood estate and I knew Tomas would not be leaving her side any time soon. Emelia's sister seemed intent on pretending that nothing strange had occurred, to the point that Emelia started pestering me to see if the Aberrants had already gone to work on Lynn. The woman simply did not want to think about the implications. To her, all that mattered was that one day she had been in Junction, and the next she had been on Vale visiting her family. I almost respected the representative's capacity for denial.

For my part, I didn't want to be anywhere that was not next to Emelia, Lea's assurances be damned. Though she outwardly groused and groaned about it, Lady Rasczek seemed intent on keeping me exactly there. Her opinion seemed to be that there was no safer place for Emelia than next to me. I debated that point, but only silently with myself.

Still, I found myself reeling when Lady Rasczek and I stood on the same side of an argument with Emelia, trying to stop the woman from going on a walk beyond the estate. I simply did not feel like going to work, and I certainly did not need Emelia escorting me. There had been no stopping Emelia, though, and I had followed her as she stomped away from the gates to be her unwilling bodyguard. Behind us, Lady Rasczek glowered and glared, but she had given up on dissuading her daughter long before I had.

"Should we be walking this openly?" I asked, eyeing the well-to-dos taking note of Emelia. It wasn't just them and their gossiping mouths I worried about.

"If I am honest, Sade, I don't really care what gossip spreads about me. I will just take it as a compliment that everybody finds it so necessary to take note of my life instead of worrying about theirs." The pinched lips and sour tone were unusual for her.

I looked at her. "Are you alright, Em?" I asked quietly.

She frowned and shook her head. "I'm sorry, Sade. I'm just tired. And everything … There is so much."

I took her elbow and casually steered her away from the main street.

"How do you keep so calm?" she asked desperately. "We could be sinking into the cloudline and the Society won't even acknowledge the danger. They have Aberrants, they have the College, by the gods, we have engineers; they must be able to do something. And, for all we know, the College does know and just doesn't care. Maybe they have been keeping us all blind. How else can nobody have noticed?"

"It is easy not to see that which you don't want to. Just look at Lynn."

Her face crumpled slightly.

I took her hands in mine, grounding her, not caring who saw and what gossip sprung from this. "What would panicking do for us?" I asked softly. "I make dresses, Em. What would panicking do for me? This is not a matter I can do anything about, except for keeping you safe while we have time."

"I don't need you to worry over me," she said. She looked at the street and the passing notables with a sigh. "I don't know, Sade. Maybe … maybe I could get the socialites talking about it. Bring some light to the matter and force the Society to address the issue. Maybe if enough people know, something will be done."

"At the risk of causing mass hysteria," I pointed out. "Or

having you packed up and shipped off. If not worse."

"I'm not worried about me. There must be something we can do." She turned her eyes to me. "I know it is not fair for me to say. I am not the Natural. Should we take any action, it is likely that much of the effort falls on your shoulders."

I swallowed. "I don't want you to get your hopes up, Em," I said quietly.

"I know. I know. They are not. But I cannot help but have a little bit of hope. Otherwise, I do not know what I would do."

"It could be years, still."

She smiled sadly at my false optimism. "I don't think it will be years."

"The Society is sinking along with the rest of us. With how many scientists they have at their disposal, I don't have a doubt in my mind that they don't already know." I checked around us, leaned close, and kissed her cheek. Taking her hands in mine, I pressed my forehead against hers. "Emelia, please, can we for a moment pretend we don't know the world is potentially coming to an end and enjoy the walk that you so sweetly forced us out onto?"

She laughed hollowly. "Well, when you say it like that, how could I possibly not think about our impending demise?" She sighed and took my hand. "If our days truly are limited, we may as well enjoy them. Come on." She drew me along, doing her best to leave the matter behind. No other topics of discussion seemed to stick, though, and we lapsed into silence with her leaning on me, hand tight in mine as though she regretted her decision to force me out once again.

We stopped outside Mrs. Sandfjord's.

"I don't know that this is the best idea," I said, feeling the need to voice my misgivings one last time. "I should be with you. Not here."

Emelia took my hands in hers. "You said the Garnet agreed to leave my family alone. Besides, Mikael will get me home safely," she said with a surreptitious glance back toward the mass of muscle that had been trying to evade our detection as he followed us. I didn't know how much I trusted the gate guard's abilities when faced with an Aberrant, but there was little I could do at this point.

"Weren't you just saying how we have bigger concerns?"

She kissed me, not caring who saw. "It will do you well doing something you enjoy for a day. Besides, it is not as though you can just disappear from your job without explanation. Can you imagine what will befall all the sirs and madams if they cannot have one of your designs at their next gala?" She laughed and I couldn't help but smile at the sound.

"Look at you," Heinrich, my fellow clothier, drawled at me as I walked in. "Playing missus with Emelia Rasczek?" He grinned and I knew the talk would be townwide by the end of the day. It didn't matter, though. We were sinking into the abyss. "I've covered your work for you since you've been out," he said, without even a hint of malice.

"Thank you. You are a good soul."

"Don't I know it," he said with a smile. "I'm glad you were gone, honestly. Gave the rest of us an opportunity to shine. But … I am even more glad you are back. Some of your customers are a bit …"

"Rude? Demanding? Insatiable?"

He grinned. "Unpleasant, let's say."

It was nice bantering with this man who had no knowledge of Death Sights, Charmers, the waning cores, or the approaching cloudline. I thought maybe Emelia had been right.

Still, when I returned to my quiet workshop, all the typical peace of my work was gone. Instead, I found the solitude only gave me more time alone with my thoughts, and the fear that Lea would actually follow through with her promise to train me. I quickly found myself moving to the front of the shop in search of a distraction. Days ago, I had been pulling Emelia from the clutches of a Garnet, only to be dropped on a frozen mountainside, and now here I was working in the display window of Mrs. Sandfjord's as though nothing had happened. Adjusting the trains of these gowns only did so much in the way of distractions. When I raised my eyes, I saw Lea watching me with tight-lipped amusement.

I backed away from the window and she entered, drawing eyes as all College Aberrants did in their flowing robes.

"I told you I would find you," Lea said, the bells jingling on the door as it closed behind her.

"I'm at work," I growled.

She looked around and chuckled softly. "So it appears. This is quaint." She looked at me. "Somebody of your power does not need to be toiling over dresses that wealthy women wear once and discard."

"Maybe I enjoy this work."

"Maybe," she snorted and rolled her eyes. "You have more important things to be doing. We can't all just disregard duty to do what we enjoy."

Mrs. Sandfjord appeared from the back room. "Aberrant …" she said in quiet surprise.

"Yes, dear woman, that is what I am," Lea said, her fingers rising and flicking a glyph of sleep into existence in only a moment. I caught Mrs. Sandfjord as she crumpled and set her gently on the floor.

"You can't just go around attacking old women," I chided, trying to make the sleeping woman comfortable behind the counter.

Lea leaned over the countertop to look down at me. "Oh, I can do whatever I want."

I shook my head and looked up at her, about to argue, only to see her finish a glyph just above my head.

A moment later, I found myself crouching on the floor of a dark room, looking around with apprehension.

"Do you recognize this place?" Lea asked as I straightened.

I drew the glyph for light, bringing clarity to the dark space, but I hadn't needed to. There had been a time I could navigate this modest house in pitch black.

"You brought us all the way to Junction?"

Lea watched me and nodded. "So, you do know it. It has gone vacant all these years because there's a powerful ward on the house. You could be standing on the street staring right at the building, and unless you are looking for it, you won't even register it is here."

I blinked, a memory snapping free in my mind.

"Are you certain they can do this, Priya?" I didn't recognize the voice, but it belonged to an older woman. "They are children."

Their voices had been hushed, but Lea and I exchanged a look. We knew they were talking about us.

"Their potential does not change as children or adults. Just their knowledge, and I will help mitigate that gap. I will be with them the whole way, and they will have each other. If the Society cannot protect itself, we will. It will be alright, Leeta."

The two were quiet for a time, and I knew the two women were not alone in their discussion. My mother had already taken on the abilities of a Death Sight at this point.

"I don't think that Fennick is too far off," my mother agreed. "Sade and

I have been visiting the cores for months. I have isolated the issue to Vale."

"You know more than you think," Lea said, pulling me from the memory as she rounded the room. Furnished with only a pair of well-aged armchairs and a simple wooden coffee table, the house was modestly kept except for the bookshelves that lined the backwall of the living space. Even from across the room I could tell the collection of elegantly bound texts had been assembled by a connoisseur. "I suspect bringing you here may right some of the damage you did to yourself." Behind me, Lea banished the dust from the long-abandoned dining table with the flourish of a finger before dropping a book onto it with a thud.

"*Foundations*," she announced. "A perfect place to start for a careless Aberrant who has no concept of economy or practical glyphs. We will train you to refine your reactions with a strong foundation of said practical glyphs."

"I don't need practical glyphs," I grumbled, turning to her.

"Oh, and what is it you need, then?"

"You want to teach me something useful, then how can I dissipate the cloudline?"

"Dissipate ..." She blinked at me as though she could not comprehend my words. "You want to dissipate the cloudline? For what? There's nothing below us."

"You don't truly believe that, do you? If that's the case, then where did all of this come from?" I said with a general sweep of my hand. "We came from somewhere. The landmasses came from somewhere. And the only logical place we could have come from is below."

"Even so, dissipating the cloudline ...?"

"It can't be impossible. We control the clouds with glyphs. We control the atmosphere to keep these chunks of rock survivable."

She shook her head. "Even our control has been failing recently."

"Which is why we need to dissipate the cloudline. With enough Aberrants—"

"No," she cut me off sharply. "No. The College will not engage in such a foolish endeavor."

"What about it is foolish, Lea? We could have the entire planet. We could be free of worrying about drifts. We could stop the acid that is eating away at the potential of life below."

"The ..." Her mouth seemed to falter as she cocked her head

to the side. "What …" She blinked. "What were we talking about?" She rubbed her temple.

"What do you remember?"

Lea blinked several times to clear her mind and looked at me. "What do you mean? We were talking about … weather patterns?"

"Not quite. Give me your hand."

The woman looked at me suspiciously, then slowly presented her hand.

I set my fingers on hers and pushed the memory of the conversation into her mind.

"That doesn't make sense …"

"Can I look?" I asked, nervous at what atrocities I may accidentally happen upon in this woman's memories.

She swallowed, then nodded once.

I prodded. Deara had said that gaps could be difficult to identify. That giving made the taking easier. That it made the search less painful. I let a memory slip to Lea. A harmless one. A night playing cards with friends.

In exchange, Lea's memories melted into mine. My mother. Further. A ceremony. The gap. I prodded the edges. A barrier. A tether.

I released from her stream of memories.

"What was that?" Lea asked cautiously, taking her hand back and holding it protectively against her chest. "There was a barrier."

"That would be your leash," I said, shaking my head. "That explains it. The College. It's a control. I mean, obviously it is. But it's deeper than that. It's years of exposure to a control. Deeper even than the Society's thought binding. You don't even notice it bleeding into you. As long as all Aberrants are sent to the College, or killed, the control remains intact."

"Why would we tether ourselves, Sade? You are misinterpreting it."

"What are the gods? Do you even question it?"

"The gods?"

"Have you even thought about it?"

"Thought about what?"

"This is going to be more difficult than I thought." I sighed and took her hand again, pushing the last few minutes back to her.

"Why do I keep forgetting?" Lea said, rubbing her temples.

"There's a barrier, a deterrent. It's making your mind slip away from whatever it is they don't want you thinking too hard about."

"Who is 'they,' Sade?" she asked, exasperated.

"How should I know? The College? More likely, the gods. Whatever the barrier is, it wasn't set up to protect against me pushing memories to you with Sight."

"But if I don't have the memories anyway, it's not as though poking around will get you anywhere."

I shook my head. "The barrier only extends so far. As I said, it was a gradual process. Like when I scrambled your memories, because it was a glyph, a rapid shift, it was easily remedied, right? This one burrowed deep over time. It must be why my mother reached out to you while you were young," I said. "I know when it started. I think that if we prod the beginning, we can determine what it is keeping you from even contemplating the cloudline."

"Why would I contemplate the cloudline?"

"Give me your hand," I grumbled.

She frowned and did so.

I went back once again. A memory slipping unbidden from me. My mother, her death. Still, the tithe was paid, and in exchange I found my mother in Lea.

"The cloudline, Lea. You are strong. You can dissipate it," my mother said.

"It's not possible, professor." Lea was young, before the barrier had fully formed.

"It is. But we need to do it soon."

"Why?"

"Because if we wait too long, you won't be able to anymore. They don't want us to know it's possible, Lea."

"Who?"

"Jespair. The other gods. All of them. They can control us like this. As long as our population is small, as long as they hold all the Aberrants, they control the Society. I know it's confusing, but that is how it is, Lea. And I need your help. I'm not an Aberrant. I can't use glyphs or magic. With you ... with your natural talent ... with the cores, we can do it."

Lea hesitated. "How?"

My mother smiled. "There are forbidden glyphs. Forbidden due to their power. Forbidden because they can free us from these landmasses and from the Society's controls. Can I show them to you?"

Lea nodded slowly, hesitantly. I could tell that already the barrier was starting to impose itself on her. That my mother had seen Lea's potential only at the end of her capability to use it.

Lea glowered with a small shake of her head. "Let's say I am willing to believe you. You want to dissipate the cloudline? Well, then you need a foundation. Practical glyphs. And proper understanding of the basics. Only then do you have any hope of being able to refine your glyphwork to handle such a load. So, are you done complaining, and are you ready to learn?"

"Are you willing to help me in this?"

Her face pinched as she considered. "Are you willing to listen?"

"Yes. Sorry."

"It's alright," she said with surprising patience.

I frowned at her, too familiar with the Aberrant's darker nature to be able to reconcile this version of her with what I had seen in Hayden's memories. What I had glimpsed in her own.

"What is it?"

I considered for a moment, then said, "You tortured the former ringleader of my gang. I saw his memories."

Lea closed her eyes and sighed. "Did you, now? That's unfortunate. Sometimes that is what the Society asks of us."

"Don't bullshit me, you enjoyed it."

"I won't deny it," she said with a shrug, seeing she wasn't getting out of it with an act of false compassion. "I remember him. The Present Sight. That boy had too many ambitions. Bigger than his capabilities."

"The Persephone was not that grand of a heist. Had you and the Enforcers not been expecting us, we would have succeeded."

"It was not the Persephone that got him killed."

"I did not say he was dead."

"He's not dead? The incompetence of …" She bit off her angry tirade. "It doesn't matter." She took a calming breath. "My job was not killing him. Just finding out why he was targeting the Gao family."

"The Gao family?"

She shrugged. "Old money. The patriarch is a Chairman; surely you know them."

"I do. Why was Hayden going after them?"

"Well, that was the question, wasn't it?"

"Surely you found an answer. With everything you put into your interrogation," I said darkly.

She narrowed her eyes at me. "It is not as though I intended to torture you. I did not tell you to go traipsing around in his broken mind."

"No. You didn't, but that is what I did. Why was he after the Gaos?"

"He was a misguided young man. That's why. A Present Sight sees too much, and the Gaos are a very dirty family with a lot of strings to pull. Your 'ringleader,' as you call him, he thought he could blackmail the father with the sins of the son, but if you know the Gaos, you know that anything their son has done, the Chairman has done far worse. Seems that Chairman Gao bought one of your compatriots because, the next thing I knew, I was being assigned to board the Persephone." She waved a dismissive hand. "Are you content with this errant rabbit hole we have wandered down? Can we return to training, finally?"

We stared at each other for a long time in silence, a touch irritated with one another. We were off to a great start.

After a time, I grabbed *Foundations* and cracked its pages. She was right. I had no hopes of dissipating the cloudline if I couldn't even manage the most basic of Tinkerer's glyphs.

36:

After the mountainside, Lea kept her lessons tamer. The Aberrant had seen the breadth of my magic with my use of the core glyph. Now she seemed intent on refining it. I accepted the foundational lessons without much fuss. I knew pushing her too quickly would result in little. Still, each day I woke up and looked out my window, I swore the cloudline seemed to be climbing higher to meet us. I knew our descent was slow. That we would die choking only after the slums had been forced to expire before us. That we would likely be held back from the upper alts by barricades and Enforcers, and that families like the Rasczeks and the Gaos would be the last of our landmass to sink slowly below.

I waited for Lea at our usual spot outside of town. The deserted mill would soon be converted into a textile factory, short-lived as that venture would be with the fall. While I waited, I practiced etching glyphs into existence here and there. Small things like bringing a bit of light to the room, heating up the space, changing the color of the paint on the wall. Lea insisted that I draw the glyphs with my fingers, rather than only summoning them to mind. The act seemed to ground the magic and maintained the glyph's stability longer under more strain. Better yet was the ability to draw one glyph, but summon a different one.

"Fancy tricks," Lea had described my new technique as when I sent her to the ground while we trained basic combat. The thin line of her mouth had been peeved, but I could read the small hints that the woman had been impressed. Still, it was difficult to pull off and too easy to confuse intent. I practiced a few times, then sighed and looked at the door to the mill. It wasn't like Lea to be late.

I walked outside and looked around. No Lea.

With a grumble, I turned to the massive combine out front and summoned a glyph to mind, carving it into existence with two fingers. As it released, the combine started picking itself apart until it was nothing but a pile of parts that had once been a machine. The magical cost took the breath from me for a moment, and I set my hands on my hips to recover.

"Economy," Lea said from behind me.

I turned to the Aberrant. "Where were you?"

"How many times have I told you, you need to learn economy? What did that achieve? Hmm? That piece of machinery could have and would have been repurposed. We have limited resources to draw upon here. Like you have limited magic to draw upon. You can't just go wasting it all on foolish displays."

"Where were you?"

She looked down and I spotted something clutched firmly in her hand. A book. An old atlas. Small and easily overlooked. She hesitated in giving it to me. When she did extend it toward me, her fingers refused to release the cover for a moment. I could see her struggling with herself and the unseen binding of the College.

"I want nothing more than to destroy that," Lea muttered. "Which tells me it may be important." She glared at the book, her hands clenching into tight fists to stop herself from summoning the glyphs of destruction. "I haven't been able to look in it. I didn't want to risk it." She growled and turned her back on me as I held the atlas.

"You found this at the College?"

She nodded. "Is it useful, or can I destroy it and relieve myself of this agony?"

"Was it in the restricted section?"

"No," she said with effort, stepping away from me, hoping distance would lessen the urge to burn the book. "It was in the wrong section, overlooked for I don't know how many years."

I looked at the glyph inked onto the flyleaf. "*Benfi.*" I read the glyph's name. "Forgotten." I translated. I looked at Lea. "Can I help you?"

"Unless I can destroy that, no. I will just have to bear this."

I nodded and hastened to flip through the pages to determine the book's worth. The tattered atlas seemed an unimpressive find, until I realized it was of the planet below. Mountains and seas, forests and deserts. The planet below the cloudline had been charted, memorialized in the pages of this book, and forgotten.

"So?" Lea ground out. "Is it important?"

I was at a loss for words, but finally managed, "Yes. Yes. I think it's the most important book you could have found."

"Damn," she said, breathing hard through her nose, trying to calm the directive to destroy.

I quickly hid the atlas in my bag and turned Lea around to look at me. I set my hand on her cheek and the lines of tension instantly relaxed as I released a drowsiness glyph. Her eyelids fluttered, but she kept her feet, and I prodded the edges of the binding once again.

While I focused on finding the source and reason for this branch of the binding, she slumped forward into my arms, my drowsiness having gone a little too far. I pressed a little energy into her, and the tension returned.

"They don't want us to know about the surface," I said as I hunted down the binding. "They don't want us to know anything exists below the cloudline but fumes. Focus."

She met my eyes with a snarl of frustration as she focused on breaking another border of the barrier enforced by years of exposure.

"Anything that evidences the planet was once viable. That we came from below. They want it destroyed. Wiped from history. Lea, think about it. How can it be that the entire Society does not even question what lies below the cloudline and the potential that the surface holds. The gods clearly do not want such thoughts to even exist."

Her eyelids fluttered, and she collapsed.

"Shit," I swore, catching the Aberrant and rapidly transporting us to my room with a hasty glyph. I dragged the unconscious Garnet to my bed and laid her down to recover.

Emelia had been bad enough, but I was certain Katarina would tear the house apart if she found a College Aberrant within her walls.

37:

I had never frequented any of the gods' shrines. I'd whispered my share of prayers to Devton before dives, but I couldn't say for certain that he had done anything tangible for me in the past. Still, failing cores and sinking landmasses seemed an issue large enough for the gods to take an interest.

"I want to speak with Devton. I demand to speak with Devton," I said in a low voice to the hooded figure standing at the foot of the statue of the god.

"You speak with Devton through me, sister."

I knew it was pointless. Still, I tried. I lowered my voice. "Then tell him I know. I know we are falling." The representative said nothing. I wondered why I even bothered. "You do not even try to refute that it is happening? Why do you do nothing? The landmasses are sinking. The cores are sick. The cloudline will kill us all. I suspect it will even kill you."

The representative was quiet a moment, then said, "All you need is devotion."

I growled. "Canned answers from a mindless drone." I turned on my heels and stormed from the shrine.

"You won't get anywhere trying to make demands of the gods like that," a woman said beside me.

In my irritation, I ignored the nosey passerby and strode from the useless shrine. The gods claimed anybody could speak with them any time, but if what they meant was that anybody could speak with a mindless drone any time, they were not much use at all.

"I didn't take you for a worshiper." In my annoyance, I hadn't realized the nosey party was Lea until she peeled from where she had been leaning against the wall of the shrine to follow me. Now Lea stood directly behind me. "What are you doing here?"

"What are *you* doing here?" I rebuffed, peeved from my pointless visit to the shrine.

"Following you, obviously."

"Please tell me Katarina did not see you when you left the house."

Lea chuckled. "Do you think I walked here? When I woke up and you were not there, I cast a net to find you. You were not difficult to find, by the way."

"Are you feeling better?"

"Is that concern for a fellow Aberrant I hear?"

I grumbled and shook my head. "What are the gods?"

Lea raised an eyebrow at me. "Even street urchins know about the gods, surely."

"Yes, I know about them. But what are they?"

She frowned, struggling with an explanation. "They are eternal. Unexplained. They are the greatest conduits of the magic of the fold, and they are the ones who determine how it is allocated to the rest of us."

"I question that, though."

I could see her eyes start to fade and knew I was on the right path. I took her hand and forced my words to echo in her memories as I spoke.

"I think they are Naturals. Old, powerful Naturals. But they are just Aberrants. Why do you think they keep other Aberrants on such tight leashes? There's no lore that makes sense about their beginnings." I shook my head. "You can feel it, I am sure, that their representatives are all Aberrants." I pressed.

I could see clarity returning to Lea's eyes as she beat back the bounds of the binding.

"I think Jespair figured out how to bind other Aberrants to her. I think that is why she is in charge. I may be new to this, but I have never known a second daughter and third born to be the head of a family while her siblings still live. Jespair must have done something to get one over on her older siblings, Albain and Espa."

I took my hand away from Lea's when I saw I no longer needed to enforce the rigidity of her memory.

"That doesn't explain their timelessness," Lea pointed out.

"I imagine holding that much magic at your fingertips does strange things to your body." I shrugged. "It is just a theory, but it is obvious the College does not want you questioning the gods. And I suspect that is because the gods are the source of the—" I grabbed her hand, seeing her eyes fading once again. "I suspect the gods are the source of the College binding," I repeated.

She glowered. "This is so frustrating. Why did it have to be me to discover you?"

"You could have left well enough alone," I reminded her.

"Perhaps I should have."

"Would you have been happier in your ignorance?"

"I would have been happier not having to listen to the theories of an uneducated, overpowered scoundrel day in and day out," she said, but I could tell she was just being querulous. "Interesting as they may be," she added reluctantly after a time. "That's not the assignment I gave you."

"No, but it seems more important, doesn't it?"

She shook her head. "An untrained Aberrant is a threat to the Society."

I gave her a hard look. "Are you parroting or is that your true belief?"

"I truly believe that an undertrained and overpowered Aberrant such as yourself, especially with grandiose and harebrained ideas such as yours, is a threat. Yes."

"Then why haven't you turned me in?"

She frowned.

"I am an abomination, after all. A Natural and a Death Sight-enabled Lock. I see you resisting the urge to kill me right now." Indeed, my reminder of what I was added strain to her hold. "It is not just because we were close as children. I imagine that has not stopped you in the past."

"Then why do you taunt me?"

"Because, for some reason, you refuse to obey a binding engraved so deeply that we have been plucking away at it strand by illusive strand without any sign of the knot holding it firm. That cannot be an easy refusal. Why not give in to it?"

She scowled. "Because you *might* be right." It looked like it pained her to admit, and not because of any deeply engraved magical binding. "Maybe we are sinking. Maybe the gods are false. Maybe ... maybe we can do something about it. But, Sade, even a Natural cannot elevate a landmass alone."

"What about the College?"

"They won't help if they are as subservient to the gods as you think," she strained to say. "And I'm starting to believe they are ..." She frowned, trying to get past the binding again. "Why would the gods not want to keep the landmasses up? The cores from failing? If they are just Naturals as you say, they cannot survive the fall either."

"Maybe they can. Or maybe they can keep the Isle afloat. Maybe they don't care. Either way. It does not seem they are taking action. The cores *are* dying."

"Did your ghost tell you that?" Lea asked incredulously.

"He did, actually."

She narrowed her eyes. "He has seen the core?"

"I sent him to check," I said. "Each time he gets closer and closer. That is sign enough for me that something is wrong."

"He shouldn't have been able to get close to any of the cores. Even dead. If that's true … Hmph. The barriers may be failing, which points to a larger issue … I will have to get the Chancellor to sign off on me even going close to a core. It will not be an easy ask, but if she will hear of such an idea from anybody, it will be me." She set her hand on my arm and a moment later we were standing in my mother's house on Junction. "You. Study," she said, pointing at the book she had left open on the table. "I'm going to have a chat with the Chancellor."

I frowned down at the open pages. "What's this?"

"Raw talent is nothing if it is not well-backed," she said in hardly an answer. She drew a glyph with her deft fingers and was gone.

I sighed and turned my eyes to the book she had delivered me to. Another restricted book for only the highest levels of Aberrants. I could feel the hum of the tracking glyphs on the pages. So much as touching the book would engrain my identity into its pages. I kept my hands in my lap and leaned over the rows and rows of glyphs that told the history of the gods. At least, what the College knew of the history of the gods.

It seemed a foolish thing to me to study a history I suspected was entirely made up, but there was power even in these glyphs. And there was power in knowledge. Even on these pages of lies there had to be some truth. The gods were siblings, of that I was certain. Five siblings who seemingly sprung into existence without the aid of their parents. Five siblings who supposedly brought life to a desolate rock face and made the landmasses liveable. Five siblings who taught the first Aberrants how to use the glyphs to harness magic.

I frowned. If the landmasses weren't livable before, where did the gods come from? Then I rolled my eyes. It would be chalked up to the great mysteries of the world. Maybe the entire Society was bound by a grand delusion. But if that were the case, why could I question what Lea could not? No. That glaring delusion had to be, at least in part, accepted by choice.

Instead of reading the words, I turned my attention to the glyphs. There was a reason this book was restricted, beyond its content showing the gaps and fallacies of the gods. No. There was more. The glyphs used were old, strict, and basic. None of the flourish of the College writings Lea had provided me.

Strict and basic. The foundation of glyphwork. The College had bound itself with its own creativity. The glyphs they trained in were adulterated, weakened by their divergence from their foundational core. They could adapt their intent in the most basic ways, but their foundation was weak and that made their magic sloppy.

I studied the page, reading the intent in the strokes as naturally as I always had. Finding the patterns and structure. With a proper base, an Aberrant could create endless intent in glyphs.

Lea actually looked proud for once when she returned. "I knew you would see it. I can't teach it. But I knew you would understand. Those who rise to Garnet are the ones who discover the true base of glyphwork and who contain the power to use it. Those who can see beyond the limitations of the glyphs taught by the College. What are ten thousand glyphs when you could have endless intent?"

"Says the woman whose first lesson to me was economy."

She rolled her eyes. "It is not the same. Reactions should be built on basics and fast economical glyphs. You don't need a lot of fancy adaptations to survive. True skill, though, that's derived from the ability to form intent in a glyph. To drive and shape magic as we need it. The College found ways to make the glyphs easier to wield even by the weakest-willed Aberrant. But to do so, we have taken away from their strength."

I knew the importance of this lesson but had other matters on my mind. "What did the Chancellor say?"

"She said she would think about it, which is as good as a no. So, keep studying." The woman was frustrated. I could see a little seed of rebellion starting to grow in the leashed Garnet. If nothing else, maybe I would actually find an ally in this woman. I could see that the girl of her past was not completely dead in Lea now.

38:

Katarina eyed me, my jumpsuit and the talons strapped to my wrist making her frown. "What are you up to?"

"I want to see the core for myself."

She laughed and shook her head. "And you plan on climbing down there?"

"I'll have Reeva."

"I'm not worried about you getting past their wards, Breaker or no. The Enforcers can kill you with contemporary weapons just as well. They will see you climbing down the side of this rock and they will pick you off with standard lead."

"I'm taking a risk, I know. But I don't think they will see us. I don't think anybody is looking. I don't think ..." I blinked, not certain what I was about to say. "I don't think the ..." I trailed off again and Katarina raised an eyebrow. I swallowed and cleared my throat. "The gods don't want ..."

Katarina pouted. "What were we just talking about?"

The two of us just looked at each other dumbly. I checked the straps on my talons, then headed for the door. "Don't wait up."

I took my leave and set off for the slums. Reeva took me in with an air of excitement when I entered her squat. "I was worried I had lost the hard-handed, tarry-lunged vagabond to those dunderheaded nobles."

Her talons looked worse for the wear, too many nights on the streets without shelter over the last year, but the woman had kept them with her. A memento of her past.

"Are we doing something stupid?" I asked, checking the streets from her small window. Nobody would notice us passing, but the talons on our wrists were a dead giveaway of nefarious intent.

"Oh, most definitely," Reeva said. "I think you might have the right idea that the s n't t any o ow the ing."

I looked at her with a frown. "What?" Her words were a jumble that slipped away the moment they reached my ears.

She rolled her eyes and grabbed my hand. "The gods don't want anybody knowing the cores are failing." Her voice was so clear now. "Maybe they really won't have a full retinue of guards surveying the descent." Her hand left mine.

"I thought the binding was broken," I said, rubbing my palm.

She shrugged. "Latent effects. Maybe it's all that time you spend on Junction these days. I'm sure they will go away. You sent Marco ahead for recon, right?"

I nodded. "He said he didn't see any guards around the core itself, at least as close as he was able to get. At the entrance there was just the usual Enforcer presence, about six Enforcers rotating through. At least for the climb we should be alright, as long as we can slip between the roving patrols and their airships."

"Not a problem. I pretty much have their schedule memorized. The Enforcers really are bad at deviating from the standard." She tossed me a climbing harness and stuffed one in her own sleek climbing pack.

"Where did you get this?" I asked.

She shrugged. "Your Charmer."

"Does she know you have it?"

Reeva rolled her eyes and led me onto the streets. "She handed it to me herself. Same with the rope and the clips."

"You didn't tell her we were doing this, did you?"

"No. Of course not. You asked me not to. I did, however, mention that if she had any climbing gear from her last expedition … we could maybe use it. She didn't ask questions. I seem to think she would rather prefer we don't go falling to our deaths on this little adventure."

I hoped Emelia wasn't worrying knowing what we were up to in the dark of night, but there wasn't much I could do about that now. I needed to focus.

When we arrived at the rails of the Grand Cross Bridge I looked over the edge and felt a familiar pang of nervousness. A touch of anxiety had always accompanied every climb, every dive, every moment where my feet were not securely planted on the surface of the landmass. Reeva, for her part, seemed to revel in the thrill of the descent over the edge of the bridge to the cliff face below.

I would have preferred to transport myself with a glyph, but I wasn't about to leave Reeva to climb on her own. The act of scaling down a cliff was one I had once been so familiar with. Now I found myself having small moments of terror if a rock slipped under my fingers or my toes scrabbled to find a hold. Yes, I would have much preferred transporting us. Reeva appeared entirely cool and collected, as though she still spent her days scuttling around the underside of the landmass.

We managed to make the climb down to the platform outside

the core's entrance. Our boots met the heavy metal plates with only the dullest of thumps as we ducked behind the guardhouse to take a few moments to recover from the long climb.

The glyph cores were always guarded, though only out of an exuberance of caution. It was the rare madman who thought attacking the glyph cores was the only righteous way. The station had mostly become an honor posting at this point. One that even the Enforcers had lost the honor in. The current group seemed to see the posting as nothing more than a nice break from the grind of the more strenuous patrols on the surface of the landmass.

They laughed and threw down cards and dealt new hands at a small table outside the entrance to the glyph core tunnel. A memory broke free. *My mother and I at the entrance of this same core. Her handing off a set of papers authorizing her access to the core as a College researcher. Patting me on the head and kissing my cheek before entering the tunnel. Me joining the Enforcers in their game of cards as though I were one of their best friends.* I noticed now how the Enforcers had barely even looked at her documents, mainly taken her word for it. How often had we come to these cores? How had she convinced the College to allow her access? I doubted the gods wanted just anybody poking around their cores.

I focused on the Enforcers, then drew a glyph for sleep. The men and women slumped in their seats, their cards slipping from their fingers as they drifted off. We stepped silently past them while they gently snored.

I understood now why Aberrants were not posted at the cores. The fold felt like it was buckling under the weight of such a high density of glyphs. My stomach turned and my eyes lost focus so close to the glyph core. The glyphs carved into the walls practically flared with light from the magical density clogging the air.

Reeva kept her hand securely on the wall, holding the defenses at bay as we approached. The Breaker looked no worse for the wear, grimy from the climb, but not nauseous.

"I don't want to get too close," Reeva said. "That thing's what's keeping us afloat and the air around us breathable. I would hate to accidentally break that."

I nodded and the two of us halted with the glyph core just barely in view in its chamber. The perfect sphere of stone shone faintly with the strength of so many powerful glyphs. The wide plinth the massive stone rested on had no physical means of keeping the core from rolling but I suspected that such a trivial matter had never been an issue when confronted with such a high density of magic.

I sat heavily, barely able to keep my dinner from spilling out of me.

Reeva set a hand on my shoulder. "Is that better?"

The pressure of the glyphs and the buckling layers of the fold receded, but so did my sight of the subtle glow from the glyphs lacing the walls and the core stone. I would have to get closer.

"Better," I agreed. I caught my breath and steadied myself. "Alright. I am going closer. I'm ready."

Reeva lifted her hand and the oppressive force weighed down on me instantly. My stomach flipped, but I had more important matters to attend to.

"Stay here," I said to Reeva, then crawled forward, aware of the glyphs lining the stone walls of the tunnel and their deadly intent.

"Don't go too far," Reeva warned.

I focused on the task at hand. The fold felt like it would crack my spine under the pressure, my wrists felt weak, and my mouth was overly damp. I was cold and hot, and for a moment I saw something that looked very much like empty air all around us. A blue sky, soft white clouds. Darkened land far below. Vertigo kicked in, making my head spin and my vision whirl as the stone beneath my hands seemed to vanish. A moment, then it was gone. The hard surface was once again certain beneath me.

I looked back at the core, focusing on the glyphs rolling across the stone in tight rows of meticulously etched strokes. It looked strong and healthy, its magic an impressive thing. But still, there was something in it. A waning. It was hard to know if the core was sick when this was my first glimpse of it, yet looking at it, I had a certainty that something about it wasn't quite right.

"—are. Sade." Reeva's voice sounded far off and distorted.

Another sickening flip of the fold made me feel like my insides were beyond the confines of my body. I collapsed to the floor of the tunnel, but with my eyes fixed on the core. Suddenly a dead stone. No light shining from its glyphs. Broken and dark. Nothing but rock.

Then once again it shone overly bright. I pushed myself against the wall to my right, using it for support as I tried to find enough strength to make it back to Reeva.

"Sade! Dammit, Sade. I can't go closer to you. And if I lift my hand from this glyph ... Damn you," she growled, and I felt a small shattering of magic from her direction as she broke the glyph at the core of the tunnel's defenses.

She took a step toward me, but I waved her off. "Don't. Don't risk it." I could feel a waning in the magic around me with her one step. It was a reprieve, but a dangerous one so close to the core.

She stayed where she was, and I dragged myself inch by inch back to her. I dropped at her boots and she wrapped her arm around me and hauled me to my feet.

The quiet of her separation from the magic was a soothing thing, but the suddenness of the loss left me cold.

She looked at the glyph she had broken. The careful etching now bore a jagged crack through its base stone. We could both see the flare of an alarm triggered by the severing.

"They will know somebody was here now," Reeva said nervously.

I leaned against her heavily and forced my feet to trundle forward. "We need to get moving," I said weakly.

Reeva dutifully helped me toward the exit, but I could feel the anxiousness in her fingers.

"Are you going to be able to make the climb back out of here?"

"I just need a minute to recover. I'll be fine."

"Can you transport yourself?"

I shook my head. "I'm not leaving you behind, Reeva." Already my strength was returning to me with distance and time away from the core.

"It will be easier for me to make this climb without your dead weight. The core didn't affect me like it did you, Sade. We could have an airship filled with Abbies headed for us right now."

"All the more reason for me to stay with you," I said, leaning off her now. The entrance yawned ahead of us, and the cool night air was a refreshing change after the intensity of the core. I hadn't realized how hot it had been so close to the stone. Luckily, the Enforcers continued to slumber, completely unaware of the events that evening.

The climb was hard work. My muscles were exhausted from the proximity to the core, my arms shaking as I pulled and pushed my way up the cliff face of the underside of Vale. Still, the act of climbing was natural and I read the rock face easily even in the dark.

"Sade. We have a problem." Reeva was looking up at a quickly approaching searchlight and the Enforcer airship it belonged to.

I swore even though I had known this was a possibility. A likelihood.

I set my hand against the stone in front of me and drew the glyphs I needed into mind.

"Hold tight," I said, then released the magic into the stone. The glyphs burrowed and crept, carving and widening the space while Reeva and I avoided the rock crumbling away from where our fingers and toes had been moments before. I watched the searchlight and the airship in its descent, creeping closer. "Get in," I said to Reeva once the burrow was large enough for us both.

"I don't need to remind you I am a Breaker," Reeva said anxiously. "Whatever you plan on doing, you won't be able to."

"Just trust me."

The woman scurried into the hole while I remained outside. I needed distance from her, and even with it, I resorted to the certainty of a drawn glyph. My fingers worked quickly to wrestle a struggling glyph into existence. So close to the core and a Breaker made the work challenging, but finally the glyph took shape and released as the spotlight swept ever closer. The glyph hung in the air just outside the hole, then expanded into a perfect semblance of a rock face. I swung into the hole, just barely large enough for Reeva and me. Reeva caught me and pulled me back away from the lip and the drop that would mean certain death. She was trying to stay as far from my illusion as possible, trying to keep it from wavering as the light swept over it.

We both held our breath. The beam shone blindingly on us, then continued its hunt.

"I thought it would be bigger," I commented about the space. The two of us crammed in, smashed front-to-front with dirt pressed against our backs in a space the size of a coffin.

"It probably would have been if I hadn't stopped your glyphs when I dove in," Reeva whispered.

"Not the end of the world," I said as we watched the airship continue on its way.

Reeva's chuckle vibrated against my chest. "That's exactly what it is, though, isn't it? Be honest. What did you see?"

"What does the glyph core look like to you?" She could see magic in her own way, but had she really been unable to see the power of the core?

"It looked like a rock held together with a lot of fraying strings."

I frowned, realizing the Breaker wasn't far off. The description fit. For all the core's apparent strength with its blinding power, it was fraying.

"I'll take that long sullen silence as agreement," Reeva said, looking out at the cloudline. "I know we are pretty low on the landmass right now, but it looks closer than it should."

I looked out over the clouds with a pit in my gut. During the Grand Cross climb with Emelia, I had seen it, too. The approach of the cloudline was slow; I never would have noticed it if I hadn't been away from the slums so long.

The airship moved off and we continued the climb. Our breaks were sparing, stopping only moments at suitable ledges, aware that at any moment another airship of Enforcers could round the landmass. Still, it wasn't until we were heaving our exhausted bodies up and over the railings onto the streets of Vale that we heard our first shout of alarm.

"You there, halt!"

Reeva and I turned from our panting recovery to the cluster of Enforcers approaching us at a run. Behind us, the port was abuzz with Enforcer activity.

Reeva shoved me into action. "Move!"

We ran. Determination and fear drove our spent legs. This wasn't the first time either of us had fled from Enforcers. We leapt crates and tossed barrels as we darted between warehouses and into alleys. It was only when we were about to pull away from our pursuit that the shot cracked through the night.

Reeva stumbled. I skidded to a halt. The glyph for sleep managed to lodge in my waning mind and release before my arms wrapped around the falling Breaker. My access to my magic cut abruptly as I held Reeva, but my glyphs had been fast enough. The Enforcers went down in haphazard heaps. There was a moment of calm as our pursuit hit the cobbles, but behind their sleeping forms I could hear the shouts of more Enforcers continuing to scour the area. I threw Reeva over my shoulders and bolted.

39:

I only stopped running when we were safely tucked away in Reeva's home. My energy was depleted, adrenaline the only thing that had gotten me this far. I knew I wasn't done yet and forced my body to ignore the fatigue.

I set Reeva down. "I'm going to get help."

She nodded, her grimace deepening as she clutched at the wound. I stepped away from the Breaker, then summoned a glyph to my hand and brought it to my mouth.

"Katarina."

"Fuck, Sade," I could hear the woman's surprise at the sudden voice in her head. She sounded strangely clear-headed. "What went wrong?"

"Reeva's been shot."

"Where are you? Start the engine." She must have been ready with the motorcarriage on hand.

"The slums. Hang on. I'm going to show you."

Katarina groaned at the prospect, but I knew she was willing. An engine roared to life in Katarina's ears.

I sketched the glyphs quickly, pushing my intent into them, then releasing the magic.

Katarina groaned again and I knew the directions had arrived in her mind.

"I really don't like that," Katarina said with a nauseated tone. "We are on our way, Sade. I have a doctor who will be discrete about what she is."

"Thank you."

I returned to Reeva's side.

"Katarina's coming."

"Oh good, the drunken cavalry," she drawled weakly. I helped her get into a more comfortable position and did what I could to slow the blood rushing from her side.

"She's not as bad as she seems."

"I don't know what happens when Breakers die," she said hollowly, her face paling. "If we are cut off from the fold in life, are we ..."

"Reeva. No. We don't need to think about that. You aren't dying today."

She closed her eyes. "It's an interesting thought, though, isn't it

...” she trailed off.

I pinched her hand and she opened her eyes again.

“Ow. You shit. I am already in pain. I don’t need you adding more.”

“Then keep your eyes open.”

Her head rolled to the side, and she took a deep and ragged breath as she looked at me. “If I die and linger, will you manifest me?”

“Reeva.”

“I hate the thought of just wandering around lost and mindless. I would want my faculties about me. I would want some semblance of control. I suppose that’s all dependent on if Breakers can even exist in the fold ...”

“R ... Reeva?” The man’s voice brought both our eyes.

Hayden stood half-clothed and groggy, rubbing his eyes as he pushed aside the sheet hanging around his sleeping alcove.

He looked down at us with recognition. “Sade?” He saw the blood. “What is this? What happened?” He shook his head and knelt beside us, his hands searching for a way to help Reeva.

“She’s been shot,” I said slowly, confused at the man’s behavior. “Enforcers.”

“He ...” Reeva’s voice was quiet and weak. “He has clear moments. More and more now ...” She trailed off and her eyes started to close again.

“No. Dammit, Reeva. Stay with me. Katarina is almost here.” I grabbed Hayden's hands and placed them over the hasty bandaging. “Hold this,” I ordered, then hurried to the door to check the street. No motorcarriage, but I could hear an engine rumbling in the distance. Maybe ...

I looked back at Hayden talking quietly with Reeva, his eyes intent on hers as he kept her conscious.

The engine’s rumble grew louder, and sure enough, there was the Norwood’s motorcarriage. I swallowed nervously at the amount of noise it was making on the quiet streets. There was no hiding the vehicle, but it would be parked only a moment.

I hurried back to Reeva. “She’s here. You ready?” I asked, preparing to lift her.

“I’m going with her,” Hayden said.

I shook my head. “You can’t, Hayden. I’ll take care of her. You’re not exactly the type of person they let into discreet clinics.

Frankly, Reeva doesn't have time for us to debate this."

Reeva had done her best to tend to the man and keep him clean, but his hair and his beard had become unruly things that she had only given so much energy to.

He scowled but relented. "Fine."

I lifted Reeva, who was barely conscious, and carried her to the waiting carriage.

Katarina made space for us, surprisingly without complaint about the blood getting on her seats and staining her dress.

"The Toman clinic. Now," she ordered the driver, who set off before I was even settled.

I quickly secured Reeva against me as the motorcarriage lurched forward and into the darkened streets of the slums.

40:

Katarina took a seat beside me in the clinic's silent waiting room, her eyes on the closed door. The clinic was small and discrete to the point that an unwitting passerby would see only another row home among many others. The late hour had kept the streets quiet. I had been glad for the privacy when Katarina and I had hauled Reeva's limp and bloodied body up the stairway to the door.

"What did you find?" Katarina asked quietly.

"Only what we already knew. The core is failing."

She took in a long inhale, then let it out with a curse. "Was it really too much to hope for better news than that?"

"It's slow. At least from what I can tell." I was certain that the more the glyphs frayed, the faster our fall would be, but there was no reason to elaborate on that fact to Katarina.

"But it's inevitable. We will hit the cloudline," she said darkly.

"Not if I can figure out how to dissipate it."

"Dissipate what?" Katarina looked exhausted. She had been up all night waiting for me and Reeva to fail.

"The cloudline."

Katarina looked at me like I was insane. "Dissipate the cloudline? Dear, you might be a Natural, but that might be asking a bit much from yourself, don't you think?"

I shrugged. "You will help me try, right?"

"Tell me. How the fuck is a Death Sight supposed to help you dissipate a planet-wide shroud of deadly gasses?"

"You can channel. You said you have an Amp's hair on hand."

"Maybe you overestimate my channeling and, for that matter, Amps. I don't see it, Sade."

"Then I will try to do it myself."

She shook her head in frustration. "You wouldn't help me with my so-called suicide mission, so why should I help you with yours?"

"Because we are friends."

"Friends? Ha. Like you were to Deara? Tell me, did she give you the go-ahead on sleeping with the love of her life?" I knew she was trying to be hurtful and let it roll off my shoulders. We were both tired and strained.

I looked away slightly then nodded. "She did, actually."

Katarina groaned and tossed the small blue pill I had missed rolling between her fingers to the back of her throat and swallowed. "Gods, you are no fun, Sade. Even when you are stealing from the dead you are so damn considerate. My personal moral compass. Next you will tell me trying to dissipate the cloudline is the right thing to do. That we have to. For the Society," she said with self-righteous pith. She sat up straight, eyes fixed on mine. "Just like her, you know, a self-sacrificing fool. It will get you killed, and you want me to help."

"Of course I want you to help me, Kat. That's not a question. But I'm not going to push you on it. You have already expressed you have no interest."

"You aren't even going to try to convince me? Even a little bit?"

"It's not my job to convince you."

"You need an Amp. I don't care how strong you think you are; you need one."

I shrugged. I would let her make my arguments for me.

"Damn it, Sade. Try to convince me."

"Why bother if you are already agreeing to help?" I smiled.

She glowered. She needed to be able to pretend I had pushed her.

I snorted and obliged. "The College isn't your target. The Aberrants don't make the choice of which magics to eradicate. They are just the pets of the gods. The gods who are not helping, even though they could. They are, in fact, enforcing that nobody try to stop this descent. What would piss them off more than if we dissipate the cloudline and allow the landmasses to safely descend to the surface without them?"

She scoffed. "That's what you are going to go with? Stick it to the gods?"

I shrugged. "Yeah. That's what I'm going to go with."

With a snort and a shake of her head, she stood. "Fuck. You must have some sort of plan, an idea even?"

"Not really. I've been working with an Aberrant to try to figure it out, and all I have gotten out of it is an old atlas and a stronger foundation," I grumbled.

"An Aberrant? A College Aberrant? I thought you promised not to go the way of those assholes."

"I needed training, Kat. Lea is the only chance I have at learning how to do this."

"Lea?" She barked out a laugh. "You are on a first-name basis now, I see. It is only a matter of time before this *Lea* either comes to the conclusion on her own that she must bind you, or she succumbs to the bindings placed upon her. The leash around all College Aberrants' necks. Shit. Maybe you will even go along with being leashed willingly at that point." She shook her head. "Stupid, Sade. Working with the College ... The only thing you will get out of this is your mind warped and bound. I won't watch you do this to yourself." She glared at me, exhaling a long breath out of her nose, trying to set aside her irritation and distrust. "Can you do anything about the cores failing? Natural that you are."

I shook my head slowly. "Not yet ... It would take the College or the gods to stop this. Alone ..."

She sniffed and nodded. "Of course," she harumphed. "What's the point in wasting our thoughts on it, then?" She shrugged and rolled her eyes. She stood. "I trust you will find somewhere else to stay."

"Katarina ..." I reached for her hand to stop her but hesitated when she turned to face me again.

She fixed me with a hard stare.

I looked at Reeva's blood on my hands, and then nodded, dropping my hands back to my lap. "I'm sorry I didn't tell you I was training with an Aberrant, Kat."

She just shook her head, mouth pinched. With a look at me, her lips parted for a moment to say something, then instead she shook her head, turned her back and took her leave.

She just needed time. I knew that, but I worried about her being alone.

I returned my eyes to the door and continued to wait, my eyelids drooping with exhaustion.

41:

"Madam," the woman's nudge roused me.

I sat up, startled, looking into the nurse's eyes.

"We will keep her here a couple days so she can recover."

"She's alive?"

The nurse smiled and nodded. "She's alive. We can't speed her recovery, as you know, so she will need her rest. She'll be safe here. You should go look after yourself for the time, madam. Get cleaned up. A good night of sleep is in order."

I looked at the dried blood on my fingers and nodded. "Thank you."

I stepped out into the quiet streets of the early morning. I couldn't walk in this part of town, covered in blood as I was. I turned to into the cover of the nearest alley and tried to pull the glyphs I needed into my mind, but fatigue made them slippery. Lea would chide me for my lack of focus.

I sat heavily, leaning against the bricks behind me, letting the cold stone lend me focus.

My fingers dragged over the rough concrete beside me as they etched the glyphs. My intent was a foggy thing, and once again I thought of how Lea would react if she witnessed my sloppiness.

The magic released, and a moment later I fell to the side, unconscious in the safety of Emelia's room.

42:

"I don't know where you came from, but it was stupid of you to come here." It was not Emelia's voice but Lea's that greeted me when I woke.

The Aberrant's back was to me as she worked at her desk, a

stack of books and papers surrounding her.

I sat up slowly, rubbing my head. Reeva's blood had been cleaned away from my skin, and I wore a fresh set of clothes.

"I heard there was an attack on one of the cores. Specifically, Vale's," Lea said tightly, still working through her papers. "Then I find you unconscious and filthy on my floor."

"I didn't mean to come here," I said.

She tsked again and shook her head. "Sloppy. Transporting yourself all the way to Junction on accident. No wonder you lost consciousness. You are lucky I have so many dampers around my quarters, or your entrance would have sent alarms sounding College-wide." She set her pen aside and turned. "What were you doing to the core?" She glared at me.

"I was just looking. I wanted to confirm if it was failing."

"How close were you able to get?"

"Close enough to see it. Close enough to feel that it is sick."

She swallowed, a look of remembered pain crossing her face. She knew the difficulty of approaching a core. "Is it as bad as you thought?"

I nodded. "It is worse now than what the Present Sight saw." I shook my head. "I don't know how to explain it. I felt a ... a waning in it."

She growled, setting her elbows heavily on her desk and rubbing her temples. "I wish you just followed directions and ignored the things that are so far above you."

"You want me to ignore that Vale is sinking?"

She closed her eyes and shook her head. "The implications, Sade." She rubbed her temples and looked at me. "Do you think you have another core trip in you?"

I blinked at her, not quite understanding. "You want to see Vale's core?"

"Not Vale's, no. If you say it's failing, I trust you." She looked at the ceiling, clearly not liking where her thoughts were going. "The cores are linked. It's unlikely that only Vale is failing, but ..."

"If we only have one landmass falling into the abyss ..."

"That would make saving the world quite a bit easier." She stood and extended her hand toward me. "So, do you have the strength for another trip? I can get us to Junction's core. It won't be any easier a trip than Vale's was."

I stood and took her hand. The Aberrant gave me a nod of

approval, then lifted her free hand and etched the glyphs.

The oppressive weight of the core nearly buckled my knees as we manifested in the tunnels of Junction's core. Lea reacted similarly, and the two of us leaned heavily on one another as we made our way down the tunnel to the core.

This core was oppressively hot, the glyphs lining the tunnel and the core stone itself shining brighter and stronger than Vale's had. But still I felt the sickness in them.

The fold bucked, and I saw a crack in the core stone looming ahead of us.

"Shit," I said, and Lea looked at me.

"What?"

"You didn't see it when the fold buckled? The crack?"

She smiled weakly and closed her eyes. "I'm astounded you can even keep your feet, Sade."

I realized how weak the woman was so close to the core. While my nausea was manageable, Lea seemed to be physically diminishing under the weight of the core's presence.

"We don't need to stay here any longer," I said.

"It's sick?" she asked, her legs failing to support her. I shifted more of her weight onto my hip, trying to help compensate.

"Yes. Not as bad as Vale's; earlier in the process, maybe."

Lea raised her hand, and with a swipe of her hand, had us back in her room.

She took a few moments to recover on her hands and knees before using her desk to get back to her feet. I was surprised to see the woman willing to show that level of weakness in front of me. I remained where I sat, leaned back against her bed, and looked up at her.

"What do we do?" I asked.

She just shook her head.

We stayed in silence for a while longer. Only a knock on the door and a timid voice broke our dour state. Lea looked at me with a moment of nervousness, a deep crease forming between her momentarily widened eyes. I ducked low behind her bed while she composed herself and admitted the student.

The young woman kept her eyes fixed on the floor. "Professor. I'm sorry to bother you. I'm having difficulty with the concepts you taught today."

Lea ushered the woman out of the room with a glance back at

me where I hid behind her bed. With the door closed, I picked myself up and examined the space I had accidentally transported myself to.

The trip to Junction was a not a short one. The distance alone precluded even some College-trained Aberrants from making the trip via glyphwork. There was too much room for error. Too much chance that the Aberrant would not be a strong enough conduit for the required magic, and they were as likely to find themselves over the abyss as on a landmass. Still, now, here I was in the College.

My fingers trailed over the spines of the books Lea kept on the shelves of her room. History, science, Tinkerers' craft. My finger stopped when I saw a familiar name: Amsel.

I frowned at the text, then carefully removed it. Doctor Priya Amsel. I thumbed through the pages as I waited.

Lea slipped back into the room. "Students," she grumbled to herself. "If the College didn't force me into being a professor, I wouldn't. That one is barely more than a Tinkerer. But 'everybody has their place,'" she said with an eyeroll as she came over to me. "Hmm. Yes. Your mother's book. She was a real visionary on the theoretical uses of glyphwork and the base knowledge of historical glyphs. If only she had been an Aberrant."

"Maybe because she wasn't, she was able to see glyphs as more then weapons and steppingstones. Maybe that is why the Tinkerers are the most inventive."

Lea smirked. "I can see your point. It is too easy being able to simply summon intent to my fingertips. Especially with that base knowledge of historical glyphs," she said with a nod at the book. "Take that with you when you go." She reached past me. "And this." She dropped another of my mother's books in my hands.

"I don't think I can muster the strength for the transport back."

Lea turned back to her desk with a sigh. "Well, then sit silently while I finish grading these assignments. Damn things."

"Have you read these?" I asked, turning the books over to look at them.

"I have." She frowned. "I can't remember exactly what was in them—I am guessing that's your fault—but I know they are highly restricted. I have considered cracking them a few times, then didn't …"

I looked at her curiously as I sat back against her bed. She looked a little concerned by her own statement, her mouth going to a thin line as she looked at the books.

"I shouldn't have them," she said slowly, as though confused why she did. She turned back to her desk and her work. There was no point in pushing further. I knew the signs of the binding taking hold. It seemed a waste of knowledge to keep so much controlled in such a way.

I stuffed the books into my climbing pack. The Aberrant wouldn't be able to read them, anyway. I set the pack on the floor to use as a pillow.

"You can use the bed," Lea said without turning. "No reason to behave like an animal."

43:

Lea was gone when I woke up. I waited, knowing the woman would not leave me alone for too long. Sure enough, minutes later she appeared with a plate of food, which she set at her desk without a word before leaving again.

I ate and then waited an hour before she returned once again.

"Put this on," she said, tossing me one of her cloaks. "I only have so much time between classes."

I pulled the cloak on and followed the Aberrant into the halls of the College. The wide corridors felt familiar to me. I avoided the eyes of Aberrants passing in the halls. Most seemed to avoid Lea regardless. As rare as Aberrants were, Garnets seemed to be only a very select number of their ranks. Even other Aberrants seemed scared of them.

She led me into a Tinkerer's workshop. Pliers and mallets of various sizes hung from the walls with a scatter of metal bands and scraps resting on the workbench below them. Bins filled with crafting materials arrayed themselves around the room and in the center sat a man focused on the delicate placement of cogs in what looked to be a pocket watch etched with an array of fastidiously crafted glyphs.

"She needs a Garnet's ring set," Lea announced to the man at his workbench.

He looked up from his work. "Those are restricted use," the Tinkerer said, eyeing me curiously. "Does the Chancellor know you are promoting a Garnet?"

"Since when has that mattered to you, Perry?"

The Tinkerer shrugged. "Fair enough." He grabbed my hand and examined my fingers before turning to his workbench. A moment later, he turned with two rings, then a thought flashed in his eyes and he snatched up a third. "No point in a pair of amplification rings if I don't give you a little control along with them." He held up the third ring, showing me the glyphs etched into its metal. "A director. Too much amplification without direction can create dangerous things. Dominant hand."

I offered him my right, and he slid the director onto my pointer finger. I felt a sharp prick that made me yank my hand back protectively.

"Did I forget to mention they need to embed with you as a conduit?" He held out his hand expectantly once more. "The director is rather pointless without the amplifiers," he said when all I did in response was look at the ring now latched onto my finger, the metal seemingly fusing with my skin.

"You will forget they are there soon enough," Lea said, holding her own hand up to display the metal bands around her pointer and middle fingers. I had never taken notice of how they laid so close against her skin, the band smoothly transitioning from flesh to metal. It didn't make me want to offer the Tinkerer my hand again, but he was right: direction alone was only so useful.

The second ring bit into the base of my middle finger before the man snatched my left hand and slid the third ring onto my opposite middle finger.

I felt the rise in power in my gut, sizzling through my hands and up my arms.

Lea gave me a thin smile. "You'll get used to that, too." She gave the Tinkerer a nod. "Keep this between us." She set her hand on my shoulder and steered me away from the man.

"The first time using those rings can be a bit jarring, so start with something small."

I nodded, intent on only transporting a few steps ahead before the magic started to swell and the memory of Reeva's door came to mind instead.

I felt a charge run between my hands, my fingers tingling, the pain of the new rings intensifying for a moment, then with a sharp intake of breath, I opened my eyes in a dark alley.

I surveyed the street I had arrived on. I had meant to take steps, and instead I had crossed the abyss to the slums of Vale. It didn't inspire confidence in me. How was I supposed to dissipate the cloudline if I couldn't even control myself while using a simple transport glyph?

My knuckles burned and I clenched my hands into fists against the sting of the rings sealing themselves into my flesh. I hoped Katarina hadn't been right, and I hadn't willingly just bound myself to the College. I looked at the rings. Lea would not have tricked me in that way. At least, not intentionally. I hoped not, anyway.

I quickly took stock. Nobody had seen me appear. The alley was deserted. I had gotten lucky. The step should have drained me, but the magical tap only seemed to have trickled a little away.

Lea's voice rang in my ear. "Dammit, Sade. Where did you go?"

"I'm on Vale," I said, quickly ducking into Reeva's hovel. "I'm safe."

Lea grumbled a string of irritated curses, then chided, "Economy, Sade. Economy. I told you to start small. Nothing to do about it now." The magic dissipated.

I sighed and looked at the rings now affixed and burning into my fingers. All I could do about it now was try to ignore the pain.

I realized I wasn't alone, and looked up to see Emelia sitting with Hayden. Marco sat in the corner unnoticed, but watching the two curiously.

She looked from the man, catatonic once again, to me. "I stopped by the Norwood estate," she said in explanation. "Katarina told me Reeva had been shot and that you were not welcome there just now," she said with a frown, standing. "I thought maybe you would be here." She took my hands in hers. "Are you alright?" She looked from my eyes to our hands, holding mine up in the flickering yellowed light to inspect the rings. "You're bleeding."

"Best to leave it." I pressed my forehead to hers. "I'm glad to see you. I meant to go to you but ... I ended up in Junction ..."

She cocked an eyebrow. "Just like that? You ended up in Junction?"

I shrugged, embarrassed. Twice now, I had let my intent slip while transporting. That was dangerous business.

"You know, even experienced Aberrants don't just jump between the landmasses like it's nothing."

I wiggled my fingers, now bearing the rings of a Garnet. "I

wouldn't quite call it nothing. I might not have gotten back if not for these."

Her eyes widened as she fully understood the significance of the metal bands. "Wait. Are those … How did you get those?"

"Lea."

Emelia's lips pinched with uncertainty at the sight of the rings and their meaning. "She must really trust you to have made you a Garnet. That is not a small move for a College Aberrant."

"I would have preferred if she had just agreed to help me with the cloudline."

Emelia swallowed. "She may not be able to. Directly, anyway. I imagine that if the gods don't want to take action, that means they do not want their Aberrants taking action. The binding is likely very strong. That she is fighting the drive she must feel to turn you in, that may be the most she can do for us. The leash the College subjects their Aberrants to is not weak. Those rings may be her way of helping. She believes you can do this. So does Reeva. So do I."

"Katarina doesn't. She kicked me out for training with Lea."

"She will get over it. And you know, Sade. She is a pessimist. An optimistic pessimist. She will come around when we need her."

"Landbringer."

We both looked up when Hayden spoke. His eyes were far away.

"What is the Landbringer?" I asked the man. "You say it often."

"The Landbringer will bring our fall."

I set my hands on the table, studying him. He still wore Reeva's braid, so he wasn't seeing anything but his own memories.

"Is that a person?" I asked, hoping something would break through to the man. "Are they the one who broke the cores? Is that why we are falling?"

His eyes found me curiously. "The Breaker breaks the core. The Landbringer brings our fall." He said it in an almost lucid way, as though he could not understand my lack of understanding. "The gods, with all their strength, sit by idly."

This was new. "The gods?" I had seen what he had. I had heard their decision. That we had made the mess for ourselves, let us sort it out. What I didn't know was if the decision had been made in the past or had yet to be made. I didn't know if that had been a reality of some other layer of the fold that would never be on ours. I had no way of interpreting the visions of a Present Sight. There were too many potentials.

"The Landbringer is as they are."

"They? Do you mean the gods? Is this Landbringer a god?"

"Is … was … will be …" His eyes were thoughtful. "The venture to dissipate the cloudline will not end as expected. There is no individual conduit strong enough to save us."

I frowned. The statement gave me a sinking feeling in my gut. The thoughts were too clear. Too lucid. For a moment, Hayden looked as he had before the Aberrants had subjected him to months of torture.

"The cloudline is getting closer. We are falling. Falling. Falling. Falling."

His eyes turned lost as his lucidity slipped. His lips moved soundlessly for a moment, then his gaze fell to my hands resting on the table. Hayden's eyes fixed on the rings on my fingers. I pulled my hand away slowly, wary of making any sudden moves around the feral man, moving the digits out of view, but his face had already shifted to something beastly. With a savage growl he leapt from his chair, taking me to the ground.

"Hayden! Wait!" I covered my face as his fists beat down on me. "Wait." His knuckles fell with a resounding thud and for a second my defenses fell. My mind spun and my arms dropped. I didn't bother raising them again. No single conduit could save us. What was the point?

Marco tried in vain to stop the man, his spectral hands passing uselessly through Hayden's shoulders. Emelia looked on in horror. I could not muster the strength nor the desire to stop him.

The fist landing against my face felt deserved. It felt right. Was this the catharsis Katarina felt when Tomas got the better of her while sparring? I stopped trying to resist Hayden's crushing fists and lay still.

A crash of wood ended the beating. Hayden crumpled on top of me in a shower of wooden legs as Emelia brought a chair down on the man's head.

With a grunt, Emelia shoved Hayden off me, then dragged me away from the unconscious man.

"Sade?" she asked quietly, an odd look in her eyes as she looked down at me, my head resting in her lap.

I closed my eyes and turned in to her stomach in a small attempt to hide myself from her. Tears came unbidden to my eyes.

Slowly she set a tender hand on my shoulder and stroked my hair lightly while I tasted blood in my mouth and salt rolled down my cheeks.

A cold hand rested beside Emelia's timidly. "Is she alright?" Marco asked in a small voice.

Emelia said nothing, but I knew she was shaking her head. The spectral hand remained and the two sat vigilantly over me.

44:

When I woke, Emelia's hand was still on my shoulder, firm and grounding. Beside it rested something hard and flat against my arm. Something that felt very much like a book. I didn't mind being used as a bookrest, and nestled closer to Emelia.

Her thumb stroked my shoulder and she asked quietly, "Where did you get these books?"

"The College." My answer was muffled by her stomach, but I knew she would understand. I savored the scent of the woman pressed against my beaten face.

"Can we talk about why you let him do that?" Emelia asked, her weary tone telling me she did not expect much of an answer.

I didn't give her one, and she didn't press. I shifted slightly, getting comfortable, and she resettled the book on my arm, her thumb continuing its comforting slide over my shoulder.

"I'm tired," I said into her stomach.

"Then rest. I'm here, Sade."

45:

The book was still open on my arm, but I could tell that Emelia had fallen asleep, her deep breathing a soothing rhythm.

Carefully, I rolled so the book wouldn't topple to the floor and sat up. My left eye was swollen shut and my left cheek attested to the damage Hayden's crazed fists could inflict. I sat beside Emelia, gently goading the sleeping woman into leaning against my shoulder rather than slumping forward.

Marco sat with his back to me and his eyes on the alcove where the man slept. When the ghost heard me move, he crawled over and sat in my lap. His cooling presence was a comfort, and I held him tight as he looked up at my face with sad eyes.

"He could have killed you," Marco said in hushed tones.

I nodded.

"You would have let him …" I said nothing and he looked away for a moment before looking back up at me. His fingers brushed over my bruised cheek. "You can fix that."

I nodded again, but didn't bother with the glyphs needed for the recovery. As a Breaker, Reeva couldn't be aided by them. Why should I? Instead, I looked at the books Lea had given me and opened one at random. Supposedly these were the words of my mother. Supposedly she had been a great scholar. Supposedly she had known something was wrong with the cores when I was only just a child. She had gotten herself, Leeta, and who knew who else killed with her theory. I was following in her footsteps.

I waited until Emelia stirred, her head burrowing softly into my shoulder as she fought the urge to rise. When her eyes opened, I set the book aside.

She looked at the binding. "Who is Priya Amsel?"

"Was. My mother."

"Your mother? Oh, Sade …"

I shrugged. "I don't remember her, so it's not as though these words are any more powerful for me than any other scholar's." I said the words, but my fingers still lingered on the print as though trying to lift some memory from the pages.

Emelia bit her lip, then turned a few pages. "She wrote things that she should not have been able to. But she also knew how to hide her meaning to get around the Society and its barriers. She was a smart woman."

"I've been told." I looked at where Emelia's finger indicated on the page. A description of glyphs. Core glyphs. Restricted glyphs. I blinked, something breaking free in my mind.

"I know you find it boring, sweetheart, but it's important you know this." The maternal tones were Doctor Amsel's. My mother gave me a commiserating smile. "How about we make a deal? If you can demonstrate that you know the seven glyphs that keep the cloudline at bay, we will call it a day. Maybe go to the park? We will do something fun today. I promise."

"I want ice cream," my child's voice squeaked.

She smiled and kissed my forehead. "Well, that's a given." She looked at me expectantly and I grabbed my pencil excitedly. "Be careful not to bring intent into your drawing," she warned, but with the tones of a woman who knew I knew better already. Still, the caution had to be made. These glyphs were lifegivers, but very dangerous lifegivers.

My pencil etched out the seven core glyphs. Restricted by virtue of their power and the danger they posed, were somebody to break their magic.

She watched with pride and something else: expectation.

Emelia was watching me.

"Where did you go?" she asked quietly.

"There are seven core glyphs that keep the cloudline at bay," I said hollowly, fixing the glyphs in my mind as I scrambled for something to write with. "Seven ..."

I had stashed a set of pencils and a sketchbook in the hovel weeks before. I hurried to grab them before the glyphs slipped or warped. Deara had been right. The memories were preserved with such clarity that there could be no question of their validity, but that would slip quickly.

"Seven glyphs to keep the cloudline at bay," I repeated again, studying the seven core glyphs. The restricted knowledge. Lost knowledge. Lea had only known three, and that only because my mother had drilled her on them as diligently as she had me. I looked at the remaining four. "The core created the cloudline. The gods created the cloudline."

Emelia's face dropped. "What?"

I looked at her, then at the book. "My mother was not an Aberrant. She could never change the intent of the glyphs, but she taught me. She knew we would need it." I shook my head at the page. "They hid the intent among the seven glyphs." I carefully redrew the glyphs to ensure they stuck fast and true to my memory, then dissected their anatomy. "Only two of the seven glyphs are known, to evidence the gods' gracious intent. To display their protection of us. They are the only two on every glyph core. Two more are restricted knowledge for only the leaders of the College to know for maintenance. The final three were considered lost. But my mother discovered them and taught them to me. Look," I said, drawing what was hidden among the seven. The creation of the cloudline. The creation of the acid rain and corrosive gasses, the death of the planet below.

"I don't ..." Emelia said, looking at the page. She had not

studied glyphs as I had.

"This killed our planet," I said simply.

"Sade." Hayden's voice made us both look up sharply. "You're an Aberrant." He shook his head. "How many years were you living under my protection and I didn't even see it?" He looked at his wrist and the bracelet. "Reeva has become a crutch to me." He untied the knot securing the woman's hair around his wrist and let it fall to the floor. "Maybe it is time I see what needs to be seen."

I could feel the man's magic swelling. He was a Present Sight. A very powerful Present Sight. How he had not lost his mind sooner, I didn't know. In the absence of Reeva's breaking, the man's eyes turned searching, far-seeing.

"We should go to the farm today," he said to himself, seeing something somewhere in some layer of the fold. "They want to go knocking where they ought not to. They want to intercede without paying what is due. Then let the bounty we have given them crumble." The man's recitation was a jumbled mess as he shifted through the layers of the fold. "Jake, come to mama. Come on. It's time to have dinner." His lips were moving absently, no doubt only voicing fragments of what he saw. "You give them too much credit. Too much compassion." He blinked several times, his eyes coming back into focus as he stabilized the rush of Sight. "Destroy the Locks. They threaten our standing. Leash the rest. Tell them we created them. Make us gods in their eyes." His mouth continued to try to catch up with his magic, failing. "You can do it, honey. One step. Two. This is wrong. So very wrong. Are we going to let this happen?"

He sat, looking up at me, his arms wrapping around his knees. "I've seen it, Sade." He finally managed to bring his words into alignment with his present. "You have to try. Even if you fail. There are too many possibilities. Too many potentials. But only one way. You have to try."

"How? What can I do?"

"Try try again. It's time for bed. Time for dinner. Time ... time ..." He was struggling against his Sight, holding back his hand reaching for Reeva's braid. "We are short on time. The cores are sick."

"The cores. Do I have to get to them?" I asked, trying to help him focus. "Is that how?"

"Try. Try. Try." He grimaced.

"I cannot get close to them without their magic overwhelming me."

He frowned at me. "What's in your pocket?" he asked.

"What?" I patted my pocket. There was nothing. I shook my head.

The man shuddered as his eyes sank again, and the rambling began again as he saw all edges of our world across all levels of the fold. With his mind so far disconnected, his hand seemed to get the better of him and he grabbed the braid from the floor, giving in to the calm of the Breaker. He sighed deeply as the Sight cut off, then lost consciousness.

"Your pocket?" Emelia said behind me as I stared at the man.

"What? I checked. There's nothing."

"That necklace Eda brought back to you. Where is it?"

"At Norwood manor," I said, shaking my head in confusion. "In ... Oh, shit. It is still in the pocket of my jumpsuit."

"Maybe it is best you keep it on you from now on," she said, looking almost hopeful. "He said you have to try, Sade. So, get over your self-pitying and try."

You have to try. Even if you fail.

Failure though, could very well mean all life.

46:

Reeva greeted me with an eyeroll. "You look like shit. You should heal your face," she said.

I chuckled. "Thank you, Reeva, for your concern."

"I am not fucking around, Sade. Heal your face," she said with a seriousness that had me feeling thoroughly rebuked. "Whatever pain you think you deserve, you don't."

I shook my head slowly. "I'll heal.

"Is this about me, then?" she growled. "Just because I cannot be healed magically does not mean I want you to suffer alongside me. It only makes me feel worse, seeing you like that. Idiot."

I considered the wall for a moment.

"How did that happen?" Reeva asked, watching me think.

"Hayden."

"I suppose Beater was an accurate name for the man," she said quietly. "Why?"

I held up my hands, showing her the rings now fused solidly. The glyphs blood red from binding with my flesh and my magic.

Reeva whistled low. "A gift from your Abbie friend?"

I nodded.

"Only Garnets have those."

I nodded again. "I jumped from Junction to Vale when I only meant to take steps."

"Ah, so you are, what? Afraid you will heal your face out of existence? Seems to me you should at least try." I was starting to hate that phrase. She narrowed her eyes at me. "Unless this," she gestured at me weakly, "is about something else entirely."

I looked down with a sigh and healed my injuries.

"Better. So, those rings, let me guess … He saw them and flew off the handle?"

I looked at the bands. "It was a Garnet who tortured him …" I said, not wanting to give Reeva the whole truth on just how involved Lea had been. I knew Lea well enough to know that she not only engaged in, but enjoyed the darker sides of the College. I tried to push that reality aside for the moment. She was serving her purpose to me as a teacher. I needed her. "Why didn't you tell me that he was recovering?"

She gave a small shrug. "What is recovering? One day he is him and one day somebody else. One day he is gibbering on the floor and the next he is sitting, conversing with me like we are now. He has his mind about him only when he is not himself," she said quietly, uncertain in her emotions.

"What do you mean?"

"I am a Breaker. He is a Present Sight. I am his self-prescribed medication. But I make him somebody other than who he is."

"He took your bracelet off."

She nodded. "He has a right to choose." She frowned. "But why did he choose to? He has always clung to its clarity."

I looked at her pallid features, trying to decide if now was really the moment. "The cloudline. I found the critical seven glyphs. He … I think he wanted to help."

She sighed. "It will be days before he is able to speak coherently enough to be of use if that's the case." She frowned. "Wait. You said you found the seven core glyphs? How? You were not able to get close enough to the core to have seen those. Another gift from your Aberrant?"

"In a way. In another, a gift from my mother."

"Huh …" Reeva winced as she shifted position, but her eyes remained intent on me. "And?"

"And I know how the cloudline was formed. I know its base nature. I know how to dissipate it. I'll need you, though, to break the adulterated glyphs."

She scoffed. "You want me to break core glyphs? Do you even know what that will do?"

I shrugged helplessly. "I don't. I don't think we will until we break them. Do you think you can?"

She looked hesitant. "That is strong magic. I mean. In theory, it should not matter. I should be able to. I've never tried something like that. What are the glyphs?"

I showed her my sketchbook and her eyes widened and she shook her head. "Sade. Breaking those won't just dissipate the cloudline, it will remove the protections they give us. We are too high up to breathe without those glyphs in place. I don't know that suffocating the populace is what we are striving for here."

I shook my head at her sarcastic tone. "They will be broken a moment only. As you break them, I will replace them with uncorrupted glyphs."

"Core glyphs, Sade," she said in a strange staccato of uncertainty and disbelief. "I know you are a Natural. I know you have those rings, but those are *core glyphs*. Do you even know which core has the corrupted glyphs?" She was searching for a way out of this particular solution.

"Vale. And only Vale. The strongest core and the one dying the fastest."

"How do you know that?"

I looked at my hands again with a heavy sigh. "I am trusting my mother."

"Your mother? You are entrusting the survival of everybody on Vale—"

"Everybody everywhere," I said quietly.

Reeva made a choking bark of a laugh. "Everybody everywhere. Fuck, Sade. Everybody everywhere …" she said in a diminishing voice. "All of that, you are entrusting to broken memories of a woman who failed before you?"

I bit my lip and, still looking at my hands, shook my head. "I have to try, even if I fail."

She swore. "That's not the most convincing, Sade."

Finally, I looked at Reeva. "My mother didn't have a Breaker. We didn't have a Breaker. I wasn't strong enough to rearrange the glyphs then."

"And you think you are now? With those rings, you think that's all you need?" she asked, incredulous.

"Rearranging a glyph is harder than emplacing a new one."

Reeva closed her eyes for a moment, exhausted in her recovery. "I'll let you rest. We have time."

She shook her head. "How did you get to the core the first time without collapsing?"

"Beater helped with that, actually." I pulled a thin chain from my pocket. I had stopped by Norwood Manor by aid of a glyph to avoid a run in with Katarina before making my way to the clinic. Just as Hayden had said, the necklace had been in the pocket of the jumpsuit. The charm now hung between us, the charm I had always worn with me as a child, somehow never losing it through the years until I had given it to Eda. It had seemed only a trinket, one I could not remember the source of. One I had known the importance of subliminally. One that Eda had returned to me in her death.

Reeva looked at the charm, then at me. "That charm? I can feel the magic on it, but what is it?"

"I don't know for certain, but I do know I had it when I first went to the core with my mother. I know it is essential." The glyphs used to channel the creator's magical intent had somehow been hidden in the metal, perhaps covered by the heads of wheat to keep prying eyes at bay.

Reeva chuckled mirthlessly. "So, we are relying on the thin trail of memories you have of a dead woman, and a charm you don't know the function of, to do something nobody has ever tried, that you don't know that you have the strength to even do, without knowing what will happen if you fail, or, shit, even if we succeed."

I shrugged. Hayden's prophecy of failure played in the back of my mind.

"What about Katarina? From overhearing the nurses gossiping, it sounds like you two had a tiff."

"Her tempers are short lived. She should come around." I hoped.

"Not the most inspiring, but I suppose you're the best we have." She snorted. "Alright. You have until I am out of this bed."

47:

I appeared in the back of Lea's class. The young woman sitting beside where I materialized jumped in surprise at my sudden appearance. She saw my fingers and stammered out a whispered, "G ... Garnet"

I understood the title now. The glyphs etched into the rings had taken on the color of the blood red stone.

I gestured for her to slide over a little on her bench, then sat beside her to wait for the lecture to finish. Lea cast me an irritated look, but continued on. I folded my fingers neatly in my lap and away from the staring eyes of the young woman.

She was looking at my face, maybe trying to determine if she knew me. She wasn't much younger than myself. Maybe if I had been discovered by the College, our two circles would have gravitated around each other. She looked away quickly when I turned my eyes toward her.

"Wh ... which landmass are you posted on?" She whispered, as though talking to an idolized actor.

I just gave her the thin smile Lea always favored me with and nodded back toward the lecture.

She returned as much focus to the end of the class as she could spare from studying me out of the corner of her eye.

When Lea put down her chalk, the girl looked at me again. "Look for me among your ranks one day."

I gave her a wan smile, and she darted off.

"She will never be a Garnet," Lea said when the room emptied.

"Why not?"

"It is all a lie that we tell them, that if they study hard enough, even those with less inherent talent can become Garnets. You can amplify a Tinkerer, but they will only ever become a lesser Aberrant."

"It cannot just be raw potential that justifies making a Garnet."

Lea shook her head, coming to stand beside me. "No. Not just raw potential. There's a reason there are so few of us, though. If you amplify somebody who cannot handle the additional load, as many cannot, they fizzle out. Or fall victim to their own intent. Or develop insatiable megalomania. Or they just lose their minds," she listed casually.

"Oh, is that all?" I was feeling less and less excited about the rings. "Yet, you gave me these?" I said, holding up my hands.

"I knew you could handle them. If the College had known what you were as a child—"

"If they had bound me."

"If they had trained you, you would have had those rings years ago." She sat down on the bench. "Why are you here?"

"I need your help. More than your training. More than these," I said, holding up my hand for a brief moment. "I need your magic. I need the help of the College."

"You are asking too much, Sade. I can't exactly tell the Chancellor to just trust some errant Aberrant with the future of all the isles."

"You trusted me with these rings."

"Making you a Garnet does not mean I believe you are right to meddle. It just means that," she took my hands in hers and looked at me pleadingly, begging me to understand. "It just means that this was right for you. Just know, if the Chancellor finds out about you, she will make you disappear. And likely make me disappear, too." She dropped my hands. "The cores are sick. Yes. I trust you on that. I told you, I will talk to the Chancellor. I will try to get her to talk to Jespair, ask for help. This is above us, Sade. This is so far above us. Leave it for those above us."

I shook my head, marveling at the woman's stoic desire to ignore what we both knew was inevitable. Her unwillingness to help. How frustrated Reeva and Emelia must have felt toward me.

"Can I show you something?"

Lea frowned at me, but nodded.

I drew the glyph for transportation, and a moment later we were at Iolde's Point on Vale. The Point where Katarina so loved training her Death Sight was quiet, no lovers tangled in embrace to disturb us.

I closed my eyes and felt the layers of the fold pinching and widening. Katarina was right that it didn't matter what your abilities were; the fold made strange things happen here.

"What is this?" Lea asked, sounding off.

I opened my eyes. The Aberrant looked sick. Perhaps the exposure to the fold was too much for her.

I offered the woman my arm, and she took it gladly.

"Don't you feel the fold?" I asked.

The woman groaned. "If that's the fold I'm feeling, then I

would prefer not to."

"Alright, we will leave in a moment, but first, come here." I led her toward the railings.

"Are you planning on throwing me off?" she asked in only half a joke.

"Not just now, but this would be the place to do it." I looked down, hoping that there would be a pinch. A flicker of the mountaintop.

Lea looked with me with sunken eyes. "What am I looking for? Oh … what …?"

I followed her eyes, and sure enough, the flicker of a snowcapped peak rose below.

"What is that?" she asked, straining to focus on the anomaly.

"Don't you recognize it? It's the other half of the valley."

"What?"

"I found where we came from in that atlas, where all the landmasses rose from."

The mountain was fading again.

"Wait, bring it back," Lea said, her knuckles white as she gripped the railing.

"It comes and goes," I said. "But when the fold pinches here, the mountain seems a constant. It makes sense. The mountain ridge spans ages. Even if the layer is future or past, it is visible. Free of the cloudline."

A woman grabbed my arm, and Lea's attention suddenly adjusted. "Where the fuck did she come from?" Lea said, still weakened but ready to fight.

"Have you seen him? Have you seen my son? He was just here. Just here …" The Whisper's hand slipped away from me.

"Where did she go?" Lea asked, on edge as she clung to my arm for strength.

"A Whisper," I said, watching the ghost search the point. She drifted here and there regardless of the railing and the bounds of the landmass. She was no jumper. When she had been here, there had been nothing to jump from. I looked at Lea; the woman seemed to be worsening by the moment. I drew a glyph to pull us from the point and back to Lea's study.

"How many times do I have to tell you how very stupid it is for you to come to the College?" she said, heaving herself onto her chaise. She sighed gratefully. "What was that, Sade?"

"As I said. It's the other side of Vale."

She shook her head and gestured for water. "That spot. What could we see through the cloudline?"

"We didn't see through it. We saw the future or the past of it. A time without the cloudline shrouding the peak. Iolde's Point is a confluence for the layers of the fold."

"And you didn't find it horrendously sickening?"

I handed her a glass of water and sat across from her. "Clearly not. I didn't realize it would do that to you."

She drank gratefully, the color already returning to her cheeks. "How do you know that mountain is the future or past and not an alternate?"

"It's too constant. I have seen alternates. A waste, a river. But they are only flickers. The mountain, though, it seems to penetrate multiple layers of the fold. If I had to guess, what we saw was a layer that lives in our past. The woman, that Whisper, I think she died on what is now the landmass of Vale, and her son died below. We came from below and we will eventually return there, one way or another."

Lea pursed her thin lips, her fingers tapping nervously. "I just … I don't know what we can do. Give me some time to think, Sade. Alright?"

I nodded. "Alright. Take a minute to recover. I'm going to visit your Tinkerer."

"What?" She sat up quickly, but I could see her mind spin with the sudden rush.

With a small gesture, I drew the glyph for sleep and the woman settled back, eyes already closing.

48:

It was not difficult to find the Tinkerer's workshop once again. Walking the halls of the College, I was beginning to understand just how small the community of Aberrants must be. A new face seemed to stand out among the students, even garbed in Lea's cloak as I was, and I worried I would be stopped. The rings on my fingers seemed to quell any desire to interrogate me, however, and I passed unmolested.

The Tinkerer eyed the charm in my hand.

"Can you make more of these?" I asked.

He held out his gloved hand and examined the charm over the rim of his glasses with a considering sound, then returned his eyes to me. "I'm not supposed to do work for unleashed Aberrants," he said, lowering the charm to his workbench.

I wiggled my fingers in the air, the rings flashing in the light. "That didn't stop you before."

He returned his eyes to the charm. "The intent of this little piece?"

I set my hands on the workbench to lean over the charm. "I was hoping you could tell me. I think it dulls the sickness Aberrants feel around the cores."

The man's eyes flicked up to me. "And why ever would you want to be around the cores?" He sat back, studying me.

"Can you make more?"

He crossed his arms. "An untamed Aberrant comes knocking on my door with a project that will give her access to a core. I don't know that I should help her. In fact, maybe I should be calling the Enforcers in right now."

I shrugged. "Then call them."

The man's eyes narrowed behind his glasses and he leaned forward once again to inspect the charm. "I can make more. I made this one, after all. Sade."

I backed away a step in surprise. "You know me?"

"Of course," he scoffed. "You really thought I wouldn't recognize you? You are the spitting image of your mother, little Amsel. I would be careful walking around this campus if I were you. There are still those of us who remember her." He tossed the charm back to me. "I'll make another. Deliver it to Lea when I am done. You really should stop coming to the College." He turned to his work.

I studied his back a moment, then drew the glyph to return to Vale and stepped.

49:

I gave Katarina her time and space, but I needed her. I found myself on the steps of Norwood manor staring up at the bronze elks, wondering how many of the animals could possibly still be alive in the wilds of the landmasses. It couldn't be many.

Emelia's hand squeezed mine as we waited. Beside us, Reeva kicked at the steps impatiently.

The grand wooden doors swung open, Katarina glaring down at us with arms crossed over her chest. "Come in," she said after a long silence. She watched us all as we stepped past her into the entryway. "Is this your 'save the world' posse, then? What, no Aberrant?"

"Only me," I murmured.

Katarina sucked her teeth at the reminder.

"I need your help, Katarina."

"Hmm."

"Please."

The maid followed us into the parlor, looking questioningly at Katarina.

"Tea," Katarina said tightly to the woman, who bowed low and backed out of the room.

"Tea?" I asked, surprised she hadn't called for something harder.

She waved a dismissive hand at me. "I don't think this return to the ground is going to be the beautiful moment you seem to think it will be," Katarina said bitterly. "Even if you dissipate the fumes. Even if we don't crash to our deaths when the glyphs fail. Even if all this works out, we still end up on some gods-forsaken planet. Think of the garbage and bodies we have thrown over. We've destroyed the ground before we've even reached it."

"You were always such a pessimist," Emelia said dryly.

"Well, she does have a point," Reeva said, looking at me. "A lot has gone overboard. Pretty much all of our crew is down there. But maybe the acid clouds took care of all of that for us."

"Which only adds to my point. There is nothing on the ground. The ages of acidity will have killed anything down there. It is not as though we will be able to grow food or raise families on so much destroyed earth."

"That doesn't matter, Kat. We can't stop the sink. We have to make the best of it."

"Maybe the best of it is a fast end, not a drawn-out one," Katarina said darkly. "Sade. Think about it. Nobody has to know it was a choice. Everybody can keep living their lives in denial of the sink until those lives end." She looked between me and Emelia. "The two of you can stop having to worry about the disparity in your status and arranged marriages. I imagine that would be quite freeing."

"You want me to not even try?" I asked slowly.

Katarina shrugged, not bothering to try for any of the delicateness she so clung to usually. No anger, no hostility, no snide comment, nor sickly-sweet sentiment. The hollowness in the woman scared me.

I looked at Reeva, who shrugged. "I'd rather not die if we can stop it."

"It's not even a question, Sade," Emelia said. "You are the only Aberrant here, though, so we are all dependent on you."

I nodded. It was all on my shoulders. The weight was taxing.

"Katarina. I need you," I said again.

She waved a hand dismissively. She would follow me, but that didn't mean she would help. Slowly, I turned from the hollow woman to Reeva and Emelia.

"We need a way to the glyph core."

"We could always climb," Reeva suggested.

"It's too dangerous. The fumes are too close now, and only two of us are hard-handed. Besides, if we are spotted scuttling around on the underside, the Enforcers won't hesitate to pick us off."

Reeva shrugged. "I guess you are right."

"I can get us an airship, but a pilot for that will be more difficult to come by," Emelia offered.

"I can pilot." Reeva said. "It may not be the smoothest ride, but you don't get tarry without learning a little something."

"What about your Aberrant friend?" Emelia asked. "Will she help?"

"I don't know that I would call Lea a friend, exactly," I grumbled. "I don't know. I've asked her. I've told her what is at stake. But the College ... because of the binding, I think she can't help more than she already has."

"Then we will do this with just us," Emelia said.

"We hardly need a Charmer," Katarina sniped. "I can't imagine what she will do for us but get in the way."

Emelia ignored the woman's comment.

"I will be coming too," Tomas said, entering the room unannounced. He stood behind Katarina as she groused.

"Did you see something?" I asked.

"Only that you were all planning on doing something dangerous." His hand set on Katarina's shoulder. "I won't be letting you go alone, madam."

Surprisingly, Katarina relaxed slightly under the man's touch as she considered his fingers. "Fine."

50:

The plans had been made; the preparations set. Reeva had recovered fully enough, and we had no more excuses. I had run out of time to prepare. The morning would bring a challenge I didn't know if I was ready for.

I wasn't surprised when Katarina lay down beside me.

"Can I stay here tonight?" she asked quietly.

I made room for her.

"You should get some sleep," she said.

"Easier said than done, it seems."

She rolled onto her side with a sigh. "You know I think this plan is foolish and reckless, but I will be with you. The whole way. Just ..." She sniffed. "Just don't die. Don't leave me alone here."

I put an arm around her and nodded, but I couldn't make that promise.

"If you do die, at least have the good graces to move on quickly so we don't have to watch each other peel away," she whispered.

When the morning came, I was surprised I had gotten any sleep at all. Katarina lay curled against my side, something loosely clutched between her fingers. A braid.

"You shouldn't have wasted your energy on charming me," I said quietly when she stirred.

"I've been channeling since I was a baby. A little charm isn't going be what breaks us today. If anything, you not getting a proper night's sleep could have been."

I yawned and stretched and started getting ready. She watched me remove a pair of trousers from my wardrobe with only a subtle pinch of her lips.

I cocked an eyebrow at her. "What, no derisive comment?"

She shrugged delicately. "I think we are beyond derisive comments. If ever there was an occasion for you to wear trousers, I suppose it is this one." She scowled. "I might even have to try them myself."

I laughed. "You never know. You might like them."

She cringed at the very thought.

Our lighthearted banter flowed with tension in its undercurrent. Today, we would either succeed, or fail to save all life on the landmasses. The pressure was oppressive. It did not exactly bring me calm knowing that if it was failure we found today, I would not be alive to experience the consequences.

51:

It was an unusual feeling boarding an airship legally. It felt too easy, just climbing on board without any circumstance. No hiding. No dive.

This one was small, nothing so grand as the Persephone had been. A simple airship meant for tours and pleasure cruises around Vale for the well-to-dos, not for crossing the abyss. The benches were furnished in intricately embroidered upholstery and a fully stocked bar sat against the back wall of the passenger compartment boasting an array of crystal. The family crest hanging just behind the bar belonged to the Tonson's. It seemed Emelia had asked a favor of her family friends to obtain this vessel.

Emelia looked at me with a curious glance, emerging from the cockpit with a checklist in hand. "You feel … unusual," she commented. "Are you alright?"

"Nervous, is all," I said in a half-truth, turning from fidgeting with my talons to look out at the cloudline below. The lower half of Vale's undercarriage was already immersed in clouds, with drifts of planetary fumes no doubt reaching even higher. The descent had definitely increased in speed as more and more glyphs failed on the core.

While there were those who noticed, there were so many more who seemed intent on disregarding the facts so long as the Society contented itself ignoring what was happening. It seemed unreasonable to entirely blame the binding at this point. Still, there were enough people at the docks watching the cloudline nervously that, even if we failed, I could only hope the Society would be forced into action.

I swallowed when I looked at Emelia again, remembering the words her mother had said to me only days before. *I don't know what you are up to, but I know you will take care of my daughter no matter what happens.* That moment of confidence the woman had shown me had ebbed only a moment later when we were no longer alone. I could only hope I didn't let Lady Rasczek down today, but I was bringing Emelia into the exact opposite of safety.

Emelia set a hand on mine and soothed away the discomfort. "I don't have much I can contribute in this venture, but I am here, Sade."

I gave her a grateful smile, but couldn't stop my eyes from dropping back to the clouds below.

I needed to bind the cores. I needed to break the clouds. I needed to see that the landmasses continued their slow descent to the surface. It all seemed like too much.

Maybe if I could bind the cores, that would be enough for the landmasses to stabilize their glyphs and keep themselves afloat a little longer. I doubted it, though. I could feel the magic snapping and breaking like thin strings trying to buoy an enormous weight. The *twang* of each faltering glyph brought Vale closer to the cloudline. I hoped that, between the glyphs and the machinery, I would be unnecessary in bringing down Vale except as a supervisor of a controlled descent.

Reeva arrived soon after, hauling a man along by the arm. Beater.

"He's an asshole, or he was, anyway, but I couldn't exactly leave him behind," the woman said, hauling the man onto the airship. "When this fuckery goes south, as we all know it's going to, the slums are going to hit the cloudline first. And even if they don't, none of those buildings are designed for big quakes. I gave the residents some warning that things may get rough and to head up, but I'm sure everybody thought I was as crazy as Beater. They will change their minds when they feel the first shakes." She pushed Beater past me toward the passenger compartment of the small airship. "The bastard is family in his own way, I guess," she said very reluctantly. "I feel a little responsible for him." She sighed and looked over the small airship.

I knew the Breaker wasn't entirely recovered yet from the way she carried herself, still protective of where the round had penetrated. Looking at the cloudline, we knew we could not wait any longer.

"Should I start getting her ready?" Reeva asked, her eyes reluctantly breaking from the clouds below.

"Best to. We should get this over with as quickly as we can."

Reeva swallowed, fighting the urge to look back down at the cloudline. "Yeah. Let's do that." Her hand rested absently at her hip.

"Where did you get that?" I asked Reeva, eyeing the ornate pistol holstered there.

"Oh, you can't expect me to go down there without some protection," Reeva muttered.

"That's not what I asked."

She rolled her eyes. "Where do I get anything?"

"Is that my father's pistol?" Emelia asked, seeing the piece.

Reeva blushed a little. "You can prosecute me after we save the world, Charms."

Emelia only chuckled and handed the Breaker a wooden box. "I was actually planning on giving that to you, anyway. I wish we didn't, but I am not naïve enough to believe we will not need protection with what we are doing. Anyway, when I couldn't find my father's pistol, I picked this one up for you instead." She nodded toward the box and Reeva opened it.

"Well, fuck me sideways. Isn't that a beaut." She lifted another pistol from the box. Engraved and flashing. She grinned as she eyed the weapon. "Perhaps you should hold onto this little baby just now. When we get to the surface though … Don't mind if I take both, then, do you?" She glanced at Emelia for only a moment before returning her eyes to the pistol.

"They are yours. I am not much of a shot."

"Well, we will have to fix that," Reeva said, offering the revolver back to Emelia, still appreciating the pistol even as it left her hand. She met Emelia's eye. "I'll teach you when we get to the surface," she said almost wistfully before moving to the front of the airship.

I didn't like watching Emelia holster the revolver on her own hip, but it was necessary.

Tomas and Katarina came next. The woman moved past me without a word and sat beside the window of the airship. I knew her apprehensions, but I also knew she would do her part. That she would stay with me as long as I needed her. She may not be an Aberrant, but she knew the magic required for this was immense. Even with the abilities of an Amplifier, we would likely fail.

For his part, Tomas gave me a smile, looking ready for a fight. He wore light body armor to protect against bullets and carried a rifle that looked Enforcer standard issue. Very illegal for him to own personally, but I was sure he had his ways of keeping secrets. A pistol rode on his thigh and knives were strapped around his body. I hoped he hadn't drawn too much attention on the trip from the manor.

"I haven't had a good fight in a while," he admitted a little shyly.

"Please don't tell me you are hoping for one," I said.

He gave a halfhearted shrug. "No … but I know that when you start going to work on the core, there will be one. The Enforcers have been on high alert recently. I'm here to keep you and Katarina safe. Whatever that might take." He moved to stand beside Katarina, the two silently looking out the window.

"What about Lea?" Emelia asked quietly.

"I wouldn't hold my breath. Best if we hurry. Each glyph that fails leaves the rest straining." Even from the landmass' surface I could feel the core's sickness now. I could feel the massive amount of energy it took to keep the glut of land that was Vale aloft straining. I didn't understand how the College or the gods could ignore the certainty of the fall now. They must be able to feel it, surely. Vale could not be the only landmass in such a state.

Reeva poked her head out of the steering compartment. "She's ready to go. You get us all the necessary clearances, Charms?"

"I got us clearances," Emelia said evasively. "I couldn't exactly get us the ones required for docking at a highly restricted location."

Reeva waved her hand flippantly. "I'm not worried about that as long as we are not set upon from the get-go. I'll have to take us the long way down so we don't draw too much suspicion, so enjoy the view."

I rubbed the charm hanging around my neck as we set off, then took a seat beside Katarina.

The woman's eyes were on the cloudline, her bottom lip drawn in between her teeth in nervousness.

"Are you alright?" I asked softly.

She shook her head. "Are you?"

"No," I admitted, looking at the yellow clouds. They looked so innocent just now, their splash against the stony bottom of the landmass appearing innocuous.

She sniffed, then rested her head against my shoulder. "Oh, Sade … You know when you have a feeling the thing you are doing is the right thing … but you know that what you are doing may not be right for keeping your loved ones safe? I have that feeling. I don't think this is going to go well."

I squeezed her shoulders. "We will have each other down there." It was a thin attempt at assurances with no promises made. She saw through it, but said nothing.

"I'm starting to wish we had the College on our side," Katarina said darkly.

I laughed, rubbing her arm. "A sentiment I never thought I would hear from you."

She sniffed, plucking at her clothes. She had deigned to wear a pair of high-waisted trousers and a fashionable blouse for her journey into the underworkings. "Well, you also never thought you would see me in pants, so." The little pompous edge in her voice made me smile. I squeezed her shoulders once more, then stood.

Marco appeared at my side. "The Enforcers know somethin' is up, sis. But still no Abbies at the core."

I nodded, patting the boy's shoulder. "Were you able to get closer?"

He looked grim when he nodded. We both knew the failing of the restrictions didn't bode well.

Emelia and Reeva were bantering through the open door to the control room. Their talk was light, but there was a tension flowing through their words.

I joined Emelia in leaning against the wall beside the control room door. "I didn't realize you two were such friends now."

"Jealous, Sade?" Reeva called back. "You should really learn how to share."

"As you can imagine, we've had a lot to talk about over the last few weeks," Emelia said.

"Like how batty it is that you want me to break glyphs on the core keeping us all alive." Reeva chuckled mirthlessly. "But we are going to make it happen, aren't we, Charms?"

Emelia took my hand. "You are going to make it happen," she said reassuringly.

"Thanks," I said quietly, closing my eyes to savor the calm of the moment. It would break soon, I was certain. The hum of the airship's engines and rotors was as familiar a din to me as the rush of wind on the underside of the Grand Cross Bridge. Even the too-loud banter between Reeva and Emelia had its place. And the quiet muttering of Hayden. The electric hum of the lights adding their unneeded illumination to the cabin. These were the sounds of my youth, of my gang, of my exploits, and for a moment, I clung to them.

"The Enforcers see us now," Reeva called back to us. Tomas's back straightened, ready to go.

I joined her at the controls. "There are six of them. No Abbies," I relayed for Marco.

"Plenty of lead, though," she commented, surveying the array of waiting rifles.

"Turn back now!" The Enforcers called through their megaphone. "Return to the surface!"

"What do you think?" Reeva asked. "Should we follow their order?"

I stepped away from the Breaker and readied the glyphs needed to stop the impending volley.

"Turn back or we will open fire!"

Reeva continued on.

I released the glyphs.

The Enforcers fired.

The bullets hit the barrier cast at the nose of the airship in an anticlimactic series of warbles, then fell. Another volley followed, with a third quick on its heels.

"Think you can put them all down from here?" Reeva asked.

"Save your magic. I'll handle them," Emelia said behind us. "You just worry about landing this thing."

Reeva looked at me, not bothering trying to hide her uncertainty.

"Alright," I agreed, hoping Emelia wasn't overestimating the power of a Charmer.

Emelia set her hand on my arm and met my eyes. "Trust me, please," she whispered.

I took her hands in mine. "I do. I'm sorry."

She grinned. "If a Charmer told me they were going to try to convince six Enforcers just to pack up and leave their post, I would have some doubts too."

"You're up, Charms," Reeva said doubtfully, casting yet another look at me before bringing the ship to the landing pad. The Enforcers had given up on wasting their rounds and instead had taken up defensive positions behind a barricade at the tunnel entrance.

"Katarina, if you would," Emelia said, holding her hand out toward Katarina.

Katarina set her hand in Emelia's, amplifying the Charmer's already impressive ability as they stepped into the doorway of the airship.

"How are all of you fine Enforcers today?" Emelia asked, her magic nearly leveling me into doing her whim. "You all wouldn't mind climbing onto your airships and flying back up to the surface now, would you?"

The Enforcers stared at her in varying levels of swoon. Two ran for their airship, fighting each other to be the first to obey her, and the rest quick-stepped in pursuit of the others. My legs nearly gave in to the desire to please Emelia by following the Enforcers.

Reeva set a steadying hand on my shoulder, breaking the Charm. I took a freeing breath.

Emelia dropped Katarina's hand as the Enforcers spun up their airship. Reeva hurried to grab Katarina's arm before she gave in to Emelia's magic as well.

"Damn," Katarina said with an appreciative look at Emelia. Tomas almost looked disappointed at the lack of resistance.

Emelia grinned, then handed me a talker. "Tomas and I will make sure they don't come back." Already the man was setting about building up a fighting position at the tunnel's entrance. I didn't like the idea of leaving Emelia to cover us in a gunfight, but I knew the Charmer could take care of herself. "You three go take care of business. And, Sade." She kissed me. "Be careful."

Katarina took my hand, and with an apprehensive look, started into the tunnel.

The oppressive heat of the core built as we drew closer. The necklace seemed to be doing its work as the crushing illness of the core was held at bay. The core's sickness still rang subtly in my gut. Reeva moved just ahead of us, stopping with her hand placed against key glyphs in the core's defenses as we passed.

"Reeva, can you break this?" I said indicating the string of defensive glyphs around the core chamber.

"I sure can," she said, cracking her knuckles and approaching the wall. She set her hands on the glyphs, and for a moment everything around her touch dimmed before her focus set.

Twang. Twang. Each of the glyphs severed from its intent and faded away.

"Any more?"

I read the walls quickly. "We should be good."

The core was familiar. The memory dragged from the pit of my mind. The overly white glow of glyphs lighting the earthen tunnel was unpleasant. My mother had brought me here. And when we had left, she had died. Had our actions inadvertently caused the sickness?

My mind went to Lea. My mother had thought the two of us capable of whatever she had brought me here for. Was I anywhere near enough on my own?

I set my hand on the core, feeling the magic.

"First, I have to bind the cores," I said, beating back my apprehension. "Get them back in balance."

The intent was easy, a simple maintenance glyph Lea had taught me. I felt the connection fire between the glyph cores. The magic balanced, the cores acting as they had been designed to do. The hum of the magic in the air was overwhelming as they all united once again.

"Bound," I panted. Simple, but taxing.

There was a tremor that shook the tunnels and brought small rocks and dust down on our heads.

Katarina ducked and watched the ceiling suspiciously.

"Can you tell if we are still sinking?" she asked, a little too hopeful.

"Yeah. We are," I said, crushing her hopes that we could let matters rest. "Now the clouds."

With the cores bound once more, the instability of earlier no longer made me nauseous when I rested my hand on the core. Seven cores all shared the burden while I steered them. I beckoned Reeva closer.

"Alright, Sade, I don't want to be next to this thing any longer than I have to be. Are you ready?" Reeva asked, eyeing the corrupted glyphs.

I took a steadying breath and held Katarina's hand, then

nodded.

Reeva shattered the first glyph, and the air felt like it was being pulled from my lungs as I carved the replacement into existence. It shuddered at the tips of my fingers as the magic required bled from me, even as Katarina doubled and redoubled it. The glyph firmed and settled, and the air became breathable once again. Reeva looked at me for confirmation that I wanted to continue. I didn't waste my energy on talking but just gave her the slightest—and a little bit apprehensive—of nods. The next glyph shattered as I finished drawing its replacement. Even the heat of the core seemed to drop for the moment that the glyph was broken before my new glyph settled. We continued on, each glyph sapping me and Katarina of strength until we were sagging against each other for support. Reeva broke the last glyph and backed away from the core, panting. It seemed even the Breaker was feeling the strain.

"Alright, Reeva. I need you to go back to the airship. If we get too close to the cloudline, just go. I'll figure things out on our end."

She nodded, looking around. "My very presence is dimming the magic in here, anyway, which is exactly what we don't need. Look after each other," she said, looking between Katarina and myself.

I placed the base of the final glyph, resealing the sustaining magics of the landmasses. The corruption of the glyphs gone, I felt a shifting in the cores as they rebalanced. My finger traced over the smooth stone as I added and adapted the glyph to break what the gods had created.

Katarina groaned as the strain of what I was doing balanced across the cores.

"I have this," she said tightly when my finger froze against the hard stone, dragging as though it was being glued into place. The flesh on my fingers felt like it was burning away as the magic locked in the digits. The magic cycled through her once more, building strength enough to allow me to finalize the glyph.

We both collapsed, panting against one another as we stared up at the core, the release of magic required to dissipate the cloudline immense and immobilizing. I could hear the sounds of gunfire echoing down the tunnel toward us from outside now. I had been too focused to notice it before. There was a sudden lull in the *crack-crack-crack* of Tomas's rifle and the returning fire, petering out to silence that I could only hope was a good sign. With all the interference from the core, I could not feel any death, but that did not preclude death's occurrence.

"Priya! You did it! You were right. The cloudline is gone." The voice belonged to a woman I did not know.

"Great Aunt Leeta ..." Katarina said slowly. "What in the abyss?" She looked at the ghost. "She was a quick burn. Here and gone. I saw her move on." Her hand slipped out of mine. "Where did she go?"

I looked from the ghost to Katarina. "She's right here; what do you mean?"

"You can still see her?"

I nodded, but when I looked back at the ghost she seemed off, distorted, her mouth moving but only hints of words reaching my ears.

"The fold ... I think it's pinching," I said as the ghost disappeared.

"Fascinating as that is, we should probably get out of here," Katarina said, leaning heavily on me. She shifted to all fours and then, using the wall to stand, managed to get her legs under her. She offered me her hand which I gratefully took, letting her pull me to my feet.

Her eyes roved the space around the core as we saw what was around us. The pinch of the fold showed us cracks in the glyph core. Clouds. Hard rock. People. Animals. Trees. We heard voices from times ahead, times past, and times that would never be.

"Who is meddling where they ought not be?" The voice was a thin whisper in the back of my mind, trying to worm its way into my brain. Another voice in the fold. A menacing voice. I pulled Katarina toward the tunnel and our escape. "Solving problems you don't understand and cannot fathom the depth of. Hmph. Fine. Solve them."

I felt a shattering in the cores, and after a sickening moment, realized that several of the core glyphs had fractured. The binding between them snapped and the balancing vanished, staggering me with another sickening wave that even Perry's charm could do nothing to abate.

Katarina compensated for my sudden lack, holding me on my feet.

"What just happened?" she asked, stepping back from the stone.

There was a laughing in the back of my mind as I reeled, trying to hold the snapping intents of the core glyph.

"Something just broke the core," I said, straining to pull intents back together again.

"Yeah. We did." Katarina said, eyeing the crack forming in the smooth stone and its glowing glyphs.

The ground rumbled beneath us and the landmass lurched, breaking any attempt at holding together the severing glyphs. "Something much bigger than us. We are falling."

"We were before," Katarina said, but any of her usual irritation had quavered away into fear. We could both tell it was faster now, less controlled. We could feel the lightening in our legs, the steady increase in the rumble. "Do something."

I looked at her helplessly, then at the core. Even broken, there was still power in the stone. I held my hand out to Katarina and she took it. We both knew this was beyond our abilities.

I formed the intent, fingers etching steady patterns of stability and control into the air. There would be no arresting the descent, but maybe I could slow it. Maybe I could diminish the impact. There were too many maybes as I drew up my magic.

"You can do this, Sade," Katarina said in the first display of outward support she had afforded me. "You can do this. Focus."

I nodded and took a steadying breath, pushing aside all other thoughts. All doubt. And became nothing more than a conduit, my intent driving my hand as I carved into the air.

My hands burned with the magic constrained within me. I felt Katarina shudder and go to her knees as she channeled and amplified. The release of the magic pent up inside my gut sent me to my knees beside her. The heaviness I felt in my bones wasn't entirely exhaustion, though. The threat of freefall had abated for a moment, but I would need to continue.

Katarina looked at me, swallowing her nerves when she realized our work was not done, then nodded. I helped her back to her feet. Even a Natural needed form and focus. Once again, I carved.

The floor under our feet quaked, only breaking my focus further. The smooth stone of the core shifted; cracks started to form in the dirt below. I grabbed Katarina as the floor shifted, then fell away. Years of practice had my wrist flicking and my talons slamming forward to catch the stone of the cave wall. They dug in deep enough to hold us, jarring my shoulder painfully as we dangled over the new hole in the floor. The drop hadn't been too far. More rock fell from above, promising to crush us to death if we weren't careful. The collapsing dirt and rock did one helpful thing, stopping the errant rolling of the now unrestrained glyph core by burying the stone in tons of earth.

Steadily, I lowered Katarina as far as I could before she dropped the rest of the way to the new cave floor. I worked my talons free of the wall and carefully picked my way down the rock wall to stand beside her. There was enough of the core showing still for us to have access, at least.

Katarina stared at the rock, then at the rubble leading to the exit tunnel.

"We can still get out of here," she said.

I shook my head. "I'm staying, Katarina."

"You can't do anything to stop this," she said, gesturing at the cavern of failing glyphs. "Sade. You have to accept that there are limits to what people can do. If the gods wanted us to survive this, don't you think they would have given us more than just you?"

"I still have to try."

"Of course you do." She sighed. "Do you know how to stop this?"

"Um …"

Katarina swore and took my hand. "Better think of something, fast."

I set my hand on the core and focused. We needed control. We needed to stabilize the descent. The glyphs came to mind and released, small chips at a massive oak of a problem. Practical glyphs and economy would never solve this. I slogged through foundations, building a glyph I was certain would have made my mother proud, had she survived this long, and carved it into the dust-filled air.

"I will need to sustain this," I said as the magic leeched away from me. The rumbling of our fall slowed and our descent softened, but the glyph needed to be maintained.

"Take what you need."

Katarina panted from the strain, her hand slackening in mine. My eyelids fluttered and the two of us sagged against each other.

"Let it go, Sade. Nobody could do this alone," Katarina said, breathing hard.

"I can't just let Vale fall."

"I don't think we have much other choice, darling."

Katarina and I sat with our backs against each other, hands still connected but the grip lost from our fingers. I felt the rumble of the failing glyphs, the rotors of the mechanical means of keeping Vale aloft struggling and failing to keep the landmass afloat. I had tried to slow the descent, but it was too much.

I felt a swell of magic behind me.

"Rhoda?" I said in confusion at the unexpected arrival. Of course the woman had noticed the sinking of the landmass and guessed something had happened to the core. It spoke to the woman's character that she chose to rush headlong toward the problem.

The Aberrant innkeeper swore, her knees buckling under the weight of the pinching fold. Still, she crawled to me.

"This better not be you and your girlfriend doing more thrill seeking," Rhoda said through clenched teeth. "What can I do to help?" she ground out. I could use the woman's magic, but without a charm to protect her from the fold, she would only lose consciousness soon, and I was starting to wonder if maybe such extensive contact with the fold was not entirely healthy for a body. Every moment near the core seemed to drain the woman a little more.

"Go. Save lives. We will try to hold here as long as we can," I said tightly.

She could tell that as long as we could would not be very long. Still, she nodded, and a moment later, after drawing a glyph with effort, was gone.

"We could have used the help," Katarina said with a heavy tongue.

I didn't say anything, but instead focused on my glyphs. I could feel myself slipping away.

Marco's cold hand touched mine. "Survive," he said, and I felt a surge of energy in my fingers that crawled to my heart. The pulsing hit Katarina's amp and doubled, channeled back, and grew.

My eyes opened, and my hand pulled back from Marco's too late. He smiled and was gone.

"No. Marco!" I reached for him, but the specter had given me what was left of him. Even so, his sacrifice wasn't enough. I knew it without trying. Vale was too large.

There was a crackle amidst the whining of metal and groaning of earth as the landmass started picking up speed in its descent.

For a moment there was a swell of magic, solid and well-formed intent amidst so much fracturing. I recognized the stability and skill behind the surge. Lea had finally decided to help.

"There you are." The hand that took mine was warm with life. Lea reached up from where she crouched beside me, seizing the hand of a terrified-looking man beside her. "Hurry up. We don't have time for this. Do you want to die or not?"

I felt Marco's contribution grow, doubling and doubling again as the Amps Lea brought all formed a ring around us, their hands linked in sweaty fear-filled grips.

"Sade. I am not becoming one of your ghostly friends today," Lea growled. "Slow us down."

I nodded, picturing the complex string of glyphs in my mind, refining the conditions and bringing only what was essential into being.

I could feel the magic faltering as it released. Even amplified, all of Marco's potential, all of mine, it wasn't enough. Katarina lost consciousness behind me, but her channel continued to pulse against my hand, so I knew she still had some fight left in her. Lea's finger etched against the back of my hand, binding our strength to each other, sharing the burden of the release. Still it wasn't enough.

A cold hand touched my cheek. The Widow Reese. Wordlessly she passed from this world, leaving behind what was left of her in a distant look and a surge of magic in my chest.

I gasped with the revitalization, and forced the slipping glyphs back under my control. The descent slowed even as the ground quaked beneath our feet and the core chamber threatened to come down around us.

I felt our magic leeching away into the core, the draw heavier than it should have been, even given the strain of our action. The other landmasses were plummeting, too.

"You are not focused," Lea said tightly.

"It's not just Vale …" I said, struggling to hold the descent in check.

"Focus on what you can control. We can't help the others. If we try, everybody dies. Vale dies," Lea said sharply.

She was right, and yet … My hand still rested against the failing core. I released my hold on Katarina and slid my fingers against the smooth stone. The tether between the lands still held. My efforts were being leeched from Vale to the others, but in diminished quantities. They were falling faster than we were. Their people would never survive the descent. I could cut them loose now and save who I could, or give them more and risk what we had.

Another cold hand touched my cheek, one and then another. I looked up into the eyes of the dead as they came to me, giving themselves and vanishing. I recognized some. The gang. The street kids. The Rasczeks' groundkeeper. Many I didn't. Strangers from ages past and strangers who had passed only recently with the cloud drift.

"This is rather morbid," Lea said, watching the string of dead come and pass. Still, she shook the Amps back into action. Their exhausted line reinvigorated with the fresh flush of magic as it bloomed through me. Lea looked at me. "*Betho, Having, Fre.*"

I nodded, already bringing the glyphs into mind, my intent renewing with each, the release surging through the core to the other landmasses, binding us all.

I felt the final glyph release, surging through the connection in a deafening ring, then grasping the falling landmasses. The clutch was like a weight crushing down on my chest, and I groaned under the strain.

Lea gasped, rocking forward and collapsing under the shared weight. Around the line of Amps, several went down, but their fellows kept their hands locked together tight, maintaining the chain.

Another cold hand touched my cheek, the magic of their life draining away into the core almost instantly. The constant drain, the constant amplification, the constant push of more magic through my body was almost too much. I felt myself losing my grip that the glyphs required.

"Focus," Lea ground out, her own eyes closed tight against the strain. "Re ... re ... resettle the glyphs, Sade."

My teeth ground together and I took a deep pull of air through my nose, struggling to focus as I felt our descent increase in speed once again.

I could feel the deaths above. I could feel the deaths on the other landmasses. Buildings would be collapsing. Distal bits of land would be falling away as the glyphs continued to fail.

Betho. Having. Fre. I focused on the glyphs, renewing their stability and feeling myself wane with the effort.

"Sade! Where are you? Damn these lights!" Emelia's voice

echoed down the corridor. "Sade. We are almost to the ground. We have to get to the airship now." Her warm fingers on my cheek drew my heavy eyelids back up. Tomas was with her, the man similarly touching Katarina's cheek to rouse the woman.

I felt a lessening on the drag of magic from the core as Junction reached the surface, then Reach, Bevilla, Dorado. Vale would not be far behind the others, my ability to slow our descent a feeble thing.

"Get the others out," I said.

"Who are these people? No." She shook her head. "Later. I'll ask later. You'll get trapped, or worse. We have to get out now."

"Get them out, Emelia. I'm right behind you."

"I don't believe you," she said in shattering tones.

"It doesn't matter right now. Take Katarina." Tomas's arms lifted the woman from the floor delicately. "The rest of you, follow Emelia. There's an airship. I can hold on my own a little longer."

The Amps hesitated, then those who could stand picked up those who couldn't between them and started down the corridor. The moment the chain broke, I felt a rope tighten around my heart.

There was only Vale left now. I hoped, anyway. It was getting difficult to focus through the ring of magic in the air.

Emelia grabbed Lea and tried to pull the woman to her feet.

"I'm staying. I have to stay," Lea protested, her hand still tight in mine, still sharing the burden as best she could. "I will get us out of here, my lady. Worry about the others." Lea's weak voice almost sounded genuine, but I knew that there was little chance either of us would survive impact.

Emelia's lips pressed to mine. "I love you, Sade. This is not the last time I see you."

"No," I agreed, but it felt hollow as the core pulled more and more from me. "I love you."

Still Emelia hesitated, but finally she grabbed the last Amp and half-dragged, half-carried the woman from the core.

Lea met my eyes, hers looking deep-sunken and grey under the strain. Mine no doubt looked the same.

"One last push," she said weakly. "*Venn.*"

I nodded, dredged the requested glyph from the depths of my mind, and released.

Lea and I collapsed together, the final glyph taking the last of us.

- 311 -

PART 3:

LANDBRINGER

- 314 -

1:

Katarina stood in front of me. "I left it all to you, my dear." She looked up at the dirt ceiling. "Though there may not be much left. You will figure it out. Of that I am certain." She crouched in front of me. "It's time for me to go find Deara. I need my sister." She pressed her cold forehead to mine. "Survive, Sade." Katarina's lips pressed to my forehead, then she vanished, her magic bringing me back from the brink with a gasp.

We hadn't been crushed. We hadn't died in the impact. But we would die trapped in this cave.

I pulled Lea against me, her limp body dragging over the rocks to rest against my chest. I wrapped my arm tight around her shoulders, raised my shaking hand, and drew the same glyph my mother had during our first escape from the core.

2:

I woke when Lea rolled off me with a groan.

"Where …" she said in a daze before stopping short. "Sade?" The woman shook my arm. "Sade? You'd better not be dead. You got us into this mess. We still need you. Sade?" Her voice pitched with a hint of fear.

I pushed her insistent hand away. "I'm alive," I groaned. "Barely." I lay where I was, flat on my back, staring at the dark sky above. No part of my body wanted to move.

"Where are we?"

I could feel the rubble under my back. "My mother's house."

Lea lay down beside me, giving up on trying to get off the rubble pile.

Above, the lights of airships tentatively approaching the ground circled.

"We made it," Lea said. "We broke a lot of stuff on the way, but you did it."

"We made it," I whispered before giving in to much-needed sleep.

3:

A hand grabbed my throat, pulling me from the rubble and hefting me into the air like a doll.

"You did this," the woman holding me up growled. She reached down and grabbed Lea, then a moment later we were in a great hall. Glyphs glowed on all the walls and floors, their magic the only thing preserving the structure during the fall. The fingers around my throat released. I hit the cold stones with a groan.

I set a hand on Lea's shoulder, shaking lightly to try to rouse her. I knew she wasn't dead, but we had certainly gotten close. She mumbled a string of unintelligible syllables, but otherwise lay where she had been dropped.

I pushed myself to all fours, feeling the threat in the air and wanting to meet it standing if I could. The weakness in my muscles did not bode well. I knew I shouldn't be alive, much less standing. The glyphs etched into the white marble walls around the massive chamber pulsed and hummed with sickening strength. Somehow, the glyph hum also seemed restorative, and with them bolstering me I managed to take my feet.

"What's this you found, sister?" slithered a voice to my right.

Around the room sat five looming thrones set atop a grand marble platform with four sets of eyes peering down at Lea and me. Behind the thrones stood an array of statue still attendants.

Outwardly, there was nothing remarkable about any of the onlookers except the stark resemblance that marked them all as siblings. They were people, elegantly adorned and with an imposing way about them, but lacking the grandeur of overwhelming height that their statues had always presented. The hard set to their faces and dismissive air as they looked down at us embodied a millennia of separation from the people who revered them. Still, I could feel the strength of their magic emanating off them as though their bodies were not enough to contain all that they were. There was no denying that these were the gods.

The speaker had been a man just cusping into middle age with a mirthless mouth and a dark look in his eye. I knew his visage. Albain. The God of Death.

I looked at the woman who had so effortlessly brought us to the hall of the gods. She watched me with her eyes narrowed and a thin line of irritation creasing her brows. Jespair.

"This seems to be the one who dissipated the cloudline and brought the landmasses down," Jespair muttered, taking her seat to stare down at me.

"These two, alone?" A thin woman with a mouse of a voice asked, staring wide eyed at us. Ralti.

"I doubt very much that they were alone," Albain groused. "There is death all over this one. What did you do, girl?" he demanded.

"What you all wouldn't," I snarled, surprised that any strength remained in my voice. "I saved the landmasses."

"You killed thousands," Jespair corrected me. "The destruction you caused never needed to happen."

"You are right," I agreed darkly. "You could have stopped it. It should not have been left on our shoulders."

Beside my boots, Lea was starting to stir. I didn't know if having the Garnet at my side would assist in anything except getting us killed faster. I knew there was little chance of escape, but I found myself forming a transportation glyph as I watched the gods assess me.

Lea muttered and I bent to help her up. When I did, I released the glyph, intent on running from this new threat.

The magic slammed back into my body, winding me like a blow to the stomach, and I fell back, struggling to breathe.

"I wouldn't try that again," Jespair warned. She was standing now, an amused tilt to her face. "A Natural." She stepped down from her throne to stand before me. "Well, would you look at that?" She pulled me to my feet by my jacket. "It seems we have a new sister among us."

"That? A Natural? No," Albain said angrily. "Even if she is, it does not make her one of our peers. And what about when the Society finds out about her? Do we simply tell them a new god has been born? Who, pray tell, would we say she was born to?"

Jespair looked me over. "We tell them she came from them. We did, after all, ascend her to our ranks to fulfill her destiny as the Landbringer."

"The what?" I asked, finally catching my breath.

"The girl doesn't even know her true name," Espa chuckled. "Your nature, girl. Your soul glyph."

Jespair crouched over me. "You are clearly a knowledgeable Aberrant to have done what you did to the cores, so you must know everything has a name."

Lea shifted beside me, drawing Jespair's eyes. I took my feet, setting myself between the god and the Aberrant.

"A Garnet …" Jespair said thoughtfully, then looked at me. "You could make use of that, you know. I can wipe her mind for you, little sister. Yoke her magic to yours without question or hesitation. Make her raw talent yours. As a welcome gift."

I kept myself between Lea and Jespair.

"No. That's not what I want. Leave her be."

Jespair's lips pinched, then relaxed into an amused expression. "You want a pet. Fine. But she must be leashed."

With a flick of her hand, she sent me staggering to the side several steps. The strength of the god was overwhelming. Jespair closed the distance to Lea. Her fingers etched a glyph just over Lea's chest. A binding of some sort.

The glyph released, and as it did, it sunk into Lea's chest. The Aberrant went to her knees, clutching at where the glyph had disappeared, crying out in pain.

Jespair didn't stop me when I rushed to Lea's side, wrapping a protective arm over her shoulders.

"She is bound to you now, little sister. Use her wisely."

Lea panted, but the pain seemed to be easing. As she recovered, I felt a new power wrap itself around my heart. A new welling of magic, and with it, more strength in my ruined body.

"What do you think you are doing, Jespair?" Albain raged, standing.

Jespair silenced the man with a look, then turned back to me. She gestured behind her and two of her blank-faced attendants stepped forward. "My gift to you," she said, sweeping a hand at the two. She stopped at each, etching the same symbol into their chests. They didn't falter when the glyph burned into them. Instead, their blank stares turned from Jespair to me, and once again I felt the warmth of yoked magic fill me. They had once been powerful Aberrants like Lea. Strong conduits, but not Naturals.

"What was that glyph?" I asked, helping Lea back to her feet.

Jespair smiled. "It's yours. Landbringer. A bit of an auspicious glyph for you, wasn't it? Not all of them are so … predictive. Hers for example," she nodded toward Lea. "Unbound, a little less so." She laughed and sneered at Lea. "You've been Bound since the day you were born."

"I don't understand," I said, shaking my head. "What do you mean, it's mine?"

"Everything in this world has a glyph, little sister. With these three bound to you, you should be able to see it now, if you focus. The power you can have over something by knowing its true being …" She shuddered in ecstasy. Her eyes refocused on me. "That is what will make you a god, little Landbringer." She returned to her seat with the others. Albain glowered but remained silent. "Right now, we need to discuss exactly that. You broke the cloudline. You settled the landmasses. An impressive feat for one with no Bound, but a destructive one, too."

"The landmasses were sinking. We all would have died."

Albain laughed. "Not everybody, *little sister*." He sneered.

"If only we had found you before you made such a dreadful mess of things," Espa said ruefully, shaking her head.

"The belief that we are needed was starting to wane," Albain explained. "The Society questioned our value. Only Jespair's blindly devoted Aberrants seemed not to question, and that only through a subtle binding. One I think you broke in your pet."

I looked at Lea, who could not stop herself from looking at the slate faces of the Aberrants ringing the chamber. The Bound. Had she known them?

"You wanted the Society to see your worth by putting it in danger?" I said, looking at the gods in horror.

"The core glyphs are hard ones to break, but—" He shrugged, as though the effort had been nothing for the gods. Given how many Bound stood behind them, it likely wasn't.

"How many would you have let die?" I asked in a thin voice.

"As many as it took," Jespair said. "It wouldn't have taken long to bring the masses running, begging for our salvation." She rolled her eyes at me. "I can see you find it distasteful, but sometimes what's best for the Society requires unpleasant acts."

"How many people died with your little exploit lowering the landmasses?" Albain asked. "Had you come to us, they wouldn't have had to."

"Meat for the machine," Jespair said dismissively. "Our little sister may have done something foolish, but we can still benefit from this. A god, risen from their common ranks; I can see the headlines already. I can see our return in it. They need us now more than ever, brothers and sisters. This little accident," she said with a pointed look at me, "is a gift when looked at through the correct lens. We gave them the planet. A dying rock, maybe, but we can change that … given the proper devotion."

"Why do you need that?" I asked. "Why do you need anything in return? The collective here must have enough magic to bring life back to the planet. You had enough to take it away."

Jespair turned dissatisfied eyes on me at my knowledge of what the gods had done, but it was Espa who spoke.

"You should not have survived bringing the landmasses down," Espa said, ignoring my question. "Even as a Natural. Without so much as one Bound, it should have killed you. You certainly should not have succeeded, even with the destruction from the act. It is impressive." The words felt coerced, more a compromise with her sister than a compliment for me.

Albain gave me a look like we shared a secret, then said, "Truly. And that is no doubt why Jespair brought you here." His hateful tune suddenly shifted. "You belong among our ranks. But that means you play by our rules."

Espa smiled. "Our game is not so hard. You just need to learn how to play it." She eyed Devton. "Seeing as she's one of your vagabonds, why don't you show her where she will be staying while us grownups talk through this mess our new *sister* has made for us?"

4:

"Landbringer," Devton said in a small, considering voice. He led us toward a secluded corridor with a subtle glance back toward the hall where the rest of the gods deliberated without him. The man was diminished compared to the rest of his siblings, save for maybe Ralti. Even so, with all of his Bound, I knew the god could crush me with a thought if he so chose. "I tried to warn you. To give you guidance, but …" He looked back the way we had come. "My siblings are everywhere and hear everything." He shook his head. "I never agreed with them about the breaking or the cloudline. It is why I am as I am, and they are as they are."

I didn't have to wonder what the god meant. I could feel the difference in his magic, the fact that he had relatively few Bound. Enough to sustain him through the ages, but not enough to make him a threat to his siblings and their will.

"It is why they will keep you less than. A pet. Something to bring devotion back to them, but not enough to give you the strength to challenge them," he went on.

I frowned at the man's verbiage. An outsider among family. The god of the vagabonds, it seemed, was as outcast as his people. Still, I didn't trust altruism from anybody with so much power, especially one so timeless.

"How did you try to stop them?" I asked. "From breaking the world?"

He swallowed and looked ashamed. "I didn't. I simply said no. You will learn soon enough, that while you hold all this power," he looked at his hands, "it is not truly yours. You are just another conduit for Jespair's will. She will give. She will take. She will do what pleases her."

"What about Albain?"

"Albain," Devton said with derisiveness. "Is a dog who bites. He goes along with Jespair only because he knows that is the only way to grow his power. That his younger sister surpassed him will never stop burning, though."

"And Espa?" I had seen the hateful glint in the second-born's eyes whenever she looked at her younger sister.

"She and Albain are of one mind."

"What about Ralti?" What deceit hid in the timid god of compassion.

"Ralti?" He shook his head. "She alone may be the only one among my siblings who wants nothing." I didn't entirely believe that.

"And you?"

"What about me?" He asked, stopping in front of a heavy wooden door.

"Jespair seeks devotion. Albain and Espa want to surpass Jespair. What is it you want?"

"To help you."

I frowned, not having expected that. "To help me?"

He nodded with a small smile.

I looked at Lea, who trailed despondently behind us with the Bound. "In that case, how can I break the binding on Lea?"

He looked at me, not comprehending. "Why would you want to? You need her to have any hope of succeeding among the others." He looked at Lea derisively. "Do you have any idea how many of your fellows she has tortured or killed? How many minds she has warped?"

I swallowed. "I have an idea."

He shook his head, eyes returning to me with a pitying edge. "I don't know that you do. She is better bound. And you are better with her bound. Trust me, sister. You will need her strength, not her free will." He opened the door in front of us, revealing a richly furnished anteroom. "I will look after you as well as I can, but you will need to fend for yourself, and for that you will need Bound. More than these three. And be careful. Your magic is much stronger than it was ten minutes ago. Try not to manifest any glyphs until you have a handle on what you are capable of."

I stepped past him into the anteroom, then turned. "Why tell me any of this? Why look out for me?"

He looked sad. "Maybe," he sighed and shook his head, banishing the thought.

"Maybe?"

"Maybe you can right what we did out of greed. Maybe you can fix what we have become," he said in a small voice before hurrying away.

I watched him go, then closed the door with a sigh.

The rooms beyond the antechamber were only richer still with high ceilings supported by columns and stone arches, tapestries hung from the walls and rich green and gold trimmed curtains draped the stately windows, while an eternity of baubles ornamented the space. I did not want to touch anything for fear of upsetting any one of the gods who only tentatively accepted my presence on their fallen isle. Still, I poked around, finding the glyphs built into the foundations of the building underfoot and stabilizing the walls on all sides. The castle should have put up a deafening hum with the magic that threaded itself into its very construction, but dampening glyphs kept the roar silent. I also found a few listening glyphs that I hesitated to break just yet, heeding Devton's advice to adjust to my new potential before exploiting it.

"I don't imagine a single stone moved on the isle when the landmass came down," I said quietly, hoping for anything from Lea. Her eyes lighted on me for only a moment before she found a corner and sat silently, her knees tucked to her chest as she stared into space. I looked from her to the slate-faced Bound and felt a disconcerting familiarness in their expressions.

"Give me your hand," I said to the female Bound, and she extended her hand, face immobile as she stared at me, barely blinking.

I prodded carefully for memories and found no resistance, but also no success. There was nothing. Only a glyph blazed in her mind. My glyph. The Landbringer.

I dropped her hand and quickly grabbed the hand of the man, only to find the same. I backed away from the two. "Go."

They bowed and left the room for I didn't know where.

"We are just steam for their engine," Lea said quietly, her eyes watching me over her knees. "I worshiped them all my life. I strove to serve them. I did not know all it meant was becoming this. A husk. A tool. A Bound."

I crouched in front of her. "Lea …"

She scoffed. "Lea. Ha. What a fool I was. Thinking myself better than you. Better than a Natural. Better than a god." She let her head fall back against the wall and stared at the ceiling. "And now I'm just another log thrown to their fire."

I could see the Landbringer glyph coiling in her chest. The edges seemed wrapped around her heart.

"There must be a way to break it," I said. "Lea. I need your help to break the binding."

"It is not a simple balancer binding. You can't just snap it away. Nor should you want to. Not if you want to stand any chance among your new *brothers and sisters.*"

"They are not my brothers and sisters," I growled. "You have a day to get over your defeatist shit, and then you need to help me."

Under her skin, it seemed the glyph tightened, and she groaned, then coughed, head lolling back in defeat. "I may be able to question you, but an order is an order, it seems."

My face fell. "Lea. I did not mean to. I'm sorry."

"I know, Sade. But it doesn't matter."

5:

I was not left alone with my thoughts for long. Albain did not wait for an invitation to traipse into my rooms. I was all too familiar with the way the god looked down his nose at me as he circled my main room. It was the same way passersby had looked at me as a child on the street and how the well-to-dos had looked at me when I had first become a Norwood. Judgement. Derision. A certainty that he was better than me.

I watched him from the couch where I had been contemplating life when he intruded. He prowled around like a cat ready to pounce and I knew the threat was intentional. I did my best to remain where I sat, hoping I looked very much like I did not care in the slightest that he stalked closer.

Lea, who had been avoiding me by taking refuge in quarters reserved for the Bound silently entered, having sensed my unease through our ill-fated connection. She leaned against the wall beside her door, unseen, watching the god.

He sat beside me, lifting a lock of my greyed hair with a thoughtful grunt. It seemed that, with the drain of the fall, the black had leached away. "I imagine consuming the magic of that many dead takes its toll on a person," he said, lifting my hair from my cheek with interest. He looked from the hair twisting around his finger back to me. "You are like a gateway that they can traipse through, now. We are not made to be in such a high level of contact with the fold. I would not recommend coming into such prolonged proximity with the fold again," he said, hawkish eyes adjusting sharply from my hair to my face as he took his hand back. He reclined back, folding his hands in his lap as though we were having nothing but a companionable chat now. "I know exactly how you survived your little act of defiance. That, my little abomination of a sister, you will want to keep to yourself. What you are can quickly be seen as a threat to what we are." He smiled. "Do you understand, pet?"

I nodded slowly. This man could blink me out of existence with a thought.

"My sister seems to believe you can bring the people back to us," he said darkly. "Don't be fooled by her kindness toward you. To her, you are just a tool."

"Are you about to tell me that you see me as anything other than a tool?"

He sneered. "You are too smart for that. You figured out how to do all of this," he said with a sweeping gesture. "So I will give you your due credit, at least." He shifted from his relaxed position to lean closer. "You—"

"Albain." The warning growl was accompanied by a swell of magic that preempted Jespair's appearance before us.

"I am just welcoming our new sister," the god said, standing with his hands up in surrender as he backed away from his sister.

"Out."

He bowed subtly, then cast me a wolfish smile. "To your health, sister." He looked at Lea. "When you change your mind about letting *that* have thoughts and opinions, let me know and I'll fix it for you." He turned from Lea slowly then bowed low to Jespair with a mocking sweep before retreating from the room, eyes never leaving his sister as he backed away.

Jespair watched the door latch behind the man before she turned to me.

"You will need to bring life to the ground. Once you have rested from your recent feat, we will start your training to apply your new strength." A tray appeared in her hand, and she set it beside me with a smile. "I see great things in you, Sade." She patted my cheek lightly with a maternal touch. "Don't let your body deceive you with your new Bound. It is tired and you need to recover." She nodded toward the tray of food. "Eat, then go and lie down, alright?"

I nodded, and the god smiled warmly.

"Good." She looked me over once more with a nod of approval, then disappeared from the room.

Lea cast me a long look, then uncrossed her arms and stalked over. Without a word, she snatched up a bun and tossed it at me before taking the tray and retreating back into her quarters with the Bound.

I stomached the bun, realizing how hungry channeling so much magic had made me then went to lay down without much hope for rest. I was surprised when I fell asleep as easily as I did, but Jespair had been right. Even with the rush of power from the Bound, my body could not deny the expense of having settled the landmasses.

6:

I had thought I would die in the core cavern. I had thought that, if not, I would be able to help rebuild. I had thought I would be doing more than standing on the Isle of the Gods, staring out over a desolate wasteland of craters and acid-worn rock.

I crouched at the edge of the former isle, now an oasis. Katarina had been right; the return to the surface had not been a beautiful thing. My fingers rubbed over the destroyed ground.

The gods had done this. They had scorched the earth to gain a devoted populace. They had created the cloudline, burning acid, and deadly fumes, then they had ascended the landmasses and called themselves heroes.

I felt the soil between my fingers. Between the scientists, Tinkerers, and the College Aberrants, the Society would find a way to make the land viable again. It would take time, though.

I sighed, looking at the grey ground as I had every day since being brought here. I had been a week on the isle. A week of wondering what lay beyond the waste that surrounded us. A week not knowing how many had survived the fall. A week of having no idea if my friends had made it back to the airship and where they had found themselves in this new world. A week of uncertainty as to what had befallen Emelia after the descent.

Lea took her time in coming to me. I gave her the space she wanted, and frankly, that I needed as well. I didn't look up when her footsteps approached, ashamed at what had been done to us. Her hand rested on my shoulder.

"I tried to stay away, but as you said, you need my help," she said, looking as if she was torn over whether she should have come or kept fighting the order. She looked tired, exhausted, defeated. She crouched beside me and looked at the soil and the line of glyphs I had absently drawn. Without intent there had been no magic, no life. I felt the slide of Lea's magic in my reserves and shied away from tapping into the pool. She looked from the soil to me. "Try," she said, her hand patting the ground next to my musings.

I shook my head.

"I am already bound; you may as well use it. The only way that we, everybody, survives this planet is with magic. You can't hide from it," Lea said sternly.

I looked at her, then swept away the glyphs. "Are you certain?"

She nodded. "Just don't do anything that is going to kill us both."

I smiled, but without much heart, and focused on the glyphs. I set my hand to the ground to stabilize the magic and drew, combining essences of the three glyphs into my intent. The markings in the dirt glowed lightly as the glyph released and took hold of the soil.

Seeds long dormant and those that had come with the landmasses in the descent found their way into life. Green sprouts reached up from the soil, seeking sun. They reached down with their roots, seeking nutrients. I looked up and summoned a fresh rain to quench the thirsty soil.

"If only I could be as reckless as you," Lea said, but she was smiling, even in her thin way.

"That's good," Jespair said behind me. "Very good, Sade."

Lea stepped back and away from the god as Jespair crouched beside me. She set her hand to the soil beside mine. A small crease formed between her brows. "Interesting. You changed the soil composition. How did you know what was needed?"

"I like to read."

She chuckled and looked at me. "It is more than that. You have an intuition about how to salvage the ground." She smirked. "Maybe 'Landbringer' means more than simply dropping the landmasses." She straightened, offering me her hand.

I hesitated a moment, then accepted the hand. I could feel the magic-amplified strength in even so light a touch.

" I admit, I was a little worried taking you in, but I am certain about you." She spoke softly, taking in the ruined landscape around us before returning her eyes to me. "You are one of us."

"Even if I do not agree with everything you do?"

She laughed again. "Do you really think that my siblings and I always agree? Far from it."

"Can I ask you what happens when you have a serious disagreement?"

She eyed me, but the smile remained. "Depends on the argument."

"You are the decision maker, though, so what you say goes?"

"I am the most powerful, but power gets you only so far. I am excited for what the two of us can do, *collaboratively*." She said the word meaningfully and I almost believed her. I doubted this woman had a single "collaborative" bone left in her body. She raised an eyebrow. "You have another question?"

I nodded, then spoke slowly. "Why does the devotion of the Society matter to any of you?"

"It is what is due to us." She cast me a pointed look. "All of us." She said it as though I weren't just some stray she had decided to take in. I knew that even if Jespair pretended I was family, I was nothing more than another tool for her manipulation of the Society. An inconvenient convenience after what I had done. "Whatever we might have done. However you see the decisions I have made in the past. However the Society perceives us. It doesn't matter. None of you, none of this," she gestured at the dead landscape, "would have existed if we had not done what was needed in our youth. This all would have ended. Been pulled into the fold."

"You are not just a Natural, then."

She grinned. "My dear. I am not *just* anything. You are not *just* anything." She looked around. "We are going to save this world."

7:

Albain was waiting for me when I returned to the castle.

"Do you know why she wants you on her side so badly?" Albain asked, peeling away from the stones of the entryway. "It's because she can feel herself waning. She knows her time is coming to an end and she is struggling in vain, grasping at anything to keep her on top. You are nothing to her but another Bound. You are not truly our flesh and blood. Did you really think you had a place among us?"

I smirked at him. "If she is waning, so then too, are you. Whether you realize it or not. You think that this is your opportunity to surpass your baby sister?" I chuckled. "Good luck with that."

He snarled, but I had already turned my back on him.

The man was stronger. My superior in strength and magic. I could be in pieces on the floor before I even realized he had struck. Still, he stayed his hand. His fear of Jespair was greater than his hatred of me.

"You should know better than to make an enemy of me," he snarled at my back.

I ignored him.

"You should be careful," Lea whispered at me. The woman had been silent for so long I had almost forgotten her following me. Around the gods, she made herself as unnoticeable as possible. "You cannot stand up to Albain."

"I don't think the two of us were ever going to be friends," I said flippantly, opening the door to our rooms for Lea.

"You should probably also stop doing that," Lea said, looking at the door. "You have to play their game."

"Well, one last time?" I said in offer at the open door, waiting for her to step past. She did so with a shake of her head, and I closed the doors behind us.

"What am I supposed to do?" I said, exasperated, flopping down on the couch.

"Sade Amsel is dead to the world. Sade Norwood is dead to the world. So be the Landbringer," Lea said.

I frowned, and she shrugged. She circled the room, her hand sketching glyphs as she moved. I could feel the intent through her, dampening, silencing. She was making the space as private as it could be. I watched her work, intrigued.

"You are drawing on me."

"We all share the same pool. Your other Bound are just too far gone to do anything with the bounty without you giving an order." She etched another glyph. "Before you ask, I haven't thought of any way to break the binding. It is not as though Jespair documented how she made herself one of the most powerful Aberrants to ever exist. Give me time to think. And you, figure out how to make this planet livable. You brought us here. We still need you. We need the gods to trust you."

I closed my eyes. I had known nothing would be the same after dissipating the cloudline, but I had thought at least I would have Emelia, Reeva, and Katarina at my side, that Marco would be lurking somewhere nearby, causing mischief. That it would not just be me and Lea alone among gods.

8:

"Landbringer." The mouse-like voice was Ralti's, barely a whisper. She had found me wandering the halls aimlessly, listlessly testing my new strength as I found control in my transport glyphs.

I turned, wondering what this wisp of a woman could want. What hypocrisy the god of compassion had at her core.

"If you are with me, you can leave. Just for a little," the woman said timidly.

"What?"

"The isle. You want to leave, don't you?"

I eyed her suspiciously, then nodded. "I need to see what happened. I need to see what I did to the landmasses. To the world. To everybody."

She swallowed and nodded, then offered her hand cautiously, as though I could hurt a god.

I considered her hand for a minute, then set mine in hers. A moment later we were standing at the edge of a broken landmass.

"Where is this?" I asked quietly, looking at the collapsed buildings and ravaged crops.

Ralti looked thoughtful. "This one is called Bevilla now, I believe," she said in her soft tones, a curious look in her eyes.

We stood in the wasteland beyond the greenery of the landmass. Here and there rises jutted into the sky where the landmass had sunk imperfectly back onto the surface.

Ralti stepped, and a moment later we were standing among the buildings. She had a disconnected air about her as she looked at the damage. Concern formed a crease between her eyebrows, but she had the look of a woman who had seen too much already for too long and had become desensitized to it all. Maybe she had been a god too long. How long had it been since she had even left the isle?

"We could have helped," Ralti said breathed, barely audible. She fixed her eyes on me. "You. We could have helped you. And all of them." Her eyes drifted toward a building relatively untouched by the damage of the fall. People moved about and sat despondently outside. A field hospital.

My feet carried me toward the structure. Ralti followed curiously.

The injuries ranged from minor to severe. Bevilla had always had relatively few Aberrants, and so rarely used glyphs in construction. The buildings had felt the tremors of the descent, and so too had the citizens. All around I felt death.

I crouched beside a sleeping boy close to Marco's age. His leg had been crushed. His face was pale, and I had no doubt there was a chance he would not survive.

"What are you doing, sister?" Ralti asked when I drew the glyph for mending over the child's leg.

"What little I can," I said tightly. "Will you really stand by, even now? Haven't they lost enough?" I asked in a hushed but bitter tone.

The god watched as the sleeping boy's leg mended, the crease between her brows only deepening. She had a young face, but old eyes. Eyes that had seen the first of the landmasses rise. Eyes that had watched as millions were left to die on the ground as the cloudline formed, strangling the planet below. The god of compassion seemed little more than the Whispers I felt on all sides of us.

"What little you can …" she said softly. Her hand set on mine and I felt the magic between us build. The woman was kept diminished as Devton had been. The soft features and disconnected look seemed to sharpen in the woman. There was a cold fire in her that built as the magic did. She was drawing on my resources, and I allowed it. "What little we can," she said, her voice still small, but strong.

The god knew healing. She guided the magic we shared with such skill and knowledge of the body that I was certain even those caught on the edge of death would pull through. There was simplicity in her glyphwork that had me in awe of its impact. I would have to get some pointers from this woman.

"Who … who are you?"

Ralti looked at the man who had been tending the wounded, then looked at me, and in a moment we were gone from Bevilla and back in my rooms.

Ralti gave me a strange look. "My brother may be right about you," she said. The woman who had seemed so diminished now appeared revitalized.

"Devton or Albain?"

The woman's placid face actually showed the hint of a smile. I could feel the swell of magic in her.

"What are you doing?"

"What little I can." She was gone in a wash of magic.

"Jespair is not going to like this," Lea said behind me.

I swallowed, knowing she was right.

Jespair did not take her anger out on me, though, and I realized there was a reason Ralti had left me behind after Bevilla. Even diminished, Ralti proved her power to be immense as she moved between the cities, healing those she could. Jespair waited until her sister returned to the isle, praising her for her feat and the devotion it was certain to generate. The next day, Ralti was in a deep sleep that she could not be roused from. While Jespair claimed the woman had overdrawn her resources and that she would recover in a few days, months, or years, I was certain that Jespair had a role in her sister's coma. Devton seemed of the same opinion as he cast me a knowing look over his sister's sleeping body, then kept his distance from me.

For her part, Jespair seemed content to pretend I had played no part at all in Ralti's actions. That I had evaded the god's wrath seemed a small thing when looking at Ralti's nearly lifeless body.

9:

The months on the Isle of the Gods were a brutal isolation. I missed Emelia, I mourned Katarina, my conversations with Lea steadily tapered to one-sided forays. I feared my own words and the potential of giving her a thoughtless order that she would have no option but to follow. I retreated into my books and my prodding at the planet's health.

I began testing my restrictions, transporting myself to parts unknown and counting the moments until Jespair either appeared beside me or sent Espa or Devton to recover me. They always found me with my fingers sifting through acid-burned soil. Steadily they stopped their pursuit, until finally I spent an entire day wandering through the wasteland unmolested.

When Lea looked up at me upon my dusty return I simply said, "Tomorrow," then retreated to the bath.

10:

Lea and I stood outside Norwood manor. It seemed the Breaker had managed to pull together quite the cooperative following the fall and had decided to lodge them all in my former home. The manor was flush with activity, people coming and going, construction raging on the western side while others tended to the cleaning. I even spotted Hayden amidst the workers, assisting in the repairs to the damaged estate.

"You wily shit."

The harsh growl behind me made me turn. "Reeva."

"Don't 'Reeva' me," she snarled. She grabbed my arm, hauling me into the house amidst all the chaos. For a second, I felt myself detach from so much magic, but even the Breaker's touch could not sever the bond between Lea and me. Reeva hauled me all the way to my old room with Lea following close behind. The Breaker slammed the door, rounding on me.

"We looked all over for you," she snapped. "We assumed you didn't make it out of the core. I mean, we all knew that was likely a one-way trip for you."

"I know."

"Emelia mourned for you."

"I know."

She glared at my cloak and its embroidered sheafs of wheat— the symbol of the Landbringer and the promise of life on the ground. I waited.

"You aren't even going to comment on the fact I stole your house?" was what she decided to break the silence with.

I shrugged. "It is not as though I am using it. If it can be of use, it is yours, as long as you take care of the place and its books."

"Yes. Yes. I made sure nobody mistreated your precious books, and I haven't touched anything of yours," Reeva said flippantly, but I could see she had avoided my room entirely, almost preserving it.

Books lay where they had tumbled in the fall and drawings lay scattered about where they had settled. Even now, Reeva avoided disturbing anything as she glared at me.

"Reeva. I am short on time. I need your help with something."

"Short on time? Fine. What do you need?" She crossed her arms and tapped her foot.

I looked at Lea. "Lea has been bound. Can you break it?"

She looked, seeing the glyph binding Lea. "I may be able to loosen its hold … fade it at the edges, but that's not a normal glyph. What is it?"

"It's a soul-glyph binding. To me," I said timidly. "It is me."

Reeva shook her head slowly. "No. That is a powerful, powerful binding. Not even a Natural should be able to do that. Not unless you did that to her while amplified?" The very thought seemed to confuse and horrify Reeva. "Why would you do something like this, Sade?"

"She didn't do it to me," Lea said, shaking her head. "I knew this was pointless."

Reeva held up a hand, stepping between us and the door as though that would prevent our departure.

"If she didn't do this to you, then who did?"

Lea and I exchanged a look.

"Jespair."

"Jespair? Jespair the god, Jespair?"

"The very one."

Reeva eyed us both suspiciously. "What … what is your true name, Sade? What is that glyph?" She asked, pointing at Lea's chest as she backed away a step.

"Landbringer," I said with a hint of shame.

Reeva scoffed. "Of fucking course you are. Lady Landbringer. Your name has been plastering the newsstands all around Vale. The gods can't seem to get enough of their new acquisition. Their handy little tool for drawing the masses back to them after nearly killing us all. And here I thought you didn't want the recognition for bringing us to this shitstorm of a planet."

"It's not a 'shitstorm.' It just needs time to mend itself," I said defensively. "And I didn't. I didn't even think I would survive to fall, much less be forced under the thumb of the gods to become another point of leverage to control the Society. I didn't ask for any of this, Reeva."

Reeva rolled her eyes, then looked at Lea. "I can't release you from that binding without killing you. Your truth is being overwhelmed by hers. I can slow it, maybe, but her self is taking the place of yours. The only way to get rid of Sade's glyph is to transfer the binding, *you*, to another. And I don't know that Sade could do that, even with you bound. That sort of power should not be used willy-nilly." She sighed. "You could have a worse master," she said in a weak attempt at reassurance and with an uncomfortable glance at me. "Not that that is what you want to hear."

"Can't you do *anything* about it?" I asked.

Reeva frowned at Lea's chest, and the glyph seared under the flesh. "As I said, I can't break it, but I may be able to soften the edges, as it were. Maybe give her a little breathing room and keep her from becoming your mindless thrall at your slightest word." Lea and I glanced at each other. "Which it seems has been an issue." She clapped her hands together and cracked her knuckles. "May I?" she asked, gesturing at Lea's chest and the glow of the glyph twisting beneath her flesh. At Lea's nod, she gently touched her chest and closed her eyes.

"This may feel a little weird," Reeva warned.

At the woman's touch, Lea almost recoiled, her connection to magic draining to a trickle. My connection with her waning.

"She's a conduit for you right now, so I can't cut her off completely," Reeva said through her teeth. "Which makes this one hundred times more difficult to pull off." Still, with the ebbed flow of magic through Lea, the glyph on her heart seemed to fade a little. Reeva's fingers seemed to grab hold and pull, lifting the fibers of the glyph away from the flesh, fraying the edges but ultimately releasing the diminished thing back into Lea's chest.

Lea, for her part, kept still, her face stone. I could see the pain sneaking in at the corners of her eyes, but she gave it away nowhere else as Reeva tore.

"That's all I can do," Reeva said apologetically, taking her hand back. Little beads of sweat glistened on her brow. She looked at me pointedly. "Watch your words with her, Sade. I have loosened the bond, but an order from you will tighten it again. So don't be a shitty friend."

"I will do my best," I promised Lea.

She nodded, knowing I would but hating the situation anyway.

I turned back to Reeva.

"Don't tell Emelia I was here, please."

"You want me to pretend you are still dead?"

"I didn't say that. Just … if she's moved on, let her move on."

"Two of her girlfriends have died horrific deaths. I don't know that she is exactly ready to move on. But, I won't let her know the gods are keeping you captive. For her. Not for you. As far as I can figure it, that's the only way to keep her safe. She's far too likely to go running in after you. If that helps."

I snorted and shook my head, trying to push back the fear at the very idea of Emelia coming to the isle. "It might."

"She's going to figure it out the moment she puts two and two together about Lady Landbringer, Sade. One of these days the press is going to demand to see you."

"Just … just keep her from doing anything stupid."

She chuckled. "You know, that's like trying to keep you from doing something stupid." She sobered. "I'll look after her. Things aren't …" She shook her head. "Things are not falling together nicely for everybody, Sade. A lot of people died in the fall. A lot of Society leadership died. Including Emelia's parents. She has done a lot to help us rebuild and it's hardly the place of her *groundskeeper* to give an opinion on anything that woman does."

I closed my eyes, trying to clear that reality from my mind.

"Sade. We don't have any more time," Lea said, growing anxious.

I looked at her and extended my hand.

She took it, and I summoned the glyph to bring us back to the isle.

When the glare of the magic cleared, Lea and I were standing back in my room. Two sets of eyes stared at our point of return blankly.

"What are you doing here?" I snapped at the two Bound. "I'm sorry," I said, taking a calming breath and shaking my head. "May I have the room?"

The two bowed and retreated.

"Sade, what's wrong?" Lea asked when they were gone.

I gave a short chop of a laugh. "I got her parents killed."

"You were not responsible for that. You were trying to stop the disaster your fellow Naturals created."

I was afraid to say anything to Lea now, nervous that even the slightest request or seemingly benign statement would tighten the binding once more. I shook my head.

"You didn't do this to me either, Sade. Jespair did." Her eyes turned sad. "Don't leave me alone here, please. This is hard enough as it is."

I opened my mouth to respond, but only nodded.

"We are trying our best. You are trying your best. Thank you for bringing me to Reeva." She smiled a sad little smile. "I'll give you some space to think."

"If the others see you …" I said carefully, eyeing the loosened glyph.

She nodded. "I'll make myself scarce."

Our half-conversations had become the norm over the several long months. My fear of a frustrated slip or an incautious statement causing Lea pain kept my tongue tied around her.

She set a few books I had not seen her grab on my desk as she took her leave. My sketchbook, the atlas, a collaboration between Doctor Green and the College on the application of glyphwork on farming. They hadn't studied farming acid-burned soil, but it was a start.

11:

"It may not feel like it now, but even you need to remember economy," Lea said, setting a hand on my shoulder as I worked through the complexities of blending glyphwork with science.

"Please just be quiet for a minute," I said, exasperated and without thinking.

Lea's hand fell away and she backed up a step.

I looked up at her, realizing what I had done too late.

"Shit, Lea. I'm sorry." I had let my irritation get the better of me; I could see Lea's own frustration at not being able to speak, but also an understanding that only made me feel worse.

"I cannot keep working like this," I complained, eyes going to Jespair who stood by, watching. "There must be a way to unbind Lea," I groused. "I need her knowledge. Please."

Jespair patted my shoulder in mock concern. "You will get over your qualms about the setup sooner or later, little sister. I see the value in you keeping her as a pet; the woman has done wonders in helping train you, but it is approaching the time when you will not need her knowledge anymore. It will be better if you allow me to make her a proper conduit for you."

"I don't want a conduit, Jespair."

She laughed. "Of course you do. You have seen how many Bound your brothers and sisters have. If you have any hope of attaining our level of power, you will need to take on more. In fact, I have a few identified for you already I was going to surprise you with." She smiled as though that was anything I would ever want.

"I don't want more Bound. I don't want more power; I want her free," I said, looking at Lea. "She is my friend, and you made her a prisoner in her own body."

"My dear," Jespair said, her voice taking on a sterner tone. "You don't need these Aberrants for friends. You have peers now." She crossed to Lea, her hand setting on the woman's shoulder. I edged closer, nervous of the danger Lea was in. "These things. These Aberrants. They are useful. But they are tools. They are fuel for the engine of our world. We are the gods. You are the Landbringer. If you have any hopes of righting the disaster that you created for all your beloved humans out there, you will need more power. You will need more Bound. And you need a backbone." She looked at Lea, her hand creeping up the woman's neck. "Maybe it would be best if I wiped this one for you."

"Please. Sister, no. Please …" I begged.

Jespair's hand stilled, fingers against Lea's temple like a gun poised to fire. "Sister?" She smiled. "That's a first from you." She looked me up and down. "Very well. But you will take on more Bound. And you will be the Landbringer." Her fingers remained against Lea's temple a few agonizing moments longer before she finally released the Aberrant and took her leave.

Lea released a long-held breath and sank to the dirt. I helped her up, only to have the woman hurry to her quarters to be alone.

12:

It was hours before Lea emerged from her room. She sat beside me on the couch. The woman's sharp face had taken on a softening sadness. Unexpectedly, she shifted, her head resting on my leg as she stared at the wall.

I looked at her under my book, then set the tome aside. "Are you alright?" I asked softly, stroking her hair. This woman and all her atrocities. This woman who had practically been a sister to me, only to be forgotten.

She didn't say anything, and that was answer enough.

As I stroked her hair, a memory slipped from her. *The backseat of a motorcarriage, a little girl's head resting on her knee as the child slept. Her stroking my hair as I was now stroking hers. Lea looked up at the rearview mirror, catching the eye of the driver for just a moment. My mother. The woman smiled. A genuine and loving smile.*

"I'm sorry," she said in barely a whisper. "For what I did to your friends. To both of them. The Present Sight and ... the woman," she swallowed, eyes still fixed on the wall. "I don't know if it makes it better, but ... she went fast. She wouldn't have suffered." It didn't make things better, but I knew Lea was genuine in her regrets. "I'm sorry for everything, Sade. I just ... I keep thinking ..." She took a shuddering breath. "What if ... what if I had gone with you that night?"

My hand stilled. "Why didn't you go with my mother and me?"

She shook her head against my leg. "The binding. We waited too long. I ... I think I was the reason you were caught. The reason she was killed." She swallowed again, and I felt the hint of wetness on my leg as her tears started to dampen my knee. "I'm sorry."

My hand balled into a fist beside her head as I thought.

"Why didn't we block the binding on you?" I asked. "We did for me, so clearly it could be done."

"I was a leashed Aberrant of the College. You were an unknown. Hidden. The Chancellor would have noticed if my binding had been altered. We all agreed it was best not to ... It proved a mistake."

My hand relaxed with effort and I set my palm on her shoulder. "It wasn't your fault."

"I should have fought the binding. Like I fought it when I learned you were a Lock, or when I found that atlas. I should have fought it."

"You are years older now, and more experienced. I don't blame you, Lea. I blame the College. I blame the Society. I blame the gods. But not you. If you had been with us, I don't know that it would have changed the outcome for the better. The gods would have reacted then as they did now. They would have cracked the cores and we would not have been able to control the fall."

"We would have had your mother …"

"*Our* mother was not an Aberrant," I said, knowing with certainty now that for a time, we had been like sisters. "We would not have had the strength to arrest the fall."

Lea was silent for a time, taking another halting breath. "Our mother … Gods … We were a family, weren't we?"

"We still are, Lea. We can make up for what was lost."

She turned her head to look up at me. "I don't know if that is true, but I appreciate the sentiment, Sade." She reached up and cupped my cheek. "You have to bind me. Properly."

I pulled back from her. "No. Lea. I'm not going to do that."

She sat up and held my gaze. "Jespair is right," Lea said in a shaken voice, torn on what she was proposing. "You are going to need to show the Society that we have not abandoned everybody on a dead planet. You need to bring life to the soil. To do that, you need more power. You need more Bound. She will only give them to you if she trusts you."

I opened my mouth, then closed it and thought out my response. The woman waited, her own thoughts far more inward. "I … I am afraid that I will become as they are."

"You won't," she said, meeting my eye. "Not right away, at least." She took my hand. "All of this is for nothing if you don't survive here, Sade. You need to start playing their game and you need to be convincing about it. You need to wipe my memory, blank me out, make me one of the Bound."

I grimaced, terror at the prospect racing though me.

"The restricted glyphs. With three Bound you should have the power for it." She took my hand again, and I knew she wanted me to look into her memories, past the broken barrier at the glyphs my mother had taught her.

"Lea …"

"You need to play the game. They can still get rid of you. You need to be able to protect yourself. You need to look like you are one of them. They will parade more Aberrants in front of you and you need to take them."

"You will be leaving me alone here," I said quietly.

She nodded slowly. "I'm sorry."

13:

Jespair came to me while I was in the training yard.

"I don't understand this love of fighting that you have, Landbringer," she commented lightly, watching me flow through the steps Katarina and Tomas had drilled me on for over a year. "If *we* are ever in a fist fight, something has failed."

I straightened and wiped the sweat from my brow. "I like a good workout," I said, stretching my arms as I walked over to her. "It helps my mind warm up. You might enjoy it, should you ever wish to join me, sister."

She cocked an eyebrow at me, then smiled. "Maybe I should try it." She looked around the training yard. "No pet today?"

I shook my head. "I thought about what you said the other day," I admitted. "Keeping her around … It was a weakness," I said slowly, still struggling with the decision. I set my shoulders and nodded. "You were right. Aberrants have done nothing but create trouble for me, so why cling to that one? It is time for me to get mine, without any of the distraction of having a shadow of my past follow me around."

"I am so glad to hear you say that," Jespair said with a broad smile, "but you didn't kill her, did you? That one was top shelf. A ringed Garnet is not a usual gift."

"No. No. No. Of course not. As you said. Top shelf. She is a powerful conduit. She's with the others."

Jespair grinned. "You made her a true Bound?"

"I did."

"Good work, little sister. I wasn't certain you had it in you. I suppose I didn't need to wrap your gift as well as I did, in hindsight," she said, gesturing toward two blank-faced Aberrants. "For you, little sister. I have taken care of the messy work with these ones. We don't always need to see how the chickens get plucked," Jespair said coolly. "We just need them cooked and served." She stood behind me, hands on my shoulders with a bit of pride in her eyes. "Can you do the binding?"

"I think so," I said, setting my hand over the chest of the first blank-faced man. I pushed away the wrong feeling climbing under my skin, looking at the man with no memories or thoughts. He was yet unbound, and my glyph would make him an eternal prisoner. Lea had told me that nothing but shells for storing magical potential remained of the Bound after the work of the gods. If I didn't claim them, Jespair and the others would, and their power would only continue to grow.

"I'm right here if the glyph proves too strong," Jespair said reassuringly.

I nodded and started drawing. A soul glyph was no small feat, and even using the physical direction of my hand, it started to get unwieldy midway through, my hand shaking and the glyph becoming less certain. Jespair's hand covered mine, her fingers joining mine in the formation of the glyph and leading me in the release.

I felt the drain of the binding for only a moment before the man's strength joined with mine. The feeling was euphoric, intoxicating. I could see how the others had become so addicted. The man's eyes raised to follow me like a moth to a lamp. My euphoria abated slightly.

"I'm impressed," Jespair said. "I thought for certain you would lose it on the first few strokes. You have better control than I thought." She squeezed my shoulders excitedly. "Let's see how you do with this one."

I took a steadying breath, drawing on the new reserve as I brought my hand to the chest of the second man. The magic pooled, and felt as though it would drip from my fingers if I were not careful. I had only held so much so briefly while bringing the landmasses down. I drew, the magic leaving my fingers to form the glyph like wet paint in the air. I didn't need Jespair the second time, the binding sealing itself around the man's heart, his eyes adjusting to mine. I gestured the men away with a flick of my wrist, and they departed. I didn't need their empty eyes following my every move.

Jespair laughed and leaned close. "Four. Do you know how many it took Albain before he could do his own bindings? Seven. For a *Natural* he isn't much of one, is he?" She turned me to face her with a beaming smile. "I am so proud of you. I am so happy you have chosen to join us." She clasped my hands in hers. "I think you are ready."

"Ready?"

Her smile broadened. "To truly become the Landbringer. You are ready for your feat. You are ready to bring the Society crawling back to us." She put her arm over my shoulder, regardless of the sweat, and led me back into the house.

"What do I need to do?"

"Bring life to the land." She looked down at me. "Just a small part of it, mind you. Just enough to give them hope. Our blessings are not free. The Society cannot just assume us at their beck and call. Do you understand?"

I nodded.

"Good. Now, for presentation: don't make it look easy, but don't make it look too hard, either. Just a little bit of strain, hmm," she said, allowing a gentle crease to form between her brows as an example. "You are a god, after all." I gave another nod of understanding and gave her a sample of my concentrating face. "Perfect. Do you know the glyphs to use?"

"I believe so."

"I know it is easier to stabilize the glyphs by drawing them, but we don't want the Society to start thinking of us as overpowered Aberrants. You will have to construct the glyphs internally. And remember, the cameras will be watching."

It was everything Lea had taught me not to do.

14:

Ralti may as well have been a corpse. The only evidence that she still lived was the subtle and all-too infrequent rise of her chest. I scanned the room, aware of the little spy glyphs hidden in the corners. Even with the woman so deeply sunk in slumber, Jespair needed to keep an eye on her.

I pulled a chair to the god's bedside and gently took her hand. I felt I had found a potential ally in this woman, only to have her dashed away from me, but maybe she still had something to give me. Her hand felt cold, but there was life there. Life and dreams and memories.

I pushed a memory to her. Something gentle. Something soft. Something too long-forgotten and only remembered at the edge of death. A memory of my mother. Her response was a dulled, groggy thing, but whatever binding was holding her in this half-life slumber could not prevent Deara's gifted Sight its wandering.

A woman hefted Ralti to her hip, her words as distorted as the memory. The language one I had never heard. Still, I knew that, as I had shown Ralti my mother, she was showing me hers. The woman's hand moved in blurred motions, the glyph she was drawing one that had faded with time. Still, it was enough to know their mother had been an Aberrant. Somehow, the knowledge that the siblings had been raised in a colony of Aberrants found its way into my understanding. They had been outcasts, but in their separation, they had found a home.

"Little sister," the sarcastic slide to the voice was Espa's, her intrusion breaking me away from the memory. "Whatever are you doing here?"

I set Ralti's hand back on the bed, covering it with the sheet, and looked up at the god. "I was just sitting with her. Keeping her company."

Espa pulled up a chair of her own and sat beside me thoughtfully. "I didn't realize you two had grown close."

I shook my head. "We weren't, but it just doesn't feel right to leave her here alone."

Espa sucked her teeth and sniffed. "Dear little Ralti, always so soft. She had a way of making people pity her."

I studied Espa for a moment while she sneered at her sleeping sister. Her face evened and she looked at me. "I know why you are really here." I said nothing, and the woman looked back at her sister with narrowed eyes. "You are nervous that Jespair will do the same to you if you step out of line. If you try to stretch that leash my sister holds you on." She brushed a hair back from Ralti's face and cocked her head at the woman. "Don't worry. She won't. You are not our blood. She doesn't have the same attachment to you that she does our baby sister." Espa levelled ice-cold eyes on me. "This little world tour of yours … I wouldn't step out of line if I were you." She smiled, but it was a false little thing, and patted my hand.

A memory slipped free from the god. *Jespair. I could tell she was more powerful then than she was now. Winds whipping around her. Chaos. The same woman from Ralti's memory, their mother, dead at her feet while Jespair faced down what could only be described as an army. On all sides of Espa stood rows of Bound; an entire colony's worth. I could feel the fear and intimidation that had pulsed in Espa at the time. Fear at their impending doom from the looming army, but terror at what her younger sister could and would do.*

The memory moved seamlessly from Espa to me in the brief touch, with the god none the wiser about my abilities. I stood and left the sisters.

15:

"Nice work," Jespair said, appraising Lea as she stood blankly in the airship's cargo hold with the rest of my Bound. While I didn't need their proximity to draw on their pool of strength, it helped balance the burden. "I admit, I was worried you had taken a half-measure with this one." She dropped Lea's chin. "I see I need not fear, little sister." She smiled, leading me up the steps of the airship and looking out over the wasteland. "Are you ready for this?"

I could see the press cameras already emplaced with their journalists poised and ready. If I failed in my feat, it would be documented for the entire world to see. Jespair had insisted upon joining me to ensure at least my partial success if the strain proved too much for me. I knew she was watching me. Keeping my leash short. This would be the moment that either won her the devotion she so craved, or sabotaged the standing of her siblings.

I nodded, taking a deep breath.

She squeezed my shoulder. "I have every confidence in you. Remember, appearances are everything."

I pulled on the gloves Jespair had required I wear—anything to hide the embedded rings on my fingers. It would not do to have the Society make any connection between simple Aberrants and the gods, after all.

Jespair stayed behind in the airship, not wanting to diminish my feat with her presence. The entire Society knew that if I had been elevated as a god, it was only because Jespair had made it so. She didn't need to make public appearances to benefit from my existence.

I took my position in front of the cameras and lowered my hood. Jespair had worried a young face and greying hair would not present the infallible image of the gods that her eternal life had won her. It had been Devton who convinced her that the grey was a strong symbol of my sacrifice during the struggle to save the descending landmasses. She had reluctantly agreed to let the world see me without a bad dye job I would be forced to maintain for eternity. Appearances were everything.

I focused, trying my best not to let the strain show on my face as I wrangled the needed glyphs into existence without the grounding aid of the motion. The gloves felt stifling as I tangled with the glyphs. The burn of the rings on my fingers as they channeled and redoubled my magical efforts had become familiar. How easy had it been for the gods to destroy everything we had? It would be an uphill battle to recover what had been lost.

The pool of magic, five Aberrants joining with me, felt like an ocean surging through my bones. Still, it wasn't enough to bring forth much. I released the building wave with theatrical sweep of my hand toward the barren landscape.

The outpouring of magic carried the unwieldy glyphs into existence, sinking deep into the ground, righting the soil composition, fostering balance, and bringing long-dormant seeds to life. The dirt roiled and settled again, turned and alive. Sprouts emerged in a bright green swath of land, covering acres. Enough to be impressive, enough to bring the masses back to the gods—of which I was only the weakest—enough to give people hope, but not enough to truly survive. Jespair had told me to restrict how much I gave them, but I knew I was limited in what I was even capable of giving them. Bringing the sprouts to life was a needless expense of magic. They would come with time, but without them there would not have been evidence that the grand display had worked. Still, that had limited me further.

The cameras flashed and the audience of rich and powerful all "Ooh"ed and "Ahh"ed. There would be critics who would see the display for what it was. But there would always be critics. Right now, we needed displays, and we needed food.

I extended my hand down toward the ground, feeling for the reserves below. What I had done already was a feat on its own, but it was trivial in the face of what needed to be accomplished. I just hoped I had held back enough magic for the next step. This would be easier, though: destruction versus creation. The water rose, and as it did the earth rumbled, terrifying the crowd and bringing memories of the fall. It needed to happen.

The water started as a puddle, a spring, a pool, a pond, and grew until it was a lake: fresh and clean.

Once again, cameras clicked and popped as I returned my eyes to the scene in front of me to take in what I had created. Slowly, I turned to the crowd. My eyes found a familiar face among the onlookers, her fixed stare causing me to falter a moment before speaking.

"This will take time. This will take care. This will take all of us. It is the slow hands that will ensure our survival down here. It will take everyone to make this work. Not just the farmers and the workers; everybody needs to contribute. Everybody needs to learn the skills needed for us to thrive. This planet was not meant to harbor us," I lied, "but we can nurture it back into health." As I spoke, I summoned the glyph Deara had shown me so long ago. The glyph for rain. As my words finished and I turned back to the swath of green, the drops started to fall. "Thank you," I said quietly, and headed for the waiting airship.

"Landbringer!" members of the crowd called in celebration.

Jespair greeted me with a smile. "I didn't know you were going to dredge up a water reservoir. Good touch." The forced lightness in her voice spoke to her true feelings regarding my actions.

I sank into one of the seats and sighed with relief. The endeavor had been exhausting, and I was spent. I could feel the Bound below, their reserves tapped, all of them sleeping it off.

"That was a big draw," Jespair said, sitting across from me. "Rest, sister. You will be surprised how quickly you recover."

I lay down across the bench, taking the woman's advice and closing my eyes. All I saw behind my lids was Emelia's face in the crowd, watching my every move.

Jespair laid a blanket over me, her hand lingering on my arm for a moment. "Next time, do less." Her voice hinted at concern, but I knew it was an order. One lapse of judgment could be forgiven, but not a second. "We can't have you falling out as Ralti did."

16:

I looked at the settlement. The ambitious settlers who struck out into the barren wastes with the hope of bringing life to a dead land. Without the help of magic, they would fail. How many more of the overeager had traveled too far from the safety of the landmasses?

I removed a glove and crouched at the edge of the hastily erected buildings. The sleeves of my cloak pooled around my hand, hiding my rings well enough, I hoped. Setting my palm on the ground, I allowed my magic to poke and prod as needed, hunting for the essential nutrients, finding the fresh water below. A camera snapped beside me, documenting the Landbringer at work. Jespair would not like an image of me bent over the dirt, but if I was supposed to bring life to the land, such an image only seemed fitting in my mind. Besides, I was getting damn tired after so long afield and so many such feats behind me. I allowed the small cluster of press that had been pursuing our travels continue in their reporting.

Jespair had returned to the isle ahead of me, content with my work at the last several stops and bored with the tedium of the airship. I was glad for the time alone as the airship lumbered from settlement to settlement. I clung to the moments away from the cameras and Jespair's watching eyes, the moments I could just be. The peaceful moments I could spend looking down at the surface from the air, pretending that nothing from the last few months had happened. That the landmasses hadn't fallen. That I had not been turned into *this*. That Katarina had not died. It was only ever moments before my mind wandered to Lea, mindlessly waiting below deck. To the reality of the weight placed on my shoulders once again. To those missing from my side.

My fingers sunk deep, and I drew up water and turned soil. The ground roiled and flipped. A rocky mass outside of town crumbled, dispersed, and added drainage to dense soil. Even with the aid of magic, this area would be difficult to maintain as more than rancher's land. The cattle needed somewhere to recover from the fall, and this plot of land just out of reach of Dorado had been designated as the spot. I let the magic flow from me and I did not straighten until the work was over half-done. I did enough to give the cattle and the settlement a chance, but held myself limited. I knew better than to cross Jespair, but I was also too exhausted to do more.

I straightened and watched the wide swath of land settle and sprout, and without a word, returned to the airship to sink into a deep unconsciousness to recover as the craft turned for home.

17:

There was a rush of wind and magic behind me signaling a new arrival in my chambers. I had grown accustomed to the feel of the gods' magic and knew without having to turn that the newcomer was not one of them. No. The newcomer was somebody I wasn't certain I was ready to face. Instead of turn, I continued to study the stark contrast between the green of the isle and the ash tones of the wasteland beyond my window.

With a thought, I silenced the wind and dampened the swell of magic, hoping it would pass unnoticed by the gods. Outside, Espa didn't seem to notice as she argued with Albain, her arms not faltering in the slightest in their determined slicing of the air. I stepped back from the window, not wanting the siblings to look up and see me watching them. Espa played nicer than her brother, but I knew about the second-eldest's jealousy for her younger sister's position and her quiet hatred of me.

"Lady fucking Landbringer," Emelia swore behind me. "I was stupid not to have seen it sooner. I just assumed the gods were going to take credit for your actions with some little puppet, but then, there you were."

"You are not off base," I said quietly, not looking at her, eyes still directed at the horizon. I could feel her frustration like a humid day.

"Lady fucking Landbringer," she repeated, storming around to stand in front of me.

"You are starting to sound like Reeva, my lady." I raised my eyes to meet hers, even though I wanted nothing more than to look away.

"My lady? My fucking lady?" she fumed.

I sealed my lips and let her vent. She did.

"I thought you were dead. I thought you were crushed under the rock you fought so hard to save. I thought ... Arg. You are a shit." She growled in frustration, then crumpled. "You're alive." Her fierce anger abated in an unsteady wave.

"After a fashion," I said, looking past her at the window. I stepped back, grabbing her hand to pull her away from the pane of glass and the gods strolling below. She yanked her hand back, rubbing her palm like my very touch burned her. "I hear you are a Chairwoman now," I said causally, as though there were nothing more than politics and the weather to discuss.

She sniffed. "Yeah. I am. A little young and inexperienced, but I suppose they wanted a familiar face in all this uncertainty." She snorted at me. "I hear you are a god now," she said with equal parts sarcasm and wonder. "Are we going to talk about that, or just pretend that never happened?"

I looked at my hands. "I don't know that I can pretend that never happened," I said quietly.

"I'm sorry, Sade," Emelia said, feeling my misgivings. "This all must be hard for you."

I chuckled mirthlessly. "As hard as it must be for you, Em." I gave her a long look. "It is dangerous for you to be here."

"I missed you," she said, ignoring my fears. With a tentative reach, she took my hand and held my fingers to her lips.

I withdrew my hand slowly, not wanting to break the contact but needing to. "How did you get here?"

She didn't answer. "I mourned you, you know that?"

"Maybe it's best you continue to think of me as dead. Who I was is gone now. It is not as though we can go back to how it was before. We cannot pretend I did not break the world."

"Break the world? You saved it."

I shook my head. "How many did we lose in the fall? How much was destroyed? Even now, all I do is hurt those trying to help me." I looked at her and released a long sigh. "I am sorry about your parents."

She frowned and nodded. "It was not your fault, Sade. I am sorry about Katarina. I … I assume you know?"

"She came to me, then passed on. She's the only reason I survived, I think."

"Is that when this happened?" she asked, reaching for my hair.

I backed out of her reach.

She dropped her hand and swallowed.

"I think it looks very dignified," she said, trying for levity.

"That is what I have always tried to achieve." I allowed a hint of a smile. I could put in a little effort, I supposed, but her presence was a risk. Still, I reached for the cooling tea pot. "Would you like some?"

She favored me with a half-grin. "Do you have anything harder?"

I nodded toward the carafe at the end of the table. Finishing my tea, I held the emptied teacup toward her, and she poured.

"Did your Aberrant friend make it out as well?" Emelia asked, staring down into the amber liquid in her glass.

"She survived the fall," I said quietly with a wash of shame. Emelia felt my discomfort and frowned. "She ... Something terrible happened to her after."

"Oh. I'm sorry. Is she ..." She looked around.

"She's not dead," I said, shaking my head. "Not in the traditional sense, anyway. I ..." I shook my head, clearing the image of the woman's slack face. "It does not matter." I turned my back to her. "I am glad we had this opportunity, but you should go."

"It's not working," she said, crossing her arms. "Don't forget, I am a damn good Charmer. You are trying to seem cold and distant, but you are happy to see me."

"It is not entirely happiness," I said quietly.

She looked at me. "Worry? For me? For yourself? Sade, talk to me. You owe me that."

I sighed and nodded toward the couch.

We sat. Her hand reached for mine. I shook my head at her. "Let's not do that."

She set her hand back in her lap with a dissatisfied sigh.

"It is dangerous for you to be here," I repeated.

"You'll protect me."

"I haven't been able to protect anybody so far."

"You protected all of us. You nearly gave your life to save us all, Sade." She shifted, sitting close to me, then, disregarding my coldness, leaned against me heavily. Her warmth was familiar against my side, and I couldn't resist the urge to soften. I had become lonely and desperate, and I gave in to it.

With a sigh, I allowed my arm to settle over her shoulders. She nestled closer, her hair releasing her scent against my nose. I breathed deeply, knowing it was reckless of me to allow her to stay, but not wanting to let her go. We stayed like that for a long time in silence.

I had to ask, though. "How did you get here?"

"I have friends. A Tinkerer." She touched the locket hanging around her neck.

"You should use that and leave. You really don't belong here, Em," I said softly.

"It doesn't seem that you do either, Sade."

My eyes flicked down to hers. "Do I not?"

"You are not like them."

"Am I not?"

She shook her head. "No. You want to help us. This is not all on you, you know that? You brought us home, but that does not mean that only you have to fix what was done to our planet."

"The other gods do not wish to help," I reminded her.

She turned in my arms to look at me. "Fuck the other gods." She licked her lips, then looked to the high ceiling. "We have survived despite the other gods. We survived living on rocks in the sky despite them. The farmers and ranchers know how to make do with what is available to them. We will survive down here despite the other gods." She looked at me with a thin smile. "We don't need you, but you certainly can help. Come to Vale. See what we have done there. Go to Antop and see what the farmers there are able to do. Learn what they know. Learn how to help them. They will teach you."

"You make it sound so easy," I murmured.

She sat up straight and held my face in her hands to hold my gaze. "You dissipated the cloudline. You brought the landmasses down. You defied the gods. You became one. I think you can handle learning a little bit about farming to help the new colonies."

"Still, you make it sound so easy," I grumbled.

"It is exactly that easy."

I took a sip of my drink and glanced uneasily toward the window. I didn't like the ferocity with which Albain and Espa had been arguing before Emelia's arrival, and I feared an intrusion by any one of the gods at this moment while I was so close to Emelia, so obviously in love. I *needed* Emelia, but I also *needed* her gone.

I set my drink down and turned to face her. "Why are you here, Emelia?"

"Do you want me to go so badly?"

"Yes. I do."

Regardless of my words, she smiled. "No. You don't."

I growled, knowing she could feel my relief at not being alone for once.

I stood and paced. "Look, Emelia. I am happy to see you. I can't *not* be. There is no point in hiding how lonely I am here. I cannot deny a part of me was excited when you came here, but also I am terrified. I am terrified for you. I am terrified that my new *brothers and sisters* will find out you are here. But yes, I am so happy to see you. And you ... you can feel it all and it is not fair, Em. It gives me no sanctuary."

"What will they do if they find me?" she asked quietly.

"I'm sorry," I said instead. She could do nothing about being a Charmer, and to fault her for it was wrong.

She stood, catching me in my pacing with her hands firm on my arms. I didn't bother trying to evade her. "You don't need to apologize to me, Sade. It's alright. What will they do?"

I looked at the door. "I'm not certain. They can't make use of you since you are not an Aberrant. But if they know about you ..." My eyes returned to her.

"It gives them leverage over you. I understand."

I nodded once.

"Where are you living?"

"The estate, still ... What's left of it."

I nodded and formed the glyph in my mind. My hands gripped her arms tight as the magic swelled and released. I hoped the dampening glyphs around my room would keep my new siblings from taking much notice of my actions, but they were used to me coming and going at all hours by now.

"Sade? What are you—" By the time she had finished her thought, we were standing outside her mansion. "—doing?" She looked around.

"Goodnight, Emelia," I said dropping her arms.

Her fingers remained clenched around my sleeves, her lips quivering with frustration. "You can't get rid of me that easily."

I backed away a step, freeing my arms from her hold. "You are right." I held my hand out for her locket. "I can't have you just popping by again like that."

Emelia frowned, but she undid the necklace and dropped it in my hand. "You know I can feel it."

I nodded and looked at the damaged house, a quick glyph for

stability releasing unseen into the stones and mortar. "I love you, Emelia," I said, taking another step back. "You cannot come back to the isle." I closed my eyes and drew up the magic to return.

My room felt emptier upon my return. Everything felt emptier now. I looked at the locket in my hand, a plain thing, but with skilled glyphwork behind it. I set it on my desk and returned to my drink.

18:

"Land … Landbringer?" Doctor Green said breathlessly as she recovered from the suddenness of my appearance beside her. Her hand covered her beating heart, shaken. I had my hood up, but she recognized the two sheafs of wheat embroidered onto my cloak's chest, and there was no denying the sudden rush of magic that had prefaced my appearance.

"I need your help, Doctor."

The woman's mouth opened with words unformed, then closed again. I knew her question. Why was a god asking for help from a botanist?

"Everywhere I go, I must assess the soil, the water, every aspect of the land. I have to find what is there and what is not. I have not studied these things as you have. It limits what I can do. Everything I have done to this point has been a best guess," I explained.

"Sometimes that is what science is at the start," she said, finally finding her ability to speak.

"I know, but it is not efficient. It is exhausting and it limits what impact I can have. The land is healing itself, but not fast enough for many of the new settlements. Not fast enough for the survivors of the fall to thrive. I know that food stores were lost in the fall, that many of the crops and the livestock did not survive the trauma."

"We have had thin years in the past," Doctor Green said, not refuting my point. She cocked her head at me. "I recognize your voice, don't I?"

It wasn't really a question. I lowered my hood.

"*You* are the Landbringer? Never would have guessed Emelia's girlfriend was a god, but you never do know with some people." She looked back toward the tents her field team occupied, then nodded for me to follow her.

She led me to her tent and the array of maps and texts that lined the canvas enclosure. "I want to help. Clearly, I do. That is why we are out here in the wilds. I just don't know what I will really be able to do for you. Perhaps if you describe your process, we can find efficiencies. I did work with the College years ago on improving yield and resistances through the aid of glyphwork …"

"I know. I read your work."

Doctor Green smiled. "I suppose I should not be surprised. Emelia is one of the greatest advocates I could have found. It is both a shame and a boon that she got pulled into politics," the woman said, but her voice canted strongly toward remorse. "I don't even know the basis of your magic, but, well, maybe that is all academic at this point," she said thoughtfully. She sat, grabbed a pen, and let out a determined exhale. "Let us go through your process. See what I can help with."

I looked at the pen, poised to document, then offered my hand. "Can I show you instead? It may be easier than trying to explain with words."

The woman raised an eyebrow, then nodded and set her hand in mine. I closed my fingers lightly around hers and crouched beside her chair, setting my hand on the dirt floor, both to steady myself and to connect with the soil. As I worked, my memory of each action and sensation slipped from me to Doctor Green so the woman saw all I did barely a moment behind reality. I found the water reservoirs within the region. The nutrients and life. The soil that could one day bear life and the land that never would. I found the ruins of the civilization the gods had destroyed. I finished by turning the soil at our feet and bringing up a patch of grass. I took my hand from Doctor Green, who sat for a long time, as though in a daze.

"You … you're self-taught?" Doctor Green said, still recovering.

"I have had help," I said, "But yes." I straightened and circled to sit across from her.

Doctor Green sat forward, knitting her fingers together on her desk while she thought. "You have a lot of raw power, but I can see what you mean. The exploration seems to be a heavy draw. If I know where you intend to travel, I could, in theory, send a team ahead to do a survey and soil analysis. We would not be able to go as deep as your magic can, but we could provide you with what exists and what changes would be optimal for the region. As you know, all regions and all life have different needs, so each locale will have different requirements."

"If you or your colleagues are willing to contribute teams, I will not say no to the assistance."

"To make this planet survivable, I am certain I can get you the resources you need. Is it too great an assumption that you can divulge your intended travel?"

"It is, but only because I need an experienced eye telling me where I should be going."

The woman nodded her understanding, but her mouth pulled down into a frown. "The cartographers are struggling to get everything mapped. Everybody is starting from zero down here."

I summoned a duplicate of the atlas Lea had given me and offered it to the woman. "Would this help?"

She flipped through the pages and nodded to herself. "Yes. Greatly. When was this made?"

"Over a thousand years ago. Before the cloudline. Before the landmasses ascended."

The woman's eyes fogged for a moment as she strove to comprehend. The binding that held the gods infallible and kept the Society in the belief that the cloudline and landmasses always had existed struggled with her scientific mind. The thought binding was broken with the breaking of the cores, but it had had a lifetime to sink its claws into the minds of the Society.

"There will be changes," Doctor Green finally said, her voice slowed as though her tongue were plodding though molasses. "But this is a good start. Can you make more for distribution?"

I set my hand on the book's worn cover and drew the glyph of duplication, bringing several more copies of the forbidden text into existence. "I don't believe the other gods will be wholly glad to learn that anything from before survived."

The woman swallowed, understanding that my actions were not sanctioned by Jespair, and were potentially bringing danger to her doorstep. She nodded. "I'll make certain the recipients know to keep this discreet. There are ruins; some more intact than others. Your *colleagues*," she said, nervous now at the prospect of attracting the attention of the gods, "cannot possibly think that nothing from before has survived. The existence of city ruins alone will start causing questions."

I cast her a look and she quieted. "I will handle those matters," I said quietly.

She nodded, knowing I was redirecting her away from the subject. "I suppose that is not my area of study." She patted the atlas in front of her. "A few of my colleagues and I should be able to direct where you can have the most impact. We will aid you as we can in revitalizing the ground."

"And I will aid you in ensuring we do not lose more species than we already have. Whatever you need, do not hesitate to ask."

She nodded, and as I stood, I could see she had a question lingering on her lips. One she tried to hold back.

I looked down at her and smiled, a glyph leaving my finger. "You can speak freely, Doctor. The others cannot hear anything that is said in this tent," I assured her.

She hesitated, then nodded. "I can't help but notice that you use glyphwork ... You are a Natural, aren't you? Are the ... the others ...?"

I nodded, understanding what she was nervous to ask. I tapped my nose and pointed at her. "I will let you ponder that one for a little bit, but I can tell you are on the right track, Doctor. Remember, if you need anything." I set a small talker on her desk, one that would communicate with only me. "I look forward to hearing from you." I pulled my hood back up, and with a nod of farewell to the woman, stepped from the tent.

19:

Hidden amidst the heads of wheat, I closed my eyes and led my exploration with subtle glyphs. The work had become second nature to me at this point. The glyphs barely manifested in my mind before releasing. Just beyond the landmass of Antop, the land was thriving. Land I had not touched. Land that only held the hints of magical intervention. The farmers had found a way to bring life to the soil.

The wheat brushed my shoulders as the wind swept across the field and I continued to pass unnoticed, huddled on the dirt as I was. The soil of the surface had not been as ravaged here as it had in other regions of the world. That had helped speed life's hold after the cloudline dissipated. The farmers had brought nutrients back to the surface, and from their efforts, they had managed this bounty. The crop was a fragile thing at the moment, but with the knowledge and the careful tending by the residents of Antop, the area would survive.

Magic swirled behind me, and a moment later Jespair set a hand on my shoulder. "What are you doing, sister?"

I cut off my study of the farmers' work and blinked my vision clear as I looked up at her. "Learning. Life is returning to this planet."

"Is that why you have been traveling here, and there, and everywhere?"

I nodded and turned my eyes back over the rolling fields. "I need to understand how the planet is reacting to recent changes to know how to help it."

"Such dedication," she said with a tone that put me suddenly on edge. "You have been talking to the farmers, learning from them?" Her hand tightened on my shoulder, and the strength of her fingers sent jolts of pain through my bones.

"They have a lot to teach."

"It makes you look weak. You have been caught on camera in these 'lessons,' and it makes you look less-than." Her hand continued to tighten, making my breath quicken as the bones groaned under the strain. "You are a god, now, Sade. We need to appear all-knowing. Not like children struggling through grade school."

My hands dug into the dirt beside me, trying to ground myself against the pain. "I ..." I steadied my breath. "You told them I came from them. Was risen from them. To them, I *am* less-than. Less than you. Less than your siblings. Less than the true gods. My shortcomings do not reflect poorly on you, sister. They only make me more relatable; they only aid in bringing more devotion to you."

Jespair's fingers tightened again, then released.

"I know you have been healing portions of the planet on your own. *Without* consulting me."

I looked up at her, clutching my injured shoulder. "I'm sorry, sister. I thought ... I thought I was supposed to bring life to the land ... I did not realize ..." The nervousness I felt looking up at Jespair brought a tremble to my voice. I hoped she saw innocence in my eyes before I looked down, cowed. "I am sorry. I will consult with you before I take any action."

Jespair touched my chin and brought my eyes back up to hers. "It is for your own good. I will see you back on the isle." With that, she disappeared.

With the god gone, I sagged forward, my forehead pressing to the dirt as I let the pain in my shoulder overwhelm me for a moment.

I didn't know how long I stayed like that, hidden amidst the wheat, swallowed by my pain, before I finally brought the healing glyphs to mind and mended the fractures that laced my bones. I sat a while longer, listening to my breath and the wind in the wheat before standing.

A memory had slipped from Jespair. *Pain. Anger. Vengeance. The first Aberrant the young woman had bound. The spiraling effect and addictive quality to the building power. The reasoning she had used to justify her actions as she moved through her colony, turning every Aberrant she had grown up beside into a mindless Bound. She had spared only her siblings and her mother. Their father had been nothing but a treacherous Reg, and he would pay for his crimes. They all would.*

She needed the power. Her friends and neighbors would have wanted this. They would have given themselves to her willingly if they had only been able to understand. The world would be theirs, and they would never have to fear the Regulars or the treacherous fold-leaching Sights and their prophecies. She would protect them all from the encroaching fold. She would own the world.

I pushed the woman's ages-old memory back. I drove away the remembered waves of power. The death and destruction she had wrought. I pushed it all back and focused on my surroundings. The calm of the wind. The sway of the field. I picked myself loose from Jespair.

I walked the countryside with my hood up and my face all but hidden. I had left all symbols of the Landbringer behind, hoping a little separation would leave me unrecognizable. My shoulders slumped around me, trying in vain to break the dignified bearing Katarina had driven into me. I didn't want attention as I took in the flourishing fields. It was grounding in contrast to the chaos of Jespair's youth. Her siblings had feared her as much as they had feared the Regs. When she issued the order, they fell in line. Only their mother had not, and they had all seen what Jespair's rage begot.

My hand ran over the heads of the wheat filling the field beside me as I walked. I stopped and took it all in. The golden field, the green beyond. The rise and fall of the hills. Even the scarred earth. We would survive this.

I closed my eyes, my hands still held over the wheat, allowing the plants to brush against my palms.

"What are you doing?" The voice was harsh with suspicion. A man peered down at me from the back of his horse, a rifle poised across his lap. I had been so lost in fields that I hadn't even heard him approach.

I turned toward the man, my hands staying visible and away from my body. I kept my head down, letting my hood shadow my face. "I'm sorry," I said softly. "I was just taking in the view."

The man's lips pinched, and he nodded back toward the city. "Well, take it in somewhere else. Can't just have every looky-loo wandering through, ruining our crops. Lot of hungry mouths to feed this winter and the abyss only knows if the gods will do anything for us." He sighed, softening. "I don't know how you got all the way out here. Do you need a ride back into town?"

I eyed the horse, extending a hand to pat the beast's neck. I had never seen one of these animals before. Horses had not been used in Vale where motorcarriages reigned supreme. I was surprised and gladdened to see that the species has survived the descent.

"I'll be alright," I said, stepping back from the horse with a smile. "Again, I am sorry for intruding."

The man sniffed and bobbed his head. "Well. You best get a move on. Don't want to be caught out too late."

"I will," I promised, and started toward the city.

Antop had been considered a dismal float by the citizens of Vale. A backwater that focused more on agriculture than industrialized progress. Antop was thriving. The people knew how to look out for one another. How to survive.

"Landbringer watch after you, girl," the man called, then turned his horse.

I glanced behind me, then stepped back into my rooms. I had visited Antop, I had visited the colonies. I had learned from the farmers and could see the benefits of even small wells of magic to feed the survivors of the fall. They would survive with only their knowledge, but I could lessen the burden a little more. Emelia had been right. We would survive despite the gods. They would survive despite me.

20:

I spent nights staring at Emelia's locket. It would be so easy to see her again. I wanted to see her again, but allowing her within the castle, within the reach of the gods, was a danger I could not allow her to put herself in.

I knew her Tinkerer could always make her another locket, but I hoped Emelia wasn't so foolish. Still, I wanted to see her. I lifted the locket from where it rested on my bedside table. I could destroy it. I should destroy it. Instead I found myself warping and twisting the glyphs that powered it and their intent. It was unwise, but I did it.

With a flick of my wrist, I banished the locket back to its owner. It was only a few minutes before I felt the embedded glyph trigger.

With a glance at the door, I summoned the transportation glyph and opened my eyes on the other side of the planet.

"Sade?" Emelia asked standing at the edge of a ravaged sea. "Where are we?"

I looked around at the green swath of grass leading to the black-sand beach and the acidic sea.

"Far away from the isle," I said.

"Why?"

"I wanted to see you."

She resisted her smile. "Why here?"

I looked around at the stark landscape. Earth scorched bare dominated the eye, but still there was this grass, the sea.

"I know you can't see it, but it's righting itself. The only magic cast here is the planet's. The sea is sick near the surface, but deeper there is life. It is the same with the ground." I crouched, setting my hand on the new grass, fingertips finding the dirt, and closing my eyes. "Try as we might, we did not destroy it all."

I heard Emelia walk over and crouch near me. Her hand covered mine, then her lips found mine.

"I worried you had changed," Emelia said when our lips parted finally.

"I have changed."

"You still care. I worried the gods had taken that from you. I …" She met my eye. "I saw Lea at your shrine. I saw what they did to her."

I sat back and looked at the sky. "I did that to her."

She frowned. "You did that? Then you know how to reverse it?"

"I can't."

"You don't know how?"

I looked hard at Emelia. "I can't." My fingers dug into the soil, magic bleeding from the tips into the ground, sinking, prodding, feeling the planet healing itself under us. The glyphs played through my mind nearly unrealized, directing my absent searching. The very act grounding me.

She took my free hand, leaving me to my absent exploration of the ground. "Why can't you?" I knew she could feel my shame.

"Because if I reverse it, Jespair will know, and she will destroy her mind irreparably. I left Lea relatively undamaged, hidden with an adaptation on *Kelta*, but I may as well have wiped her clean because I will never be able to free her again."

"Look around you, Sade."

I frowned at her, not understanding but following her direction.

"You dissipated the cloudline. You brought us to the ground. You have given the ground life."

"Life persisted," I said quietly.

"Don't lessen it, Sade. The gods did this to us. They created the cloudline and killed the planet," she said with disdain. "You bested them. You will best them again."

"Why do you think I want to?"

She laughed. "Oh, Sade. Your every act reeks of opposition to them. I saw Jespair watching you from the airship. I saw her irritation when you brought up the lake. Being here with me. Protecting Lea as you did. You will figure this out, and I will be here to help you in whatever way I can. Even if it is just to call you on your despondent attitude."

I smiled and squeezed her hand. "I am putting you in danger."

"Stop it," she warned. "I don't care. I chose to come here. Well, not *here*. But I did choose to use the locket. That was rather unsettling, by the way. I was assisting with a restoration when this appeared around my neck," she said, lifting the locket.

"I am sorry about that."

She shook her head and kissed me again. "I am glad you sent it." She looked at the sea. "You could heal the sea now, couldn't you?"

I shrugged. "There is life that has grown accustomed to the

state of things down here. They will need time to adjust again. A sudden change may suit us, but we are not alone here."

She gave me a considering look, then rested her head on my shoulder. "Thank you for bringing me here."

21:

I watched Emelia trigger the locket, disappearing in a swirl of magic. With a lingering stare at the sea, I stepped, finding myself at the gates of the College of Aberrants. Jespair's summons had been clear, and I had been swift in responding, not wanting the god to come in search of me. She cocked an eyebrow at me from where she leaned in the shadows of the walls. I could feel the ward around her, making her nearly invisible to the Aberrants standing guard. Her entrance had been silent where mine had been loud.

The Aberrants jumped into excited action at the sight of me. How many alarms had my magic set off around the College?

With a shake of her head, Jespair joined me, dropping her wards with a click of her tongue. "I had intended for us to walk in unmolested, but the inexperience of youth ..." She sucked air in through her nose and gave me a look that said she forgave me as Aberrants darted here and there to make their god comfortable. She ignored them entirely as we walked. "Where were you this time?" Jespair asked lightly, but there was no hiding her intense curiosity.

I was glad her anger toward me had cooled again. I had made an effort to stay away from the cameras for a time to allay the god's concerns over how I was being perceived.

"Bevilla. They have been successful in establishing their farmland." I looked at the dirt still marking my fingertips. "I was checking soil composition." I rubbed my fingers together, clearing away the dirt.

Jespair made a small grunt of approval. "You really have leaned into being the Landbringer. Soil composition ..." she said wistfully. "I remember all the work we put into the cores. The attention to detail of each and every glyph. Everything with its purpose. Everything they needed for life," she said, as though in a pleasant memory. I fought back the frown that threatened to appear at the contradiction of the woman's memory. She looked down at me. "It is refreshing to see that vigor again. Maybe we have grown too comfortable on our isle," she said, leading me through the halls of the College.

Eyes followed us and I recognized the Tinkerer, Perry, among them. His eyebrow raised, and I could not tell exactly what emotion I saw there. Judgment, maybe. Jespair led me past the man without even seeing him.

A young woman turned from her whispering friends to watch us pass. The young woman from Lea's class. Instead of the awe I had seen in her when she recognized me as a Garnet, there was something else. Confusion. A touch of fear. She quickly turned her eyes away. I swallowed, but otherwise pretended not to have seen her.

"Your Grace." The woman waiting for us at a wide set of double doors bowed low. Her robes and the grandeur of carved wood behind her marked her as the Chancellor. Her eyes shifted to me with a hint of curiosity. "Landbringer."

"Chancellor Yedira," Jespair said with the slightest bob of her head in acknowledgement as she stepped past the woman into her office.

Yedira gestured to the guards standing just to the side of the doors. They nodded and turned, as though to retrieve something. When they entered the office behind us, they hauled a dazed captive with them. The woman's head hung and her feet dragged, boots bouncing uselessly on the stone as she tried to get her legs under her.

"We caught this one running some sort of halfway house, orphanage, or some such," the College Chancellor said with an unimpressed air about her. "We would have just done away with her, but I assess her as Garnet potential. I don't know how she went undetected for so long, but I suppose when we returned to the surface it flushed her out." The Chancellor looked at the restrained Aberrant like she was a rat sneaking from the sewer. She turned to Jespair hopefully. "I thought maybe she would be of some use to you."

My jaw was tense. I recognized the woman on her knees. Rhoda. The same woman who had made a refuge for those on the climb. A safe haven for those with nowhere else to go.

Her eyes raised, groggy but defiant.

"Garnet potential, you say?" Jespair said, evaluating the

innkeeper. "Yes, we can make use of her. What do you say, sister?" She looked at me with a beckoning smile.

I forced a smile and approached the woman on her knees. I looked at the two Aberrants keeping her fettered with glyphs. They refused to meet my eyes, but at my signal, struck the glyphs from existence. Without a word, the two departed the room. This was a matter best kept between only the gods and their pet Chancellor.

The woman's eyes raised. Found me. There was recognition there. "Is this saving lives?" she growled weakly.

"Yes," I whispered, watching as her rebellious gaze sank to nothing as I carved her from herself, finishing the act by cutting the glyph of the Landbringer into the air over her chest and binding yet another soul to mine.

"Ah." The small groan escaped my untamed throat as the woman's magic merged with mine.

"Still assess her as Garnet potential?" Jespair asked, seeing my quickening.

I nodded, feeling the raw potential of the woman. Only Lea outstripped her so far.

Jespair set a hand on my shoulder. "I hope her contribution brings success to your ventures, sister," she said, taking my hand and wiping away the last flecks of dirt. "Take her back to the isle. I have matters to speak with the Chancellor about."

I pulled Rhoda, now a Bound, to her feet. Her eyes watched me dully, but I saw her defiance superimposed upon her features.

Jespair had already turned to matters of business, forgetting me altogether.

I summoned the glyph and stepped, drawing the Bound with me. Her hate and judgment boring into my spine. I knew it was my own hatred of myself that I felt, though. This woman felt nothing anymore.

How many more would be taken? How many more would I bind, with only a thin hope of ever being able to release them again? This was the role, though. I knew the importance of never once slipping while on the con. I knew now what Gan must have felt as his arm had been held down and the cleaver had raised.

It was only a matter of time before I either lost myself or found myself under the knife.

22:

"My Lady Landbringer," the Aberrant said in awe, nervousness peaking in her voice as she looked at the array of bored gods. I descended from my seat to stand before the woman. She was wildly unprepared for this, but I could feel the power in her; she would be a valuable addition.

"Why do we continue to throw our little sister more fish?" Espa complained. "She is a figurehead only. But we give her more and more. If we continue to feed her, she will outgrow her role."

"She has yet to even near that level," Jespair said coolly.

The Aberrant's eyes flicked to the arguing gods.

I redirected her eyes back to mine and set my fingers against her forehead, allowing the glyph to form in my mind and bleed through me to her. Her face slackened and her eyes emptied. It was almost too easy to wipe away an entire existence now.

While the gods continued to bicker behind me, I drew the binding over the woman's chest, then sent her away with a quiet word before returning to my seat.

I felt the surge of magical strength that had become all too familiar now, but something else. A distant pull. Lea?

"Does it bother anybody else that our new *sister* is drawing more followers than any of the rest of us?" Espa asked. "The Society begs her for salvation. Was this what you were hoping for, Jespair? Was this what you had in mind with this great scheme of yours? *She* gives them enough that they don't seem to think they need *us* anymore."

"She is new and exciting to them, is all," Jespair said. "She is in the public eye. If you crave attention so badly, go and do the Society some service. Go get your photo taken. You cannot rally against Sade without taking any action yourself."

"Maybe I will," Espa groused; still, I knew in the back of the god's mind she saw Ralti in her coma and feared what Jespair may do to her for drawing too much devotion to herself.

I felt another pull from Lea on the pool and lost my focus on the bickering siblings. I had slipped back into being unnoticed and forgotten among them, anyway.

When the first of the siblings stood and stormed from the room, I was able to slip away in their wake, the rest trickling away slowly behind.

I etched the glyph swiftly with my finger, wanting to keep my footprint small as I stepped from the hallway into the hastily erected temple to the Landbringer.

I ignored the excited calls from the praying masses and set my hand on Lea's arm. Within the cover of my sleeve, I traced another hurried glyph, and the two of us stood at the edge of the acid sea.

"I thought you might feel that," Lea said, her voice small.

"How?"

"You hid me; you didn't kill me, as much as you seem to convince yourself you have," she reminded me. She still sounded distant.

I pushed back her hood so I could see her face. The binding still held, though it was a fractured thing.

"Did Reeva come to you?" I asked quietly.

She shook her head and looked out over the sea. "I don't need a Breaker to break your sorry excuse for a glyph," she said. Her voice was flat, but I could see the hint of mirth at the corner of her mouth. "I think I know how to break the binding. I share in your power," she said. "All Bound do. The more of us you take on, the larger *our* pool. You are the only one who can take on the full press, though. We store and you balance. But that does not mean we cannot access what you own. If we can surface long enough to do so … Erg." She closed her eyes tightly, struggling through a wave of pain.

"What's wrong?"

"*Kelta* remains." The glyph I had use to hide her mind. "I can suppress it for a time, but …" her face slackened for a moment before Lea returned once again.

"I will remove it. It is only causing you pain now."

"I can hide behind it, still," she said with effort. "Leave it be for now."

"If any of my brethren discover you, they will wipe you."

She nodded. "They don't come to the temple. It is a good place for me to remain and think." She looked back at me from the sea. "You should return me. I wanted you to know I am not gone so you can get over your defeatism." She grinned, then her face slackened again and she returned her hood into place.

I spent another moment with the now-silent woman, then returned her to the temple. In a step I was back on the isle, at the edge where I had first brought life back to the soil with Lea.

"Where, oh, where do you disappear to on your little walks, I wonder?" Albain said behind me.

"Does it matter where I go as long as I come back?" I asked, not bothering to look at him. The small spot of magically turned soil was larger, spreading deeper into the destroyed landscape an inch at a time. It would be slow progress, but I smiled.

"You were a dressmaker. An orphan. A vagabond. A thief. What makes you even vaguely worthy of what you have been given?"

"What makes you worthy?" I asked coolly, knowing he could kill me with barely a thought.

"We were born to it, my siblings and me. We took what should always have been ours. You, I don't know what you are. Circumstance. A lucky draw. An abomination."

I turned to face him. "Are you able to reach across the fold?" I asked innocently. "You are the god of the dead, so surely you must be able to?"

His jaw tensed. "We should never do so. The living should not touch what we should not touch."

"You created Locks, though. That's the belief, anyway. That the gods dole out the magic of the fold. Why would you create something that can touch the fold if we should not?"

Again, there was a flicker of hesitation shielded by irritation. "It was a foolish thing remedied."

I grinned at his loyalty to the lie. "You didn't create my mother, did you? You didn't create any of them," I said, narrowing my eyes at the man. "Not Locks, not Death Sights. None of them. They were around before you and your siblings gave in to your fear and thoughtlessly fell in behind Jespair and her war." His eyes widened. "So, when you tried to wipe out all Locks, did you succeed? Was my mother's existence a gift from the planet? A gift from the fold? Or did you simply fail in your genocide? Did a few inferior humans manage to hide so much from you for generations?"

"You would do well not to try me," Albain growled.

"I don't think that Locks are all they seem," I pushed, ignoring his growing anger. He reached for me, his hand sliding through my chest with a harmless tickle. I looked down at his wrist buried where it was. "That's interesting." I looked out over the desolate landscape and saw it lush with life. "Very interesting."

He growled with rage, but he could not touch me now.

"I don't think you can reach across the fold. Not even with all your Bound. I think you are nothing more than an Aberrant with a bit of sensitivity toward such things. Have you ever seen what I see now?"

"A desolate landscape? I have seen it every day since you decided to drop us down here."

I shook my head slowly, looking out over the foreign landscape. A small city rose to the right. A meadow beside it that led to a forest climbing into the mountains. I blinked and the image shifted somewhat. Another plane? A different time? There was so much unknown.

I looked at Albain.

"So, what do you think it is? Does the fold continue to give us its gifts, or do you and your siblings truly think you have any control over anything? Do you know what Jespair told me the other day?" I asked casually. "That she willed me into being. That she knew a Natural was coming. Not that she chose my mother. Not that she chose me. Just that she hoped, and here I appeared. Do you think she has deluded herself into truly believing she has control over such matters? Has she convinced herself she does?" I looked at him. "How long had she been hoping? Years? Decades? It was inevitable another Natural would appear. We have been born several times before, but your family finds them and does with them as they did to the Locks." I shifted back from the fold, the barren landscape returning. "The planet is in the midst of a course-correct now, and I have a feeling you may be part of what gets corrected."

"You little ..."

I narrowed my eyes at him. "Did this conversation not go the way you were hoping? Were you thinking of waving your magic around and threatening me, working me into a state of fear so I bend to some crooked will of yours? Hmm." I brushed past him back to the house.

I knew I was acting foolishly. It didn't matter. I was getting tired of the game.

23:

"She thinks herself better than us. She is a threat," Albain complained to his siblings before I entered the throne room. His voice boomed out of the chambers, his irritation greeting me along the halls as I approached. "We cannot continue to pretend that she is one of us."

"You almost sound afraid of an undertrained, underpowered figurehead," Espa commented as I walked in. Her eyes followed me like a predator's.

"Have I done something to upset you, brother?" I asked innocently.

"We both know you have access to power beyond your pittance of Bound," he snapped at me.

"Do we both know that? That's interesting, and did you choose to share that with your siblings? Am I no longer under threat of death if I share this with them?"

He scowled, and I could see in Jespair's expression that he had not told them how I had survived bringing down the landmasses.

"I wanted to come to all of you, but Albain wanted secrets," I said, acting timid as a mouse. "Any of you could kill me. I was scared."

"What did he make you keep from us?" Jespair asked softly, her eyes hard on her brother.

"She can touch the fold. She's a Lock," Albain growled spitefully.

"A divine gift from the god of Death," I said with a slight swoon at the man.

"You made her a Lock?" Espa asked tensely.

"You know full well I did not make the little wretch a Lock," he snarled.

"Albain," Jespair said warningly. "Aberrants cannot be Locks. Aberrants cannot touch the fold." She looked at me. "Why do you believe you can?"

I looked at Albain. "Because he told me I could. He said it was the only way I could have survived bringing the landmasses down."

Jespair turned accusatory eyes on her brother. "If my brother is trying to convince you to try and touch the fold, it is only because he wishes harm for you," she said with a warning growl at Albain. She returned her eyes to me. "We have had Aberrants try before.

The fold has drained the life from them. Do not attempt it, sister."

"You are not listening to me," Albain growled.

Jespair leveled him with a hard stare. "And you are not listening to me, Albain. Sade is our sister now. I will not tolerate you and your jealous little heart trying to trick her into killing herself."

He cowed, but only slightly. "I'm telling you Jespair. She's a Lock. That aberration you feel on her, it is not just that of a Natural. You have been too long divided from the chaff, perhaps, to tell the difference. She is an abomination: a Lock and a Natural." Albain snarled. "Her innocent act is all a farce. She was the one who convinced Ralti to go against your orders. I wouldn't be surprised if she is scheming behind your back at this very moment. She's a threat to us. Like *all* Locks."

"What do you mean 'a threat'?" I asked. "I would never harm my family."

Jespair looked at me, her lips puckering with consideration, then she turned to her brother. "Don't you think you are taking things a little far?" The woman was willing to believe my innocence if it meant she could keep me close. She did need me, and I did not like how much.

Albain growled, his hands slapping against the arms of his throne as he stood, glowering at me. "Hide behind her skirts all you want, Sade. Maybe it is safe for you there now, but not long." He stormed from the room.

Jespair's eyes followed her brother, then switched to me. "Don't worry about him." Even with her reassurances, I knew my time was coming to an end.

24:

I stood in the shadows of the temple, watching Lea. She stood stock-still as offerings were laid at the foot of the statue behind her. I could hear the whispered prayers and petitions of the pilgrims through her ears. I felt no stirring of the Garnet within the husk.

"Why did you bring us here? Why did you commit us to this life? Why did I survive the fall, and my son did not?" The pleadings of the old man were not uncommon. The sorrow he felt was as familiar as the fear that the child kneeling beside Lea tried to whisper away in prayer. I had brought the landmasses down. I had destroyed lives and ended lives. I had committed all of these people to the struggles of life on a ravaged planet.

Lea shifted ever so slightly, her hooded eyes finding me. Another of my Bound stepped in to take her place, and I followed the Garnet away from the main hall. We entered a room where two more of my Bound rested. One slept, while the other spooned gruel into his mouth with a blank stare that found me as I entered the room. I hated that stare, but suffered it because I had done so much worse to him.

"Why are you here?" Lea asked.

"Why have you endured? I've used *Kelta* on the others to keep their minds intact. Yet, they do not find themselves as you do." I asked her quietly. As though to confirm the difference, the others did not react.

Lea's face slackened slightly for a moment before she found herself again. "I think it is our glyphs."

"Do you mean how Jespair said they can be prophetic?"

"To a degree. Our glyphs: Landbringer, Unbound. They are prophetic only because they speak to our nature. My glyph, it gives us a way to break the binding. At least, I think so. It is a soul glyph. Its strength matches yours. But while your glyph's very nature is life, mine is breaking, specifically unbinding." She winced as she nearly was pulled back into her slate state. I waited while she fought for control. Finally, she returned with a peeved look, but no worse for the ware. "It is why you were able to help me break free of the College's leash. It is why my glyph has endured so well against yours," she said through her teeth. "As unconvincing as that may be at this particular moment."

"You think we can use Unbound to break Landbringer's binding? Your glyph. It endures. Its inherent power. Do you think we can use it to help free the Bound?"

"It is theoretical … Even if we could, it would not do anything to save those whose minds the gods have already wiped. Only *your* Bound will be freed," she said thoughtfully.

"The others will still be freed. Just not as they were before. Maybe we will be able to find a way to help them. But first I need to figure out how to restore their glyphs. I'm running out of time."

She closed her eyes tightly again as Landbringer nearly overwhelmed her. My proximity was not helping anything, and I knew I needed to leave.

"I will think," Lea said tightly.

"Thank you," I said, backing away a step before transporting myself away.

25:

I waited at the edge of the sea. My fingers dug into the dirt under me, my senses sinking into the earth and the life that had survived so long. By dissipating the cloudline, we had brought the potential of life to the surface, but it would not be without its costs. The life that had adapted to so much turmoil would have to change again.

The swell of magic behind me brought my senses back to the surface as I heard Emelia's soft steps approach. I felt the breeze play in my hair and smelled the salt it carried.

"I thought you might be here," she said quietly, sitting beside me.

I kept my eyes closed, rubbing the soft grit of the soil between my fingers, and smiled. "And I knew you would come."

The shifting of fabric marked her turn to look behind us. "What's all that?"

"A house," I said simply, opening my eyes to watch her. A small simple house. "I made it for us. I wanted us to have a place away from the prying eyes, chaos, and expectations. A little haven of calm. Somewhere that can be just ours."

"You built us a home." She smiled, then looked down. "You know we cannot have somewhere that is just ours. Somebody will always find us."

"I know. But for a little bit, it will be nice to dream. Do you want to see inside?"

Her eyes flicked to me, and she nodded. Her hand found mine as we climbed the hill to the seaside home. "How long do we have this time?"

"How long do you want?"

"The rest of my life, if I could, but I will take as long as you can give me."

I smiled at her. "The rest of your life, you say?"

She grinned and shrugged. "Is that asking too much?"

I only squeezed her hand tenderly, not having an answer for her, and led her into the house.

26:

I took one last look at the sea before taking Emelia's hands in mine and transporting us both to her estate. She held tight, not wanting to see me leave, and I found myself lingering.

"Reeva will be by shortly. I am sure she would not mind seeing you." Emelia tried to entice me into staying, refusing to release my hands.

"I'm sure. But I should go. I don't have the same dampers established here. The others can see my magical footprint now." My eyes moved around the expansive foyer of the lonely mansion. I hated leaving her here alone. The eastern wing had collapsed in the fall and Emelia had not bothered putting any effort into its reconstruction. She had kept the staff on who had wanted to stay, and paid those who wished to strike out into the new frontier a healthy sum with which to start over. The house was quiet.

"I will be alright," Emelia said, knowing my thoughts without me having to give voice to them. "If you truly have to go?"

I swallowed, blinked a few reluctant times, then finally nodded. "I should. I am sure I will see you soon."

"You better, or I will come find you on that damn isle of yours." She smiled and pulled me tight against her, and again I dreaded leaving.

The surge of magic in the room made me turn, putting myself between Emelia and the god. Already I was bringing glyphs to mind, but Espa was faster.

Immobilizing, thought-crushing pain raced through my body and I collapsed to my knees, the glyphs slipping away from me.

Emelia wrapped her arms protectively around me and dragged me back and away from the smirking god. I reached for another glyph, but another wave of pain lanced through me. Espa was stronger, faster, and more experienced. I stood no chance. Another peak of magic from the woman stilled my body, freezing it in place so I could barely even blink. Emelia stiffened behind me, wrapped in her own paralysis.

"Well, isn't this charming?" Espa said, looking down at the two of us on the floor.

My worst fears were realized as I watched the smirking god sink down into a crouch.

"I'm hurt you never thought to introduce us, little sister," Espa said, feigning sorrow. "I am Espa." She offered her hand to Emelia, then laughed. "Oh, right." Her hand dropped heavily to my frozen shoulder, eyes slowly sinking to meet mine. "Do you know the problem with the likes of us being in love with the likes of them? They are just so fragile. Spoil easily, too, don't they? One day here, and the next in the ground."

She flicked her wrist and a knife appeared in her free hand, its blade dancing in the light as she considered it.

Cold fear shot through me. I had brought the gods to Emelia. What was about to happen to her was my fault.

"My sister did a fool thing," Espa said, turning the knife this way and that, then setting it flat against my shoulder and glaring at me. "She gave you enough Bound that we would not be able to overwrite Landbringer." She pulled the knife back, then sank it slowly into my shoulder, letting me feel every inch of its descent into my flesh. "None of her siblings, at least. No. No. I think she's fattening you up to take for herself. I think that ungracious sister of mine has enough strength to take even you at this point." A second knife appeared, and this one she stabbed quickly into my gut. Were my lips able to move, I would have cried out. As it was, tears dripped uselessly from my eyes. She grinned and summoned yet another knife into her hand. Her eyes shifted to Emelia, and she sneered. She flicked my chin and said, "Don't move," then stabbed the knife through my hand where it supported me against the floor, nailing me to the wood.

She straightened and moved behind where Emelia and I were held trapped; where I couldn't see her or what she was doing.

"I don't intend to let my dear sister get that grand of an upper hand. Indeed, I do not." Her words accompanied a blade sliding painfully into my side. "I could kill you now. I *should* kill you now. But, oh. The idea of the disillusionment and betrayal I will see in her eyes when I tell her that her little pet has run off to conspire against her ..." She laughed. "That may just make keeping you alive worth it. Just imagine what she will do to your darling co-

conspirator. You haven't seen the cruelty my sister is capable of. Just know the College learned their methods somewhere."

Behind me, Emelia uttered a muffled whimper of pain.

Espa circled around to my front again, a bloody knife in her hand. I tried to free myself from her restraining magic, but was stuck firm. My mind raced with images of what she might have done to Emelia with that knife. Espa grinned and crouched again. She drew the flat of the bloodied blade across my cheek, covering my face in a streak of Emelia's blood.

Trapped inside my body, I raged and railed to no avail. When even a hint of magic drew up in my core, Espa sank the knife into my chest, breaking my focus.

"No, no. As fun as it would be to watch you and your girlfriend be carved down into your most basic forms, it will be better to kill you here and now. Best not to give Jespy the option to make you her Bound," she snarled. "No. That wouldn't do at all." She patted my cheek. "From what I hear, my younger sister's folly granted you two Garnet-class Bound." She shuddered with delight. "I am excited to inherit those from my darling baby sister." Another blade sank into my chest, its handle standing proudly alongside the others. "But who says I can't have fun of my own? Come here."

The magic holding Emelia frozen shifted, and Emelia moved from behind me. Even in my haze of pain, I was relieved to see only a shallow cut on Emelia's cheek, but I knew any relief was coming too soon.

Emelia moved stiffly, as though trying to resist the commands of her body. Espa placed a knife in Emelia's hand and then stepped away to watch.

"Take your time with it, dear. No need to rush this."

Emelia crouched. Her eyes poured with tears and her hand worked in Espa's intent. A quick slash across my face, another down my chest. Espa laughed. The knife carved into my leg, and when I saw the blood spurt, I knew that would be the fatal wound.

"Oops. Got a little excited, didn't we?" Espa said.

"You psychotic fuck." I barely registered the growl of rage; blood loss, pain, and terror all kept me slow-witted. In a rush, Espa's hold on me vanished, and my previously restrained cries of pain erupted in a sob as my body suddenly broke free from Espa's magical restraints.

The knife dropped from Emelia's hand, and she quickly pressed the heels of her palms against the deadly wound in my leg. "I'm sorry. I'm sorry," she sobbed.

"It wasn't you." I struggled to sit up to set my hand on hers, groaning as the knives left in my body tore through yet more critical tissue. My mind was slowing but I found the glyphs I needed, formed their healing intent, then released. Under her hands, the wound in my leg sealed and the loss of vital blood slowed. I fell back panting.

"Sade. I could use a little help here," Reeva said, struggling to keep her hands on the god.

"Lea," I groaned. "I need you."

I lost consciousness as Lea's boots materialized beside my head.

27:

"As long as you can keep Espa unconscious, we should be alright. Think you can do it, Perry?" Lea.

"I've never tested my work against a god, but if all we need to do is keep her from conscious thought, then yeah. I think we can pull this off." The Tinkerer considered the trussed god like a bug in a dish. "You don't happen to have a few Garnets on standby if I need a little backup, do you?"

Without a word, I sent out the summons and Rhoda appeared beside me.

Lea turned at the newcomer's sudden approach, her eyes going from the woman's blank face to me. Rhoda moved to stand beside the unconscious god, poised and ready if needed.

"You called, and I answered," Lea said to me.

Emelia sat beside me, her hand tight around mine. Lea stood with Perry beside Espa, the god slumbering in chains. Reeva stood away from the rest, eyeing Epsa suspiciously.

"I am glad you did," I said, looking at the blood stains on my clothing.

"As though I could not." Still, she gave me a sparing smile. "Do you suppose letting you die would have broken the binding?" she mused darkly. "Maybe I shouldn't have been quite so attentive."

"She's joking," I said when Emelia moved to stand between us.

Lea's eyes closed tight, and she shook her head. "I don't have much more time," she growled, then looked at Espa. "If you are ready, Sade. I don't think Jespair is just going to ignore the disappearance of her sister."

"You would be surprised. But you are right. If Espa was willing to do this, Albain won't be far behind. I'll draw him to the seaside house."

"What are you talking about, Sade? You were nearly killed just now," Emelia cut in, her voice peaking with worry.

I held her hands in mine and stared into her eyes, trying to will understanding into her. "What has started cannot be stopped until it finds its resolution. The gods have no intention of allowing the Society, the people, to grow and flourish. They will always find a way to subjugate the world. It is the only way they can remain eternal."

"So you are just going to go and attack Albain now?"

I shook my head and backed away a step. "I assume he will be the one attacking."

"And that is supposed to assuage my concerns?" Emelia shot.

I looked at Reeva. "You will look after her?"

"You don't have to ask."

I nodded and grabbed Lea's arm lightly. In a step, we were in my chambers on the isle.

"Funny thing," Albain said from behind me. "Espa followed you to Vale, and the next thing I know her Bound all look a little paler."

I turned to look at the man. "She shouldn't have attacked me."

Beside me, Lea was a slate, having given in to the glyph binding once again.

He cocked an eyebrow, taking in my bloodied state. "Did she, now? And yet you survived?" He drawled with a hint of bewildered amusement.

I shrugged, waiting to feel his magic rise.

"Did she?" he asked, intrigued, reclining into my couch.

"Do you really think *I* could have killed Espa? She's sleeping it off, is all."

He laughed. "If that's the case, you have put yourself in quite the predicament. She is not one to forgive easily."

"Why are you here?" I asked.

He smirked, and I felt his magic start to build.

I released the held glyph and, in a blink, I was standing alone on the peak of Vale.

Albain followed a few moments behind me, and I summoned a hasty barrier against the swath of fire that accompanied his arrival.

A moment later, we were not alone. Devton was struggling to hold his brother, growling, "Let her do what needs to be done, brother. Let this end."

Albain threw his brother aside, rounding on him. "You. Ralti. We should have drowned you both as children. You were both so weak-willed. No wonder you were never much of an Aberrant. No wonder only the weak and helpless flock to you."

Devton's eyes flicked to me as he pulled himself to his feet and squared against his brother.

I swallowed and stepped again. Fleeing the mountaintop and the clash of gods.

I emerged from the swell of magic at the seaside house. I started when I realized Emelia was waiting for me.

"What are you doing here?"

"Trying to talk some sense into you. You cannot stand up to the gods," Emelia said.

I grabbed her arm and pulled her into the house, sealing the door behind us. "I don't exactly have a choice, now. Albain was waiting for me as soon as I returned to the isle." I said, checking the windows.

"He was? Where is he?" Her breathing hitched.

"Vale. Devton is fighting him."

"Devton is on your side?"

"I guess," I said with a shrug as I set increasingly powerful protections on the house. "I suspect that, if Ralti was ever allowed to wake, she would be, too." I turned to Emelia. "You should not be here. There is no way that Jespair has not taken notice of all of this activity."

"I'm not leaving you." Noble but foolish.

"Sade!" Albain's voice sounded from outside, his call a savage snarl. "Making a man kill his own brother with his bare hands. A dirty trick, girl."

I peeked out the window with a sinking feeling. If Albain had killed Devton, there was little chance I could get the better of him. I was in too deep now, though.

The god stood with his hands dripping in his brother's blood, an army of Bound behind him.

"He ... he killed Devton," Emelia said, peering over my

shoulder, sounding less certain about her insistence on staying.

"I admit, I didn't think he would *kill* him," I said, trying to push down the bile rising in my gut. I had known I was going into a battle I would very likely lose.

"Sade," Albain called from outside the house. "I know you are here. This quaint little hovel won't hide you. I will find you. It would be better for you to surrender yourself to me." He waited only a moment before turning to his Bound. "Find her." Albain's order was a harsh rasp.

I took Emelia's hand and drew her through the house. "Stay silent," I whispered, etching a concealment glyph into the air, glad for the dampers drawn throughout the house. We ducked into the bedroom and slunk behind the protection of the bed and watched the door.

A Bound entered the house, the sounds of their progress through our home drawing closer to our room. Emelia and I stayed still, going so far as to hold our breath as the Bound inspected the doorway of the bedroom before he slunk in. I summoned a glyph for silence, and, in the unsettling hollow, grabbed the man, my hand clasping firmly over his mouth, and drew the Landbringer glyph over his chest. My fingers dragged through the air like they were held fast in molasses, struggling against Albain's glyph, but the god's hold on so many Bound made each individual tether weaker. His muffled shout of warning to his master died in his throat as the glyph sunk under his skin and his eyes adjusted to me.

I broke the silence and leaned close to the man's ear to whisper my instructions, then sent him on his way.

I took Emelia's hand again and waited. It seemed Albain had neither heard the subdued scuffle, nor felt the loss of a single Bound from his collection. I felt my new Bound draw on the collective pool of magic as he seized another of Albain's Bound and their strength joined with ours. I wondered if the god even felt the losses as the two Bound turned another.

"What are you doing?" Albain's angry shout told me he had figured it out.

"I'll be right back," I promised Emelia, signaling for her to wait where she was hidden then walked outside to face the god.

"You think that this little trick will save you?" Albain snarled.

"No." I admitted, grabbing the arm of one of my new Bound and summoning the glyph. One step and we were on the isle;

another, and I had returned to the house on the sea. "That may help, though," I said.

"What did you …?" he trailed off, feeling the losses now. He clutched at his chest. "My siblings will not stand for this," he said, waning as I grew stronger.

"It's not really up to them," I said softly, as he crumpled under the weight of his own body. "You grew too accustomed to being carried by your Bound."

He laughed. "You will die with me, abomination. You cannot hold the power of so many Bound."

I knew he was right as the pool of magic continued to grow within me. His alone were overwhelming at such a rate. I hid my pain. I only needed to bear it a little longer.

"The moment my siblings realize what you are doing to me, they will kill your ill-gotten Bound, and they will kill you," he threatened, but with no teeth, sagging to his knees.

"Which siblings might you be talking about? You killed your brother. Espa is out of commission. Jespair put Ralti in a coma."

He growled. "Jespair will not stand for this. Even if you are her pet."

"Lucky for me, she will be as weakened as you." I grinned, even though I felt like I was being shredded from the inside out. "The order was not just to convert your Bound."

"You are insane," he groaned.

Lea would be taking care of the Bound at the temples and shrines. The new glut made my heart feel like it was going to give out with the sudden influx, and I could no longer hide the pain. I clutched my chest and groaned.

Albain gave a choking laugh as he continued to diminish.

Lea appeared at my side and held me up. She drew Unbound over my chest, binding me to her as she was to me. I gasped at the suffocating grip and felt the glyph ripple through the binding connecting all the Bound now. "Give the order," she whispered to me.

"Unbind yourself," I said in her ear, the order echoing through the ears of all of my new Bound. The order carrying the method and my intent. I could only hope it would not be too much for the individuals.

The draw was immense as so many Bound did as Lea had and restored their soul glyphs, but the pool was now equally immense.

Lea held me up as she traced the glyph of the Landbringer back over my chest, replacing that of the Unbound. The surge and then sudden withdrawal of so much magic left me panting, and my heart ached as my glyph was restored. My eyes fluttered and I nearly lost consciousness.

In my distracted state, Albain managed to summon a glyph with his waning strength and disappeared. No doubt, back to the isle and the safety of his little sister's protection.

"We are not done yet," Lea whispered, keeping me on my feet still. She traced a glyph onto the back of my hand, the same we had used to balance our magic while bringing down the landmasses. "You have only had Bound for months; they have had them for centuries. Imagine what condition Jespair must be in."

Spent as I was, she harnessed my magic and we stepped.

Bound wandered aimlessly through the halls of the isle mansion as Lea half-dragged me through.

"La ... Landbringer?"

I looked up, my eyes focusing on the woman. One of my former Bound.

"Lea?" she said, realizing who supported me. I hadn't known the woman before binding her, but it seemed the circle of the College was small as the two Aberrants recognized each other.

"You were one of the lucky ones, it seems, Veena," Lea said, nodding for the woman to help support me.

"What's wrong with her? What's wrong with the others?" Veena said, watching a directionless Bound amble by. "What is happening?"

"We are tearing down the gods," I said weakly, not at my most convincing.

"As for the others," Lea said, frowning as we passed a Bound staring blankly at the wall, "we will find a way to help them once we deal with the greater threat."

"The gods? Are they a threat?" Veena looked at me, drawing back a little even as she helped carry me. "Is ... is this one a threat?"

"Not yet," Lea said, casting me a look that was both playful and suspicious. "When that changes ..." She shrugged, and I knew well enough her meaning. "How many did you manage to hide?" she asked me.

"Seven. Very few."

"More than none," Lea said reassuringly before her face

hardened. "We are almost there. Can you make it the rest of the way on your own?"

I stopped, focusing on my legs and the strength there. Reminding the muscles that they still knew their work even after the loss of the magical support they had grown so fond of. I had been a hard-handed, tarry-lunged vagabond before I had been an overpowered Aberrant. My body just needed to remember that. My knees strengthened under me, and I managed a step without assistance.

"Let's go," I said.

We rounded the doorway into the hall of the gods with our hands raised and glyphs half-drawn and ready.

The magic we had built up in our collective fizzled away when we saw Jespair collapsed on the floor in front of her throne, struggling under her own weight as her body fought to adjust back to reality. Albain had only just made it back to the isle to warn Jespair before the full impact of my rebellion had taken them both down.

"Sade!" Jespair growled, clawing her way to her feet with the aid of her throne. She struggled to keep herself standing at the sudden loss of so much magic. Albain barely even bothered trying to rise. "Did you do this to us?"

Lea swiftly drew the glyph for sleep, causing the struggling Albain to topple the rest of the way to the floor in a stupor. Even with the draw on my magic, I kept my feet. I understood the need for appearances to be upheld. Behind me I felt Lea's glyph of strength burn into my lower back in an invigorating and terrible way. We didn't know how strong Jespair still was, even cut off from her Bound. On her own, she had been a powerful conduit.

Rhoda appeared, dropping Espa's unconscious form on the floor before coming to stand beside me. She sniffed, but gave me a subtle look of appreciation.

"What have you done?" Jespair raged, but her bite was gone with her strength. Her feeble attempt at standing gave in, and she toppled to the stone floor with a frustrated growl. As long as she could focus, she could cast a glyph, and that kept me wary, but she looked a pitiful sight.

I hadn't spent the better part of an overly extended life with far too many Bound strengthening me, and so had managed to recover faster than the siblings. I pulled the woman to her feet and sat her in her throne, where she slumped uselessly.

"It is no longer your time," I said. "It hasn't been your time for ages. Ever since you and your siblings decided the world was yours to own."

"You can't bring this planet back without us," she said in a half-threatening, half-pleading sound.

"This planet does not need us. It doesn't need me. It just needs time to heal from what you and your siblings did to it."

"You will commit your beloved people to toiling and struggling to survive?"

"I intend to toil beside them. Some things cannot and should not be rushed."

She glared hard at me. "What will you do with my siblings?"

"The Society will decide."

"Even with the revelation of what they have done, there will still be those who revere them, Sade," Lea warned me quietly.

"Yeah. I know. It is a risk."

"It is too big a risk," Lea growled, eyeing Jespair.

"They are too public to just kill," I said.

"Bind them to you. A proper binding. Not the feeble thing they have been doing. We might still have enough strength to do it."

I looked at the Aberrant, knowing the glyph she was thinking of. The woman's knowledge went deep. She was the only reason we had made it this far.

"It seems wrong."

"More wrong than what they have done?"

"It is not a matter of more or less." I shook my head, knowing there was little point in arguing ethics with the woman. "I have another idea. We will give them to the Society to judge, but I will take away their ability to bind. We won't have to worry about them getting their hands on a willing Aberrant. I will lock their access to magic."

"Can you even do that?" Lea asked, an uncomfortable look in her eye at the very thought.

Jespair's eyes widened, and she forced herself back to her feet. "You cannot do that. It is not possible," she protested.

"You forget I am a Lock."

"That does not mean—" she grasped at me, but her hand faded through my flesh as I stood on the other side of the fold.

My mother stood before me with Marco at her side and

Katarina and Deara just behind. In the infinite possibilities of the fold, my family had found each other. My family had found me. My mother gave me a reassuring nod, mouthing the words I couldn't hear, her hand tracing the glyphs in the air between us.

I nodded my understanding and seized Jespair's hand.

"I know the reason your family was so afraid of Locks. It's not simply because we can touch the fold. It's because we can manipulate it on this side. It's because I can create gateways, and I can break them down." Half in the fold and half out, I found her connection to her magic and closed it. "Where once there was a conduit, now there is not."

Jespair wailed in frustrated anguish. I left her to it. She had grown dependent on her magic and now was trapped within her own body.

"What gives you the right?" she raged. Lea put the woman to sleep so we could have silence.

Veena shrieked and Rhoda spun with her hand poised. Ralti stood, clutching the wall for support. She released the stones and crumpled at my feet. She looked up at me pleadingly, and I acknowledged. Closing her off would be a loss, and I hesitated.

"Please," she whispered weakly, looking from me to her siblings. "It is the right thing."

"Alright," I agreed quietly, cupping her cheek and sealing her magic. With a glyph I returned the woman to sleep and settled her beside her siblings.

"A binding would have given you their strength," Lea said quietly as I worked.

"I don't need their strength." I sealed the last of them.

"You could have done a lot with it," Lea said almost wistfully.

"Says the Unbound," I pointed out.

She smiled, looking at the sleeping gods. "Fair enough, I suppose." Still, there was a longing in her eyes before she turned them to Veena. "You call the Enforcers. I will summon the College heads."

"That's my cue to leave," Rhoda said with a slight tip of her head toward me. "If you need me, I'll be saving lives." She cast me a wink before flicking a glyph into existence and vanishing.

"What do we do with all of them?" I said, looking at the collective of former Bound. They watched us, some lost, some fearful, many confused.

"We won't be able to restore what they had. The gods were thorough in their wipe, but unbound, they can start again, at least. The College will take care of them. The lives they had before are gone, but we can give them another," Lea said. "You should return home. I'll take care of cleaning this up."

I watched her as she drew the glyphs necessary for summoning the College heads to the isle, a flicker of suspicion from a lifetime of fearing Aberrants fluttering in my chest, then I carved a glyph and returned to the seaside house.

Emelia worked to keep the Unbound calm and together.

"Landbringer!" the first Unbound to spot me cried out, running from the cluster to grovel at my feet. "Take me back! Please! Take me back!" the man pleaded. "I don't know anything else. Please!" He clung to my arm.

"I will not bind you," I said, setting a hand on his grasping ones. "But maybe you can help me. We have a world to rebuild. There is work for everyone."

"Show me."

- 387 -

- 389 -

EPILOGUE:

"So, this is where you've been hiding out."

I hadn't heard the woman come in. Maybe too focused on the dress in front of me. Or maybe because Reeva hadn't bothered with the front door.

"Lady Landbringer," she sneered.

"Nobody knows about that here, Reeva," I chided. "I prefer to keep it that way." But I knew we were alone. I set down my work and watched the woman as she rummaged through my workspace. "How did you find me?"

"Charms wrote me, of course. Were you trying to hide?" She looked up from thumbing through my sketchbook with a quizzical eyebrow raise.

"Not from you, no."

She shrugged and let the sketchbook fall closed again. "I actually bought a ticket for an airship to come here. Can you imagine? The number of times we illegally boarded them, and this was the first ticket I ever bought. More expensive than I would have liked, but I suppose I did swing for one of the upper-crust suites." She looked around the dressmaking shop. "Living the dream?"

I smiled and offered her some tea. "This is all I wanted."

She snorted, but there was nothing malicious in it. "Why Junction, though?"

I laughed. "Oh, didn't you know my father lives here?"

She grinned. "He still thinks you are his daughter?"

"We all know I'm not … I think … But it makes him happy to believe it. So …" I shrugged.

She smiled and sipped at her tea once before pulling a face and setting it aside. "You know Lea has taken over the College."

"I know."

"And you are not nervous about that? You two might have been friends, but she is still an Aberrant. Not that all of you are bad, just …"

I nodded. We had seen enough brutality in our youths to know how questionable the College and the Society could be. I knew Lea well enough to know that she had not been a kind and harmless Aberrant in her time.

"I hear you are doing your part to help bring change," I said.

Her lips pinched and she looked around my shop again. Was she disappointed in me? Were my dreams too small for her? Nights with Emelia in our seaside home and days in my shop.

"It would help if I had some support from the Landbringer."

"You have Emelia backing you," I reminded the woman. I had kept the Landbringer out of the public eye and away from the news for nearly a year, and I had no intention of changing that. The time of gods was over, as far as I was concerned.

"I do, but saint that she is, she still represents the old society."

"And so does the Landbringer. Besides, I am not called the Vote Winner, now am I?"

"You are not called the Dressmaker, either," she drawled, and I laughed.

"You will be fine. According to the news, you are polling high on all the isles as well as the new provinces. You don't need me to help you get elected to the senate."

She sighed. "Maybe I don't need the Landbringer. But *you, Sade*, I may need." She went back to my sketchbook. "At least to make me something dashing. Not a fucking dress, though."

I smiled. "In that case, I will see what I can do."

Thank you for reading Landbringer!
If you enjoyed this book, please leave a review to help other
readers find my work.

BOOKS BY KAREN LUCIA

THE WARRIORS OF HELSVERN SERIES:
The Golden Valia
Daughter of Helsvern
Son of Helsvern

STORIES FROM EARTH TO THE UNKNOWN
The Divide
Funeral Singer
Blackburn Station
Greystone Alliance

A Second Life Worth Living

ACKNOWLEDGMENTS

Thank you to my partner who puts up with the chaos that is my writing process and to my son who provided me with ample distraction along the journey of writing this book. To everyone who did a beta reading of my book, thank you for your feedback and for giving me the support needed to make this book even more enjoyable for my readers. I want to say thank you to my parents for always being supportive of my endeavors. Thank you to my editor, Kelly McLennon, who gave me plenty of things to think about as I worked through finalizing Landbringer. And, of course, thank you to all my readers who continue to support me and my writing.

ABOUT THE AUTHOR

Karen is a Minneapolis, Minnesota based author. During the long, cold winters she has learned the value of a good story, good friends, and a strong internet connection. Writing has been a passion project for her since childhood. It took that passion, her love of stories, and her friends to get her books out into the world. Check out her website at KarenLuciaWrites.com for more of her writing and updates on new releases.